HOLY DEADLOCK

BY THE SAME AUTHOR

MISLEADING CASES IN THE COMMON LAW
MORE MISLEADING CASES
STILL MORE MISLEADING CASES
'NO BOATS ON THE RIVER'
HONEYBUBBLE & CO.
THE WATER GIPSIES
THE SECRET BATTLE
THE HOUSE BY THE RIVER
THE OLD FLAME
TANTIVY TOWERS
DERBY DAY
HELEN
THE BOMBER GIPSY, AND OTHER POEMS
THE WHEREFORE AND THE WHY
'TINKER, TAILOR . . .'
WISDOM FOR THE WISE

HOLY
DEADLOCK

by

A. P. HERBERT

The strength of sin is the law
I COR. XV. 56

SECOND EDITION

METHUEN & CO. LTD.
London

First Published . . . . . April 5th 1934
Second Edition 1934

PRINTED IN GREAT BRITAIN

NOTE

I WISH to thank the many legal friends who have assisted and advised me in this difficult affair. They will agree, I am sure, that there are good reasons for not recording their names.

Numerous judicial and other offices are mentioned in the story: but no personal reflections on their holders, present or past, are anywhere intended.

A. P. H.

So here he was at last, travelling down to Brighton with a strange young woman in a first-class carriage.

What a situation for a publisher of schoolbooks!

And this was only the beginning. A whole week-end waited ahead of him, as elastic and uncertain as a week-end in the trenches.

So far, Miss May Myrtle had given no trouble at all. At Victoria she had said 'Good afternoon': on the platform she said it was a nice day: in the carriage she said she preferred back to the engine: and there she was, sitting quietly in her corner with the *Happy Magazine*. No facetious remarks: no ferrety questions. She was the well-trained expert, discreetly doing her job, no more. Moreover, the little thing had brought an 'attaché-case' which had a solid and even an official appearance. This lay upon the seat beside her: and together, he thought, they must present a convincing picture of a public man, confidential secretary, and important papers on their innocent way to a Conference.

John Adam, of Heddle, Feather & Co., was free to read the typescript which he had brought with him—a book on the History of Christian Marriage. But it seemed unsuitable to his present voyage. He could not concentrate on the worthy writer's opinions. He put it away in his case.

He put away the evening paper too; for at once he saw a letter about the divorce laws which saddened him: a letter signed 'Candid'; one of those brief, emphatic letters from some happily married man—or more probably woman —who could see no point of view but his own:

What is the real meaning of 'Citizen's' complaint? Is it not that he has made a bad bargain and is not man enough to stick to it?

LEWISHAM.   CANDID.

I

London, sliding swiftly through the rain, and wondered what he would have done if he had been as wise and good and clever as 'Candid'. He looked back at his life, and could think of nothing which he would do differently if he 'had his time over again'. And he looked at his life critically, not with the warm self-pity which was fashionable then among the unfortunate: for he had never thought enough of himself to consider himself. What he was doing now he was not doing for his own sake, but for other people's: and even for that he had never patted himself on the back. But he was the son of a Civil Servant: he liked things to be orderly, sane, and decent; and what he was doing now seemed to be crazy and wrong. He wished that the sagacious 'Candid' could be magically deposited where May Myrtle was sitting now, and be compelled to tell him exactly what he should have done.

What year was it? 1929—November. Nine years since his marriage. Two years since he parted from his wife—his lovely wife—his golden girl. And three weeks since he received from her that wild, foolish, disgraceful, but so characteristic, and, if one knew her, so innocent telegram. He had it in his note-case still; foolish—for Boom had said that it was not merely indiscreet but a danger to the whole proceedings. He took out the folded pink paper and read the message again. How absurd it looked, in the round and featureless post-office writing:

John Adam 19 Adelphi Terrace London darling do hope you will behave like gentleman because really decided want to marry Martin impossible do anything this end all nonsense but think you know why and hurry please darling because very much in love tell you more later much love and kisses writing Mary.

Many people, he thought, would blame the woman who sent that telegram. 'Candid,' probably, would want to have her whipped in public. But to him, her husband, who understood her, this frank communication was neither surprising nor shocking. What was the time of dispatch? 10.21 a.m. Yes. John Adam smiled: for he could see his Mary sitting up suddenly in bed—her sweet face rosy with sleep, her hair a gleaming tangle of gold—snatching the telephone from the little table, pushing the tawny spaniel off the bed, purring into the receiver, so fresh and so polite, 'Good morning! I want "Telegrams", please'; and then dictating this outrageous message to the astonished operator as if it were the most natural thing in the world. Made up as she went along, probably, with maddening emendations and monstrous explanations—A for Athenaeum; D—for—Dear—Basil—Dean, J—for—Augustus—John, and other naughtinesses. It would not occur to her that she was doing anything unwise or wrong. For to Mary it could never be wrong to be open: and she knew very well that he was ready to do anything he could for her. Somebody would have told her (as somebody had told John Adam) that in these days divorce was an easy matter. The husband 'behaved like a gentleman'; good lawyers were engaged, a good many pennies had to be put in the slot, but the divorce emerged from the machine at last as easily as a motor-licence, and rather more easily than a passport. Having heard that, and knowing the special difficulties of Martin Seal (who was employed by the British Broadcasting Corporation and must not be so much as breathed upon by scandal), she would have said at once: 'John will behave like a gentleman, *I know*,' and sent off the telegram at the first opportunity. The only surprising thing was that it was not marked 12.30 a.m. and dispatched by the head waiter at the Savoy Grill.

Veracity, passionate veracity—that was Mary. Here was her letter, too—a glowing, generous, ridiculous scrawl, from which it would have been difficult for a stranger to discover whether she loved John Adam or Martin Seal the more. But much about the B.B.C.—and, of course, she was right. They were mad, compromising, indefensible documents, and it had been silly of him to keep them; but they were the last things he had had from Mary, and there might be no more. He tore them slowly into very small pieces, and lowered the window; and the wind scattered the evidence of Collusion across the wet fields of Surrey.

Collusion certainly. Probably Connivance. Perhaps Condonation and Conduct Conducing as well. Mr. Boom, the lawyer, had bombarded him with so many dreadful words, and he could not have said clearly which of the various improprieties he was committing at this moment, travelling to Brighton with Miss May Myrtle. But the sum of it all was clear. If two young persons made a mistake and married: and did their best to make the partnership work: and after seven years agreed that it could not be done: and decided that the false partnership ought to be brought to an end: and made friendly, honourable plans to do so—that was some kind of criminal offence. There was no decent way in which that mistake could be wiped out.

'Quite right too,' dear 'Candid' would say. 'Teach you not to make mistakes again!' But the human world, even the State, was not, in other matters, so ungenerous to the mistakes of young men. In those far-off days of the Great War the State had been very grateful for the impetuous decisions of young men, and very ready to forgive their errors. It had been a mistake for John Adam to enlist in the infantry as soon as he could escape from Oxford (they would not have him at first, because of his eyes). They said then that, with his education, he ought to be an officer. He took a commission: and that was a mistake: for he was shy, a little slow of decision, and could never really persuade himself that he was fit to command soldiers. He could remember mistakes which he had made in France—wrong judgments, foolish orders—by which good men had lost their lives. But those were not held up against him now. After the war they had given him a vote: and he had voted for those who said that the Kaiser ought to be hanged. Probably a mistake: but, if so, he was free to rectify it, and to vote at the next election for those who said that the Kaiser was a much misunderstood man, and that if any one could be blamed for the Great War it was Sir Edward Grey. All very odd. A man might jeopardize the lives of soldiers by his orders, the safety of the State by his vote, the property of his employers by his arithmetic, his own welfare by his choice of a partner or profession; but all such errors were forgotten, or could, at least, be corrected, by a man of character. Only in the most difficult choice of all—the choice of a partner, not for business, but for life—was a young man expected to be infallible, considered caddish if he confessed to error, and treated as a criminal if he attempted to correct it.

Very odd. And yet the wise and pious State took no trouble at all to prevent the young man from making the mistake, to impose delay between the decision and the fatal step. A decree of divorce was not made absolute until six months after the wise Judge had decided that there ought to be a divorce—for fear the wise Judge might have made a mistake. But there was no decree nisi for marriage: the foolish young man could tie himself up for life seven days after he made his decision by walking into a register office and filling up a form or two. Very odd. All those laws and regulations to prevent a man from eating the wrong things, drinking the wrong things, seeing the wrong pictures, reading the wrong books, working in the wrong way—but nothing at all to prevent a man from marrying the wrong wife. But what a fuss if he admitted his mistake and wanted to marry the right one! There sat Miss Myrtle, half asleep now over the *Happy Magazine*—a stranger: but, if he were free, he could be her lawful husband in a week or two. Very odd.

But probably he would have made the same mistake if he had had to wait six months, or twelve. No, perhaps not: for dear old Mr. Figg had turned up only a week or two after the marriage; the first stage-engagement was two months later: and that had been the beginning of the trouble. No, that was not really true. The trouble was visible from the very first night. And that was a trouble no law could provide for. Nor could any law prevent a man from being enchanted by the first sight of Mary Eve. The law might have kept her out of that hospital, perhaps, as a menace to the peace of mind of wounded officers: but they would have come together in the end, over the Children's Country Holiday affair. He could remember still the thrill of that first meeting; July, 1918, and his last day in the pleasant hospital at Hampstead, to which, after two years with the infantry in France, an inglorious but painful wound in the left buttock had delightfully brought him. He had been washed, and was waiting for breakfast, thinking wearily that he would be soon back at the lunatic and filthy war. Then through the open door came a golden-headed girl, carrying a bowl of roses—a slim, golden girl in a green overall, with the bloom of youth on her lips and skin. 1918? And Mary's birthday was in June. She must have been just seventeen. But she might have been twenty: for she was tall, for a girl, and moved with a mature grace: and her large grey eyes were confident and wise. She glanced at the warrior, and said 'Good morning', with a happy little upward inflexion at the end, which seemed to say that all was glorious this sunny morning. She put the bowl of roses down and went out. He remembered the foolish phrase which had come into his mind— 'a walking daffodil'. He had stared at the empty doorway as he would have stared after the exit of an angel. And that might have been the end. For John Adam was a shy young man: he had never had anything to do with women, even at Oxford; even at Amiens. For one thing, he did not think that he could ever be attractive to the strange beings, and for another he was good—or under-educated. He would not have dared to ask the name of the golden girl or what she did there. But his nurse, remembering the names, said: 'You two ought to meet, Mr. Adam. That was Miss Eve.' So, after the doctor's visit, she brought the golden girl to see him: and the golden girl sat on his bed and talked to him with perfect self-possession: and John Adam shyly stammered back at her, enchanted. Her voice, he thought, was golden too: there were deep, surprising notes in it, and now and then there came that little upward leap at the end of a sentence, which must be the voice of daffodils and brooks and cherry-trees in blossom. But she seemed to contain the serenity, as well as the laughter, of Spring: her eyes were grave, her forehead high, and she did not, like so many golden girls, smile without a reason. She was serious-minded, he discovered, and after the war she was going to do social work in London: she did not know what. Her father was a Rector in Sussex, but she was staying with an aunt in London, because there was nothing to do in the village. Here was a bond with the golden girl, for John had worked during vacations at the Oxford House Settlement in Bethnal Green: and eagerly he began to tell her about the East End. But then the nurse returned and chivvied the golden girl away. John went back to the war, and did not hope to see her again.

But the children of Whitechapel brought them together again a year later—in August, 1919. John looked across at little Miss Myrtle and wondered how she would have carried herself that day.

The young man returned from the war very serious-minded indeed. The idea of service (provided it was not military service) possessed him. He had formed a deep affection for his 'men' in France; he got on with them well, and found that he was more of a leader of men than he had thought, though neither were persuaded that he had any special strategical genius. It was a pity, he thought, as so many thought then, that that close and chastening companionship of the classes should perish utterly as soon as the common danger was defeated; and he determined to do what little one man could to keep that part of the war-spirit alive. He had his war 'gratuity', and a few hundred pounds his father had left him, but no job; and until something turned up the obvious thing was to go into residence at the Settlement in Bethnal Green, where he had worked spasmodically as an undergraduate. He had spent many short periods there during vacations, helping at the Boys' and Mens' Clubs, and with the Children's Country Holiday Fund arrangements. He did not delude himself that he was helping to solve the problem of poverty by this work; but he thought humbly that he could add a little happiness and order to the lives of a few: and he knew that he was learning much that every citizen ought to know.

Those brief undergraduate visits had been a little alarming to the diffident young man: he felt himself a stranger, without the knowledge or the right to exercise authority, even at a Boys' Club—indeed, the wild Boys were the most intimidating. But now, with the experience of the war, he had more confidence, was given a club to manage, was happy, and did useful work. He had no thought of marriage, and thought sometimes that, if he had an income, he would be content to devote his life to the East End, as three or four of the fine fellows at the Settlement had done. But each of them had a few hundred a year: and he must find employment. He had hopes that Heddle & Feather's, the publishers, would give him a job in the end: he had taken a 'first' in History, they specialized in Education and Social Reform, and he was already reading a few manuscripts for them. If that came off he might be able to live on in Bethnal Green and work at his club in the evenings. The 'Head' of the House said that he would be delighted.

Pondering these plans, one sticky August morning in 1919, John Adam walked into the yard of Paradise Street School, Bethnal Green, E., and beheld Mary Eve, the golden girl, standing like a lighthouse in a sea of small, stormy children.

Best of all the work, John thought, was this business of the Children's Country Holiday Fund: perhaps because there was so much to show for the work, from the happy faces of the mothers as the children departed for their fortnight in the country to the pink and lusty faces of the children when they returned. For weeks the workers had been busy at the preparations, calling on mothers, compiling lists, distributing labels and information, collecting (where possible) parental contributions—hard house-to-house visiting work in the hot and dusty side-streets. And here at last were eighty-three small children, one batch only of the first tribe of emigrants, all washed and dressed and ready for the voyage. Pinned to every breast was a label, which advertised the name, age, address, and destination of the child. They carried bags of gooseberries, and bottles of milk, and loaves of bread, and cages of white mice, and bulbous bundles of personal baggage. The little yard was paved with children, tumultuous, mad, hot, shouting, singing, laughing, and crying. They were bound for the country, most of them for the first time, for the war had suspended the operations of the Fund. For many months their parents had been saving pennies towards this day; for weeks they had thought and dreamed about little else. They were almost Bacchanalian with happiness, and heat, and impatience. The news had spread among the tribe that the golden lady, Miss Eve, was to take them to the station, and they surged about her, demanding to start at once, for they would miss the train.

John stood still in the gateway. So it really was the golden girl. Two weeks earlier, in the Bethnal Green Road, walking home along the sticky pavement between the costers' barrows and the fried-fish and butchers' shops, he had seen a golden, hatless head bobbing along in front of him above the short inhabitants of Bethnal Green. He had observed how all the costers, all the men at the doors of shops, turned and stared and made remarks as the golden head went by. He had thought for a moment of the young girl in the hospital; but the head bobbed away down a side-street, and he thought no more of it. And here she was, without a hat, and dressed in forest green.

One of the organizers of the Fund led him delicately through the crowd of children. Something had gone wrong. There should have been three escorting adults for this large party, but one of the helpers had had to go with another party, and another had not turned up. Miss Eve, of St. Hilda's Mission, had kindly volunteered to fill one of the breaches. They would have to do the best they could.

'Miss Eve—Mr. Adam.' And then came the old joke; 'You ought to get on well. I hope you will—for you've a large flock to deal with.'

They shook hands over the heads of six riotous children. Mary looked at him gravely and critically, as if she were wondering whether he was man enough for the job. She liked what she saw, a plain-looking, honest-looking, pale-faced young man, in grey flannel trousers, with metal spectacles and a nervous manner. His best features were a high forehead and a strong chin. She seemed to know his face, but could not think why.

2

He said, 'We've met before, Miss Eve. At the hospital. You—you sat on my bed.'

What a thing to say! thought the shy young man.

But a lovely smile lit up her face, and she gave him her warm little hand again.

'Of *course*! Mr. *Adam*! But you didn't have glasses then.'

'No,' he said. 'I don't wear them always, except for reading. But when there's a glare——"

'Take them off, please,' she said, surprisingly, but very sweetly.

Extraordinary conversation! The children clutched at her skirt, and clamoured at his knees, and mutinously yelled on every hand. The organizer stared at this strange pair of social workers. But solemnly he took off his glasses, and solemnly the golden girl inspected him.

'That's better,' she said. 'Much better. I remember you well.'

And John solemnly put his glasses in his pocket. That had been the beginning of it, he thought, looking at Miss Myrtle, who was now asleep. Something happened in his heart then which had never happened before. He knew that he, of all people, was in love; and, stranger still, he felt the first stirrings of an infantile, fantastic belief that the golden girl liked him.

'You'd better be off,' said the organizer, looking at his watch.

The eighty-three children were paraded in the street outside in an uncertain formation of twos and threes. They were counted a fourth time and voted correct; and then the noisy procession moved off, Mary at the head of it, and John, embarrassed but excited, at the rear. The children occupied the centre of the greasy street, the little ones dragging their feet and stumbling over the cobbles among the cabbage-stalks and horse-dung: the anxious mothers skirmished along, like Arab scouts, on the flanks of the column, some laughing, some crying, divided between delight that their young ones were to see a real cow for the first time and fear that the cow would do their young ones a mischief. From time to time some mother would

dart across from the pavement, fasten like an eagle on her
Maggie or Jane, and shout or whisper some final warning
against bulls or Deadly Nightshade or drinking out of
ponds. One mother, whose little Martha was just ahead
of John, instructed him twice that on no account was
Martha to have any mushrooms, which her father died of.
From time to time a bag of gooseberries burst, and the
precious droppings were trampled by the advancing army:
from time to time a loaf of bread fell and was retrieved,
with shrieks and agitation. But all the time the main body
shouted and sang and swept ahead under the hot sun, as
irresistible as a swarm of locusts. Policemen at the cross-
roads saw the host approaching: and the gross lorries and
omnibuses had to stand and snort while the children went by.
Somehow, the great joke about the names had spread among
them; and soon they began to chant '*Adam and Eve! Adam
and Eve! The animals went in two by two! Adam and Eve!
Adam and Eve! Hooray for Adam and Eve!*' Mary, when she
heard that, far-off at the head of the column, turned round
and waved a green sleeve at him, and threw her head back
and laughed aloud. And John, the old soldier, thought
that this was the most exciting march of his life. He was
carrying two bundles, one bottle of milk, and two sets of
eighty-three railway tickets: and he moved as in a dream,
divided, like the mothers, between terror and delight.

He could not now remember the details of their difficult
route: but they reached some station—Bethnal Green—
or was it Whitechapel?—at which the clinging mothers,
now almost all in tears, were at last shaken off. And then
the nightmare began to gather strength and swiftness.
The eighty-three children, still yelling hilariously, streamed
on to the platform, and with one accord rushed to the edge
and peered perilously at the electric rails. Never, thought
John, had two mortal adults borne so heavy a responsibility
—eighty-three small children, belonging to other people,
and bent upon electrocution. 'Stand back! Stand back!'
the ex-officer shouted: but not a child stirred a foot. Sick
with anxiety, he glanced towards the tunnel from which
the train would come. Then, turning back, he saw that at
the other end the line of children was rolling back from the
edge, like an irregular wave on a shelving shore. Mary was

walking along the edge, saying very quietly, 'Stand back,
you little idiots, and keep still till I say "Go".' Presently
the whole herd was standing three paces back, an orderly
line, absolutely quiet, and gazing in adoration at the golden
lady, while she told them for the fourth time at what
station to get out. Then little Martha piped, 'Adam and
Eve!' and the other eighty-two, in hearty unison, cried
'Adam and Eve! Adam and Eve!' and Mary laughed at
John along the platform, and the train came in.

The children scrambled into three different carriages:
and John and Mary could only be in two. They were bound,
if he remembered right, for one of the Northern terminuses
—King's Cross?—Baker Street?—and they had to change
once—it must have been twice—at Underground or Tube
Stations. He could not remember the details: what he
would never forget was the general madness of that enormous
and exceptional convoy, and Mary's coolness, efficiency,
and power. The changes were as mad as battles, for as the
train moved on it was joined by other parties of children,
equally hilarious and indifferent to advice; and these
parties mingled with John's party and all the children
seemed very much alike: so that, though the other children
might have different destinations and differently coloured
labels, it was a problem at the change-station to extract
from the train all the right children (with all their bundles)
without extracting any of the wrong. At the first change,
the eighty-three tickets had to be counted by an inspector,
while the eighty-three children fumed and sang and shouted
'Adam and Eve'. After the second Mary found that they
had collected two alien Hoxton children who were labelled
for Victoria. Here they were being hurried northwards:
and here for the present the distressed pair must remain;
but their tears were disturbing, and some of the normal
passengers looked at Mary with suspicion. The normal
passengers, here in the dignified West End, were not less
ill-disposed towards the shouting of the eighty-three, and
the strange song about 'Adam and Eve'. But they reached
—was it Oxford Circus?—some dreadful station with a
moving staircase—and here the convoy reached its unforgettable climax. Not far from the moving staircase the
eighty-three tickets had to be counted again: and Mary

confessed to the inspector that, by misadventure, they had the bodies of eighty-five children. 'Adam and Eve' the children sang. ' Adam and Eve! Go on, Mister! Adam and Eve! Go on!' The inspector said that it would be well to count the children: they were counted, but on the count there were only eighty-three. If that was correct Mary and John had lost two of their own party. But the children jumped and jiggled so that it was like counting gold-fish in a pond: it would be well to count the children again, more carefully. John and Mary began to count from the tail of the column and the inspector from the head. And when all three were approaching the middle of the column a devil entered into the head of it: and with one accord, like the Gadarene swine, all the children rushed violently past the barrier towards the Moving Staircase, the glorious, the exciting, and their first Moving Staircase! So many were they, and so narrow was the gap, that it was impossible to reach and stop the head of the column without trampling on the children behind. The inspector, fanatical for duty, was still finishing his count as the last children rushed by: he had the tickets and somebody must stay till he delivered them. 'Get the tickets!' John said to Mary, and he scrambled over the inspector's barrier and ran to the foot of the staircase. He was in time to hold back about a dozen children, but the other seventy were on the staircase, soaring happily heaven-ward under the bright lights, delirious with excitement, and shouting 'Adam and Eve!' with more zest than before, because in that place their voices sounded so delightfully loud, they knew not why. John Adam stared up at the extraordinary spectacle for which he was responsible: and he did not know what to do. He thought vaguely that it would be a good thing if someone were at the top to super-intend the disembarkation of the children from the stair-case, for few of them would be careful to step off with the left foot first. But he could not be at the top: for he could not climb over the children, or force a passage through such a mob in time. And there was no other way. He glanced at the 'Down' staircase. But there were many respectable citizens sailing down upon that, looking like moving targets on a rifle-range, and regarding with mild surprise the mounting ladder of children on their right; and

something in John Adam's disciplined soul said that it
was wrong to run up a 'Down' staircase while respectable
citizens were coming down it. Then Mary, breathless, was
at his side: and at once—that was the whole difference
between them—she knew what to do. 'Quick!' she said.
'They'll never get off!' She sprang for the 'Down' staircase
and ran up it as fast as she could—which is not an easy
manœuvre, as John, following, found. She pushed indignant business men aside; twice she stumbled and once she
fell. He could see those slim, pink legs twinkling up the
staircase under the green skirt now. But the first of the
children reached the summit well before Mary. Some of
the older children stepped off carefully, but with the wrong
foot, and fell down: some of the younger ones were carried
into the curving barrier under which the staircase disappeared and span off like tops, delighted by the sensation:
the smaller ones fell down: the mischievous ones lay down;
and all rolled off together, clutching their little bundles,
crying aloud with rapture or apprehension. When Mary
reached the top there was already a small but increasing
mountain of tangled children and bundles and bags of fruit,
as if some fantastic children-ship were unloading cargo by
an endless conveyer on to an unattended wharf. If relief
had not come instantly there might have been bad trouble.
But Mary plucked a child from the mountain, and passed
him to John, and John to a friendly passenger, and the
passenger to a porter, and, working desperately, like a
chain of helpers at a country fire, they dispersed the
mountain and made the way clear. When the host was
marshalled in order again the casualties were seen to be
less severe than the noise and swiftness of the catastrophe
had led them to expect: for the children knew how to fall,
and they lived in streets where the arts of self-preservation
are soundly taught. There were a few dusty white frocks, a
crushed loaf or two, and one scratched face, which belonged,
unhappily, to little Martha. But little Martha had nothing
to say except, 'Ma says I'm not to have no mushrooms, lady.'

That adventure, no doubt, had been the beginning. It
belonged to that class of experience which can turn two

strangers into firm friends in the twinkling of an eye. After they had dispatched the eighty-three (or rather eighty-one) children to Hertfordshire, they took the two strays to Victoria and committed them to a guard. Then they took a cup of tea at an A.B.C. and laughed and sighed together, like two survivors of a battle. That tea and talk was the most intimate approach that John Adam had ever made to a woman: and he could recall the excitement of it still: the tremulous adoration which he felt already for this golden, fearless, forcible girl, who looked like a film-star (but an exceptionally refined one) and was a social worker. She was more than a year older since the morning in hospital, a year before; she seemed a grown woman now, firmer, though not yet full, in face and body and mind. They had laughed, as who would not, recalling their adventures; the clamorous march of the eighty-three, and the ludicrous predicament of the moving staircase. But Mary at once was serious again, questioning and facing things, blaming herself and not the children or their mothers, as the West End lady generally did. 'Isn't it cheek,' she said, 'taking other people's children and treating them like that? You and I deserve to be lynched.' 'We shan't,' he said. 'The mothers are very grateful. It's the best thing we do.' 'Perhaps; but that's not the point.' It was so strange to see that thoughtful little frown on the face of his 'walking daffodil'. 'Isn't it just a—what's the word—palliative, or something?'

'Palliatives are better than nothing—if you're very ill.' And there, for a long time, in the empty A.B.C., they had pursued that old and endless argument, and, as usual, arrived at no conclusion. Mary wondered whether all these Missions and Settlements did any real good. But what else could humble individuals do? It was bad to appear patronizing, but worse to be indifferent. She thought she would stay in the East End for a year at least: she too was helping to run a club, for mothers—absurd, wasn't it?—but the mothers seemed to like her (for she could play the piano and sing their favourite songs) and the Mission seemed to think well of her. John hoped with all his heart that she would stay, and said so. 'Though I wonder,' he added, 'you don't go on the stage.' 'Don't say that,' she said. 'Everybody does. I sometimes feel it's Fate. It's so silly. Does every plain man have to go into the Church?'

That had been good to hear: and she had stayed—though not for a year. One thing, as one thing does, led to another. The golden girl, marching hatless through the streets, became soon a famous and befriended figure in the borough: the costers always had a greeting and a joke for Miss Ginger. The children in the side-streets trailed after her like sea-birds pursuing a ship: and always they had the same cry. 'Adam and Eve!' 'Adam and Eve!' The great joke had spread everywhere, with the story of the moving staircase. It was a commonplace at the Settlement, and John became so well accustomed to hearing it that he no longer blushed. All the world seemed to have agreed that Adam and Eve were destined to mate. It was, to John, a proud and thrilling but lunatic thought: but what the world thought so openly he might with propriety think secretly too, though, but for the compelling power of words and popular suggestion, he would as soon have thought of proposing to a princess. The kind and wise old head of St. Hilda's had heard of the 'Adam and Eve' joke also: she knew John (for the work of the Mission and the Settlement touched at many points) and she thought that the sooner her fascinating and mature Miss Eve was married the better—though she did say she was only nineteen. So John was asked to tea at the Mission House: and he and Mary found themselves on the same Committee; and ran the Margaret Institute Fun Fair and Dance together. The world which frowns most fiercely on the breaking of a match conspires most recklessly to make one. They met on duty: and they began to meet off duty: they went to matinées and concerts: they went for wanders round the docks: they walked arm in arm along the wide Whitechapel Road. In November Heddle & Feather's said that John could begin work with them in January. And one December evening, on the top of the bus which goes from Liverpool Street down the Bethnal Green Road, John found that he had kissed Mary ineffec-tively on the side of her nose, and asked her to marry him. She said that she would, he could not imagine why: and why she had said so he did not understand to this day.

Mary had been a little surprised herself. The truth was, perhaps, that, like John, she had never really met any one else. The war, and the seclusion of the country rectory, had kept her girlhood free of young men. She had shot up suddenly from girlhood in the hospital to womanhood in the East End, and had missed the preliminary trials and errors of the Modern Girl. The few acquaintances she had made at the hospital had been disappointing and brief. The simple young officers took her to musical plays which she thought were silly: and they thought that a blonde ought not to be so serious. She was fond of John: he took the same grave view of life as she did: and it seemed to be generally expected that they should marry.

And that was why he was travelling to Brighton with Miss May Myrtle.

They were married in April, 1920—at a register office in Bethnal Green. That had been a blow to the old Rector, and to the Head of St. Hilda's too. But Mary had revealed strong opinions on the subject, and was not to be shaken, even by her sad old father, whom she loved. She hoped that she was a Christian, but nothing would induce her to be married in a church. The words of the Marriage Service puzzled and repelled her, and if she took part in it most of the words would be lies. She hoped that she would have children one day, though not till they could afford to look after them properly: but she could not agree that the 'first cause' of matrimony was the procreation of children. The third 'cause', she thought—the 'mutual society, help, and comfort'—ought to come first; and if 'holy matrimony' was the other way round she could not swear before God to undertake it. The words of the civil ceremony said nothing about the body, nothing about procreation, nothing about permanence: they trusted every citizen to make what he could of marriage according to his conscience—in short, they were civilized. She did not express herself quite so bluntly to the Rector, with whom she spent an unhappy but affectionate week-end of argument, going through the Service and the texts with him, and trying hard to let herself be persuaded. What about

'Whom God hath joined let no man put asunder'? He said that meant that divorce was wrong. She said it must mean that nobody ought to come between husband and wife; but, if he was right, that made it impossible for her. Her marriage might be a bad one: she did not believe that a bad marriage ought to be endless: and therefore they must not be joined by God. It was not honest, surely, if one was prepared for divorce, to promise and vow 'till death us do part'? That was an ideal—but it could not be a positive rule, much less a clause in a contract.

The old man sadly shook his head, consoled himself with the thought that it was honesty of mind that made her say such dreadful things: and gave up the struggle.

He might have forbidden the marriage until she was of age: but, he said, it was no use forbidding the young to do anything in these days—they only did the same thing in a worse way.

So Mary's father did not come to the wedding. But the ceremony was not without a flavour of the Christian spirit, though the material display of most weddings in church was absent. The Heads of the Mission and the Settlement stood as witnesses: workers from both of them crowded the little room: the coster-women of Mary's club brought their barrows to the door, and those of their husbands who possessed 'pearlies' had come in them: the boys from John's club had provided their drum and bugle band: and the embarrassed couple, emerging from the office, passed under a triumphal arch of flowers and vegetables—daffodils and early rhubarb, and long sticks blossoming with bunches of radishes, carrots, and spring onions, bright white turnips, and bright French beans. A taxi had been commanded to take them to the Mission House: but the costers had commanded the taxi into the background, and in its place stood an empty coster's barrow, devoid of vegetables but brilliant with spring flowers and coloured ribbons and little Union Jacks. The donkey, too, was dressed in his best, his harness polished and the metal-work shining: and at the donkey's head stood old Joe Holt, the Pearly King of Bethnal Green, glorious and beaming in his suit of pearlies, which carried, so they said, many thousands of buttons. They seized, they pushed, they carried the couple on to the bridal barrow:

the boys' band formed up ahead of it, the Heads of the
Missions and their workers followed after: the band began
(for no clear reason) the 'March of the Men of Harlech',
the procession moved off, and behind and upon both flanks
followed a cloud of children crying, 'Adam and Eve! Adam
and Eve! The animals went in two by two.'

The beginning of Brighton. John Adam sighed. Those
were the days. Now, perhaps, it would be different: but
often he wished himself back in the Bethnal Green Road,
a young man with no prospects but plentiful faith, tramping
along the greasy pavements over cabbage-stalks and paper
bags, the costers crying on one hand and the fried-fish
shops sizzling and smelling on the other; tired faces and
cheerful voices: costers' flares and shawls and shopping
baskets and shouting butchers and scampering children:
the strong compendious odour of humanity and fried fish
and rotting vegetables and unwashed stones, the strong
and unforgettable flavour of brave, ironical, companionable
people—and, far in front, a golden hatless head bobbing
along in the light of the flares beside the costers' barrows. . . .

Brighton!

'Wake up, Miss Myrtle,' said Mr. Adam to his paramour.
'We're there.'

The thought plagued him, as they walked out of the
station, that his chartered lady was much too young.
Twenty-five, Miss Mortimer had told him: his own judgment
said nineteen. And she seemed smaller than before, in her
little purple hat and close-fitting tailor-made coat. He felt
that if any one did take them for lovers he would be
accused of baby-snatching.

Driving down to the hotel, Miss Myrtle whispered in her
far-away respectful manner, 'Which hotel is it, Mr. Adam?'

'The Capitol.'

'I'm glad,' she breathed. 'I've done jobs at all the
others.'

This utterance, so slight and childish in volume, so vast
in significance, shocked Mr. Adam; and this surprised him,
for he had thought that nothing could shock him again.

But surprises lay in wait for him everywhere. There was

the signing of the hotel register, unexpectedly distressing.
It seemed a simple matter to write down

> *Mr. and Mrs. Adam   London.*

But his heart fluttered, his mind rebelled, and his hand
delayed. So often he had written 'Mr. and Mrs. Adam',
with Mary at his side. He remembered the first time, in
the little honeymoon hotel; he remembered Mary, pressed
close to him, peeping round his arm to see him write the
magical words.

Now, for the first time, those words would be a lie. He
felt that he was betraying Mary, though it was for Mary's
happiness—at her request.

But here he noticed that the clerk was eyeing him, and
he wrote quickly

> *Mr. and Mrs. Adam   London.*

'Room forty-one,' said the clerk.

Going up in the lift, he thought, in a stronger mood, 'Why
in the world should I, of all people, be made to feel guilty?
I'm a fool. And next time, after all, they will be true.'
For he would be married, then, to his comfortable Joan,
and all this horror would be behind.

Miss Myrtle took off her hat and coat and began to un-
pack. She took from her suit-case a rose-coloured silk
night-dress, and said softly over her shoulder, 'Which side
of the bed do you prefer, Mr. Adam?'

'Er—I really don't mind,' he said. 'I shan't be using it
much,' he added, mindful of what Miss Mortimer had said.

'You'd better have the right,' she said, 'opposite the
door—for the morning.'

'I don't quite follow.'

'So's the maid can see you and get your face fixed, you
see.'

'Ah, yes, of course,' said Mr. Adam.

What a thing it was, after all, to have perfect service!
A cheap secretary from Mooney's, would never have
thought of that.

'I think I'll go for a stroll,' he said, 'before dinner.'

'All right,' said Miss Myrtle. 'Send up a cocktail, will
you?'

The command was issued in the same flat little voice,

easily, as if the voice had often said the same thing. 'More surprises?' he thought, and went out.

He walked out on to the cold 'Front' and turned towards the Aquarium. The wind blew bitterly from the east. The Channel stormed in a mournful manner on the beach, and a few stooping invalids crept along the asphalt, hopefully inhaling the celebrated air.

He hoped that Miss Myrtle was not going to be a trouble, for it had been trouble enough to get her.

It was easy enough to send telegrams, but not so easy, John Adam had found, to behave like a gentleman. He took both Mary's documents to his old friend and adviser, Hilary Boom: and Mr. Boom, over a dozen oysters, had fired at him those explosive words beginning with C: for Mr. Boom was a solicitor whose business was divorce.

Mr. Boom spent his working hours in practising the law and his spare time in trying to amend it. He was of the breed of the true reformer; for he tried to change things because they were wrong and not because he wanted to attract attention by denouncing them. He worked quietly and patiently, and, like a mole or beaver, almost unnoticed —an article to an obscure weekly here, a letter to a solemn daily there, a little, but good, book every other year. Nearly always he had had to work so long upon his causes that when at last they triumphed he was no longer interested. He would protest for many years in his modest, scholarly way that two and two did really make four; but when at last the whole world shouted with astonishment that this was true Mr. Boom was busy at another problem, and some young 'modern' received the credit for the discovery. But Mr. Boom did not resent that. So long as there was light he did not care who switched it on. He had been at Oxford with John's father, had known John since he was 'so high', given him his first bicycle and prepared his Will (not that there was much in that). He was a very large man and loved good port, good wine, good words, good writing, and honesty, and country pubs, and swimming. He had been happily married for twenty-seven years, so that none could say that his interest in the reform

of the divorce laws was selfish—though many people did.
He lunched always, rather late, at a little restaurant in
Chancery Lane, on white wine and oysters. Here, as a rule,
he put aside professional cares; but when his clients were
also his friends he would sometimes take them there, feed
them with oysters, stupefy them with wine, comfort them
with wisdom, and send them away bewildered but the better.

He took John and his two preposterous documents to
the 'Maison Boom' (as his friends called it): and after the
seventh oyster he consented to talk business.

'So you want to know how you are to behave like a
gentleman?' he said.

'Um,' said Mr. Adam, gulping down an oyster.

'You realize, do you, that you are asking me to take part
in a criminal conspiracy?'

'Good God, no!'

'You are asking me to assist you to arrange a collusive
petition for divorce, to pervert the processes of justice, to
withhold material facts from the Court, to aid and abet
perjury. I am an officer of the Court, and for all these
offences I may be struck off the rolls. We may both be
committed for contempt of Court or sent to prison for
conspiracy. And you the son of a Civil Servant. Have
some more wine.'

John listened with alarm to this recital.

'I only want to give poor Mary her freedom,' he said.
'It seems simple enough.'

'It is never simple to give any one freedom. It is only
simple to shut people up. As you know, it is the simplest
thing in the world to get married or get into jail. It is
quite another thing to get out.'

'What am I to do?' said John.

'Hush,' said Boom. 'The waiter is listening. My friend,'
he said to the waiter, 'kindly withdraw a little way. I
am about to take part in a criminal conspiracy. And bring
another bottle of Chablis.'

'Let me see,' he continued. 'You were married in 1920.
You separated in 1927. Seven years. A fair trial. You
have no children. Why have you no children?'

'I don't know,' said John. 'We didn't want any at first,
and then, when we did, they didn't come.'

'Unfortunate. But not a crime. Nor is it really relevant to the law of divorce. However, since you have no children, the affair should, as you say, be simple. You have no obligation to anybody but yourselves: and if you wish to release each other, why not?'

'Why indeed?' said Mr. Adam indignantly.

'Because the law is not a hass, as somebody remarked, but a mule. I think myself——' Mr. Boom paused and wiped his large lips with a napkin.

'But surely——'

'One moment,' said Mr. Boom, 'here is the wine——' He beamed benevolently on his impatient friend; he was in no hurry: he was enjoying himself.

'I think myself,' he continued, 'that in such a case as yours the wise provisions of the Partnership Act, 1890, should be applicable.'

'What the deuce are they?'

'You and your wife should be able to go to the Court, hand in hand, and say: "My lord, long ago, when we were very young, we entered into the difficult partnership called marriage. We made a mistake, but an excusable mistake. We made a long and honest attempt (seven years) to keep the partnership going. It's not a case of recklessness or wickedness. We've tried hard, but we cannot live happily together. Our nerves, our health, our work, and our usefulness to the State are suffering damage. The partnership is a failure. It has failed to provide children for the country or a reasonably contented life for ourselves. We wish to be free, either to live alone or marry again. And so, my lord, we ask you, in your discretion, to say that the partnership ought to be honourably dissolved under Section 35".'

'That sounds reasonable enough——' began Mr. Adam.

'And therefore it is no part of the divorce laws of England. Cheese? Coffee? Port?'

'No,' said Mr. Adam. 'What would happen if I went to the Court and said that?'

'The Judge would say: "Pardon me, Mr. Adam, but have either of you committed adultery? We are not here, Mr. Adam, to secure your happiness, but to preserve the institution of marriage and the purity of the home. And

therefore one of you must commit adultery. Have either
of you committed adultery?" And if you answered "No,"
the Judge would say: "In that case, Mr. Adam, the Court
cannot help you. One of you two must go away and
commit adultery and then come back and tell us all about
it. We may then be able to do what you wish. *One* of
you, not both. For if both of you behave in this way, the
marriage must stand, according to the ecclesiastical
doctrine of Recrimination——" '

'What the deuce——?'

'Recrimination? Why, if one spouse petitions for
divorce on the ground of the other's adultery, it is in theory
enough to show that he or she has committed adultery too.
Tu quoque—the retort of the schoolboy, and the Canon
Law. The law regards physical fidelity as the vital element
in the marriage bond. Thus, without an act of adultery
on one side or the other it is impossible to obtain a divorce.
And a single act of infidelity is sufficient cause for the
dissolution of a long and happy marriage, though that act
may be begun and ended in five minutes—a sudden, unpremeditated act, the fruit of a passing craziness, jealousy,
temper, or desire. So dearly does the law regard the purity
of the marriage bed. It is, as we lawyers say, of the essence
of the contract. One would think, then, that where *both*
parties have violated the fundamental clause of the contract, there was twice the reason for dissolving the partnership. Not a bit of it. We say that in that case there is
no good ground for a divorce at all—except in special
cases by the discretion of the Court. Normally, the guilty
couple must remain united in law, though the only bond
between them in fact is that each is living in sin with
somebody else. They are, as somebody said, "joined together in unholy matrimony." Or, shorter still, "married
alive!" '

'Are you raving?' said Mr. Adam. 'Or am I?'

'Neither.'

'Sorry.'

'Not at all. Whenever I explain certain sections of the
law my clients conclude that I must be mad or drunk.
That is why I like to explain the worst parts here: for I
would rather be thought intoxicated than insane.'

'I think, after all,' said Mr. Adam, 'that I will have a port.'

'Of course. The Doctrine of Recrimination, I find, very often leads to drink. Henri, another port! However, all this is academic. For I assume that you have not both committed adultery—by the way, I mustn't use that word. Charles complains that it shocks his waiters and frightens his lay clients away. Do you mind if we call it intimacy?'

'Intimacy?' repeated the publisher.

'Intimacy. Don't you ever read the divorce reports? "Petitioner alleged that acts of intimacy took place at a West End hotel." . . . "Acts of intimacy took place!" Glorious! The language of Shakespeare! "Misconduct" is the favourite euphemism in the papers, but that annoys me. It might mean drunkenness or persistent unpunctuality. "Intimacy" makes me laugh. Nobody but the English could use such a word for such a purpose. I sometimes think of re-writing the classics in the language of the newspaper law-reports. Paris was "intimate" with Helen of Troy. Thou shalt not commit intimacy. Ha!'

Mr. Boom laughed heartily at his fancies and drank gently of his wine.

John Adam said patiently, 'Well, what am I to do?'

'I've told you. One of you must commit intimacy—not both. And you must not consult together which one it is to be: for that would be collusion. By the way, tear up that telegram of your wife's. That's enough to put the King's Proctor on your track. Most indiscreet.'

'She always telegraphs. The first thing that comes into her head.'

'Well, she must stop it.'

'I couldn't stop it when we were together; it's hardly likely I can stop it now.'

'And I suppose she sends them over the telephone, to ensure publicity?'

'Yes.'

Mr. Boom sighed. 'You and your wife are the kind of people who ought never to be allowed out without a solicitor. You say she's in love with this fellow—what's his name?'

3

'Seal. Martin Seal.'

'I seem to know the name. Why don't you divorce her? That seems the simplest thing.'

'He's on the B.B.C. and is afraid of losing his job. They're very particular.'

'I remember now. He used to run the "Children's Hour". Uncle Somebody-or-other.'

'Yes. He's one of the announcers now.'

'I see. It would never do for the British public to hear the "Weather Report" from the lips of a co-respondent. But how about your own office? Are publishers of school-books less moral than the B.B.C.?'

'It will be unpleasant, of course, but not fatal. I shall explain everything to my chief.'

'Tell him you're only behaving like a gentleman?'

'Yes.'

'With whom?'

'That's what I don't know.'

'Nobody you want to marry?'

'Yes. As a matter of fact, there is.'

'Well, then——?'

John Adam flushed, and spoke with spirit. 'I'm not going to drag her into that filthy Court! She wouldn't agree if I did,' he added.

'No intimacy yet? Pardon the impertinence—purely professional.'

'No. And there won't be.'

John described to his adviser the parentage, history, and character of the gentle Joan Latimer, Second Mistress of St. Bride's College for Girls.

'H'm,' said Mr. Boom. 'Do you suppose that your wife has committed intimacy with her Mr. Seal?'

'This is a very odd conversation,' thought Mr. Adam.

'I've no idea,' he said. 'I don't suppose so.'

'Why not?'

'She'd probably telegraph if she did—bless her! She could never keep anything back.'

'We might inquire.'

'Well, we won't!' said Mr. Adam, stubborn. 'I've not the smallest feeling against her. I'm not going to have her badgered by detectives. And I'm not going to have her

name on the placards of the evening papers. . . . Please
understand that.'

'This is going to be a difficult case,' said Mr. Boom.
'Three parties with principles, and one with a job at the
B.B.C.'

John Adam looked at him, as one bewildered. 'Do you
really mean,' he said, 'that what you call "intimacy" is the
only way out of this mess? Supposing I go to Mary's flat
and beat her—really knock her about? Wouldn't that
do?'

'Not at all,' said Mr. Boom cheerfully. 'More port?
Even persistent physical cruelty is not sufficient ground for
a divorce. It would help your wife to get a judicial separation, but she would be no more free to marry Mr. Seal than
she is now. If you violently knock your wife about every
night the ordinary person will conclude that you have not
much affection for her; but the law requires you to prove
it by sleeping with another woman. For that is the only
act of a husband that the law regards as really important.
It would be the same if you were certified a lunatic: or
became a habitual and besotted drunkard: or were sen-
tenced for embezzlement to fourteen years' penal servitude:
or were found guilty of murder but reprieved, and so let
off with imprisonment for life. Such trifles mean nothing
to the divorce laws of this Christian country. Adultery,
misconduct, intimacy, or nothing—that's the rule. Human
love, and Christian marriage, are rightly contrasted with
the brutal mating of animals, which has no spiritual element,
no mystical union of soul and mind. But if, as the law
insists, the one thing that matters is the physical act of
love, we are not, after all, so very different from "the brute
beasts that have no understanding".'

'It's disgusting,' said Mr. Adam.

'On the contrary,' said Mr. Boom, 'the whole idea is
purity. I must say, John, that I find your objections to
our excellent divorce laws a little childish. After all,
until the year 1857 you would have had to secure an
Act of Parliament to get a divorce. By the Matrimonial
Causes Act, 1857——'

'What am I to do?' said John.

But Mr. Boom's discourse rolled on like a flood, irresistible.

'The trouble is, you see, that our law is an attempt to combine two irreconcilable notions. It's possible, and honest, to hold, as the Catholics do, that marriage is a holy sacrament, and therefore cannot be terminated by men or the courts of men: and we may, and should, respect those who govern their own lives upon that principle. It is possible, again, to hold that marriage is a civil contract, a practical arrangement by which two reasonable beings agree to share certain rights and duties, an arrangement made by men and dissoluble by men. And that ought to be the point of view of any secular court of law, which is an institution designed for the practical assistance of men on the material and not the spiritual side of their lives. What is impossible is to combine the two—to say that marriage is both a sacrament and a civil contract, governed at one moment by the principles of Common Law and at another by the remnants of ecclesiastical tradition—enforceable by one set of rules but not avoidable except by another. For that's making the worst of two worlds. But that's what we're trying to do—in England—not, or not so much, in Scotland. If you claim your just rights under a contract of marriage you're supported by the doctrines of the civil law—you can get damages, for example, from the man who goes off with your wife, as if she were a side of beef (that doesn't fit very well into the sacramental theory). But if you want to surrender your rights under the contract of marriage—or partnership—you're impeded by obstacles which have a purely ecclesiastical origin. For example, it's impossible to imagine a civil action in which, both parties having violated clauses which were essential to the real purpose of a contract, the Court would nevertheless insist that the contract should still endure and be binding on them both. But that's what we do to married couples in England—though not in dear old licentious Scotland. Our old friend Recrimination.'

'What happens in Scotland?'

'The presence of guilt on both sides doesn't preclude a divorce, but the comparative guilt of each does affect the monetary arrangements. The spouse, for example, whose conduct provoked the backsliding of the other will suffer in costs, the amount of maintenance, and other ways. Both parties, therefore, can tell the whole truth without fear that it will cost them their freedom: and one, at least, has a direct monetary incentive to tell the whole truth.

'It pays to tell the truth. And so in Scotland they have no King's Proctor, because, where there is not so much temptation to lie, no special officer is needed to detect the liar. Likewise, there's no six months' suspense between decree nisi and decree absolute. They're down on collusion, of course, but the Court trusts itself to find out everything at the first shot, as other Courts do.'

'Very interesting,' said Mr. Adam, 'but it doesn't help me much.'

'No,' said Mr. Boom, and went on smoothly. 'To go back to the Church influence, the odd thing is that you have the same trouble whether you're married in church or married at a register office. Which were you?'

'Register office. Mary insisted.'

'I remember. You didn't have to say that you took your wife "till death us do part"?'

'No.'

'But you'll be treated by the law in exactly the same way as if you had—as if you'd been joined by God and had sworn a number of vows before the holy altar. One might, perhaps, have two sets of laws—one for the people who faced the Church Service, and another for the registered unions. Logical—but perhaps impracticable.'

Mr. Boom ruminated a while.

'What am I to do?' said the distressed husband.

'I was coming to that. The position is that some one has to commit intimacy for the general good; some one has to behave impurely in order to uphold the Christian ideal of purity; some one has to confess in public to a sinful breach of the marriage vows, in order that the happily married may point at him or her and feel themselves secure and virtuous. The delinquent, you say, is not to be your own wife; therefore it must be yourself. You cannot commit intimacy by yourself: there must be A Woman. But it is not, you say, to be the woman you would like to marry. Therefore you must be intimate with some woman whom you do not wish to marry. You must be a good boy and have a slice of bread-and-butter before you come to the jam. Now, is there any other woman you would care to be intimate with?'

John Adam stood up. 'If you're going to laugh at me——' he angrily began.

'Sit down,' said the large lawyer calmly. 'I'm not laughing—far from it. I'm trying to make you study the chart before you put to sea. You've no idea what rocks are ahead. Few people have. For the poor devils who do make the passage keep quiet about it. You're all the same. You prance into my office and ask me to get you a divorce as you'd ask me to get you a dog-licence; and sooner or later you all open your innocent eyes and say, "I'd no idea that it was all so difficult." I'm fond of you, John, and I'm determined that you shall go into this business with your eyes wide open.'

'They are,' said Mr. Adam wearily.

'No, they're not. To begin with, there's a film of bogus chivalry over them. Does it occur to you that in order to behave like a gentleman to your present wife you propose to behave like a cad to your future wife? She is, I understand, a pure and sensitive young woman. You will not "have relations" with her (another charming phrase, that) until you are married: such is her character that you couldn't if you would——'

'No.'

'Quite. Yet you propose to go to this virtuous girl and say, "Darling, take me to your arms. By means of an adulterous union with a strange woman I have obtained the right to woo you. The King's Courts have certified that I am impure and our holy married life can now begin".'

'Don't,' groaned Mr. Adam. 'It's ghastly.'

'It's true.'

'It can't be helped.'

'Why not? What does it matter to you if the Seal fellow loses his job? Why should you worry about your wife? Nobody thinks twice about the divorce of a leading lady. Probably it will prolong the run of her play. They're in a hurry, and you, I gather, are not. Tell them you decline to behave like a gentleman. Put detectives on them and, if you get your evidence, divorce her.'

'No,' said John, and the chin came out. 'You must

understand,' he went on shyly and slowly, 'that, in spite of everything, the Mary part of my life still means a lot to me. I'm fond of her, I respect her; I couldn't hurt her, I couldn't spy on her; and as for detectives——' Mr. Adam's pale face expressed disgust.

'Very well,' said Boom, with sympathy. 'I might say that you were sacrificing the future to the past: but I don't. I understand. The position is, then, that you are determined to behave like a gentleman and commit adultery with a strange woman.'

'Yes. How do I get one?'

Mr. Boom laughed deeply. 'My dear fellow, this is Chancery Lane, not Jermyn Street. You mustn't ask your lawyer to provide you with a lover.'

'But I don't understand——'

'At this point,' said Boom, 'I must remind you of my remarks about criminal conspiracy. The Court does not approve of gentlemen who behave like gentlemen: it would be improper for me to provide you with a lady, and I am not sure that I ought, at this point, to give you advice. I can, however, throw out a few hints about the present practice. As a rule, the gentleman takes the lady to a hotel—Brighton or some such place—enters her in the book as his wife—shares a room with her, and sends the bill to his wife. The wife's agents cause inquiries to be made, and eventually they find the chambermaid who brought the guilty couple their morning tea. A single night used to be sufficient, but the President has been tightening things up, and we generally advise a good long week-end to-day. What you want to suggest, you see, is that there is a real and continuing attachment, not merely a casual fling or a put-up job. That is why Brighton is good, for all the wild lovers are supposed to go there, though I never saw any one at the Capitol but clergymen and family parties. For the same reason it's better for the lady to be of your own class, or as near as possible. For, remember, you are supposed to have left a very attractive wife for love of the lady, and you must not put too much of a strain on the credulity of the Court, though in an undefended suit the woman hardly ever appears. At one time her name didn't appear, but Hawkhurst has put a stop to that.'

'Tell me,' said Mr. Adam, hesitating, 'do I actually have to—to—you know?'

'To sleep with the lady? Technically, no. But you must share the same room and you must be in the same bed in the morning, when the tea comes up.'

'Good God!' said John. 'What a world!'

'True,' said Boom, and slowly raised his great bulk from the chair. 'Well, I must go back to the office.'

'Half a minute. You haven't told me where to find the lady.'

'Ah!' said Boom. 'That's your affair. Good-bye, and good luck.' He took a step up Chancery Lane and stopped. 'I have heard,' he said darkly, 'that there are agents—and even agencies. Most improper.'

'I'd no idea,' said John, 'that it was all so difficult.'

'I warned you,' said Boom, and he ambled away.

For three days John Adam did nothing in the matter. Going about London he marvelled at the number of women there were: and wondered how he was to persuade one of them to be intimate with him. The problem gave him a new interest in the entire sex. At the office, in tea-shops, in the Tube, he found himself studying the female clerks and secretaries, waitresses, and passengers in a manner quite unusual to him. Shopgirls, returning home, thought that he was staring rudely at them, and gave him sharp looks. But he was thinking, 'That's a poor, pale girl. She'd be glad of a free week-end at Brighton. But how could I ever invite her?' Dictating letters about works of education to his secretary, Miss Frame, he tried to imagine himself saying, 'Miss Frame, would you care to come to Brighton with me, purely as a matter of form? I want to behave like a gentleman to my wife.' He could not imagine it. After the word 'Brighton', he was sure, Miss Frame would indignantly leave the building. It was, he concluded, an impossible proposition to put to any one.

Yet the thing, it seemed, was done, and done often. Other gentlemen successfully behaved like gentlemen: and why not he? Not for the first time John Adam wished that he were a 'man-of-the-world'. A man-of-the-world would know at once how to find a suitable person, or would have among his friends men-of-the-world who could help him. John did not even know any men to whom he would dare to put the question. The members of the Addison Club would, one and all, be horrified. Boom knew well enough, he was sure; but Boom had been in a maddening mood, alternately expanding and shutting up like a clam. Boom's dark remark about 'agencies' was his only hope. But where were the agencies? Evidently an Agency for the Supply of Intimate Women would not be in the telephone directory. He looked: and it was not. There was a *Matrimonial Post* and a *Matrimonial Times*; but the purpose of these agencies was, no doubt, to make, and not to unmake, marriages.

Mr. Boom had mentioned Jermyn Street. And after a week's inaction Mr. Adam, in despair, decided to try Jermyn Street. There could be no greater insult to a wife, surely, than for a husband to associate with a prostitute: so, at least, he thought, he would satisfy the law. Perhaps, indeed, in the case of a prostitute, this week-end visit to the seaside would not be necessary. After all, there were hotels in London.

But the prospect was repugnant. He belonged to a famous club in St. James's, almost opposite to the west end of Jermyn Street, and, after one experience of the dangerous thoroughfare, he had been careful at night to walk home another way. The ladies of the town affected him with horror—more physical than moral. He thought of them conventionally and compassionately as 'unfortunates': he was aware, from the utterances of certain advanced thinkers, that they were victims of the economic system, and he had gathered, from certain plays and books, that every one of them had a heart of gold. Many of them, he understood, had been dishonoured in their youth by the sons of clergy-men and squires, and, expelled from their native villages, had come by inevitable stages to Jermyn Street. It was not, then, the righteous revulsion of the innocent that made him go home by Pall Mall. Only, when one of the ladies came near him, he shuddered, as if he had touched a snake.

So it was not far from a heroic moment when this sensitive man decided to go into Jermyn Street and seek a prostitute for the sake of two pure women. That evening he remained in the club till most of the members had gone home. While waiting he drank two brandy-and-sodas, an unusual indulgence, partly to give him courage and partly as a disinfectant: for he was ill-informed about certain diseases and had a vague belief that some of them could be communicated almost by a look.

He set forth at last at 11.45, determined for the first time in his life to 'pick up' a woman. He said 'Good night' to the hall porter with a sense of shame. St. James's Street seemed more brightly lighted than usual, and the windows, he felt, were full of watchers who had guessed his guilty secret. Crossing the street, he remembered that he had made no plans about the hotel. Like most Londoners, he knew little of London hotels. Probably there was some special and (by everybody else) well-known divorce hotel such as the famous hotels at Brighton. There must be some place to which the citizen of Brighton could go when he wished to behave like a gentleman. Where was it? He supposed that the ladies of Jermyn Street would know.

He entered the long narrow canyon of Jermyn Street, where the dim light was better fitted for his horrid enterprise. A sharp easterly wind met him. The street was empty: only, very far away, a single stout man moving towards him past a lamp-post and, a little nearer, a female figure moving away from him. The small boy, idly poking a stick into a quiet pool, sees live things scuttle from every stone and corner. And thus, when John had gone no more than twenty yards, the street seemed to burst, or rather, melt, into life. Dark, shadowy shapes, sometimes in couples, detached themselves from shop windows or floated out of sheltering doorways, and, with a strange swaying movement, silently approached him. He felt as if he were about to be attacked by bats. A whiff of scent came down the wind.

Ten feet away the first lady cooed: 'Hullo, dearie.'

She was tall and substantial: she wore a long fawn coat topped by a spacious collar of fur, which was of an unpleasing yellow colour. Her painted face seemed to be nesting

in the fur. She advanced upon him with an extraordinary
gait, setting one foot in front of the other, like a cat picking
its way across a muddy farm-yard.

When they were nearly level she put her head on one side,
and smiled very tenderly and said, 'Where are you going,
dear?'

John Adam shuddered in his soul. He was quite sure
that he could never behave like a gentleman with this lady.
He felt unreasonably that he ought to answer the question
put to him, but no words would come. He smiled apolo-
getically and walked straight on, feeling that he had been
unpardonably rude.

She called after him, very softly and precisely, 'Won't
you change your mind, sir? I can promise you will not be
disappointed.'

Her politeness increased his sense of guilt. 'I ought at
least,' he thought, 'to stop and say something.'

But now two other ladies were approaching, each fas-
tidiously picking their way, as if the pavement were in parts
red-hot, and each wearing a succulent smile. One of these,
like the first lady, was a vast blonde, flamboyant and furry;
but the other was smaller, neater, dark, and less overwhelming.

'That would be more the sort of one,' thought Mr. Adam,
'but what does one do if there are two?'

The smaller lady, at the usual range, said in the same
precise style, 'Hullo, dear. Can I give you a little pleasure,
sir?'

She halted. The mountainous blonde passed on, and
John Adam very nearly halted too. The problem of
etiquette was solved: the woman seemed a decent, quiet,
sort: close to, she was seen to be older and plainer than he
had thought: but, after all, he was not looking for beauty,
only for some one who would not make him feel sick. She
might do. He would stop and speak to her. But merely
to stop, he found, was a frightening and difficult feat: it
would be final—once he had stopped he would never
escape: and it was in his mind that to stop would be in some
way illegal. He glanced up the street. The stout man on
the other side was only thirty yards away now, beyond the
first street-lamp. Good heavens! old Pottifer, on his way

to the club! John Adam, in a panic of shame, marched on ahead again without a word to the lady, who said wistfully, 'Won't you change your mind?' and rejoined the blonde.

The stout man came into the light of the street-lamp, and was not Pottifer at all. John walked on, cursing his ineffectuality. What a fool! He had been rude to two unfortunate women and had achieved nothing. The moment he saw a lady who seemed suitable he would stop, he determined; he would be decisive and a man-of-the-world. At least, he knew now what kind of lady would be endurable —small and neat and quiet, probably dark, not one of those gaudy monsters whose every movement proclaimed their profession. The next five ladies were all of that description, and he shrank from them all. But at least he could be polite. When they said 'Hullo, dear,' he answered 'Good evening'; and when they said 'Where are you going, dear?' he answered 'Home'; and when they said 'Come home with me, dear,' he answered 'No, thank you': and once, to soften the blow, he added, 'Not to-night.' But even these efforts did not dispel the sense of discourtesy and wrong which oppressed him. He felt that he was the only guilty person in the street, though he was only seeking to behave like a gentleman and they were far from behaving like ladies.

He was near the end of the street now, but no nearer to being divorced than he had been before he entered it. Suddenly, on the other side, he saw a small but evidently naughty lady sheltering from the wind in the door of a shop. Her age, he judged, was about twenty-five, not too old and professional therefore; and her dress was dark and quiet. She stood perfectly still, but slightly bent her small head sideways, the most delicate inquiry. John Adam's heart fluttered with fear, but, remembering his vow, he crossed the road like a true man-of-the-world.

''Ullo, *chéri*,' said the lady. '*Bon soir, monsieur*. You coming 'ome with me?'

French! An unexpected complication. He wondered whether there was any legal objection to his behaving like a gentleman with a French lady.

'Good evening,' he replied inadequately.

'You come to my flat, *chéri*? I give you a good time.'

She was cold and shivering, poor thing, but she was haggard and horrible, he thought, and painted like a roundabout. He could not face it. But he must try. He said, 'Isn't there some hotel we could go to?'

'What for hotel? I have a nice flat in St. James's. I show you nice pictures.'

He ought now to explain about the divorce laws of England, about hotel bills, and registers, and evidence. But he could not. Anyhow, she was French and would not do.

'It's late,' he said. 'I think I'd better go home, thank you.'

She became pleading, voluble, and much less Continental.

'Won't you change your mind, *chéri*? I'll go anywhere you like, do anything you like. Only a short time, dear. I've taken nothing to-night, dear, and it's crool cold.'

'No, really, thanks. I'm awfully sorry.' He had encouraged her with false hopes and felt himself shamefully responsible for her sufferings. He took out a pound note and gave it to her.

She said, 'You're a gentleman, dear. I can't hardly pay the rent this week. Sure you won't change your mind, dear? You won't be disappointed. All the gentlemen come back to me.'

'Are you French or what?' he asked.

'No, dear. Walthamstow. But a lot of 'em fall for a bit of French, when they wouldn't look twice at an English girl.'

'Good night,' he said.

'Good night, dear.'

John Adam, coming out to the healthy lights of Lower Regent Street, drew a deep breath, like a man welcoming the clean air on his emerging from a dungeon. As he left the street yet one more lady said 'Hullo, dear,' but now he could not even reply. He had done with all that. Not even for Mary would he ever attempt it. It was refreshing to be among ordinary clean men and women again, hurrying home. He wondered what Joan would say if she knew how he had spent the last quarter of an hour: and he grew hot at the thought.

But he had failed in his purpose, and that was dispiriting.

Other men would not have failed. What was the matter with him? It ought to be easy to behave like a gentleman.

Mr. Boom listened attentively to Mr. Adam's sad story of Jermyn Street.

'It sounds,' he said at the end, 'like the story of the starving nobleman who died in an orchard because he couldn't stoop to pick up a fallen apple. But I'm glad you failed, John. The tale does credit to your taste, though not to your intelligence. I think I told you before that you ought not to stir out of doors without a solicitor. Do you really want to read in *The Times*: "The Court found that John Adam, Secretary to the Society for the Advancement of Education, had had relations with a prostitute who gave an address in Shaftesbury Avenue"?'

'No,' said John gloomily. 'I suppose not.'

'Unpleasant. And, perhaps ineffective——'

'What d'you mean? I thought you said that a single act was enough——'

'Ah, yes, but you must remember that in the Divorce Court the presumption is that every one is lying. If you swear that your "relations" with a woman have been confined to a kiss under the mistletoe the world will suspect the worst: and a very little circumstantial evidence may land you in the cart. But if you confess that you have committed adultery the Court, as if affronted by the suggestion that an Englishman could be capable of such a thing, pricks up its ears. In the former case five minutes may be sufficient, in the latter a day and a night may not. Adultery, you see, is nearly always a matter of presumption, and if the Judge refuses to presume you can't make him. One would say that the worst insult a man could pay his wife would be to go with a prostitute: and, if an injured wife complained to the Court that she saw him coming out of a brothel, it would probably be useless for him to swear that he was engaged in rescue-work and had done nothing inside but have a drink and a smoke. But if you confess that you spent a night with a prostitute the Court, quite likely, will say, "We do not believe that this distinguished and cultivated gentleman is capable of sleeping with this abandoned woman.'' You must get it into your head that you are putting your name down for an obstacle-race: and the Court cheats all the time. For the object of the Divorce Court is to make divorce difficult, and old Hawkhurst has been on the warpath lately.'

'It's all very difficult,' said Mr. Adam.

One day at the office he thought suddenly, 'One of Mary's stage friends will surely know.' But then, to write to her for advice in the matter would be collusion—or was it recrimination? Still, if the letter were destroyed no harm could be done: and he could disguise the subject-matter. He would risk it.

He wrote that evening:

DEAR MARY,

A friend of mine is very anxious to behave like a gentleman, but so far has been unable to find a suitable companion. He understands that there are agencies for this purpose, and I thought perhaps that one of your stage friends might know of one.

Yours affectionately,

JOHN

He added:

PS.—Burn this, and for God's sake don't telegraph.

He received a telegram the following morning:

Adam Heddle and Feather Sussex Street Strand darling too sweet of you but why the mystery and bugaboo of course go at once to Mortimer's Secretarial and Typing Bureau Holiday Street and hurry dear because want settle down present life so very unsatisfactory thanks kisses Mary.

Collusion certainly. Condonation probably.

John Adam concluded that his wife had not yet consulted a solicitor. He did not, however, know that, after sending her telegram, she kissed his letter and carefully put it in her hand-bag, in order to show it to Mr. Martin Seal.

On a fine Monday morning in October John Adam left the office early and walked up to Holiday Street..

The Secretarial Bureau occupied the whole of a second floor. As John passed through the glass door he heard the multitudinous clicking of typewriters, and was glad that by way of precaution he had brought a manuscript to be typed. A young woman came out into the lobby, and through the door he saw a dozen female heads, all hung like drooping flowers over typewriters. It might be that Mary's information was nonsense, and the place no more than it pretended to be, a respectable assembly of typists and secretaries. He felt hot.

The young woman took him into a bigger room. A robust, elderly woman sat in a swivel-chair behind a roll-topped desk. She had an expansive bosom, and large tortoise-shell spectacles. Her mouth was a long, straight line, and Mr. Adam formed the impression that she was rugged and alarming.

'Good morning,' she said primly.

'Good morning,' he said. 'Can I see Mr. Mortimer?'

'I am Miss Mortimer.'

'Oh!' said John, stupidly.

Somehow he had expected Mortimer to be a man. He was quite sure now that he had come to the wrong place.

'There's not *another* Mortimer Bureau, I suppose?'

'No,' said Miss Mortimer. 'This is the only one. I founded it, so I ought to know. What can I do for you?'

John produced from a breast pocket his manuscript.

'Can you type this?'

'Certainly.'

Miss Mortimer took the document, put a business-like clip through one corner of it, and in a business-like manner made some notes in the margin.

'How many carbons?' she asked.

'Oh, one, please. No, two.' He did not want any; but one seemed inadequate.

'Two carbon copies. Single or double spacing?'

'Er,' said John, 'I really don't mind.'

'Double spacing. Any particular margin?'

'No. Oh, no,' he said feebly; 'just a good margin.'

'The work will be completed by 6 p.m. Call or send?'

'I beg your pardon?'

'Will you call for the work, or shall we send it to your address?'

'Oh! Ah! I'll call for it.'

Everything, thought John, seemed to be much more difficult than it seemed to be.

'Our charge is one and sixpence for a thousand words and half-rates for carbon copies.'

'Thank you.'

'Thank you. Will that be all?'

'Yes, thank you. Good morning.'

'Good morning.'

Miss Mortimer sat back in her swivel-chair, executed a little waggle to starboard, and looked at him keenly.

John Adam looked at Miss Mortimer. Now, surely, was the time to speak. He opened his mouth, and shut it again. His eyes fell: for he was ashamed of the improper purpose with which he had visited this worthy institution of hard-working women.

'Good morning,' he said, and walked sadly to the door.

Very sadly: for once more he had failed. Once more he had to begin all over again.

When he reached the door Miss Mortimer spoke—in a different tone, higher, and, he thought, suggestive.

She said, 'Any time you wish for a Confidential Personal Secretary——'

He halted, trembling. The difference was slight: but, yes, he thought, the tone was suggestive, encouraging. Hope, but not courage, returned to him. He went back to the desk, and said, blushing: 'Miss Mortimer, forgive me if I am wrong—though I fear you may find it difficult. But —er—ah—those who sent me to you led me to understand that—er—ah—there was another side to your business. I'm quite sure there's been some mistake,' he added quickly, expecting to be blown out of the room by a gale of feminine anger.

But Miss Mortimer said surprisingly, with a wide and happy smile: 'Don't beat about the bush, my good man. You want a divorce.'

'I do,' said the publisher, and sat down heavily. The relief was so great that it amounted to shock.

4

An extraordinary change had come over Miss Mortimer. A warm humanity replaced her prim efficiency. She took off her spectacles, and her face miraculously became round and gentle. She came to Mr. Adam, took both his hands, and sprinkled him with cheerful words.

'Oh, poor man,' she said. 'But why didn't you utter before? Whoever sent you here must have forgotten to give you the password. "Confidential Personal Secretary", remember that always—or C.P.S. in a wire. The typewriting side of us is perfectly genuine, and profitable too: and in every way it's better to keep the two separate. Poor man, how you must have suffered! I thought from the first that you were a major client—you and your little manuscript—ha!'—Miss Mortimer here laughed richly—'but I can't be too careful. Now tell me all your trouble. Those odious laws! I've fought them all my life. Be quite at home, do. Will you take a glass of sherry?'

John Adam was not in the habit of taking wine in the middle of the day, but he said, 'Well, thank you, I will.' It seemed to be customary among the experts in divorce. Besides, at that moment, a glass of wine seemed to be right. He felt suddenly and strangely at ease with Miss Mortimer: he felt himself at last in harbour after a long and doubtful tossing on the hostile sea.

Here at last was somebody who understood this horrible business and was on his side, without reservations.

Over the sherry he explained his situation. Miss Mortimer listened without a word of interruption. How rare a creature!

At the end she said, 'Poor man, you're just the kind of case my little show was made for. The rough stuff of this world, they don't need me so much. Do anything, sleep with any one, and don't care who knows. But a man like you—it must be agony. I know—I've been through it all. Twice.' She paused a moment, as if pondering that surprising confession. 'Not that we don't cater for the rough stuff,' she went on hurriedly, as if it might turn out that Mr. Adam was rough stuff too. 'Oh, no, we provide for every sort. I think that's right, don't you? After all, a man who's behaving like a gentleman deserves to be treated like one. A little sympathy, a little special care. It's a big

thing, say what you like. To go off for a week-end with a
strange woman in order to give yourself a bad name and
allow some fool of a wife to be rid of you—it must be an
ordeal at the best, well, mustn't it? Most men feel it, I
believe, though often enough they don't let on. And if
the woman's uncongenial, Mr. Adam, *imagine* what a man
like you must suffer! That first night, the dinner, playing
cards in the bedroom—and then the bed-drill—the waiting
for the maid to come with the tea—you know the routine,
of course, Mr. Adam?'

'Yes, yes,' said Mr. Adam quickly, and felt at last a
man-of-the-world. He knew about the tea.

'Well, my dear man,' said Miss Mortimer. 'IMAGINE all
that with a temperamental misfit! And so our object all
sublime is to make the intervener fit the respondent——'

'I beg your pardon?'

'The girl,' she explained, 'the man—though, of course,
strictly, she's not an intervener at all.'

'Ah, yes,' said Mr. Adam, mystified.

'Yes. In there, Mr. Adam'—Miss Mortimer pointed
proudly to the inner room—'we have personal secretaries
for every type of gentleman: girls who can talk to stockbrokers and athletes, girls who can talk to highbrows and
lawyers, girls who can spend a night throwing poker-dice
with racing-men, girls who can argue with journalists and
politicians, and girls who can be perfectly quiet with a man
like you. Yes, Mr. Adam, I know exactly what you require
One of the mouse type: one of our dear little restful mouses.
And, as it happens, I have the very thing free. Won't say
a word.' She blew into a speaking-tube and said, 'Send Miss
Myrtle, please.'

'Secretaries,' she babbled on. 'A happy idea, don't you
think? It solves the class problem. As a rule, when a
man behaves like a gentleman with a woman who is not
quite a lady it looks like a fishy case, and that old President
is very hot. But if it's a secretary the thing is quite different.
Every man falls in love with his secretary—very often he
marries her, and nobody thinks the worse of him. It's a
recognized thing: people rather like it: they think it's
romantic. When two people have been working together
at the Atom or Trade Unionism or something and decide to

get married it all sounds rather intellectual and democratic. Union of two minds. Humble girl from Balham real inspiration of celebrated scientist. Shows there's a chance for every girl. Shows women really run everything—and that's so popular. So when the Judge hears that the respondent has run away with his charming secretary he's not a bit surprised or snoopy. It looks much better in the papers too. . . . Come in, Miss Myrtle.'

Miss May Myrtle, the Mouse, came shyly in and stood by the door, looking as if at any moment she might scurry away into some secret hole.

She was small and neat: she had a small, neat, honest face, with brown eyes, and nose slightly snubbed, and many freckles. Her little feet were almost invisible, her little voice almost inaudible. She wore no lipstick or paint. Mr. Adam was much relieved by her appearance: he had feared that any professional partner would be scarlet from head to foot.

'Miss Myrtle, this is Mr. Adam, who has some confidential work for you.'

'How do you do, Mr. Adam?' whispered Miss Myrtle, and gave him a limp little hand, which seemed scarcely prehensile.

Miss Mortimer had resumed her spectacles and her businesslike manner.

'You've not been out lately, I think, Miss Myrtle?'

'No, Miss Mortimer. The Duke was the last. There was something said about his wanting me again, but I haven't heard nothing.'

The voice came faintly, a tiny Cockney vibration from some far-off wireless station, imperfectly tuned-in.

'When would you want her, Mr. Adam?'

'As soon as possible.'

'This week-end?'

'If convenient.'

'Very well, Miss Myrtle, will you keep this week-end free, please? That will do now.'

'Yes, Miss Mortimer.' The Mouse evaporated.

'Satisfactory, Mr. Adam?'

'Perfectly. A charming young lady,' he added, thinking it was wise to show some enthusiasm.

Miss Mortimer glanced sharply at him. 'Now, as to terms. We charge twenty guineas down, Mr. Adam, and another ten on the absolute.'

'I beg your pardon?'

'On the absolute,' said Miss Mortimer patiently, as if instructing a backward child. 'On the decree being made absolute another ten guineas is payable.'

John Adam, taken aback, said, 'It seems a great deal of money.'

Miss Mortimer sat back and shrugged her ample shoulders.

'You have to pay for the best,' she said. 'Good service, a splendid staff, and results. Results, Mr. Adam. There's never been any Court unpleasantness in a case I've handled yet. That's a great consideration, Mr. Adam. If you want cheap work, go elsewhere. Go to Mooney's and see the treatment you get. You're going to lose nerve-tissue over this business, Mr. Adam. It's a strain, at the best, a cruel strain. Our policy is to ease the strain by psychological service. And that's worth money. Besides, our business is expensive, Mr. Adam. I don't overwork my girls in this department; it wouldn't do. Very few of them do more than two jobs in the year. For every girl you see in there I have three on my books outside. Mooney's are after all of them, and they have to be retained. You can't——'

'Yes, yes, I quite understand,' said Mr. Adam. 'I beg your pardon.'

'Not at all. And then, of course, there's the deposit for good behaviour. A mere matter of form in your case, Mr. Adam, but——'

'What is that?'

'We employ a very respectable class of girl, Mr. Adam; we have to. And we do what we can to make sure that they're not interfered with.'

'Interfered with?' This was a new expression to the innocent publisher.

'Intimacy, Mr. Adam. You know what I mean. It's very seldom that we have any trouble, but there are one or two gentlemen who think that when they are behaving like gentlemen to their wives they need not behave like gentlemen to our staff. Your little mouse, now—that Duke she was speaking of, he thought that he could take advantage of her simply because it was her duty to spend a night with him. Well, he lost his deposit—twenty good guineas. Now he wants the use of her again—what we call continuity evidence: the girl doesn't guess it, but I've turned him down. I wouldn't have a hair of that girl's head touched, Mr. Adam. She keeps a blind father at Greenwich, and five brothers and sisters, and if it wasn't for her confidential work she couldn't do it.'

'Admirable,' said Mr. Adam. 'But——'. The thought in his mind was that, the whole point of the transaction being to persuade the Court that he had been intimate, it was odd that he should begin by giving a guarantee that he would not be intimate. He felt that Boom would have a word for this.

Miss Mortimer seemed to read his mind. 'Of course, we can't make it a matter of contract, because we could never sue on it. So we have this deposit system. As I say, in your case it's a matter of form, I know, but I have to treat every one the same.'

'Naturally. So I shall send you a cheque for forty guineas?'

'Fifty.'

'But I thought you said—the absolute——'

'Yes, it's payable on the absolute, but we like to have it in advance. You can trust us; we can't always trust our clients. And, as I say, we can't sue them. What it comes to is that if there's no absolute we return you thirty, or ten if the good-behaviour money is forfeited. Is that clear? Perhaps,' said Miss Mortimer, 'you would fill in this form.'

Mr. Adam sat down meekly and filled in the long form which she thrust towards him. Name and address, profession, age, whether any previous experience of divorce, whether free from contagious diseases, for what period confidential secretary required, and where, and, finally, an undertaking to regard all transactions with the Bureau as confidential, and to hold the Bureau harmless in the event of loss of property, damage to reputation, or whatsoever.

.   .   .   .

When he returned from his stroll the Mouse had put on a simple evening-frock of pale-blue-satin, square-cut in the bosom. She was busy at her finger-nails, which were now, he noticed with dismay, a lustrous plum-colour. Her face, too, was not the modest little face he knew, her lips were nearly the same colour as her nails, and her cheeks an artificial rose. John Adam had an old-fashioned dislike for cosmetics, and the change disturbed him.

'I've unpacked your things,' she said.

His blue pyjamas, he saw, and the rose-coloured night-gown lay intimately upon the pillows. He saw also that there were two cocktail glasses on the dressing-table, both empty. For no clear cause, he felt uneasy. But the Mouse remained silent, working hard at her nails: and he dressed for dinner in silence and the bathroom. Clearly it was her professional duty not to speak unless spoken to.

In silence the adulterous couple descended, and in silence crossed the great lounge. But as they approached the coffee-room Mr. Adam felt a tiny pressure on his arm. He looked down and saw the little hand of the Mouse like a crumpled flower on his sleeve. He looked then at her face, and saw, to his dismay, that she was gazing up at his own with a very tender expression.

'Good heavens!' he thought, 'has she fallen in love with me?'

This fear was at once dispelled: for the Mouse, still with the light of adoration in her eyes, whispered fiercely, 'Say something, you dumb fish!'

'I beg your pardon?'

'Say something. Smile,' was her reply. 'They'll think it's a cod's funeral.'

Mr. Adam realized that Miss Myrtle was conscientiously acting her part and expecting him to do the same.

But he could think of nothing to say.

He said, 'My dear'; and again, 'My dear': with a grave and wooden countenance.

'My God!' the Mouse replied. 'Can't you smile?'

He forced a sickly light into his face and gazed into her glowing eyes: she pressed close to him, and thus they entered the coffee-room, Mr. Adam still murmuring foolishly, 'My dear.' And, their eyes occupied with each other, they nearly knocked over a table at which a lonely clergyman sat reading Jane Austen.

The head waiter took them for lovers at once, and led them to a small table for two in a distant corner.

'Will you take the dinner, sir?' he said.

'Yes,' said Mr. Adam, not caring what he took. He saw that the Mouse was making a cross face at him, and he added, 'And two cocktails.'

'Yes, sir. Any special kind?'

'No,' said Mr. Adam, who did not know any kinds.

'White Donkey,' said the Mouse.

'Two White Donkeys?'

'What are they?' Mr. Adam was about to ask, but he checked himself and said, 'Very well.'

When they were left alone, the Mouse leaned across the table and said strongly, 'Pardon my rudeness just now, Mr. Adam, but you are serious about this job?'

'Undoubtedly.'

'Then you ought to act serious. *Act.* I mean act. Play your part, see? When we're alone I leave you alone, that's understood. But when we're in public we're lovers, see? Everything you do, you've got to think the King's Proctor's watching you, you see. It's ten to one there's no trouble at all, but, in case he does get his knife into you, you want to leave the hotel something to remember you by. And if the head waiter says, "Oh, yes, I remember the couple, more like father and daughter they were," well, where are you then? That's why I pushed you into the table just now.'

'I see,' said Mr. Adam.

'Besides,' she went on, 'it's disheartening for me, you see. While I'm on the job I like to make a good job of it. I take a pride in my work and make things easy, if I can. But if there's no co-operation any one loses interest, well, naturally. This dinner, now,' she went on, without a pause. 'Don't you ever take your best girl out to dinner?'

'We sometimes go to Simpson's,' he said, 'and have a saddle of mutton.'

'Well, I don't know about that, but I do know for this business you ought never to order the regular *dinner*. I might be your wife. *À la carte* always—remember that to-morrow, won't you?'

Mr. Adam sighed in his soul, thinking, 'All this has to happen *again*!'

'What I mean, you ought to take *trouble* about the ordering—ask me what I like, and that—and then order something special I never heard of. I know with the Duke it was generally half an hour before anything was ordered, what with all the talk about it. Nothing shows you're gone on any one like the way you order a meal. And there's another thing—you don't mind my telling you a few things, do you?'

'Not at all,' said Mr. Adam, and added lamely, 'my dear.'

'Well, there's another thing, now,' said the Mouse indignantly. 'What's all this "My dear" about? Don't you realize, *darling*, you've left your wife and home for me, *darling*, and this is the first night we've had away together, *darling*, and you can't hardly speak you're so excited, *darling*?'

'I see,' said Mr. Adam.

'My God!' said the Mouse, ' you'll give me fits! Here comes the waiter, now—squeeze my hand, darling, and look soppy at me.'

She thrust her little hand across the table behind the lamp, and looked into his eyes with an expression of humble yearning. Mr. Adam reluctantly took the little plum-clawed hand and blinked at her through his spectacles.

'I must say something,' he thought miserably. 'I must call this formidable young woman "darling". I can't.'

And he couldn't. The waiter approached, Miss Myrtle withdrew her hand with a little sigh, and sought consolation in her White Donkey.

'What wine have you ordered, pet?' she next said brightly.

'I haven't,' said Mr. Adam. 'Pet!' Good Heavens! 'What would you like? A little claret?'

He was surprised to receive a sharp kick on the shin. It could not have come from the waiter, who had just stepped away to beckon the wine-waiter.

Miss Myrtle hissed at him, 'Fizz! Bubbly! The love-wine, darling.'

It was extraordinary how she managed to maintain at the same time her ferocity of tone and sweetness of expression.

Of all drinks John disliked champagne most. But he ordered a bottle: and Miss Myrtle chose the brand.

The dinner proceeded. They ate the oysters in silence, save for one remark from the Mouse, which was, 'Oyster—that's you, Mr. Adam. Soft and nothing to say. More like a baby, aren't you, dear?' At the same time she kicked him again (but more kindly than before) and said, 'Go on—laugh, darling! Laugh, dear old whelk!'

John produced a sudden, short, staccato laugh—'Ha!' and the clergyman looked round angrily at the licentious couple.

The soup was a quiet course too. But when the waiter had filled their glasses and left them with the fish Miss Myrtle raised her glass and said, 'Clink, darling!'

'I beg your pardon? Oh, yes, of course. Clink.'

The golden glasses solemnly kissed, and, as the waiter approached again, a deliberate radiance, a slowly swelling glory, spread over Miss Myrtle's face.

The waiter moved away and the small face at once returned to normal. She sipped her wine. 'Not bad,' she said, and emptied her glass. John Adam drank a little of the high-priced liquid and refilled the lady's glass. It did him good, though he disliked it. It did Miss Myrtle a great deal of good. She began to bubble with gaiety and giggles: and with every draught of champagne became more and more the happy lover.

'Chatter away, John,' she said. 'Now you ought to say, "Tell me the story of your life." That's the line.'

'Very well,' said Mr. Adam, benevolently. 'Tell me the story of your life.' And he drank some more champagne.

She was not a bad little thing, he thought, when she was not abusing or kicking him: and now that she had become talkative the strain was eased.

She ate voraciously, and chattered volubly. She told him the story of her life, to which he did not pay much attention. He was thinking of other things. At the age of fifteen she had taken on the duties of mother and housekeeper to her five brothers and sisters. Then a year as programme-seller at the Fun House Theatre, followed by a year in a perfume shop. Then there had been a small legacy; she learned to type and became a Professional Secretary. Her young man was in a film-studio. But half of this Mr. Adam did not hear.

'A sociological anæsthetic,' he was thinking dreamily. 'A sociological anæsthetic in an intolerable environment.' That was perfectly true. He had noticed the phrase in a pamphlet recently published by his firm for a worthy Society which was opposed to the consumption of 'alcohol' and desired that the pamphlet should be studied in the elementary schools. There had been a long list of the Uses of Alcohol, of which Number 3 was, 'As a disinfectant' and Number 1 was this, 'A sociological anæsthetic in an intolerable environment.' It was true. He had never expected to be grateful to this gaseous, golden, artificial beverage. He had always treasured in his memory some lines from a comic opera song about champagne:

> This wine is full of gases
>   Which are to me offensive;
> It pleases all you asses
>   Because it is expensive.
> But not a chimney-sweeper
> Would touch it if 'twere cheaper—
>
> It's only fit for weddings . . .

That was all that he could remember. But now, having drunk more champagne than he would drink in a week of weddings, he admitted that the wine had praiseworthy properties. Though not exactly devil-may-care, he felt almost resigned to his environment. Redeeming qualities, not perceived before, stood out in Miss Myrtle's appearance and character. How gay and understanding she was—relieving him of the necessity to talk but keeping up the necessary appearances. He had been afraid of a mute and embarrassing dinner, and he filled her glass again.

His next fear was that the Mouse would become too gay. Her little laugh became more and more frequent and girlish. Now at every laugh he looked round the room with anxiety. At every new arrival he glanced guiltily at the door. More than half the tables were full; and the guests seemed to grow

more and more respectable. There were three family
parties, and two clergymen; but he could see no one else
whose appearance suggested that they were behaving like
gentlemen. He, John Adam, seemed to be the only liber-
tine there: and he expected, at any moment, to see two or
three friends from the Board of Education march in.

When the champagne was finished the Mouse asked,
simply and naturally, for more. He hesitated; but she put
her little purple talons on his hand, and said (the waiter
being behind him), 'You couldn't be crool to your little
May—not to-night.'

And she smiled so tenderly that he said, 'Very well.
Another half-bottle, please, waiter.'

'O *darling*! A *whole* one! May's *thirsty*.'

Miss Myrtle's lip trembled, and she seemed about to cry.

'Certainly, my dear. Another bottle, waiter.'

The waiter, grinning, departed.

The Mouse made a face at him.

'Horrid old moneybags, aren't you, darling? Well, then,'
she babbled on, 'I heard of this place, at Miss Mortimer's,
where you found me, and since then I've had a good time,
and the family too. My boy was ever so wild, though, when
he heard, because he made sure that I should be interfered
with, you see. Of course I told him I could look after myself,
and it was all a matter of form, and that, but he kicked up
alarming and went to Miss Mortimer, you see, and he said
if any one touched me he'd go straight to the police; not
that it would matter, because no one could *prove* anything.
Still, Miss Mortimer didn't want any trouble, naturally, so
she started this deposit arrangement—I expect you had to
make a deposit, didn't you?'

'Yes. Twenty guineas.'

'That's right. Well, that was all my Bill's doing, and
a good thing too, I say, because you never know what you
may run into in this class of work, you see, though I must
say they're a very decent class of person we deal with on
the whole. Well, it isn't every one that could afford the
money, is it, not the riff-raff, I mean?'

The new bottle arrived, and a generous draught refreshed
the narrator. 'Well, here's all you wish yourself, darling.
But Bill wasn't satisfied even then—not at first. Well,

when I tell you, the first two or three jobs I had he used to follow me down and hang about outside the hotel. In fact, the first time, he came right up to the bedroom—believe it or not—to see I was all right, you see. He slipped up the back-stairs. Well, I thought my client would have seven fits, well, naturally, but he saw the funny side of it, artist, he was, and he was ever so decent to Bill, and we all had a good laugh, and he gave Bill some bubbly, in the tooth-glass, and we played poker half the night, the three of us, and then I went to bed and the two of them played cribbage till it was daylight—believe it or not. And then when we rang for the tea Bill hid in a cupboard. Laugh? I did give my face a treat.' Miss Myrtle here laughed like a crazy flute, and all the room looked round. 'He was a nice gentleman, that,' she continued reflectively. 'Got his absolute the other day, I see.'

Mr. Adam found that he was becoming interested in this strange traffic.

'How do you manage about the names?' he said. 'I mean, if the same name comes up two or three times, don't the Courts——?'

'Change the name after every job,' said the Mouse. 'I was Rose the last job, Harriet Rose, and Ivy something the time before that. Always flowers, me. Flowers or trees. The men like that, you see. Always seem to go for a flower.'

And she laughed again. She laughed more and more: and at last Mr. Adam noticed that he was laughing too, easily and naturally, as one queer adventure followed another.

'Yes, I'll take a brandy, dear,' said the Mouse. 'And you might have some bubbly sent up to the room.' She went on to discuss the law of divorce. 'Of course,' she said, 'I think it's all a lot of nonsense—well, don't you? Well, if there's children that's another thing, I say—there they are, and they've got to be looked after, the same as if it was a dog or anything else. You can't leave 'em. But if there's no kids, and two people don't want to be married, I don't see what right any one's got to make them, any more than you'd make them sleep in the same bed if they didn't want—well, would you?'

'No,' said Mr. Adam, signing the bill.

'I mean,' she continued, 'if there's going to be all this fuss about people getting divorced there ought to be more fuss made when they're married. Well, if they've a right to interfere with you, that's the time, isn't it. But you know what it is, don't you, with some people, it's engaged to-day and married to-morrow, as easy as getting a wireless licence, and nobody can't say nothing to stop them. I mean, you can tell at once about some couples, they'd never stay the course, but the law don't say nothing until it's too late. And then there's all this trouble and strife. You ought to be able to go to a registry office, *I* say, the same as you do to get married. Oh, well,' she concluded philosophically, 'we mustn't grumble. It's all good for *our* business, anyway.'

'A sociological anæsthetic,' murmured Mr. Adam, sipping his brandy, 'in an intolerable environment.'

'Pardon?'

'A sociological anæsthetic. A description of alcohol.'

'What d'you mean, dear?'

'This,' said Mr. Adam, holding up his glass.

'Oh! I thought yours was brandy, same as mine. Here, clink again, darling, and then you tell me the story of your life.'

They clinked and emptied their glasses. Miss Myrtle laughed merrily, and now Mr. Adam did not even trouble to observe the effect of her laugh upon the other guests.

Without intending to do any such thing, he began to tell her the story of his life.

'You've heard of Mary Moon?' he said. 'She's my wife.'

'Go on!' she said, incredulous, excited.

'Yes.'

'Funny. Two M's, like me. Cool! How'd she come to marry a fish like you?'

'That's the puzzle,' he said mildly. He did not seem to mind now how much the little thing insulted him, for she did it in such a friendly way. He found, as he continued, that, though it was an extraordinary thing to do, it was a pleasure to tell to a sympathetic listener the story of his

life. Miss Myrtle was the first to hear the whole of it. She
listened well, and greedily, but exclaimed like a child
whenever the story became particularly interesting
or improbable. The moving staircase and the costers'
wedding-procession were punctuated with 'Go on!', an
expression which by a subtle variation of tone meant sometimes 'Tell us another!' and sometimes 'Tell us some more.'

'Well, then, you see, the idea was that we should live
in the East End and go on with our work there——'

'The clubs, and that?'

'Yes. But somehow it never came off—and that was a
disappointment to me.'

'She wanted the West End, I bet. Don't blame her.'

'No, I don't think it was that. But it was difficult to
find a place—and my wife thought it would be too much
for me—working all day at the office and going out there
and standing about at a club every evening as well. Anyhow, in the end we took a little flat in London: we said we'd
go over to B.G. two or three times a week, and so we did for
a bit, but after a bit that dropped off.'

'She tired of it, I dare say.'

'No, I don't think it was that,' said Mr. Adam loyally.
'Have some more brandy?'

'I won't say No.'

While he was filling the little glass he thought sadly of the
gradual dropping-off of the expeditions to Bethnal Green.
No, she never tired of them—it was the blasted stage.

'Figg saw her somewhere, you see—you know, the
theatrical man. Heard her sing a song at a party. And
he said he would turn her into a star.'

'So he has too. Go on.'

'He gave her a sort of a job at once. Show-girl. And
had her voice trained, and so on.' Mr. Adam hurried on:
for, though he loved still to see his Mary perform as a star,
he hated the memory of his Mary as a 'show-girl.' 'Eight
guineas a week. Well, we needed it. I had had an illness:
and we spent too much money. In the next show she had
a part—and you know the rest——'

'That's right. Better and better.'

'The trouble was then, you see, that we hardly ever met
—except on Sundays. Just when I came back from the

office she'd be going off to the theatre. I got up early, and
she stayed in bed till late—had to—because she never ate
anything till after the show and didn't get to bed till one or
two. Even on Sundays, often, she'd be rehearsing—or
doing a Charity Matinée——'

'And lots of friends, I dare say,' said Miss Myrtle wisely.

'Yes. Of course. Well, people used to take her out to
supper. I didn't mind that, because I couldn't myself on
account of my work. But there was never anything in it.
I was never jealous—not really—though I thought I was,
once or twice. But I was really jealous of the whole
profession—and I never got on with the actors very well.
I——'

He broke off: he was not going to tell her what agonies
he had suffered trying to get on with the actors—the smart,
successful ones: he could not keep up with their specialized,
elusive talk, did not understand their 'shop', was always
the last to laugh at their jokes. He admired their courage,
their industry, their gaiety; but he felt himself a dull
stranger in a tribe of fireflies. Mary too had been frightened
of them at first, and was shy, he remembered, of the stagy
restaurants. But as she grew into a star he had watched her
slowly changing, gaining every year a little glitter and losing,
he thought, a little sweetness. Every year a little piece
of the old grave Mary seemed to drop away (though she still
slaved for charities and was beloved by everybody in the
theatre), and every year she seemed to shoot up a little
farther out of his reach. Even in her dressing-room he had
felt himself an alien, in the way. He had tried sitting there
in the evenings, when he had been late at the office and they
had not met all day. But that was not much fun—to see her
dash in, tear off a costume, paint her face a different colour,
and dash away again. Or one of those smart young actors
would come in and discuss meticulously in what way and
when he ought to say some silly line. She was not pleased
by pipe-smoking in the dressing-room, because of her voice;
and at the end, when he wanted to carry her off home, Mr.
Figg would come in and carry them both off to the Savoy.
There would be more theatrical shop, more swift, easy-
speaking people; and the educational publisher would sit
mum and unhappy. He never blamed Mary. She did her

best to make him at home with her friends: she loved her
work, it was her life, as publishing was his. She had a right
to it. But that was the truth: he was jealous of the whole
profession—her profession.

'And I dare say,' said the Mouse, 'you were thinking the
whole time it was her money you were spending—she
earning more than you did, I mean, perhaps.'

What a knowing girl the Mouse was!

'Yes, there was that too,' he said. 'Have a little brandy?'

'Well, I don't mind.'

'I think I will too. The fact is,' he went on, 'our lives
didn't fit—anywhere—after the stage began. They did
before,' he added sadly.

'I wonder,' said Miss Myrtle gently. 'If the truth were
told, dear, I expect you were too much of a dear old oyster
for a lively girl like that—right from the beginning—only
when she took you she didn't know enough.'

'Well, perhaps——'

'They all say the same,' the surprising woman continued.
'If the bedroom's not right, then every room in the house
is wrong.'

He stared at the Mouse. 'You know too much,' he said.
'I say, we're getting very confidential.'

'What of it? Now don't get blushing, dear; the room's
empty. Tell us some more.'

'There isn't much more. We stuck it for seven years——'

'No kids?'

'No.'

'Unlucky.'

'Yes. I wanted them, so did she—once. But I don't
think that would have made any difference. We just got
more and more on each other's nerves.'

'Just what I said.'

'We had rows—terrible rows——'

'What about? Men?'

'No. Well, not really. She was never that sort. There
was one man annoyed me rather—the one she wants to
marry now. He took her out a lot, but there was never
anything—you know. But everything he said she seemed
to agree with—and everything we talked about we seemed
to disagree about. And whenever we had an argument we

seemed to have a row. We had one terrible row, I remember
—about the time of the General Strike. I can't remember
how it started, but I know it went on for days. After that,
for a bit, we tried not talking at all—because, you see, it was
making us both ill. She had headaches, and I couldn't
sleep: and our work suffered. Then we'd make it up and
try again, and down would come some terrible row again.
And at last I said I'd better leave her because we were only
making each other unhappy, and she said "Yes," and so
we did.'

John Adam stopped, as if exhausted by his dismal
memories.

'Have a little brandy, dear. You look all done-up.'

'No, I'm all right, thanks.'

'I dare say you've been happier, really, since. And better
in health, too, I shouldn't wonder."

'I believe I have really. And I believe she has too.'

'Still, it's unsatisfactory, isn't it?' said the Mouse compassionately.

'Don't think I'm blaming her in any way, will you?
She's the best person in the world.'

'That's right. Proper misfits, you were. And I wonder
you both stuck it so long—I do really.'

'I say, I've been talking a lot. Look at the time.'

'Yes, and look at that bottle of brandy, what a mess
we've made of it.'

'Miss Myrtle, you've been very kind to me,' said the
publisher, regaining some of his normal formality.

'A pleasure to listen to you, dear, I'm sure. Let's go
to the pictures.'

As they passed down the lounge Mr. Adam began to
hum 'This wine is full of gases,' but his eyes fell on the
clergyman and he stopped, surprised by his own behaviour.

Miss Myrtle hung like a heavy vegetable on his arm,
and she yawned and said, 'I say—do you know?—I feel
a weeny bit under the influence. Do you?'

Now that she mentioned it, Mr. Adam did: that is, he
felt strange, but he had put it down to the central heating.
Possibly the dinner had something to do with his sensations,

but characteristic caution forbade him to make a damaging admission.

'A little sleepy,' he said. 'It's the heating.'

'So do I,' she said. 'It's the sea air, p'r'aps. We'll have a shut-eye at the pictures.'

They went up to Room 41 to get their coats. A bottle of champagne and glasses stood on a tray. Miss Myrtle said 'Oo! Let's have a little bubbly, dear, before we go. Freshen us up, p'r'aps.'

'I won't,' said Mr. Adam. 'But if you like——'

Miss Myrtle lay down on the black eiderdown and closed her eyes and said 'Oo!'

He sat down in the only arm-chair and began to wrestle with the wire entanglement securing the cork; and he sang, gently:

> This wine is full of gases
>   Which are to me offensive;
> It pleases all you asses
>   Because it is expensive . . .

'What was it you said it was?' she murmured drowsily.

'What, dear?'

'The drink.'

'Expensive.'

'No, the other one. What you said at dinner.'

'A sociological anæsthetic?' he began slowly, and not without stumbling.

'That's right.'

'In an intolerable environment.'

'You're clever,' she sighed with sleepy satisfaction. 'I like that. Shouldn't like to type it, though. Not to-night.'

The cork of the sociological anæsthetic flew out with a loud report.

'I'll have a little water with mine, dear.'

Mr. Adam gave her a lot of water with hers.

She said, 'Have some yourself, dear. Don't be a camel.'

'Very well.'

He poured out a thimbleful and sat down. He was very glad to sit down, and disliked the thought of going to the pictures.

'I hope my Bill doesn't come up to-night,' the little voice whispered.

Mr. Adam sat up in alarm.

'Because I'm too sleepy to talk to him.'

'Good Lord! Is he about?' said Mr. Adam.

There was no answer. He stood up. Miss Myrtle was asleep, still clasping her empty glass.

'Well, I'm——' said Mr. Adam, and sat down, much disturbed. His brain was a little foggy but very active— like a sea-mist sweeping inshore before the wind.

Wasn't it enough, he thought, that he should be compelled by law to spend a night of sin with a strange woman without having to be pleasant to her *fiancé* as well? What in the world was he to do with Bill if Bill should arrive? He had no cards; he had had enough talk; and he was sleepy. Would Bill expect to sleep in the room? There was only one couch. Would he be expected to give up the couch to Bill? And perhaps Bill would not be pleasant. Miss Myrtle had clearly had too much champagne and brandy, and this might annoy Bill. Mr. Adam imagined Bill a tall, broad, unusually strong young man. Evidently he was both distrustful and pugnacious. The smallest false step with Bill and there would be a scene. The manager would be called, the King's Proctor would hear of it, and he would not get his divorce. He tiptoed to the bed and gently drew the incriminating glass from Miss Myrtle's small fingers. He went to the window and, through a chink in the curtains, peered out on to the Marine Parade to see if there was a tall young man staring fiercely up at the windows. He could see nobody but old men walking with hunched shoulders into the wind. There was a soft knock at the door.

'Good God!' he thought. 'Bill!' His heart beat. He put the champagne bottle in the bathroom. Then, cautiously, he opened the door.

'Did you ring, sir?' said the waiter.

'No.'

'Sorry, sir.'

Mr. Adam went back, shaking, into the bathroom, and filled a tumbler with sociological anæsthetic.

.   .   .   .   .

He woke at midnight and found himself in the arm-chair. His first thought was Bill. Had Bill arrived? He looked at the bed. Miss Myrtle was asleep. He went into the bath-room, prepared to find Bill asleep in the bath. Bill was not there. He drank two glasses of water, for he had a rough, tormenting thirst. Champagne—never again! he thought. He went back to the bed and looked down at the sleeping Mouse. What now?

She lay on the eiderdown in her pale-blue satin, looking very fragile and childish. One hand was under her cheek, the other lay crumpled in front of her little flushed face. The blue frock had slid up to her knees, and her small feet and thin, silken legs looked like the limbs of a doll on the spacious eiderdown. She breathed deeply and rhythmically (and not very prettily) through the nose. Mr. Adam was filled with a sort of paternal tenderness as he looked upon her—so young, so lamblike and innocent. He gently pulled the blue frock down to her ankles. The little creature stirred in her sleep and said, 'Don't, Bill, don't!'

Mr. Adam was very tired: he longed for sleep: and he was tempted to go at once to his couch and sleep. But some-thing had to be done. The words 'necessary action,' a relic of his military youth, hammered in his head. It was all very well to think paternally about Miss Myrtle, but in the morning he was to be found not merely in a compromis-ing situation but actually in bed with her. And if in the morning she were found lying on the eiderdown in full evening dress the law, he felt, might not be satisfied. Besides, she would be cold. She must wake.

He took the tiny left hand, hot and damp, and pressed it. She said something that sounded like an attempt to say 'sociological anæsthetic'. He pressed the hand again. He said, 'Miss Myrtle—Miss Myrtle,' loudly, so that his voice alarmed him. He pinched her cheek. He slapped her hand. He said 'Wake UP!' The girl slept on, breathing peacefully through the nose.

He ought, he thought, to put her to bed. But he shrank from the shocking task. At least she must be covered; and she must not sleep in her shoes and stockings. He locked the door. It occurred to him that Bill might be hiding in the long wardrobe. He looked, but Bill was not.

He took off the little blue shoes and set them neatly together on the floor.

The stockings intimidated him. Never in his life, even for Mary, had he discharged this service. He knew from music-hall jokes and club anecdotes that to undress a lady was one of the supreme delights of man: and that silk stockings were perhaps the most exciting garment of all: but the thought of removing Miss Myrtle's stockings only embarrassed him. He knew that they were held up by things called suspenders, but to reach those suspenders would involve, he feared, explorations outrageous to Miss Myrtle's modesty, and his own, although they were techni- cally engaged in being intimate. Moreover, if Bill ever heard of it, Bill, he felt, would strongly object. He pulled gently at one of the silk stockings, near the ankle, in the faint hope that some sort of magic would assist him. But, this being vain, he decided that Miss Myrtle would have to sleep in her stockings. He pulled down the bedclothes on the other side of the bed, lifted her delicately (for he did not want her to wake in his embrace and misunderstand his intentions), and deposited her on the sheets. She was as light as a child in his arms, he thought; she lay curled up in her sleep like a child: and Mr. Adam wished that he had a daughter. It occurred to him that she was likely to crumple the blue satin by sleeping in it; but he could do no more, and he tucked her up. So began Mr. Adam's night of sin.

He undressed, lay down on the couch at the foot of the bed, and covered himself with an overcoat. He lay on his back and stared at the ceiling, and listened to the beat of the breakers on the beach, and thought about the Laws of England. From the bed came long and delicate snores, like the purring of a baby tiger. The Laws of England were not troubling the Mouse.

He slept in patches, cold and uncomfortable. Whenever he woke a little snore reminded him of his situation and the duties still before him. Towards morning he slept deeply. He dreamed that an angel stood at the Gates of Heaven, constantly saying 'Oy!' 'Oy!' said the angel. 'John Adam, come in! Oy! Oy! Oy!' He woke and the voice was still saying 'Oy!'

'Oy!' said Miss Myrtle, standing by the couch in the rose-coloured night-dress. 'Oy! John Adam! I want my tea. Ring the bell and get in.'

The climax of the drama, the crucial moment of the expedition, was at hand. John Adam, publisher, was about to be discovered in bed with his paramour, in order to enable his wife to marry a gentleman of the B.B.C.

He entered the bed nervously, averting his eyes from his little pink partner in guilt. In doing so his elbow touched her side.

'I beg your pardon,' he said.

'Granted,' she said. 'I say, was I a bit tiddly last night?'

'Tiddly?'

'Tiddly. Skew-whiff. Fog-bound.'

'You became very sleepy,' he said mercifully.

'Oh, did I? I'm ever so sorry. I know I've got a head like a stale onion.'

Miss Myrtle was silent, wondering why she had gone to bed in her clothes.

John Adam was silent, wondering what his next duty might be. Should he embrace the girl? Would he ask for the tea, or she? And what——

'They don't answer that bell,' said Miss Myrtle.

'I haven't rung it,' he said.

'Oh, dough-nuts!' exclaimed the Mouse with irritation, and, sitting up, she energetically pressed the bell-push. 'I don't wonder your wife's making a change—really I don't.'

'And now,' she said, becoming swiftly business-like again, 'for the doings. I'm sorry to trouble you, Mr. Adam, but this is where we have to be matey. Allow me.'

The Mouse lay down close to him, put her tiny arms round his neck and her face against his cheek. Thus they lay and waited for the bell to be answered. John Adam's heart beat strongly: but he was conscious of no sensation but mental discomfort and fear.

'Do you always wear spectacles in bed?' said Miss Myrtle.

'No,' he said. 'But sleeping on the couch I forgot about them.'

'Take them off, I would. It looks funny.'

Obediently he took his spectacles off, and was about to put them on the little table by the bed when there was a knock at the door.

'Look out!' said Miss Myrtle, and Mr. Adam, feeling like a naughty child, hastily returned to the affectionate pose he had abandoned, but with the spectacles still in his hand.

There was a second knock.

'Shall I say "Come in"?' he inquired.

'No, I'll say "Come in". You ask for the tea.'

'Come in,' she chanted, in a high and aristocratic voice, charged with delicious drowsiness.

An elderly chambermaid came in and drew back the curtains.

John Adam, as nervous as a young actress playing in her first part on a first night, raised himself on his elbow and said, 'Oh. Ah. Good morning. Can we have some tea?'

Miss Myrtle's arms were still clinging to his neck, his glasses were in his left hand, and he brandished these nervously above the counterpane, like a politician enforcing his points with pince-nez.

The maid stood and regarded this eccentric visitor, without apparent surprise. Her face was square and weary; she had left her bed at six and walked a mile on a cold morning. A hippopotamus in the bed could scarcely have excited her.

She said, 'Tea?'

'For two,' said Mr. Adam, with a flourish of the spectacles.

'Toast?' said the maid.

'Toast, darling?' said Mr. Adam.

The Mouse at last withdrew her arms, yawned enormously, as one just wakened from sleep, and said, 'No toast, thank you, my sweet. Just a weeny orange-juice.'

'Two teas, one orange-juice,' said the chambermaid flatly, and departed. The great moment was passed, the ritual done, the laws respected. John Adam was bathed in a warm relief; he felt as one at last released by the dentist. Also, and strangely, he felt a little proud of himself. That 'Toast, darling?' he thought, had been superbly said.

'Can I get up now?' he asked.

'Better not. You want to fix your face in her mind, don't you? Talk to her a bit, where you are. And get her name.'

John lay down again. Yes, he would talk to the maid and 'fix his face'. For the first time since his quest began he felt that he was in command of the situation.

'And, if I were you, I'd put your glasses on now, so's she'll recognize you in the photograph.'

'I had thought of that,' said Mr. Adam, rather coldly. He would have to show this girl that he also knew a thing or two.

He fell to thinking of the queer human cogs which composed the machinery of his divorce—Boom, Miss Mortimer, Miss Myrtle, and now the chambermaid. Here was a humble servant at a seaside hotel, a stranger to him and his affairs, and yet, quite unconscious of her doom, she was being made the essential pin in the machinery. She was to be the principal agent in putting asunder those whom the registrar had joined in Flower Street, Bethnal Green. What right had he to descend like an eagle from London and carry her off into his odious private affairs? She would be dragged up to London into solicitors' offices, questioned by clerks and barristers, rebuked by Judges, stared at by the public, photographed by journalists, not through unavoidable accident but by the deliberate design of himself and his advisers; not to serve the ends of justice, but to assist at a meaningless ritual made necessary by a senseless law. It seemed a shame. He was sorry for the chambermaid, and he thought, 'For two pins I would chuck the whole thing and find another way.' But then, there was no other way.

His meditations were interrupted by the return of the chambermaid with the tea. While she was placing the tray he studied her with compassionate eyes. How simple, he thought, how useful, how pale, how pathetic! And he was going to have her subpœnaed, put in a public witness-box, and made to swear something that he knew to be a lie. Well, at least she should be rewarded. He left the bed suddenly, and took his note-case from his coat. It was his nature to see both sides of a question, and while he concealed a one-pound note in his palm it occurred to him that his sentimental act might bear practical fruit by helping to 'fix his face' in the woman's mind. Naturally, he thought, in her situation, she must see hundreds of couples in bed, and one, to her, must be very like another.

'What is your name?' he said.

'Parkins.'

'Well, Parkins,' he said with a genial smile, 'you will remember me, won't you? Mr. Adam.'

He thrust the note into her hand in the furtive and almost guilty manner with which any Englishman of the upper classes is bound to transfer money to a member of the lower orders.

Rose Parkins was not secretive. She looked at the thing in her hand, openly, and was amazed and overjoyed. Although she had served three years in the celebrated hotel it happened that she had never had any divorce business. No one before had given her a pound for bringing up a cup of tea on the first morning, and it delighted her. Tears appeared in one eye. She said heartily, 'That I will, sir. God bless you, sir—and you, lady.' And she went out, wiping her eyes with her apron.

'Good egg,' said Miss Myrtle. It was the first mark of approbation he had received from her, and he said, with a touch of conceit, 'Yes. I think she'll remember me now.'

'You bet your life,' said Miss Myrtle.

Basely, he did not mention the original motive of his act; for he did not think that Miss Myrtle would approve of that.

Mr. Adam now found that, occupied with his thoughts, vainglorious or compassionate, he had unintentionally gone back to bed. There was no longer any good legal or strategical reason for his being there: but there he was, and, after all, he had had a bad night. What was extraordinary, it already seemed a natural and unremarkable thing for him to be sharing a bed with this innocent maiden.

Miss Myrtle, like a large pink kitten, curled up close to his side. She said, 'I'm sorry I was tiddly last night. Champagne! my ruin every time. I ought to have warned you. I say, who put me to bed?'

'I did what I could.'

'Well, you've done for my frock,' she said with soft reproach. 'You might have taken it off.'

'I didn't like to.'

Miss Myrtle looked at him with wondering eyes. 'I never met any one like you,' she said. 'Funny old fish, aren't you?' and she kissed him softly on the cheek.

Mr. Adam, to his surprise, found that he enjoyed this gesture. She was a good little thing, he thought. She had served him well: together they had done a difficult deed: and he was more at peace in his mind than he had been for a long time. He turned his head and, to his astonishment, he kissed her forehead.

'Now then,' she said teasingly, 'you'll lose your deposit!'
Then she put her little hand in his and said, 'Let's go to sleep.' And almost instantly she was asleep.

'What an odd situation!' thought Mr. Adam. But he was tired, and he slept also. They slept till lunch-time, and after lunch they went on the pier.

Mary Adam sat up in her large, low bed and sipped her tea and read her husband's letter:

DEAR MARY,
It is with great regret that I write this letter, but it seems only fair to tell you that I have been unfaithful to you, as you may wish to secure your freedom. I have given my heart to another, and if you cause inquiries to be made at the Capitol Hotel, Brighton, you will find all the information you require. I cannot ask you to forgive me for all the suffering I have caused you, but I can at least give you the opportunity to be rid of one for whom you were always too good.
Good-bye, Mary.

JOHN ADAM

PS.—I enclose a hotel bill. The woman's name is May Myrtle, 25 River Road, Greenwich.

Mary Adam looked at the bill and felt in her heart a sharp little pang. '*Mr. and Mrs. Adam.*' What sort of person, she wondered, was 'Mrs. Adam'? And how dared she be 'Mrs. Adam'? Surprisingly, she found, Mary was jealous of 'Mrs. Adam'. She thought of John in the hot school-yard, bashful and stammering, John marching behind the eighty-three children, John silent at the Savoy, John in this bed of hers, John always gentle, considerate, and shy, John, with a flushed face, saying what he thought about the stage—John quite impossible to live with—but still John Adam, who belonged to her. And now he had gone to Brighton with somebody called May Myrtle.

Well, it was what she wanted. And now she must go and see her solicitors and sign a writ—was it a writ?—against her John. Why in the world, she thought, must the thing be done in this way, this playing at being enemies where there was no enmity at all? Why could she and John not go privately to some nice Judge and say, 'Please, Judge, we want to part'—and finish hand in hand as they had begun?

Mary Adam sighed, and turned to the telephone, that ever-ready comforter of lonely folk. She rang up Mr. Martin Seal's flat, and the voice that nightly charmed the millions replied.

'Martin? Good morning, my dear.'

'Good morning, dear. Did you sleep well?'

'Marvellous. . . . And you?'

'Satisfactory.'

The words were not remarkable: but if any stranger had heard the conversation he must have admired the diction, the unusual conjunction of two voices perfectly employed. For, as a rule, on the telephone, there is one who speaks clearly and one who mumbles, one who gabbles and one who says 'What?' Mr. Seal's voice, the voice that charmed the millions nightly, had the quality of a high-bred purr, an elegant, cultured, unhurrying, electrical purr. It was this voice, requesting murmurously that Agnes Potts would go at once to 14 Peckham Lane, where her father was dangerously ill, that had first attracted Mary to Martin.

'Darling!' said Mary excitedly; the sound of the voice had already dispersed her brooding fit. 'What d'you think? John's done it!'

'Done what, Mary?'

'Behaved like a gentleman. At Brighton.' There was no reply from Mr. Seal's end.

'Rather sweet of him, isn't it?' said Mary. 'So quick. Aren't you excited?'

'Well——'

'Say you're excited, Martin!'

'Not on the telephone, Mary,' said the voice, with a warning note.

'Oh, you pig!'

'I'll see you to-night and we'll have a talk. Good-bye now.'

'All right, stuffy. Good-bye, then. I must go and see the lawyers, and to-night I'll tell you all the doings—— Hullo?'

But at the word 'lawyers' there had been a faint click. The cautious Mr. Seal had replaced the receiver.

'There is one question,' said Mr. David Freebody, 'that I am bound to ask you before we go any further, Mrs. Adam. I am assuming that you yourself will not have to ask the Court to exercise its discretion in your favour?'

Mary looked blank. 'I've no idea,' she said.

'I mean——' said Mr. Freebody.

Mr. Freebody, of Freebody, Freebody & Thring, was nice, Mary thought. He had been highly recommended by two different friends whom he had escorted with delicacy and success to the blessed state of divorce. He did not, they said, seem like a lawyer at all—or what they had thought a lawyer was like. Human and understanding: took endless trouble about everything: and never made his clients feel that the one idea was to get their money, and hope for the best. One felt, the other ladies had said, that he was really interested. Perhaps he was, for he couldn't be much more than forty, had a handsome moustache, a noble brow, friendly eyes, and the figure of a Guardsman: and was not without interest to the ladies himself. In fact, rather a charmer; and a surprising fellow to find in a little room full of black deed-boxes and books about the Law of Drainage.

This was always a difficult matter, the framing of the safety question. A solicitor is an officer of the Court. It is his duty to disclose to the Court the fact that a petitioner for divorce has herself been guilty of adultery, if he is aware of it. It is his duty to his client to warn her that if she has committed adultery she must disclose it: for otherwise she may wander innocently into trouble with the King's Proctor. The conscientious solicitor, therefore, satisfies himself before he begins. That is to say, he puts to his clients questions the answers to which may 'tend to show that she has been guilty of adultery'. Such questions may not be put to her in Court by counsel or Judge, and need not be answered, unless she has already given evidence to the contrary effect. But since the good solicitor is almost bound to ask the questions and is bound to disclose the answers if he does, or else refuse to proceed, he does, in effect, for the Court what the Court is forbidden by Parliament to do for itself; and what the law nobly bestows with one hand it neatly sneaks away with the other.

Mr. Freebody knew that there were many methods and degrees of satisfaction. Each solicitor had his own favourite formula, and was surprised to hear that any other was in use. A few made no bones about it, but tackled a lady in good plain English. 'I must ask you if you yourself have committed adultery?' Mr. Freebody was strongly opposed to this frank formula: it was brutal, it was embarrassing: and it might provoke the question, never completely answered by the law, 'What exactly is adultery?' or 'Does this and that amount to adultery?' There were objections too to the more benignant phrase, 'Have you anything to confess yourself?' For this might include anything, according to the conscience: and if every person unhappily married was expected to confess every little aberration from the marriage vows, the practice of divorce would be quite impossible. Some solicitors, again, were content to throw that learned sentence about the discretion at the lady, and, if she mumbled vaguely, then assumed that she understood and hurried on. But Mr. Freebody thought that this was neither scrupulous nor safe. And, if the lady did not understand, he followed up the Discretion with a second barrel, a question clear enough but not embarrassingly precise.

'I mean,' he said, 'you've not yourself been living with another man?'

'No,' said Mary. 'Certainly not.'

'Forgive me. A mere matter of form. Now tell me the whole story.'

Messrs. Freebody, Freebody & Thring sent a young man down to the Capitol Hotel, a Mr. Sylvain Thomas, who was short and sallow and round-shouldered but active. At the reception bureau he was coldly referred to the manager: and by the manager he was coldly received. The manager was tired of these cases, of which there had recently, he thought, been too many. He saw no reason why his hotel should be employed as a sort of unofficial department of the Law Courts; and if it was to be so employed he thought that he should be paid for it. But neither he nor his office staff received any payment for the time and trouble devoted to solicitors' inquiries; and when his maids and porters were carried off to London to give evidence, and detained there, sometimes for three or four days, the hotel received no compensation for the loss of service. He had thought of charging a special tariff for divorce clients, but the difficulty of that was that their character was not disclosed until after the bill was paid. When a man wrote 'Mr. and Mrs. Adam' in the register the reception-clerk could hardly ask him to show the marriage lines, or sign an undertaking that he was not behaving like a gentleman. For this would anger the respectable visitors. On the other side, it had to be remembered that the divorce visitors, with all the trouble attached to them, were better than no visitors: they spent money handsomely, always drank champagne, and as the law was 'tightened up' stayed longer and longer. In the winter the business was roughly divided between divorce and tuberculosis: and in late years the consumptives had been dwindling: so the hotel could not afford to drive the gentlemen away. The simplest thing, the manager thought, would be to run the hotel openly as a branch of the Divorce Court, where gentlemen could behave like gentlemen without being disturbed by the general public— and at special rates. But then the law would step in and call it a disorderly house: for the law had no gratitude. It was all very difficult, the manager thought.

Reluctantly, then, he gave Mr. Thomas the information

and assistance desired. Mr. Thomas saw John Adam's waiter, who remembered the gentleman with glasses and the little dark lady with him. And Rose Parkins, who was about to leave the hotel for her Thursday afternoon out, was detained for an interview with Mr. Thomas.

This was a longer affair. Parkins looked at Mr. Adam's photograph, and identified her generous benefactor with the spectacles. Yes, she remembered them both very well. 'Such an easy couple, and as happy as the birds in the air. Honeymooning, *I* shouldn't wonder.'

At this point Mr. Thomas took from his case a foolscap sheet headed 'Proof' and began to make notes of the things to which Parkins was prepared to swear. Yes, she had seen the couple in bed, well, naturally, taking the morning tea and that, but what business was it of his? Suspecting that some harm was intended to the kind Mr. Adam, Parkins became resentful and reticent. But Mr. Thomas assured her that nothing but good was intended to Mr. Adam. Indeed, the more she said the better it would be for him. The couple wished to part, and this was the only way. She would have to come to London and tell the Court what she knew: she would be given so much a day, loss of wages, and her travelling expenses; and Mr. Adam would be pleased. Parkins had only once been in London and was very ready to spend a free day in the capital and help Mr. Adam. Mr. Thomas said that if she was not ready she would be subpœnaed, so it was all the same.

John Adam was alarmed by the cost of behaving like a gentleman, and inquired whether it was necessary for him to be represented by a solicitor, since he was not defending.

'Yes,' said Mr. Boom, after his seventh oyster, 'and no. There's not much to be done, and some of it you can do yourself. You can go to Somerset House, for example, and enter your appearance, fill up a form and sign your name and so on. After that there's nothing more till the case comes on for hearing. You're not bound to be there, or even to be represented. But things may crop up, not so much now as after the decree. There's no question in this case of the custody of the child or damages. But there is the question of costs—and maintenance—and perhaps a little matter called alimony *pendente lite*. You and your wife may think you understand each other, but her lawyers may spring something clever on you. Your wife, I think you said, earns more money than you do?'

'Much more.'

'Just as well; for, as the "guilty" party, you might be ordered to pay to her one-third of the joint income during your joint lives.'

'Even if she married again?'

'Even if she married a millionaire. Even if she lived in sin with a succession of millionaires. Unless by leave of the Court there is a stipulation to the contrary at the time of the application for maintenance. I remember one case— the husband was a poor man—he was ordered to pay a third of his annual earnings to his wife by way of maintenance, and did so for a year or two. Then the wife married a rich man and the husband allowed his payments to lapse, thinking they were no longer necessary. Nothing was said for ten years, and then the wife hauled him into Court and demanded her arrears. She didn't need the money—the whole thing was vindictive, or possibly mad: but the man had to pay. It nearly ruined him. Now, if you've got somebody looking after you, you can at least avoid that sort of trouble.'

'Very well,' said Mr. Adam. 'About how much is all this going to cost me?'

'An ordinary undefended divorce, without complications, ought not to run you in for more than a hundred and fifty pounds.'

'I've spent fifty or sixty already.'

'Oh, well,' said Mr. Boom, 'if you will go to a place like Mortimer's——. I only hope Miss Myrtle was worth it.'

'Hardly,' said Mr. Adam.

     ·   ·   ·   ·   ·

'No trouble about other women?' said Mr. Freebody.

'Not really,' said Mary. 'He's got a great friend. But she's a schoolmistress. Nothing in it, I'm sure.'

'Can we put it that at a certain date you noticed a cooling in his attitude towards you?'

'If you mean we had red-hot rows about everything—yes.'

'But not about women?'

'No. He was just as fond of me. We simply couldn't get along together, that's all. Isn't that enough?'

'Getting on together? It ought to be. But it isn't. What the law is interested in is sleeping with somebody else. H'm.'

Mr. Freebody thought for a moment or two.

'It would help,' he said, 'if you remembered that at a certain period you noticed a cooling in his attitude towards you.'

'Very well. When?'

'That is a matter for your recollection, Mrs. Adam,' said Mr. Freebody, writing.

'Well, it must have been 1927. Because we parted in August.'

'Early in the year 1927,' wrote Mr. Freebody.

'And did you form the suspicion that he had transferred his affections to another?'

'I suppose I did,' said Mary, wearily.

'You were unable to confirm this suspicion?'

'No. I mean "Yes".'

'And in August of that year your husband left you?'

'Yes.'

'That's better,' said Mr. Freebody. 'We'll run through your proof again, of course, before the hearing.'

'Oh, dear!' said Mary.

Mr. Sylvain Thomas walked down to Somerset House and filed Mrs. Adam's Humble Petition for Dissolution, with her Affidavit.

.   .   .   .   .

In the High Court of Justice.

PROBATE, DIVORCE AND ADMIRALTY DIVISION
(DIVORCE)

TO THE RIGHT HONOURABLE THE PRESIDENT OF THE SAID DIVISION

The 19th day of November 1929

THE HUMBLE PETITION
Of MARY ROWENA ADAM.

SHEWETH:

1. THAT on the 29th day of April 1920 your Petitioner then Mary Rowena Eve Spinster was lawfully married to Mervyn John Adam (hereinafter called 'the Respondent') at the register office in Flower Street Bethnal Green in the County of London.

2. THAT after the said marriage your Petitioner lived and cohabited with the Respondent at divers places and finally at 14 Aurora Gardens Knightsbridge in the County of London and that there has been no issue of the said marriage.

3. THAT the Respondent has committed adultery with May Myrtle.

4. THAT from the 2nd November to the 4th November 1929 the Respondent and the said May Myrtle lived and cohabited together as man and wife at the Capitol Hotel Brighton in the County of Sussex and during that time habitually committed adultery together there.

5. THAT there have been no proceedings previous hereto in the Divorce Division of the High Court with reference to the said marriage by or on behalf of either of the parties to the said marriage.

6. THAT your Petitioner resides at 14 Aurora Gardens Knightsbridge in the County of London and is domiciled in England.

7. THAT the Respondent resides at 19 Adelphi Terrace in the County of London and is a Publisher and is domiciled in England.

YOUR PETITIONER THEREFORE HUMBLY PRAYS:

That your lordship will be pleased to decree that your Petitioner's said marriage may be dissolved and such further and other relief in the premises as may be just.

MARY ADAM

To MERVYN JOHN ADAM, of 19 Adelphi Terrace, Strand, London.

TAKE NOTICE that you are required within eight days after service hereof upon you inclusive of the day of such service to enter an appearance either in person or by your Solicitor at the Divorce Registry of the High Court of Justice at Somerset House Strand in the County of London should you think fit so to do and thereafter to make answer to the charges in this Petition and that in default of your so doing the Court will proceed to hear the said charges proved and pronounce judgment your absence notwithstanding.

To MAY MYRTLE, 25 River Road, Greenwich.

TAKE NOTICE that you are entitled within eight days after delivery hereof to you inclusive of the day of such delivery to apply upon Summons for leave to enter an appearance either in person or by your Solicitor at the Divorce Registry of the High Court of Justice at Somerset House Strand in the County of London for leave to intervene in this cause should you think fit so to do and thereafter to make answer to the charges in this Petition and that in default of your so doing the Court will proceed to hear the said charges proved and pronounce judgment your absence notwithstanding.

This Petition is filed and this Notice to appear is issued by Freebody, Freebody & Thring of 15 New Square Lincoln's Inn London W.C.2, Solicitors for the Petitioner.

DATED at London this 19th day of November 1929

A. K. MEWS
Registrar

Over her Haddock Monte Carlo in the Savoy Grill Mary Adam complained to Martin Seal that she, it seemed, had to do all the work. Rehearsals for 'Happy Girl' had begun and were in the worrying stage—she did not know all her words, and disliked what she did know. She was still giving eight performances of 'Say When!', there was Christmas shopping, and, as if she had not enough to do already, the solicitors were always badgering her to sign things, answer things, send them photographs, or attend at their dreary offices. To-day, in the brief luncheon interval ('All back at two o'clock, please') she had been hustled off to Chancery Lane and made to swear an alarming oath.

AFFIDAVIT

of

MARY ROWENA ADAM

In the Matter of the Petition of

MARY ADAM for Dissolution of Marriage

I, MARY ROWENA ADAM, of 14 Aurora Gardens Knightsbridge in the County of London, the Petitioner in this cause, make oath and say as follows:

1. THAT the statements set out in Paragraphs 1, 2, 5, 6, and 7 of the said Petition dated the 19th day of November 1929 are true;

2. THAT the statements set forth in paragraphs 3 and 4 are true to the best of my knowledge, information, and belief; and

3. THAT there is not any collusion or connivance
between me and my said husband in any way whatever.

MARY ADAM

Sworn at 369 Chancery Lane
   in the County of London
this 19th day of November 1929.

        Before me

   EDWARD MAKIN
      A Commissioner for Oaths.

It made her hot to think of it now. She felt that she had
lied and had not realized that she would have to lie.
What exactly the technical meaning of connivance and
collusion might be, she knew not, but she felt in her bones
that she had committed both of them. As for paragraph 3,
she was secretly prepared to bet that her John had not
committed anything. He was not, she thought, that sort
of man.

Mary Adam heard with dismay that she must assist at
the serving of the Petition and identify her husband. It
seemed absurd, she thought, that so many solicitors, with
so many clerks, so many files and registers and affidavits
and tin boxes, should not be able to find out who her
husband was without her personal attendance. She was
expected, it seemed, to meet him face to face in a room and
say, 'Yes, that is John Adam, my husband': and at first
she refused. She had quite enough ridiculous things to do
and say in the play she was rehearsing by day and the play
she was performing in by night without doing ridiculous
things in her brief periods of real life. Mr. Freebody explained gently that the chain of evidence must be complete.
The hotel manager and the chambermaid had identified the
man sitting down in the picnic photograph as the man who
had signed the register and been seen in bed with a woman,
and now Mary must identify her husband as the man sitting
down in the picnic photograph. Everybody would then be
satisfied that her petition for dissolution was being served

on her husband and not on somebody else's. There was really nothing in it, said Mr. Freebody. Indeed, many couples welcomed this opportunity for a final meeting on neutral ground before the Court proceedings began. She might think herself lucky that she had not to identify her husband in company with the woman who had taken him from her. But, as it was, the other woman would not appear at all, either now or later.

'Well, she ought to,' said Mary, illogically. 'Why doesn't she?'

'There is no reason for her to appear,' said Mr. Freebody.

'I thought there was always a co-respondent?'

Mr. Freebody smiled indulgently at the ignorant lady.

'Where the petition is brought by a husband there is always a co-respondent. For the husband is bound to make the alleged adulterer a party unless excused by the Court, and he may obtain damages from him. But a wife cannot obtain damages from the adulteress, and there is no reason for her to appear unless she wishes to intervene in the proceedings in order to deny the charges against her and to clear her good name. She is then, not a co-respondent, but an intervener. In this case, we understand, she does not propose to intervene.'

'It sounds mad to me,' sighed Mary. 'All right, I'll do my bit.'

So, in the luncheon-hour, with the brown spaniel Bootle, she hurried to her solicitor's office, and from there, with the dog and Mr. Freebody, to the respondent's solicitor's office, that is, to the offices of Mr. Boom, where the respondent sat with Mr. Boom uncomfortably waiting for her.

The thing was admirably staged. The two solicitors were conveniently situated in the same building. Mary tripped down the two flights of stairs, talking busily to hide her nervousness.

'Will it be collusion if I kiss him?' she said.

'Condonation,' said Mr. Freebody. 'Better not.'

'I knew there was a C in it.'

The dog Bootle sniffed at a door on the right and barked loudly. They entered. John stood up, uncertain of the correct form of address.

'Hullo,' said Mary.

'Hullo, dear.'

Mary felt guilty. Poor John looked so woebegone, as if he really was an adulterer. Well, she thought—healthier than when they parted. But she could see by the mark on his nose that he always wore those glasses now; and he was a little thinner on the top.

'Do you identify this gentleman as your husband?' said Mr. Freebody with a solemn face.

The dog Bootle answered for her. He barked with wild delight, and leaped up and down in front of John, bouncing off his chest.

'Down, Bootle,' said Mary. 'That's condonation, or something.'

'Are you satisfied?' said Mr. Freebody, less solemn, to Mr. Boom.

'We are satisfied,' said Mr. Boom, smiling.

Mr. Freebody handed a sealed copy of the petition to Mr. Adam. Bootle, with a long leap, knocked it from his hands, and Mr. Boom picked it up. Mr. Adam signed his name on the back of a plain copy, acknowledging service, and all was in order.

'Good dog.'

'Good old Bootle.'

The dog, like the little child in a film, had brought sunlight into a gloomy situation. Bootle barked, John and Mary grinned affectionately, but could think of nothing to say: and the two solicitors whose business it was to separate the pair smiled stiffly on their reunion. Mr. Freebody, on the surface such a stickler, was at heart a sentimental soul, and it was in his mind to leave the two together for a little. But he knew that Mr. Boom, so easygoing in conversation, was opposed to all irregularity in practice, and would not approve.

He cleared his throat and said, 'Then that is all, Mrs. Adam. Good day, Mr. Adam. Good day, Boom.'

'Come, Bootle.' Mary moved to the door. The dog halted, irresolute, looking from one to the other, wagging his tail and panting, delighting in the joyful scene.

Mary wanted to kiss John. John wanted to take her hand. Nothing happened.

'Good-bye, John.'

'Good-bye, Mary.'

'Come, Bootle.'

Bootle barked three times at the respondent's solicitor, and went out.

Mary and Mr. Freebody and Bootle shared a taxi into the West End.

Mary, sad and brooding, said at last, 'Why shouldn't that be enough?'

'You mean——?'

'What we've just done.'

'Divorce by mutual consent—before witnesses? My dear Mrs. Adam,' said Mr. Freebody, 'you should have lived elsewhere. It is nearly three years since your husband left you. In the virtuous country of Scotland you could have a divorce after four years, for desertion. In the wicked land of France also: for if a *séparation de corps* has existed for three years it may be turned into a divorce on the application of either party. In Germany you could have been free a year ago—and also, I think, in Austria. In Sweden you could have got a judicial separation, on the grounds of aversion, and a year later, failing a reconciliation, a divorce. In Norway and Denmark it is much the same: and in Norway, after a three years' separation, a couple may obtain a royal decree of divorce by mutual request. In Holland, failing adultery, you would have to wait another two years. But in Belgium or Switzerland a marriage may be dissolved by mutual consent, subject to the approval of the Court; and in Switzerland three years' desertion is enough. In Japan also; and in Japan complete divorce is allowed by mutual consent with notice to the registrar. In Russia too. If you lived in the countries where Rome still flourishes—in Italy, Spain, Portugal or Southern Ireland—you would, of course, be worse off than you are now, for there is (nominally) no complete divorce—only what we call the judicial separation. But there still remains a large area of Europe where you and your husband would not be treated as criminals or forced into immorality. It is rather amusing, by the way, to look at the list of European countries where divorce is easier—dear little Belgium, dear little Switzerland, Norway

and Sweden, Denmark and Scotland—all countries whose
moral character we English respect, quiet, peaceful countries
notorious not for pagan licence but for moral solidity and
the practice of the domestic virtues. There's nothing like
our laws in the world. However, you have chosen to be
English, and so either you or your husband must commit
adultery, whether you like it or not. This is part of the
English heritage.'

'Thank you very much,' said Mary.

'It's amusing, too, to think how we like to look down on
the Americans, because they have one lot of divorce laws
in this State, and another, over the border, in the next.
But the States of America are rather large places. We
don't realize that in these two tiny islands we have no
less than three different sets of divorce laws—one set in
Ireland (no, two in Ireland), one set in England, and
another, and superior, set in Scotland!'

'Very amusing,' said Mary. The cool way in which these
lawyers discussed their bat-witted laws!

'It's queer,' continued Mr. Freebody happily, 'how many
things cannot be done in this great country which are
done successfully and well in most of the civilized countries
of the world, including the potty little Switzerlands and
Belgiums which, in our hearts, we despise. Take the
children question. If ever you pin the opposition down on
the divorce laws the last refuge is the children. "Quite
agree," they say, "that the whole thing's rotten: but we
must think of the children." And that's the most humbugging excuse of all. As if there were no children in
Scotland, or France, Switzerland, Belgium, Denmark, and
the rest of them! If a marriage breaks up, the children
must, of course, be provided for—and the law's doing it
every day. But what good it does to children to tie their
mother to a lunatic or a man who beats her, or compel their
father to commit adultery because their mother's had
enough of him, has never been explained to me. And the
children argument would be more convincing if the law
made things any easier in a case like yours, where there
are no children. But it doesn't. If the main purpose of
matrimony is the procreation of children, as the Prayer
Book says, you'd think the law would be delighted to

dissolve a childless marriage, if only on the principle of "Second time lucky!" But, as you know——'

'I get out here,' said Mary. 'Good-bye, Mr. Freebody. Thank you so much.'

Mr. Thomas, with Rose Parkins, travelled down to Greenwich to serve the petition on Miss Myrtle.

Miss Myrtle (or rather, Miss May Rogers) was engaged upon domestic duties, and little Gladys answered the door. The moment she saw Mr. Thomas she knew what his business was. The children were very proud of their sister's connexion with the law, though they were not quite clear what it was. They knew that it was profitable: and the visits of pale young men carrying long documents with pink ribbons were always welcome. Sometimes on wet Sundays their sister would lend them her little bundle of documents, and Gladys and Arthur and Albert would play solicitors, serving each other with petitions, and entering appearances in Arthur's drawing-book, though May could not tell them exactly how this was done.

So Gladys cried joyfully up the narrow stair, 'May, it's a *s'licitor!*'

'Tell him I'm bathing the twins, but if he's in a hurry he can come up.'

'Come up,' said Gladys, beaming. 'Can I have the pink ribbon, please?'

'No, my dear.' Mr. Thomas was a little shocked.

May Rogers sat before a small fire with a damp twin on her lap, drying, as Mr. Thomas would have said, the same.

'That's her,' said Rose Parkins and departed down the stairs. Mr. Thomas entered the room cautiously, holding the petition before him like a weapon of defence.

Before he could speak the two boys, Arthur and Albert, rushed at him, crying in unison, 'Bags I!' The petition was torn from his hands and became at once the prize and instrument of a tug-of-war in the passage outside.

May stood up without a word, transferred the naked twin to Mr. Thomas, and pursued the combatants. Mr. Thomas heard the sound of blows and the strange threat, 'If you don't let go at once, Arthur, you'll never play solicitors again, see?'

May returned with a crumpled document and relieved Mr. Thomas of the twin. 'Thanks,' she said. 'I'm ever so sorry. Is this for me?'

Mr. Thomas had never served a petition in similar circumstances, but he could think of no legal objection to it, and, since the party appeared to have none, decided to proceed.

'Are you Miss May Myrtle?'

'That's right. Gladys, you leave that tape alone.'

'I have called to serve you with this petition.'

The naked twins regarded him with round, wide eyes. Arthur and Albert crept back to the door and watched the proceedings with professional interest.

'That's right,' said May cheerfully. 'Gladys, if you don't put that paper down I'll tell the King's Proctor about you.'

In the Rogers family the King's Proctor was a figure of terror comparable to the Emperor 'Bony', and this threat was at once effective.

The bewildered Mr. Thomas said, 'Then that is all, I think. If you don't mind signing here——'

'Thanks ever so. Arthur, show the gentleman out. And don't ask him no questions or you don't get no supper.'

As Mr. Thomas went down the stairs he heard May Myrtle say in softer tones, 'All right, Gladys, you can have the ribbon now. And you can put that paper on the fire. I'll teach those boys to go grabbing my things.'

On Monday, November 25th, Mr. Adam went to Somerset House to enter an appearance. This was a simple thing, Mr. Boom said, and it was a waste of money to pay a lawyer to do it.

'Where is the Divorce Registry?' he asked at the gate, self-consciously. But the porter seemed to think none the worse of him. The Divorce Registry (Contentious Dept.) was in the south-east corner. John Adam walked slowly across the great courtyard of Kings, which was crowded with the parked cars of junior Civil Servants, and admired the building. He might have pondered on the strange tricks which history had played with it: but he did not. The noble pile stood splendid in the sun, designed for Kings and

occupied by clerks. Here, with what pride, had the Lord
Protector Somerset begun to build his palace, unaware that
he would be executed before it was completed. Here, for
a time, dwelt Queen Elizabeth and here the wives of James I,
of Charles I, and Charles II. Here the remains of Oliver
Cromwell lay in state, and here Sir Joshua Reynolds delivered his closing 'Discourses'. The ghosts of generals,
explorers, and statesmen, fine ladies, courtiers, and handsome hounds walked beside John Adam, chattering in
deathless wonderment—wonderment at the strange ways
of posterity, who had turned their palace to such ignoble
and dreary uses. On his right was the Board of Inland
Revenue, and the Estate Duty Office; on his left the
Registrar of Births, Deaths and Marriages, and the Chief
Inspector of Taxes; ahead of him the Principal Probate and
the Divorce Registries. 'Registrars and Tax-collectors!' muttered the ghosts. 'Files and officials and interferences!
Black coats and pallid faces! What have they done to our
glorious palace?' Here, in this capacious pile, the private
life of every citizen is stored away—his birth, his marriage,
his income, his investments, his divorce, his death, and
dying testament. The citizen should shudder as he passes
this place, for it holds more than half the story of his life
and may in time possess it all. 'It belonged to the King,'
said one ghost to another. 'Now it belongs to the Crown.
Why should there be so much difference?' 'That is the
history of England,' said the second ghost, sententiously.

But John Adam, the son of a Civil Servant, did not
attend to the complaining ghosts: for it seemed to him to be
a good and natural thing that this fine building should be
occupied by the servants of the State, recording and con-
trolling the lives of their fellow-men. Moreover, as usual,
he was embarrassed by the task before him.

He entered a dingy and diminutive room, divided into
two by a counter, behind which was a clerk, a large clock,
and a great many pigeon-holes oozing documents. On the
counter was a stout wire grille, after the style of a post
office, as if the clerk required protection, as if in the old
wild days some desperate petitioner had leapt across the
counter and sought to extract a divorce by violence.

There was an air of quiet bustle about the place—clerks

coming and going, and questions called from an inner room about petitioners and co-respondents in a casual manner which made the respondent feel more at ease.

The clerk was busy with a solicitor's clerk, and Mr. Adam looked about him. The little room had the depressing dullness of every place in which the Crown has dealings with the citizen. The walls were done in a dull green distemper, and the only decorations were the clock and a few typed notices pinned to a board and fluttering in the draught, announcements concerning the Hilary Sittings and faded 'Directions' from the President of the Divorce Division. John Adam, a loyal servant of the State, was often distressed by the citizen's lack of affection for the State: and now he thought suddenly, 'I know why it is: the State does nothing to make itself attractive. The State should make its places beautiful and pleasant, like an Underground station. If every State place suggests the entrance to a police-station no wonder the citizen wants to have nothing to do with it.' He made up his mind to have a word with his friend Henderson, of the Office of Works.

He read one of the yellowing Directions of the President:

'It is directed by the President that in cases where the only specific charge of adultery contained in the petition is of misconduct with an unknown woman at an hotel, the order for venue shall direct hearing in London.

(13th July, 1928).

John Adam turned away, feeling guilty and apprehensive. 'A single act at an hotel.' That was his own case: and the President had his eye upon him.

The clerk was free, and John said nervously, 'Can I make an appearance, please?'

A lunatic question, he thought: for he was already making one. What was the correct phrase? Ah, yes—'enter'.

'Enter, I mean.'

The clerk handed him a form and said, 'There's the index. Put your name in it.'

He jerked his head towards the wide window-sill on which lay two large ledgers.

Mr. Adam opened that which was labelled DIVORCE— APPEARANCES TO PETITIONS.

Inside, the book looked like a dirtily kept address-book at a low-class hotel, the pages covered with names in innumerable sprawling hands. There was none of the formality to which Mr. Adam was accustomed in official records—no columns, no printed headings or instructions, nothing about block capitals, nothing but untidy and apparently uncontrolled writing in pen and ink. It reminded him of the Withdrawal Book in the house library at school. Considering how much importance the State attached to his divorce the thing seemed strangely casual and slovenly. 'At least,' he thought, 'no one can complain about red-tape here.'

His eye halted at a familiar name and a handwriting which he knew—'*Perivale, K. M. T.* v. *Perivale, W. S.* Appearance for the Respondent.' Poor old Perivale! What a mess that was! And here was the other side of the medal: '*Watkins* v. *Watkins and Perivale.* Appearance for the Respondent and Co-respondent.' Two marriages on the scrap-heap there! Poor old gentle, fastidious Perivale! He must have hated standing here, writing his name in this grubby book. It was a shock to come upon these, as it were, real names in that waste of names which meant nothing—it was like walking among the dead on a battle-field and finding suddenly the body of a friend. Yet all these names belonged to real people too: and all of them were casualties in this same queer battle of divorce.

Mr. Adam turned quickly to the 'A's' and wrote (wrongly):

> '*Adam* v. *Adam and Myrtle.* Appearance for the Respondent.'

He filled up his form: he paid half-a-crown for a stamp and hurried away. He had duly entered an appearance. But as he walked across the sunny courtyard he wondered why, and in what sense, he had done it. For Mr. Boom had made it quite clear that he would not have to appear.

Mary Adam was badgered again. 'It seems an age,' she told Mr. Seal, 'since I had lunch in peace.' This time it was an Affidavit as to Place of Hearing.

MARY ROWENA ADAM
v.
MERVYN JOHN ADAM

I, MARY ROWENA ADAM of 14 Aurora Gardens Knightsbridge in the County of London the Petitioner in this Cause make oath and say as follows:

1. I reside at 14 Aurora Gardens Knightsbridge in the County of London.

2. The Respondent has entered an Appearance but has filed no Answer to this Cause. The witnesses I intend calling other than myself are Rose Parkins (Chambermaid) and Benjamin Macintosh (Hotel Manager) of Brighton in the County of Sussex.

3. For the foregoing reasons I desire the hearing of this Cause to be in Middlesex.

On November 30th Mr. Thomas had gone to Somerset House and looked in the great book to see if Mr. Adam or the Woman Named had entered an Appearance. On the 16th of December he went again to see if Mr. Adam had filed an Answer to the Petition, and he made an affidavit, to which was affixed a seven-and-sixpenny stamp:

No. 108.

Affidavit of Search for Answer.

MARY ROWENA ADAM

against

MERVYN JOHN ADAM

I, RUPERT SYLVAIN THOMAS, Clerk to Messrs. Freebody, Freebody & Thring of 15 New Square Lincoln's Inn in the County of London Solicitors for the Petitioner make Oath and say that I did on the 16th day of December one thousand nine hundred and twenty-nine search the Court Minutes at the Divorce Registry of the High Court of Justice to ascertain whether or not an Answer had been filed by or on behalf of Mervyn John Adam the respondent in this Cause and that I find no Answer has been filed by him or on his behalf.

R. S. Thomas

Sworn at the Divorce Registry
    Somerset House
    in the County of London on
the sixteenth day of December 1929
        Before me
          Ernest Hale
        A Clerk authorised to administer Oaths

Having filed three affidavits, Venue, Search for Answer, and Service of Petition on Woman Named, Mr. Thomas filled in Form 130 applying for the Certificate of the Registrar that the proceedings in the cause were correct and the pleadings in order. He filed this, together with the Marriage Certificate of Mr. and Mrs. Adam, and went across to the 'Blue Moon' to have one. It had been quick work: and it was careless of the respondent to commit his adultery so late in the term; but with any luck the case would now come on before Easter.

Divorce No. 13	MARY ROWENA ADAM
	against
Notice of having set down Cause for Trial.	MERVYN JOHN ADAM

TAKE NOTICE that this Cause was this day set down for hearing before the Court itself at Middlesex.

DATED the 20th day of December 1929.

Freebody, Freebody & Thring
of 15 New Square, Lincoln's Inn, W.C.2
Petitioner's Solicitors

To Boom & Wallett
    of 15 New Square, Lincoln's Inn, W.C.2
    Solicitors for the Respondent

7

Rose Parkins was visited again by Mr. Thomas, who handed her one guinea conduct money and a strongly-worded message from the King, being a *Subpœna ad Test*:

No. 3.	George the Fifth, by the Grace of God, of Great Britain, Ireland, and the British Dominions beyond the Seas, King, Defender of the Faith, to ROSE PARKINS
Divorce	
Spa. ad Test.	

Greeting: We command you and every of you, to be and appear in your proper persons at the Sittings of the Probate, Divorce, and Admiralty Division of Our High Court of Justice at the Royal Courts of Justice, Strand, in our County of Middlesex, on Monday the 13th day of January 1930 by half-past Ten of the Clock in the forenoon of the same day, and so from day to day whenever the said Division of Our said Court is sitting, until the Cause or Proceeding is heard, to testify the truth according to your knowledge in a certain cause now in Our said Court depending between Mary Rowena Adam

. . . .

Petitioner and Mervyn John Adam. . . . .
Respondent and . . . .
~~Co-Respondent~~ on the Part of the Petitioner . . . . . .

. . . .

and on the aforesaid day, between the Parties aforesaid to be heard. And this you or any of you shall by no means omit, under the Penalty of each of you of One Hundred Pounds.

Witness the Right Honourable CHARLES LUCAS, BARON HAWKHURST of RADSTOCK, President of the said Division, at our High Court of Justice, the 20th day of December One thousand nine hundred and twenty-nine in the Twentieth year of Our Reign.

N.B.—*Notice will be given to you of the day on which your attendance will be required.*

Rose Parkins had never before been directly addressed, much less greeted, by her Sovereign, whether each or every of her; and she was pleased. She listened carefully to what Mr. Thomas said, and together they prepared her 'proof'.

PROOF OF ROSE PARKINS

ROSE PARKINS....................will prove:

I reside at 3 Medina Villas, Brighton.

I am 47 years and 3 months of age.

I am a domestic servant at the Capitol Hotel.

On the nights of November 2 and 3 1929 the person whom I now know to be the respondent occupied Room 41 with a woman. On both mornings when I took up the tea they were in the bed together.

On Sunday they left the room at 1.0 p.m.

On Monday they left about 8.0 a.m.

In the picnic photograph marked 'A' I identify the person I know as Mr. Adam as the man sitting down in a bathing-costume.

ROSE PARKINS.

That evening, at the 'Medina Arms', Rose Parkins with pride displayed her 'letter from the King' to a circle of friends. But, in spite of the skilful instructions of Mr. Thomas, she did not yet realize what an important person she was.

Mr. Basil Ransom, counsel for the petitioner, took from a neat and enviable pile the papers in *Adam, M. R.* v. *Adam, M. J.*, and slipped off the red tape. The documents in the case were already numerous—Petition for Dissolution, Affidavit of Petitioner, Appearance to Petition, Notice of having Set Down Cause for Trial, *Subpœna ad test, Subpœna duces tecum*, Affidavit of Service of Petition on Woman Named, Proof of Petitioner Mary Rowena Adam, Proof of Rose Parkins, Proof of Benjamin Macintosh, Brief

to Counsel on behalf of the Petitioner (Brief 5 guas. Con.—
1 guas. 6 guas.).

Mr. Ransom looked quickly through the petitioner's
proof and one or two other documents. But he read very
carefully the proof of Rose Parkins.

The petition was in the list for hearing—*Adam, M. R.
v. Adam, M. J.*—with twenty-seven others, on April 1st,
1930.

On that morning at ten-thirty the President of the
Probate, Divorce, and Admiralty Division took his seat on
the Bench under the sign of the Foul Anchor and with a
frown surveyed the list of undefended petitions. He had a
fine head and presence, a fine brain, and a fine character.
In his long and distinguished career he had done many
things: he had rowed 7 in the Cambridge boat and represented Dunton (South-West) in Parliament: he had been
Attorney-General to the Prince of Wales, Recorder for
Vexham, and a Lord Justice of Appeal, Chairman of the
Royal Commission on Beet Sugar, Chairman of the Royal
Commission on Agricultural Co-operation and President of
the Docks and Harbour Commission of Inquiry after the
big strike; he had married happily and had three children.
For seven years he had held with dignity his present office,
one of the most odd and various of all judicial offices:
Probate, Divorce, and Admiralty—'Wills, Wives, and
Wrecks', as a cheerful young barrister put it. To the
studious foreigner who inquired on what principle of reason
these three departments of justice were joined together in
a special Division under a single President the only answer
would be: 'There is no reason about it: like many of the
grandest things in our Constitution it happened by accident.'
The President by now was well accustomed to his mis-
cellaneous functions. As a barrister he had specialized in
Admiralty practice; in the law of Salvage, Piracy, and
Bottomry, the duties of sea-captains in fog or narrow
waters, questions concerning helm orders, charter-parties
and the law of general average. As a Judge he was required
to specialize as well in the troubles of executors and the
intricacies of attestation, the tantrums of wives and the

passions of lovers. But this no longer seemed odd. One day he was at work upon collisions at sea, the next upon collisions in the family; and he was expected to be equally at home with the law of intestacy and the law of intimacy. There was, after all, a certain congruity, though not of logic, between the three sections of his Division. In each he was engaged in clearing up a mess, and these messes were inimical not only to the interests of individuals but to institutions essential to the State—Property, Inheritance, Marriage, Monogamy, Family Life, and the Safety and Good Order of British Ships at Sea. All these were part of the foundations of the British Isles. And the great Foul Anchor over the President's head did stand in a sense for all his departments, something solid and important which needed attention.

Mr. Freebody, walking to the Courts with Mary, told her not to be frightened of the President, however terrible he looked. 'He's a very fine old fellow,' said Mr. Freebody. 'We don't always agree with him, but we all respect him: and at the end of a case before him most people in Court feel that substantial justice has been done—as the law stands. People say that he's made divorce more difficult: so he has in some ways, though in others—discretion cases —he's made it a little easier. But that's not a fair way of putting it. A Judge is like a chemist—he has to make up the prescriptions the doctor gives him, and he can't keep on altering them because he thinks they're wrong or unwise. That's the doctor's job. Old Hawkhurst is not one of those Judges who continually denounce the law in the same breath with which they enforce it. Nobody knows what he really thinks about the divorce laws. He may think, as I do, that they're illogical and cruel: but he wouldn't let on if he did. And that's one of the reasons why we respect him.'

'I don't quite see why,' said Mary.

But Mr. Freebody was right. The President had so high a regard for the laws of England in general that he would have been loath to shake the public confidence in them by public criticism of any particular law. Good or bad, the law was the law. Until the supreme Parliament saw fit to make an alteration it was not for a Judge, however high, to twist the law, or for the citizen, however unhappy, to evade it. And always in the background, behind the unhappy husband, wife, and lover, he saw, so much more important than the individual, the Institutions—Marriage, Monogamy, and Family Life.

On this 1st day of April, 1930, then, the President of the Probate, Divorce, and Admiralty Division of the High Court sat under the sign of the Foul Anchor and surveyed the list of undefended Petitions for Dissolution with a frown. There were too many of them: and in the last year or two their numbers had increased. What, after all, was the meaning of an undefended petition? It meant that two citizens (by default) confessed to the world that they had committed the sin of adultery. Either the offence was so open that they could not deny it or they thought so little of it that they did not care to try: and an increase of such cases must be bad from the standpoint of public morals. But there was a third possible alternative—that they had not in fact committed adultery at all: and that, perhaps, was the worst of the three, for it showed not only loose morals but a loose legal system. Yet, in spite of the stern front he had shown, the cases had increased. He had dropped hints and warnings; from time to time he issued a formal 'Direction' which was posted up in the Divorce Registry; but still the cases increased; and still the President suspected that the people were making a fool of the law, using his august office as a mere convenience, or inconvenience, to register arrangements which they, not he, had made.

What he called the Hotel Bill class of case was a particular worry. A man took a strange woman to a hotel, wrote his name in a book, was beheld in bed for a few moments—and thought that that was enough for the dissolution of the holy tie of marriage. Too often it was: for it was the fact and not the motive of adultery that mattered: and when the fact must be presumed there must be a divorce. He had done what he could to tighten things up. At one time there had been impudent cases in which the woman was not so much as named—so that the same woman might serve an unlimited number of respondents. The next thing would have been to dispense with the bedroom scene altogether. But he had issued a Direction that the woman, where possible, must be named and served. Then, too, there had been the Direction of July 13th, 1928.

Yet it went on. Here was this troublesome Crew case— the first case in the list to-day—*Crew* v. *Crew*—a wife's petition. The resolute Mr. Crew seemed to think that he could defy the Court and put the clock back to the bad old days of the Nameless Woman. The President had decided that he should not.

The evidence was that the husband had passed two nights in a hotel bedroom with a woman. He then informed his wife of the fact and sent her a bill: but he disclosed no name or address of the woman in question, either to his wife or her solicitors. Mr. Justice Rait, at the first hearing, expressed his dissatisfaction and adjourned the petition for further inquiries with the object of discovering the woman's name. Solicitors wrote to the husband but he refused to disclose the woman's name. 'I may add,' he said, 'that this lady is a perfectly respectable and honourable lady and most naturally I would not think of behaving in a most dishonourable way by disclosing her particulars.' The case came back to the Judge, who referred it to the King's Proctor. The King's Proctor was unable to discover the woman's name; nor could he find any evidence of any kind of intimate association with any woman other than the wife, much less of an illicit association.

While the King's Proctor was engaged upon his vain inquiries Mr. Justice Rait retired from the Bench, and the case now came before the learned President. It shocked him. The husband's choice of language was unfortunate. In his second letter he had written: 'I am very sorry indeed to hear that the judge refused to make my decree nisi for the dissolution of my marriage until he has ascertained the name and address of the woman.' '*My*' decree nisi! So that the respondent had become the petitioner. It was he who was seeking a decree nisi, which, according to English law, a guilty spouse may not do. And then that talk about 'behaving in a dishonourable way'. What sort of topsy-turvy business was this?

The petition was dismissed.

Learned counsel seemed to suggest, said the President at the end of a weighty judgment, that if one spouse offered evidence of infidelity and the other was willing to accept it the Judge must shut his eyes and say 'Very well, you may have a decree.' That was not, at present, the law. A Judge had not to make or mend the law, to twist the law or manœuvre against its proper effects. He was there to administer the law; and in this case, being asked to find upon proofs provided by the husband that the wife was entitled to what the husband called 'my' decree nisi, he was unable to find that adultery had been committed.

Many barristers not engaged in the Court had come in to hear the President's judgment, for there had been much speculation concerning it. The volcano had been muttering for a long time, and an eruption was expected by many. They now walked out whispering excitedly. What was all this about 'adulterous inclination'? New law, surely? What did it mean? 'It means,' said Mr. Tompkinson, K.C., dryly, 'that a man must sleep with two or three women in order to persuade the Court that he has slept with one. I foresee a boom in Jermyn Street.'

'Will it stand?' a junior asked him.

Mr. Tompkinson thought that, on appeal, the President might be reversed. But would there be an appeal? The parties might already have exhausted their resources.

'One of the most unsatisfactory things about our legal system,' he told a junior, 'is that so many important points of law are left in doubt simply by the accident that the litigant concerned cannot afford, or does not choose, to appeal. A point like this ought to go straight to the Lords, and if the parties can't afford to take it there the community ought to pay. It would be worth the while of

the solicitors to finance an appeal, for this decision is going
to be expensive.'

'Not to the solicitors,' said the junior naughtily.

'True,' said Mr. Tompkinson, K.C.

Left behind in Court, Mrs. Adam's advisers, whose case
was next but one in the list, conferred together in anxious
whispers. With the President in this mood anything might
happen: and the circumstances of Mrs. Adam's petition
were dangerously similar to those of Mrs. Crew's. They
congratulated themselves that they could at least produce
the name and address of May Myrtle.

'Bad luck coming on just after that lot,' said Mr. Basil
Ransom.

'Yes,' said Mr. Freebody. 'You'll have to tread delicately.'

'Pity he's an education man. They're not supposed to
have any passions, much less "adulterous inclination".
But we're all right, I think—the old gentleman's thawing.'

The President, his normal geniality restored, was granting
a decree nisi to a stockbroker.

Rose Parkins sat with her married sister, Mrs. Ponder,
on a narrow bench at the back of the Court. Her rheumatic
knee was painful in the confined space. Her mouth and
eyes were opened wide in awe and mystification. She had
not understood all the President's words, but she knew as
well as any one else when there was rumpus in the air; she
saw the anxious face of Mr. Thomas and the other gentlemen, and said to herself that there was a rumpus. She
was surprised not to see the nice Mr. Adam and his little
lady, and looked expectantly at the door whenever it
opened.

Mrs. Ponder, a handsome woman in an ample style, the
wife of a street bookmaker, took a keen interest in the
proceedings: for she had been separated from her husband
by a magistrate's order only two years earlier. In Mrs.
Ponder's world divorce was a luxury almost unknown.
One went to the magistrate and complained about Henry.
The magistrate was very kind (Mr. Read especially) if a

person didn't talk too much or give back-answers in Court. But what he was after, as a rule, was to get husband and wife to go back and try again. If he couldn't do that it was a separation order and so much a week. That didn't take anybody much farther: but divorce cost money, and what was anybody to do? Mrs. Ponder did not begrudge the rich their divorces, for she could have done with one herself: she had her eye on a certain publican. But Ponder had never gone with the girls: the only complaint she had against him was that two or three times a week he would come home drunk and knock her about: and after a year or two she had tired of that. She had heard that there were arrangements for Poor Persons' Divorces now: but her case, it seemed, was not provided for. She didn't begrudge the rich one bit. But what seemed funny to her about the rich was that nobody seemed to try to get them to go home and try again. It was divorce or nothing. 'Some of this lot,' she whispered, 'ought to go before Read on a Tuesday. I'd like to hear him setting about 'em.' This King's Proctor, now—what was *he* for? He seemed to do nothing but put a spoke in the wheels. No help to nobody.

Mary Adam sat behind her counsel, with Mr. Freebody. She felt alarmed, indignant, guilty, deserted, injured, miserable. She felt as she felt during the half-hour before her first entrance on a first night, that is, that she had no stomach and would very soon be sick. As a rule, on a first night she was sick, sooner or later, from nerves; and the fear that she might be sick in Court increased her nervousness. She felt guilty because she was soon to go into the witness-box and tell what to all intents and purposes were lies—and tell them on oath, brandishing the Book. The President's profound voice and piercing eyes frightened her: she could tell from that long judgment that he was angry, and, if anything upset him, he would look right through her and see that she was lying. Not long before there had been a sensational stage divorce, and she remembered the awful things the President had said about 'the woman Smith', a famous actress. She prayed that nothing would provoke him to say awful things about 'the woman Adam'. She felt deserted and injured because neither of her men was there: John and Martin were safe in their offices and she had to go through this ordeal alone. She was angry with her own men because they were not there, and with all these funny other men because they were, and with all the men who ever existed because they had made these pantomime laws and arrangements. If she had guessed how awful it would be, what bogus documents she would have to sign and swear to, she would have behaved like a lady and made John divorce her, whether Martin lost his job or not. As it was, the papers would be maddening enough. It was a mercy having a stage name different from her own. No one yet, she thought, had spotted in Mary Adam, the petitioner, Mary Moon, the star. If they had, all those barristers, no doubt, would still be sitting in Court. There had been two men who looked like reporters scribbling in a corner during the Crew judgment, and there was one still. She had dressed very quietly, with a faint hope of escaping publicity, and she wore a hat that hid most of her golden hair. But the moment she confessed that she was an actress, no doubt, the news would fly round and she would be on the evening-papers' posters by lunch-time. She had asked the lawyers if it was necessary to announce that she was an actress: but, yes, it seemed it was the rule—every one must say who and what they were, in case they might be somebody else. 'Damn,' said Mary to herself, 'and blast them all!'

'*Adam* against *Adam*' was called.

Mr. Basil Ransom's opening speech was always brief on an undefended petition, but on this occasion it was extended by some unusual interjections from the President. At the fatal word 'hotel' he looked up from the pleadings before him, and looked down at Mr. Ransom. It was clear that the genial interlude had passed, like the calm area at the heart of a cyclone.

'A hotel? At Brighton?' he said. 'All this seems very familiar, Mr. Ransom. And now you are going to tell me, I suppose, that the respondent and the woman Myrtle spent two nights at this hotel, and were seen in bed by a chambermaid, and the respondent sent the bill to his wife—and so on?'

'That, as it happens, my lord,' said Mr. Ransom uncomfortably, 'was roughly the course of events.'

'Did you say that the respondent was a publisher?'

'Yes, my lord.'

'In what position?'

'My lord, I understand he is a director of Messrs. Heddle, Feather & Co.'

'A highly placed and responsible person?'

'Yes, my lord.'

The President looked hard at Mr. Ransom. Mr. Ransom looked innocently back at the President. But he thought, 'Christmas! Old Thunder is after "adulterous inclination"!'

'And who is May Myrtle? What is her station in life?'

Mr. Ransom stooped and exchanged whispers with Mr. Freebody.

'My lord, our information is that she is a secretary, a confidential secretary.'

'At the publisher's office?'

More whispers.

'No, my lord.'

'H'm.'

That 'H'm' was like the deep soft report of a distant heavy gun. Mr. Ransom waited in silence, as the soldier waits, to hear the shell approach and burst. Rose Parkins trembled. Mary Adam felt weak. The President opened his mouth and shut it again. No shell, it seemed, was on the way.

He said at last, 'Were you present in Court this morning, Mr. Ransom, during the observations I made in the case of *Crew* against *Crew*?'

'Yes, milord.'

'Very well, Mr. Ransom. Proceed.'

Mr. Ransom proceeded, scrambled through the rest of his statement, and called the petitioner.

Once she had said or sung her first line Mary Moon's first-night nerves departed, and, unless the play was disastrously received, she enjoyed the rest of the performance. Now, as soon as she had recited the oath and bowed to the President, she felt better.

The President liked the look of her. He liked the quiet manner of her dress, which showed a proper respect for the Court. He happened to notice the clear way in which she recited the oath. Most witnesses mumbled it secretly, as if it were a vulgar limerick. An actress, it seemed, but she did not look it.

Mary answered the questions clearly. She was Mary Rowena Adam. She resided at 14 Aurora Gardens, Knightsbridge. She was an actress. Her maiden name was Mary Eve. She married the respondent on April 29th, 1920. There were no children. They lived happily for some years. Then there were quarrels. Her husband was jealous of her stage life. He did not like her stage associates. No, he was not jealous in the ordinary way. He had no reason. She was devoted to her art. The quarrels became more frequent and worse. They got on each other's nerves. In the spring of 1927 she noticed a marked coolness. Her husband left her. She was living alone. In November she received a letter from her husband. Yes, that was the letter. She caused inquiries to be made. She filed a petition. Yes, that was her husband, sitting down in the photograph, in a bathing-dress. Yes, that was his hand-writing in the book. Yes, she was present when he was served.

'Thank you, Mrs. Adam,' said Mr. Ransom: and Mary turned to leave the box. The ordeal was over: and it might have been worse.

'One moment, please, Mrs. Adam.'

The President! The terrible old man! Those eyes!

'Before your husband left you, Mrs. Adam, did you ever have cause to complain of his association with other women?'

Mary thought quickly, 'Oh, Lord, what's he after? I know I ought to think this out.' But instead she said at once:

'No, my lord. Never.'

How, after all, could she say anything else about John?

'Would you say that he was a man who "ran after women"?'

'No, my lord. Certainly not.'

The President compressed his lips and looked at Mr. Ransom, as if to say, 'Take that!' Then he turned back to Mary.

'Your husband, in the letter to you which has been produced, says that he has given his heart to another woman, that is, to the woman named in the petition, the woman Myrtle. Are you acquainted with this woman?'

'No, my lord.'

'Prior to the receipt of this letter had you heard her name?'

'No, my lord.'

'She was not acting as secretary to your husband during your life together?'

'Not to my knowledge—no, my lord.'

'Thank you, Mrs. Adam. That will do.'

'Mr. Ransom,' he continued at once, mercifully covering Mary's retreat from the box, 'will you be calling evidence to show an association between the respondent and the woman named prior to the date of the alleged adultery?'

'No, my lord,' said Mr. Ransom respectfully: but he thought rebelliously, 'What next? Is the old bird altering the law?'

'It would assist me,' said the President.

'My lord, with great respect——'

But the President's rumbling voice rolled over him.

'The respondent is a man of good position and education. His wife says that he is not a man given to running after women. He is not, that is, likely to be given to promiscuous adultery. There is adultery, you say, on a single occasion, but no evidence of any previous association—no evidence, therefore, of an adulterous inclination generally, or of an adulterous inclination towards any particular woman. You heard my observations in a previous case.'

'What the devil is all this?' thought Mr. Ransom; but he said, 'My lord, with great respect, the evidence is very clear.'

'If you have direct evidence of adultery, Mr. Ransom, that is another thing. But if the Court is asked to make a presumption the Court must insist that the foundation is sufficient. Well, let us have the evidence.'

'Hell!' thought Mr. Ransom, 'we're sunk!' But he called the manager of the Capitol Hotel.

Mrs. Ponder whispered, 'He don't think he done it, you see?'

The manager sulkily entered the box. Yes, he was the manager. Yes, he had the custody of the hotel register (in which Mary had identified her husband's handwriting). Did he now produce the register? He did. Yes, he recognized the gentleman in the photograph.

The manager was released, left the Court at once, indignantly, and went back to Brighton, not caring whether the parties were divorced or not.

'Go on, Rosie. Fear nothing.'

Rose Parkins, the arbiter of at least four destinies— Rose Parkins, her knees knocking, her wits whirling, miraculously reached the witness-box: miraculously, because, as she afterwards said, any one could have knocked her down as soon as look at her. She made a mad mumble of the oath: she gripped with both hands the ledge of the box and clung, as she would have clung to the rail of a reeling ship: she threw a quick, terrified glance at Mrs. Ponder, so very far away, and another at Mr. Thomas, who was much too near for her liking: then she turned and, with her mouth wide open, gazed steadfastly at the President, whom she liked.

'More luck,' thought Mr. Ransom; 'our principal witness is barmy.'

Rose Parkins liked the President because there was no nonsense about him: the other men in Court were neither one thing nor the other, whispering and smarmy, like Mr. Thomas and the lawyer in the wig. She had never quite known where she was with the snoopy young man: he seemed to be saying one thing and meaning another. But it was quite clear what the old gentleman meant: and she turned to him as one rugged character to another.

She liked the President too because he was on the side of Mr. Adam. Though her wits whirled and her knees knocked there was fixed a firm purpose in her heart—or wherever the purpose of a determined woman reposes: and that purpose was to stand by Mr. Adam, who was a nice gentleman and had given her a pound. Nor would all their wigs and swearings prevent her. The proceedings, at first, had puzzled her more and more, especially the colloquies between the President and the gentleman in the wig: the atmosphere of rumpus was unmistakable, something had happened that nobody expected; but Rose Parkins did not quite know how she was affected and where she stood. If Mr. Thomas had been a wiser man he would have gone to Rose and reminded her where she stood. But he and his superiors were too much occupied with the President's disquieting pronouncements to bother about the mental processes of Rose Parkins. It was assumed, as the experts assume too often concerning race-horses, that she would run true to form and stable orders.

Rose had been persuaded, against her instinct, by Mr. Thomas, that Mr. Adam would like her to say that she had seen him in bed with the little lady. But the rumpus and arguments had restored her distrust of the snoopy young man. Slowly the impression grew that they were trying in some way to do the dirty on her Mr. Adam. The old gentleman did not think that Mr. Adam had done anything wrong, and he, she thought, could see through a brick wall as soon as any one. Mr. Adam's own wife said that he was never a one for running after the girls, and she ought to know. Mrs. Ponder's whisper about the President—'He don't think he done it, you see'—came at a crucial moment, and turned the impression into a conviction: for the President, she thought, was the only straight man there. That dratted manager, she knew, was crooked: and he too seemed to be in the plot against Mr. Adam. What the plot might be exactly she could not guess, and she had no time to try—some of this 'blackmail', as like as not; but Rose Parkins determined that she would help the President to stop it.

Yes, her name was Rose Parkins: and she resided at 3 Medina Villas, Brighton. She was a domestic servant at the Capitol Hotel. Yes, on November 2nd and 3rd she remembered attending a man and woman in Room 41. She knew them by the name of Mr. and Mrs. Adam. On the Sunday morning the bell rang and she was asked to take up two cups of tea. What did she see? She saw the gentleman in bed with the lady. She had her arms round his neck, added Rose: and Mr. Ransom shuddered in his soul, for this piece of information was not in the proof, and sounded, he thought, too good to be true.

'Thank you,' he said. 'Would you kindly look at this photograph?'

'In that photograph, do you see any face you know?'

Parkins looked at the photograph and said firmly, 'No, sir.'

The President sat up.

Mr. Ransom, raging like a leopard within, said smoothly, 'Be careful, Miss Parkins. You remember the gentleman you saw in Room 41?'

'Yes, sir.'

'You would know him if you saw him again?'

'Yes, sir.'

After every answer Rose turned her eyes from Mr. Ransom to the President, her ally, as if appealing to him for succour against the enemy gentleman in the wig.

Mr. Ransom said, 'Then do you still say, Miss Parkins, that you do not know any face in that photograph?'

'Yes, sir.'

Mr. Freebody leaned forward: Mr. Ransom stooped and they whispered together.

Mr. Ransom tried again, slow and despairing.

'Have you ever seen the gentleman in the bathing-dress —the one sitting down?'

'No, sir. Nothing like him.'

A few minutes later Mr. Ransom gracefully surrendered, having put Rose's signed proof to her in vain.

'My lord, I must ask your lordship's pardon—some mistake, no doubt. In the circumstances, my lord, if I might ask for an adjournment——'

'An adjournment, Mr. Ransom? Why should you have an adjournment? Have you any further evidence to call?'

8

'No, my lord; but——'

'I appreciate your difficulties, Mr. Ransom'—the President's voice was merciful—'but you have pleaded an affirmative issue, and if you cannot establish it I cannot help you. This witness is perfectly clear. The man identified by the petitioner as her husband was not the man the witness saw in bed.'

'My lord, the evidence of the manager——'

'What use is that, without more? He says that the respondent booked a room for himself and a woman. There is nothing to show that either of them so much as entered the room.'

'No, my lord; but, there may be a mistake, my lord—the wrong chambermaid——'

The President now looked severe, and spoke sharply.

'The respondent,' he said, 'is charged with adultery. He is not to be kept in suspense while you ring the changes on the chambermaids of a hotel. I have every sympathy with the petitioner, whose *bona fides* I do not question, but her case appears to be thin in substance, and has not been prepared with due care. I have no alternative but to dismiss the petition. I might say more, but I think upon this class of case my mind has been made sufficiently clear this morning. The petition is dismissed.'

Mary shook off her apologetic advisers and hurried away down the corridor. Her mind was a fiery furnace. All that agony for nothing! She could not believe it. What muddles men made! She swung furiously round a corner and charged into one of two elderly females going slowly down the spiral stairs before her.

Mary apologized, and saw that the woman she had trodden on was Parkins.

'That's all right. Oh, it's you, mum.' said Parkins. 'I hope I done right, mum.' she finished anxiously.

Mary looked at her. Rose Parkins' eyes were uncertain and humble. She was more mystified than ever. Nobody seemed to love her. Mr. Thomas had muttered something angry to her: that was only natural. But she had expected, somehow, a kind word from somebody. There would be somebody there, surely, who was on the side of Mr. Adam and would give her a pat on the back. But she had had no kind word, much less a pat on the back. Not even the President had said she had done right: and she was beginning to wonder whether she had. Mrs. Ponder thought not.

Mary looked down at the chief agent of her misfortunes. This was the woman who had messed up her life, she knew not why. Because of this fool, knave, liar, or lunatic, she would not be able to marry her Martin.

But Rose was trembling, she saw—poor creature. So Mary gave her a sweet smile and said, 'Of course you did right. Don't worry. Good-bye.'

'I'm ever so glad, mum,' said Rose in great relief. 'Thank you, mum.'

But Mary had gone. And Rose, who had been so queerly imported into her life, passed out of it, content and proud.

John Adam, leaving the Board of Education after a Conference, saw a newspaper placard:

WELL-KNOWN ACTRESS IN THE BOX

He bought the paper and read the report with an unquiet heart. It was brief: for the dashing divorce reports of the old days had been killed by the Act of 1926. He could not make head or tail of it—the reporters and sub-editors had been more interested in the personality and career of the petitioner than in the legal aspect of the case. The one thing clear was that all his efforts had gone for nothing. He was branded in the public press as a quarrelsome fellow who had deserted his wife: but he was as firmly married as he was before.

Mary, driving to the theatre in her little car, saw the placard too, and swore quietly. Waiting in a block in the Strand she watched, with a mutinous mind, the British Public buying the paper. Quiet little elderly men in bowler-hats. Young men with their girls. Smart men in evening dress. What, thought Mary, had her private life to do with any of them? Why, thought Mary fiercely, don't they print how many times I wash my neck or take a laxative medicine?

While she was dressing, the stage-manager, a fatherly, old-fashioned old fellow, came to see her, full of sympathy. He regarded her, she gathered, as a Wronged Woman: she had been tied to a brute, and now, trying to escape, she had been thwarted by the Brute, basely employing some legal quibble.

'Poor John,' she thought miserably, and began the difficult business of 'eye-black'.

'I think I told you,' said Mr. Boom, after his seventh oyster, 'the presumption is that every one is lying. If you had hotly denied misconduct the evidence of the manager alone might been quite enough to condemn you, but, as things turned out, he was worthless. You had bad luck, John, coming up for hearing on the old boy's Field Day. Nobody could foresee that. But it was the solicitors' fault. Some one bungled the maid badly.'

'What's to be done now?' said John Adam.

'There's nothing to prevent your wife from presenting another petition, but it would be wiser to wait a little till this blows over. Meanwhile, you'd better cultivate Miss Myrtle.'

'Oh, Lord! Must I? Why?'

'The old boy wants evidence of adulterous inclination. It's not enough for you to sleep with a lady, you must advertise your intentions as well. It's brand-new law, but until he's reversed he has to be obeyed. He's right, of course, according to his lights. A self-respecting Judge is bound to kick against evasion. The trouble is that he can only make it more difficult, and this is one of the laws which will always be evaded, however difficult they make it: because it's based upon a wrong principle—the idea that adultery is the only marital offence that really matters; and since it's the only one that's hardly ever done before witnesses it's the easiest of all to lie about. The only result of tightening things up is that it makes the thing more unpleasant for people like you, and quite impossible for most of the poor, because of the expense. The Poor Persons' procedure works pretty well, but it doesn't provide for prolonged visits to the sea-side. Divorce, I suppose, is the only privilege the income-tax payer gets for his money. Henri, more wine.'

'Take Miss Myrtle out a bit,' he continued. 'Late suppers and so on.'

'That's going to be expensive.'

'I told you, divorce is a luxury. Take her home to her flat, not before midnight. Freebody——'

'She lives at Greenwich, with five brothers and sisters.'

'A difficult woman. Then you'd better take a flat for her. Freebody must put detectives on you. I'll have a word with them——'

'Won't that be improper?'

'That depends on what I say.'

John Adam sighed. 'I'd no idea——' he began.

'Don't say that again,' said Mr. Boom. 'I warned you.'

'I'm very sorry, Mr. Adam, but Miss Myrtle is going to be married and is retiring from business.'

Blow upon blow!

Miss Mortimer, he thought, did not look sorry at all. Strangely, he had expected a little comfort from this inter-view. After the dry discourses of Boom, who seemed to take the lunatic business as a matter of course, the warm-hearted Miss Mortimer, passionate enemy of the laws, he had thought, would be soothing. She would smother him with sympathy and give him a glass of sherry. More and more, as his divorce proceeded, he appreciated a glass of wine.

But this morning she was the first Miss Mortimer he had seen—the one with spectacles, the long, straight mouth, and the sharp speech. Why was this? After all, she had had his money and he had nothing in return. He had hoped, indeed, to get special terms for the further use of Miss Myrtle.

Miss Mortimer explained immediately.

'To be frank,' she said severely, 'I should not, in any case, have been able to let you engage Miss Myrtle again. I must say you have surprised me, Mr. Adam.'

'I don't understand.'

'Miss Myrtle's report was very unsatisfactory—highly

unsatisfactory. It appears, Mr. Adam, that you plied her with wine and spirits, and then, while the girl was under the influence, attempted to take advantage of her.'

Mr. Adam stared at her.

'I cannot believe,' he said, 'that Miss Myrtle said that.'

'She did,' said Miss Mortimer: and her mouth shut like a rat-trap. She thrust a cheque towards him. 'I am sorry, Mr. Adam, but in the circumstances I am afraid you must forfeit your deposit. I am determined to keep this business clean.'

There are situations and events so monstrously unjust that the mind can hardly register a protest. No man can complain when he is struck by lightning; and for a few moments John Adam was unable to speak. To lose his divorce because he had not been intimate with Miss Myrtle —and then to lose his money because he had!

'But,' he stammered at last, 'can I see the report?'

'It is not in writing.'

'Can I see Miss Myrtle?'

'Certainly not. Here is our cheque for ten guineas, Mr. Adam. Perhaps you will kindly sign this receipt.'

John Adam, without a word, signed the receipt and went out.

It was spring, and Mary hungered for her Martin. She loved him truly, and, she discovered now, deeply: for the Court fiasco left her not angry only, but despairing.

All through the divorce preliminaries she had been like an engaged maiden, excited, expectant, impatient sometimes, but looking forward to a favourable event almost as a matter of course. She had understood that if you employed good lawyers, did what they told you, and were careful, to get an undefended divorce, upon modern scientific lines, was a tiresome but at least a certain proceeding. Now all was uncertain. Mr. Freebody said that she had had exceptional bad luck and could try again; but she had better wait for a month or two, for John must get a new woman and, in view of the decision in *Crew* v. *Crew*, go about with her for a bit. She had given him formal instructions: but at the best it would be three months before the case came on;

October probably, if all went well (she had lost what faith she had had in the law now), and on the top of that there would be the silly six months the law insisted on. Ten months—say twelve. And all that time, though madly in love, she was expected to 'be good'.

Mary, for the first time, began to wonder whether she would continue to be good. What was the use? For nearly three years now she had been alone. In June she would be twenty-nine. And the law said, 'You made a silly mistake when you were nineteen, and now you must be good for ever.'

Few of her friends, she knew, would have been good so long. Few of them believed that she was being good. But they were not the daughters of clergymen; they had not her upbringing and passion for truth. It was ridiculous; but she knew that if ever she ceased to be good she would never be able to face her old father again. It was ridiculous; she disagreed with all his opinions: she was the celebrated Mary Moon, and he was a poor old Rector—sixty-eight, or was it more?—pottering about the lawn with a mower in his hands and a sermon in his mind—watering his roses and reciting the Old Testament—old, feeble, ineffective and, she thought sometimes, a little mad. Yet he was her father, who had taught her, before all things, to speak the truth. And to speak the truth meant that one must not pretend a lie. If she should ever, technically, cease to be good, she would, she knew, have to keep away from the Rectory (which would hurt him), or else confess her wickedness the first time she saw the old man, which, she thought, would kill him.

'I don't,' she said to Martin, 'see how a law *can* be right which compels a person either to commit adultery or tell lies.'

'Or both,' said Mr. Seal.

As it was, she had not gone home since the divorce proceedings began, because she knew that she would have to tell her father the squalid truth about them, and that would upset him enough. She had spent one week-end with the Merridews at 'White Ladies', where she had had such fun in the old days, trying to teach poor John to sail a boat, which he could never do. She had had a grand blow with old Sam

Hardy, the boatman. But it was spring: she wanted other company than old Sam Hardy's.

It was spring, and John Adam met Joan Latimer at Victoria. Term was over and she had shepherded six of the youngest girls to London. She looked tired, end-of-termy. Joan Latimer was thirty-three, but looked less. She had a very smooth and youthful skin, high cheek-bones, and a high, clear voice. At the end of term the smooth skin was too pale, the cheek-bones too prominent, the voice, from endless lecturing and irritation, a little shrill. But she had candid eyes, a lithe, free carriage, and a charming crooked smile: and at the beginning of term the girls always said it was a wonder the Latimer was never married.

The six girls having been noisily restored to parents, she took John's hand and shook off school with a sigh of relief.

'Oh, dear!' she sighed. 'What a term!'

'Poor Joan.'

'Poor John,' she said. 'You must be tired too.' They stood for a moment hand in hand, forgetful of the crowd: and both at once felt rested. How clean and honest and refreshing, he thought. How solid and comforting, thought she.

A little man in a black hat, who was leaning against a lamp-post, made a little note in a little book.

'Oh, dear,' said Joan, with a sudden smile. 'I feel better. Where's the luggage?'

They dumped the luggage at Charing Cross. Joan was to go to her home in Kent that evening. They had the whole day before them: and they wandered out into the Strand like two children with a new toy, not quite certain what to do with it. They went into a tea-shop to discuss what they would do. Joan ordered an ice-cream-soda. A little man with a black hat sat at a table not far off and reluctantly ordered a cup of tea.

They would go to the Zoo in the morning, lunch at Simpson's, and in the afternoon go out to Kew and see the bluebells.

They took a taxi. The little man in the black hat, whose name was Wilkin, thankfully took another taxi and followed. A taxi going north—that would mean one of those shady little hotels near Euston. This suited Mr. Wilkin—quick business and no walking.

Mr. Wilkin's instincts were sedentary; for he had short legs and corns. But unkind Fate had led him into the private detective business, which involved much walking and standing about. And he strongly approved of couples who took taxis and proceeded straight to the scene of intimacy.

He was disappointed, therefore, when the taxi stopped in Regent's Park: and when the couple set off down the long Broad Walk towards the South Entrance of the Zoological Gardens he was disgusted.

Twice before he had had jobs at the Zoo: and it was the worst possible place for him and his work. A large space, with four or five exits; continual watchfulness needed, continual walking and standing about: tedious animals, and gravel underfoot. He hoped that, being lovers, the couple might at least have the decency to sit down somewhere and have a good jaw.

But it was late April, a fresh spring morning, and Joan and John, like young horses let out to grass, were impelled to celebrate their freedom with a caper. They turned left, and set off briskly, walking as if they were training for a race. And Mr. Wilkin, swearing, trudged after them.

They paused outside the old Reptile House, but decided to go on. 'There's only one thing, *really*,' Mr. Wilkin heard the lady say. 'And that's the Aquarium.'

'Well, that's quite close,' thought Mr. Wilkin gratefully, 'if you go the right way.'

But they did not. They marched off past the Wolves and Foxes, swinging their silly arms and breathing through their silly noses. Past the Swine and Antelopes—past the Sea-lions and Southern Aviary. They did not so much as turn aside to study the Sea-lions, as Mr. Wilkin hoped. They marched on beside the boundary of the gardens, talking busily, but now far out of earshot. On they went past the Mappin Terraces and round the corner by the Monkey Hill. Mr. Wilkin trotted painfully after them round the corner, and caught sight of the quarry, halted near the Aquarium. Mr. Wilkin thanked his Gawd, for there was only one exit to the Aquarium.

But Joan was saying, 'No, no, when we come back, my

dear. Let's walk and walk and walk.' And off they went through the Western Tunnel.

'Gawd!' said Mr. Wilkin, and trotted on. There were two exits in the other part of the Gardens, as he knew from sad experience, having once lost an important prey through the North Entrance. He was not to know that these two were coming back: he did not number rapid walking among the pleasures of illicit love, and he concluded that, mad with passion, they had decided to omit the Aquarium and go to a hotel. He followed.

Sharp left after the Tunnel, past the Gazelles' Shed, the Hippopotamus, and the Giraffes' and Wild Asses' Paddocks, and round by the Zebra House. Joan thought it would be fun to make a complete circuit of the Gardens, and John, delighting in her spirits, was ready for anything. Mr. Wilkin had counted on the Hippopotamus for a little respite: but Joan saw two girls from the school gaping at the monster, and they strode ahead.

'They don't,' said Mr. Wilkin bitterly, 'seem to take any interest in the blasted animals.'

Along the Canal Bank they went, past the Elephant and Rhinoceros House, not stopping even for the Parrots. They paused for half a minute at the Beaver Pond, and Mr. Wilkin picked up fifty yards: and the same at the Kangaroos, where one of the Wallabies reminded John of the President of the Board of Education. Mr. Wilkin was sure now that they were going to slip out through the North Entrance. But no, they turned right, and went back into the main garden through the Old Tunnel. Then left again and round past the Small Cats and Foxes and Jackals. Mr. Wilkin had half a mind to bet on the Aquarium and take a short-cut to that. But then, as like as not, they would go out through the South Entrance, the way they came in. His corns hurt, his shins ached; the spring day had developed an unexpected warmth, and, still in his winter clothes, Mr. Wilkin was unpleasantly hot. But on he went. Past the Refreshment Rooms (the couple seemed to have no sense), and past the Birds of Prey and Aviaries to the South Entrance. And there the two fools turned right and marched down the broad walk towards the Aquarium.

At last, near the Bears' Dens, they sat down and lifted

their faces to the sun. And Mr. Wilkin, lame and sweating, reflecting gloomily that the painful chase had not been necessary, limped after them and sat down too.

Joan said, 'And now tell me all about it. Poor John, what a time you must have had!'

John looked sadly at the Stork and Ostrich House, wondering how much he ought to tell her.

Mr. Wilkin, watching them, said to himself, 'It's a case, no mistake. Why the hell can't they go somewhere and get on with it? All this messing about.'

Mr. Boom had been right, John was thinking. Boom had warned him that his behaving like a gentleman might not be pleasant for Joan. And here he was wondering how much he should keep from her, a bad beginning for their life together. He hated the idea of keeping anything from her; yet it seemed impossible to tell Joan 'all about it'—all, for example, about Miss Myrtle. He could have told Mary, he thought, and they might have laughed together about it. But Joan was so different. She was so clean and sensitive and straight. So was Mary: but Joan belonged to another world. She knew, he thought, even less about 'life' than he did. He shrank even from using such words as 'adultery' and 'bed' in her presence. She would be shocked to her depths to hear of the things which he had had to do. She might say, he thought, that, if this was the only way, it would be better that they should never be married. For she would always put her standards before herself.

'Well——' he began doubtfully.

'And tell me everything, John,' she said. 'I'm not a wax flower you know. And I don't want a glass case.'

Mr. Wilkin thought, 'At this rate the pubs will be shut before anything happens.'

'Oh, dear,' said Joan. 'And you actually had to get into bed with her?'

'Yes. That's the whole point.'

'The whole point! What a law!'

She thought for a moment.

'What was she like?'

'A common little person. Not bad.'

'Poor girl.'

John was surprised and relieved by Joan's reception of his story. He had suppressed much of it, and now was sorry. He should, he thought, have had more faith in Joan's unshakable sanity. Unlike the law, she thought more of the essence than the form.

'I kissed her,' he said, doubtfully. 'Twice.'

'Why not?' said Joan. 'She deserved it.'

John, without perceiving the compliment, thought, 'She's a wonder.'

'And now, what next?' she said.

'They say I must begin again, with somebody else.'

'I wish it could be me, John,' said the school-teacher softly.

'So do I.'

'I suppose it mustn't——' she mused.

'Don't talk nonsense, dear.'

'Why not?'

'The school!'

'I know. But that's only selfishness, really. I want to go on teaching. I want to get the school. But why should you have all this trouble because of that?'

'It's nothing,' said John, stoutly. 'Soon over.'

'It isn't nothing. It won't be soon over. You'll never forget it. It's bad for you. It's been bad for you already.'

'What do you mean, dear?'

'All this faking and humbug. You're catching it, poor John. You've not told me everything, even now, have you?'

'No, dear.'

'Tell me. I don't know why you should think that a schoolmistress knows nothing about anything—but I believe you do.'

He told her about Jermyn Street. She clenched her strong fists and said, 'Oh, it's a shame!' And she added strangely. 'The Bishops ought to go through that. And that old Judge too.'

He told her how he had put Miss Myrtle to bed, which he had thought would shock her more than anything. But she smiled at that and said 'How sweet!'

She put her hand on his; and Mr. Wilkin made a note.

'Poor John. You feel better now, don't you?'

'Yes, dear.'

'That's the horrible thing about this law, it seems to me,' she said. 'It does just the opposite to what it wants. It makes the straight people tell lies, and it makes the decent people behave like pigs. I don't suppose your wife is very fond of lying, is she?'

'No, she hates it.'

'It must have been horrible for her, going to that Court.'

'Yes.'

He had not, in fact, thought much about that. Compared with his own part, it had seemed a simple thing. How understanding and wonderful was this Joan of his!'

'Well,' she said, 'shall we do it?'

'What, dear?'

Softly she said: 'Shall we go to Brighton?'

'You really would?'

'I would, John.'

He looked at her, amazed and worshipping. What a temptation! To stop behaving like a gentleman and be honest: to stop monkeying with the law and get what he wanted immediately, with no more trouble. But at what a price! He knew how much the school meant to Joan— much more, he thought, than the theatre meant to Mary.

'Well, I wouldn't,' he said. 'And that's that.'

Joan was one of the rare beings who do not argue where argument is clearly vain.

'That's naughty of you, John,' she said, 'but nice.'

Simpson's was fine. And Mr. Wilkin was quite happy, resting his feet in the downstairs bar. For the drinks, in the end, would be all paid by the respondent, thinking, poor fool, that he was having an economical meal upstairs.

Kew was glorious under the gentle sun. Cherry-blossom, the first rhododendrons and azaleas, sparkling air, delicious birds, two simple lovers—and the unhappy Wilkin.

They walked down the great glade to the river (angrily pursued by Mr. Wilkin) and looked across the water to the rich water-meadows of Zion House, where herons fished and flopped about lazily among the reeds. Then they walked back (never in all his experience of guilty lovers had Mr. Wilkin encountered such walkers) to the dusky little wood which at that time of year is carpeted with bluebells.

Mr. Wilkin regained some hope. Nobody could predict anything of so crazy a couple, he thought, but surely in such surroundings there might be some event worth putting in a report, if it was only holding hands. He sat down behind some rhododendrons, took off his brown boots, and rubbed his corns. There was plenty of time. Next time he peeped round the corner, with any luck, the couple would be engaged in intimacy, or something like it.

Joan and John lay on their backs like two boats floating in a sea of bluebells. They looked up through the tangle of branches and young leaves and watched the little clouds roll by, like small flat-fish in a rival ocean. Joan thought suddenly how odd it was that John had kissed Miss May Myrtle (twice) but had not kissed Miss Joan Latimer at all. The spring was in her and she said, 'Kiss me, John.'

'What?'

They both sat up.

'Kiss me,' said Joan.

'Is it wise?' said John, and guiltily looked about the wood.

'No, it is not,' said Joan. 'Don't look round yet, but I have an idea that we've been followed.'

'Followed?'

'There's a little man hiding behind those rhododendrons —just behind the sixth—no, the seventh—tree on your left. A little, little man in a little black hat.'

'With brown boots?'

'Yes.'

'I saw him at the station before your train came in.'

'And I saw him twice at the Zoo. I didn't say any-thing——'

'Nor did I. But I saw him at the tea-shop too.'

'That settles it.'

'Well, I'm damned!'

'What does it mean?' said Joan.

'I know very well what it means,' said John furiously. 'It's those damned solicitors. They've put detectives on me.'

'What for?'

'Boom—that's my man—said the other side would put detectives on me when I'd got somebody else—you know, instead of Miss Myrtle. For adulterous evidence and all that. And, as usual, they've bungled things and gone straight ahead. My Lord,' said John furiously, 'what bunglers they are! They don't *begin* to know their job!'

Joan had never seen, and never saw again, her John so angry.

She laughed—a long, rich, gurgling, affectionate laugh.

'There's nothing to laugh at!' said he. 'Don't you see, this man will think that you're the Woman!'

'Well, so I am,' said the schoolmistress; and she lay back among the bluebells and laughed.

John rose without another word, adjusted his spectacles, and strode away among the bluebells towards the rhododendrons. Joan watched him, laughing but loving, and tried to adjust her disorderly mind. What had happened to the Second Mistress of St. Bride's—lying on her back among the bluebells in a public park and inviting a distinguished 'educationist' to kiss her! It was the spring. But the spring, she knew, would be no defence before the Head Mistress or the Senior Common Room—to say nothing of Parents. What would Everybody say if they could see her? But hang Everybody! What fun! Here she was, the Second Mistress, plain, she thought, and unattractive, couched upon bluebells in a romantic wood—plain and unattractive, yet beloved. And there was her Knight, marching sternly (in spectacles, true) to the detection and discomfiture of a peeping enemy. Perhaps it was the spring. Perhaps it was lunacy. Whatever it was, it was delicious.

Her Knight strode round the corner of the rhododendrons and found the enemy at a disadvantage; for Mr. Wilkin, concluding from a quick inspection that the couple were neither intimate nor mobile, had taken off his boots again and was rubbing his corns.

'What the devil do you think you're doing?' said Mr. Adam, very fiercely.

'Beg pardon, sir? My feet are bad.'

'Why are you following me about?' the Knight thundered.

'Beg pardon, sir. All in the way of duty. Here's my card.'

The Knight, contemptuously, flung the caitiff's card into the bushes.

Mr. Wilkin, disturbed by this unprecedented gesture, stood up in his stockinged feet, and said with deference, 'Beg pardon, sir, but all's correct, isn't it? I've had my instructions. Follow gentleman and report relations with lady.'

'I don't care a damn what your instructions are,' said Mr. Adam. 'But, whatever, they are, will you kindly understand that THIS—is NOT—the LADY?'

'Certainly, sir,' said the awed Mr. Wilkin. 'Whatever you say, sir.'

'Is it quite clear?' said the implacable Knight. 'You never saw me in Kew Gardens? You never saw me at the Zoo? You never saw me with *that* lady at all?'

Mr. Adam emphasized each of these three points with a sharp thrust of the fist towards Mr. Wilkin's stomach, after each of which Mr. Wilkin retreated a pace.

'No, sir,' he said. 'Never.'

'If ever you *should* see me with a lady in the course of your disgusting duties, the only lady in the world it could never be would be the lady you have seen me with to-day. Do you understand?'

'Certainly, sir. Absolutely, sir.' Which said a great deal for Mr. Wilkin's intelligence.

'Very well, then.'

The Knight turned on his heel, and was about to return, with dignity, to his Fair. The victory had been unexpectedly easy, but it was victory, and he was proud of it.

But Mr. Wilkin had been in the divorce business much longer than Mr. Adam, and he began to whimper.

'Beg pardon, sir—don't be hard on a man, sir. This is a bad day for me, sir—anything you say, of course, sir—but there's been a mistake, sir—no fault of mine, sir. No information, no pay, sir—that's the rule in our firm,' he lied. 'You wouldn't be hard on a man, sir—I've a wife and three children, sir——'

Mr. Wilkin stopped, judging he had gone far enough. He was right. The Knight had already disappeared, and there was left Mr. John Adam, the compassionate citizen and humane social worker.

'Oh, well, of course——' said the social worker, and fumbled in his pockets.

Unhappily, he found nothing but sixpence and a crumpled pound note.

'Thank you, sir. God bless you, sir,' said Mr. Wilkin, and pocketed the pound note.

John marched back across the bluebells to his love: and, as he marched, the Knight returned. After all, he had triumphed in the difficult encounter.

'I dealt with him,' he said shortly, and sat down among the flowers.

'Well done, John,' she said.

'Kiss me, Joan,' said the Knight.

'You're coming on,' said the schoolmistress lovingly. 'You didn't even look round.'

The educationists kissed. It was the spring.

Mr. Wilkin, putting on his boots, observed the kiss, but without interest. It was no good now.

It was the spring: and Martin hungered for his Mary. Unlike Mary, he was determined to have his way: and, unlike Mary, he saw no reason to publish the truth about it if he did. He was, in short, an average Englishman, a decent fellow, reluctant to do wrong, but more constrained by convention than by morality, not fearing God very much but fearing scandal greatly. Moreover, he was an official of the British Broadcasting Corporation, whose moral standards were higher than that of any other British institution known to history. In that pious building it was whispered that even the innocent party to a divorce would find himself, sooner or later, unwelcome, or, to use the language of the licensing justices, redundant.

And, though at heart he did not share the moral opinions of his superiors, he was at one with them concerning the importance of their work. That is to say, he thought that nothing else quite so important was being done in the world. Kings, Dictators, Governments, Democracies, Churches, Armies, Navies, and Judges, Commerce, Literature, Newspapers, and even the Arts, had their little places in the scheme of life. But above all stood the British Broadcasting

9

Corporation, which was able to distribute to the millions in the English language whatever news, views, sentiments, or songs it pleased. Though every other channel of communication were blocked by civil strife or natural disaster, though railways, newspaper offices, ships, aeroplanes, and motor-cars stood idle, the Corporation, through the unobstructible ether, would still command the people to keep steady, and request Agnes Potts to proceed to 14 Peckham Lane, where her grandfather was dangerously ill. The Army, the Navy, the Civil Service, the Police—all other agents of authority might be mutinous or powerless: but the Corporation, like some mechanized Vicar of Bray, would still communicate to the People the voice of the Government in power for the time being. Had not someone truly said that the first act of a revolutionary conspiracy would be to seize not Whitehall, not Parliament, not even Scotland Yard, but the teeming offices at the foot of Savoy Hill? And, in the worst event, if civilization should crack, when every other organized activity of man had ceased, the last survivors in a dying world would draw comfort from a little faint orchestral music, a Talk or two about the Future Life, and the gentle intimation that they were not expected to survive much longer.

Martin Seal had never expressed himself in such precise, outrageous terms: but this was the luminous, though hazy, background of his life. The B.B.C. was the one essential and enduring thing in the complicated machinery of the country, and he, Mr. Seal, was essential to the B.B.C. It was not every man whose voice could address, without irritating, the millions every night. Prime Ministers, bishops, actors, and literary men—there were few who could be safely allowed on the air for more than twenty minutes twice or three times a year. Only a few, a very, very few, were always acceptable to the People.

Sometimes, musing in his secret heart, Mr. Seal allowed himself fantastic visions. He thought that one day the whole direction of his country might be taken over by the B.B.C. Already it supplied to the People more rich and various benefits than the People had had from any Government, from any single institution, before. It provided them, by wireless, not with entertainment only, but with education,

with practical instruction, and philosophical teaching, with
political talks and religious services. Not content with
the air, it was already invading the earth. It published
weekly newspapers and pamphlets: why not its own daily
papers and books? It had its own orchestra, its own concert-
hall: why not its own theatres, music-halls, and film-studios;
churches and schools; and universities? The world of
language and thought was boundless; and wherever the
English tongue was communicable the British Broadcasting
Corporation held sway, was alone and irresistible. Statesmen and Ministers could say what they liked in the House of
Commons, on the platform, and in the papers: but not at
Savoy Hill. Indeed, they had to come there hat in hand
before they were permitted to say anything at all. Scotland
Yard knew very well that if they hoped to apprehend a
criminal the best thing was for him, Mr. Seal, to breathe a
few delicate words into the microphone. The step was short
from the mastership of Ministers to the management of
their Ministries: and, in that event, there would be nothing
for it but a B.B.C. Army, Navy, and Air Force. . . .

At this point, as a rule, Mr. Martin Seal woke up and
rebuked himself. But the general message of the dream was
abiding. He could see no limit to the swelling empire of the
Corporation, and the basis of it all was the human voice
—not any human voice but a Voice continually acceptable to the Millions. And his was one of the rare human
voices which answered to that description. Therefore he
drank little and smoked not at all.

And therefore, though he was determined to sleep with
Mary, he was not prepared to be pilloried for it, or even to
have the fact that he was friendly disposed to her whispered
abroad. 'All for Love and the B.B.C. well lost!' was not a
phrase which Mr. Seal was likely to employ.

Nor did Mary expect it of him: for she too, unlike the
poets, thought that Work was more than Women. She
thought that what people did in the daytime was more
important than what they did at night. And if Governments would accept that simple principle a great many
vexatious laws could be done away with.

Nevertheless, she hungered for her Martin: and he for her.

·   ·   ·   ·   ·

Late in May, 1930, there was an event of great importance to the world of divorce. The petitioner in the Crew case, Mrs. Crew, appealed against the judgment of the learned President—and won.

If it were a matter of interfering with the President's discretion, said the Master of the Rolls, politely, the Court would hesitate long; but he had added something to the law. Appeal allowed. Decree nisi granted.

The decision of the Court of Appeal brought cheerfulness to many solicitors and fresh hope to many lay clients.

'What does it mean?' said Mr. Boom after the seventh oyster. 'It means that we're back where we were. That is, the law is.'

'But does it mean,' said Mr. Adam, 'that no name will be necessary now?' If so, he thought with a glow of excitement, perhaps Joan and he might after all go to Brighton together.

'No,' said Mr. Boom. 'Not exactly. That is, if the case is watertight otherwise, the old man won't be able to turn you down simply because the woman isn't named—that is to say, where it's impossible to discover it. But he can still use his discretion to make things difficult if her name's not given. He's asked to make a presumption from a single incident: and he can say that the identification of the woman would help him—for instance, the wife might know her and be able to speak of a previous association. So he can still ask the petitioner's solicitors if they've taken all possible steps to find the woman: and if they haven't he can adjourn the hearing till they have. The old gentleman's been defeated in law but not in practice: for I've no doubt that from now on the name will always be given where it can be.

'Things will be a bit tighter, though not so tight as he'd like. He won't be able to jump on the hotel case, as such, and there's no reason why your second shot—I beg your pardon, your wife's—shouldn't be successful. I'm sorry to hear about Miss Myrtle. Have you got another lady?'

'No.'

'Then have a glass of port.'

'No, thanks. Yes, I will.'

.   .   .   .   .

The only matter in which it can be recorded that fortune favoured the brave Mr. Adam was the finding of Miss Laura Tott. She fell, as it were, like a ripe apple in his path, the perfect accommodation lady.

He spent a week-end near Godalming at the house of his friend Henderson of the Office of Works. Miss Laura Tott was acting as temporary governess and companion to the two girls before the summer holidays. She had always been a governess, it seemed, and was generally temporary: for she was fond of life, and fond of London, and independent of mind, and she did not like to incarcerate herself indefinitely in the heart of any home.

'It's a mistake,' she said, 'to get too fond of children. They grow up and let you down.' Between her spells of duty she lived at a boarding-house for unmarried ladies at Earl's Court, which was, it seemed, a great place for gossip.

In her youth she must have been good-looking, in a sharp-featured style. She was pleasant-looking, now; dark and aquiline and neat, with a sharp, questing nose and a spare body; her face was freckled, her neck was thin, and the children called her affectionately 'Hen'. Age perhaps forty; perhaps not.

The children, young ladies of fifteen and sixteen, pitied Miss Tott because she was an Old Maid and would never now be married. But Miss Tott was perfectly happy: and she would not have changed her lot with any of the numerous wives and mothers she had served. She had shared in the domestic joys and agonies of twenty families while most married women had to be content with one. Even now there were four or five homes where the children welcomed her and remembered her birthday; so long as she had such a welcome here and there, could keep herself and her rooms in Earl's Court, read a few books, go to a few films, and gossip a great deal, she asked no more of life.

'Hen,' Mr. Adam heard Virginia say once in frank surprise, 'I didn't know that at your age you *could* have a real thrill.'

'Don't you worry,' said Miss Tott, 'the older I grow the more thrilling life is.'

John Adam liked her at once. He liked always to talk to any one who had a hand, however humble, in the mighty business of education. Miss Tott liked teaching and could talk about it; but she was, for a teacher, refreshingly a woman-of-the-world as well. So many keen 'educationists', he found, seemed to regard the child as the scientist regards a rabbit, a subject for interesting 'experiments'. The experiments might or might not be good for the subject, but when one rabbit was done with there would always be more rabbits to come. Miss Tott thought of her charges not as arguments for or against the What-not System, but as young human beings. She held the balance nicely between the modern theories of Free Development and the old tradition of authority—between always saying 'Don't' and never saying 'Do'.

She was very talkative. She had a sense of fun and her tales were amusing. And her favourite topic was not education but scandal in high places. In the Earl's Court boarding-house, it appeared, there was nothing the ladies did not know about the love-affairs and divorces of the rich, the habits of actresses and the vices of dukes. Miss Tott bubbled with anecdote and comment, spicy but not malicious. She had been often at the Hendersons' and was on terms of almost impudent familiarity with them. She addressed Mr. Henderson as 'Daddy' and, though virginally discreet before the children, put very few checks on her tongue when her audience was adult. Mr. Henderson was a widower: he saw little 'life' at the Office of Works, and he enjoyed hearing about the wild deeds of the wealthy. Gossip and Scandal are close relations to Literature and the Drama, and, like them, enable the audience to enjoy vicariously sensations denied to them in their own experience.

Over her night-cap (Miss Tott liked a little whisky last thing at night) she told the two gentlemen the truth about the Compton case. They had read a little about it in the papers, but Miss Tott told the tale with such assurance, with such a suggestion of first-hand testimony, that it was like seeing a good play beautifully acted—the two men felt themselves almost eye-witnesses of the scenes described. (Miss Tott had, in fact, got the story from a Miss Broom at the boarding-house, who had heard a vague rumour from a hairdresser and had used her imagination: but the gentlemen were not to know that).

Encouraged by her reception, she went on to tell them about the recent case of Mary Moon, the actress. She knew all about that too. Famous actresses were her favourite interest, and she spoke of Mary Moon as if they had been playmates or relations. Mary Moon had once autographed a programme for her, and she was loyally on Mary's side. 'Of course, you know,' she said, 'the husband used to beat her, but that didn't come out.'

Mr. Adam blushed to hear this information, and Mr. Henderson, with a loud cough, stood up and said, 'Now, Miss Tott, no more scandal!' And Miss Tott, to her surprise, was firmly ushered upstairs.

The next morning, walking to church, Mr. Henderson sent the children on ahead, and informed Miss Tott of the relations between Miss Mary Moon and his guest, Mr. Adam. Knowing her appetite for such affairs, he had carefully refrained from telling her before. Miss Tott said, justly, that he had been foolish.

Before lunch Mr. Adam walked on the lawn alone, reflecting on many things: on Mr. Garvin's disturbing article, on the news from China, on the case of *Adam* v. *Adam*, and on the wounding words of Miss Laura Tott. It was grievous to think that middle-aged ladies were going about the world saying that he had beaten his wife: and it was odd to think that, though he had that reputation, the law refused to release her from her cruel lord.

Miss Tott, back from church, came across the lawn to him, more excited than penitent, but explosive with apologies. She had never been in such close touch with a famous actress as now, apologizing to the husband of one for saying that he had beaten her.

Mr. Adam was kind and begged her to think no more about it: but he also assured her that the accusation was erroneous. Miss Tott continued to talk, for she wanted to hear more. She talked about divorce in general: she criticized the divorce laws; hoping that she might hear something about the Woman in the Case. Was it a 'romance', she wondered, or a put-up job? Mr. Adam was not to be drawn; but suddenly Miss Tott was saying, in natural tones, quite without archness, that she had once helped a gentleman to get a divorce herself. A matter of form, of course.

She had been governess to the children. They went to Folkestone.

Mr. Adam was all attention at once. But the gong sounded for lunch, the children bounded across the lawn, and no more could be said.

But all through lunch the thought possessed his mind, perhaps Miss Tott would oblige. That afternoon he would manœuvre to get another conversation with her.

It was not necessary. They all went for a walk, and very soon Miss Tott's shoe came off and he and she were walking behind the others. Mr. Adam diffidently approached his theme. Did he understand that she had helped some one to secure a divorce? Yes. An unpleasant task, he supposed? Not a bit. She had enjoyed it. Anything for a change, she had always said, and she was fond of Folkestone. Then would she, he wondered—she must forgive him— would it be too much to ask—could she possibly—help him—in the same way?

Why, of course! She would be delighted. As soon as she left the Hendersons, which would be in a fortnight. She would come and see him the moment she was free. Nothing was said about terms. Miss Tott made only one stipulation, just before Virginia bounded up to her:

'Only,' she said, 'I *must* meet your wife, Mr. Adam. . . . Yes, darling, what is it?'

This time, to satisfy the law, the thing was done more thoroughly. Before any arrangements were made for a visit to the South Coast, steps were taken to show the world that Mr. Adam had an adulterous inclination to Miss Tott, though he was as likely to have such an inclination to a lamp-post. John telephoned to Mary and Mary said a word to Mr. Freebody and Mr. Freebody had a word with Mr. Wilkin and Mr. Wilkin was instructed to watch Mr. Adam on certain dates, and make a note of adulterous events, but only so long as Mr. Adam was accompanied by a dark woman of forty with a sharp nose who answered to 'Hen'.

A delay of a fortnight was caused by Virginia Henderson's developing measles: for Miss Tott stayed on to look after the child. But at last the operations began.

The first day on Mr. Wilkin's list was a Saturday, and Mr. Adam enraged Mr. Wilkin by taking Miss Tott to the Zoo. Moreover, the fellow followed the same route as before. John wanted to make his own task lighter by reviving sentimental memories of his day with Joan, and all the way round the Zoo he talked to Miss Tott about Joan (whenever he was given an opportunity to talk). Mr. Wilkin concluded that a man who walked round and round the Zoo with one woman after another must be some sort of lunatic. But the lunatic appeared to be consistent, and Mr. Wilkin (whose corns were bad) was not going to be caught again, so he went straight to the neighbourhood of the Aquarium and sat there resting till the couple arrived.

During the next few weeks Mr. Wilkin reluctantly added much to his knowledge of London: for John betrayed his adulterous inclination by taking Miss Tott to the Tower of London, the Victoria and Albert Museum, the Tate Gallery, Westminster Abbey, and the Caledonian Market. He did not quite know what he was expected to do with Miss Tott on these preliminary skirmishes, beyond being seen about with her, and he thought it a good opportunity to see some of the familiar spectacles of London with which the Londoner is rarely familiar.

All these expeditions involved much walking and standing about for Mr. Wilkin: but duty compelled him to follow. And on four occasions they led to something more worthy of his attention. Three times Mr. Adam dined with Miss Tott in a public place—twice at Simpson's and once in Soho (in Mr. Wilkin's experience the sharing of food and drink was always a bad sign). Once they went to a cinema afterwards, and once, at the dangerous hour of eleven p.m., Miss Tott accompanied Mr. Adam to his flat. Mr. Wilkin made a note of the time and leaned against the railing opposite.

Inside, Miss Tott took charge of the proceedings. She went to the window and stood there for half a minute, looking down at Mr. Wilkin. Then she blew a kiss to Mr. Wilkin (which he regarded as an unprofessional gesture), and carefully drew the curtains. Mr. Wilkin made a note of that.

John gave Laura a whisky-and-soda: and the adulterous couple sat down and discussed Education.

John was interested in the New Education already being practised in some of the schools for the children of the well-to-do. No forcing: no competition, marks, or prizes. And the children were 'free'. When in their innocence or curiosity they made 'shocking' remarks nobody was shocked or told them to be quiet. All subjects, however difficult, were gravely discussed with the child: and their abnormal repressions and obsessions were avoided. John was attracted by the theory, and thought that in the private schools it might bear good fruit. But, he said, he was not sure how far it was practicable in the public elementary schools—or even in the home. What was Miss Tott's experience?

Miss Tott laughed: she had a pleasant laugh, which, unlike many laughs, really expressed amusement. She had had a brief experience of a very advanced school, where the pupils were not compelled to do lessons at all, but were told that, if they liked, they could climb trees instead, or go boating on the lake.

'Well,' said Miss Tott, 'I argued about this in the Common Room till I was sick. The children just did what they liked. I was the Latin mistress, and none of them liked Latin. Well, one week the English mistress was ill and I had to take her work. They all liked the English lessons because the mistress was a charmer: and she used to read them bits of poetry while the class pinched each other's behinds. I couldn't do anything with them. So one day, when the little blighters were all sitting there ready for the English lesson, I said, "What's right for the children is right for the teacher, I suppose. I don't like English to-day." And the Head Mistress found me at the top of the cedar-tree! I was sacked on the spot—and glad of it.'

Miss Tott laughed again at her improbable tale. But she continued seriously: 'All the same, there's something in it. *You'd* have been better for a little of that. You're all shut up, aren't you, Mr. Adam? Like an oyster.'

John opened his mouth wide as if to show that he was not shut up, but could not at once think of any suitable reply. It occurred to him that Miss Myrtle had said that he was like an oyster. Perhaps he was. The odd thing

was that he did not at all object to Miss Tott saying that
he was like an oyster.

She went on: 'You'd be shocked if I said adultery, wouldn't
you? I mean, just said it. You wouldn't be shocked if I
said murder. But murder's much worse, I should say.
That's what these New Education people are after, I think.
The English are afraid of words: and they're afraid of the
wrong words. So they get the wrong ideas. "Divorce"—
that's another of them. Everybody looks down on a divorced woman; but if a woman commits a murder they get
up petitions for her, and if she gets off all the newspapers
want to publish her reminiscences. They wouldn't do that
if it was a divorce case.'

'That's because you can't be divorced unless there's——'
He paused.

'Adultery! There, you daren't say it!' declared Miss Tott
in triumph.

'But the point is,' said Mr. Adam, evading the charge,
'you wouldn't talk like this to children you were looking
after, would you?'

'No,' said Miss Tott. 'Not quite. Because I should never
get a job. But I do think they ought to know more. The
trouble is that if you tell children anything they talk about
it. They come out with it in the drawing-room when
Granny's there, or the Vicar. And, of course, I do think
there are things you don't want to talk about in drawing-
rooms, just as there are things you ought not to do in a
drawing-room. It's just a question of drawing the line, the
same as everything else. Manners, you might call it. You
can't lay down rules, one way or the other. If a dog's
trained to the house you can let it into the drawing-room
and all's well. And if children are properly trained you
can tell them anything they want to know and they won't
let you down. That's the way I always look at it. But if
you let them say anything they'll say everything, and then
where are you?'

'Yes,' said Mr. Adam vaguely.

It was half-past twelve. Mr. Wilkin muttered, 'Gawd,
she's not going to stay all night, is she?'

'Do you know,' said Miss Tott reflectively, 'I shouldn't be a bit surprised if this divorce business did you a lot of good. Clear your mind.'

'Do you believe in a classical education?' said Mr. Adam.

Miss Tott did believe in a classical education: and they discussed this thoroughly. At a quarter past one she looked at her tiny wrist-watch and said she must go. They went downstairs, still discussing the classical education. Mr. Adam opened the door for her and followed her on to the pavement: they stood there for a minute or two, still discussing the classical education, clearly audible to Mr. Wilkin, and quite forgetting they were supposed to have just committed adultery.

'Gawd!' said Mr. Wilkin to himself, 'he's barmy, and no mistake.'

'Good night,' said Mr. Adam at last, and shut the door.

Miss Tott, tripping away, looked across the road towards Mr. Wilkin and said sweetly, as one dismissing a chauffeur: 'That will be all to-night, thank you'; and she added, 'Tootleoo!'

'Good night, all! All right, Martin! Curtain up!'

Mary had decided she could stand it no more. The Merridews wanted her to go down to 'White Ladies' for the week-end again. She had hedged a little: and Alice Merridew, sitting in the dressing-room after the show on Wednesday, had said slyly, 'Why don't you bring that nice man with you?'

'Which one?' said Mary defensively, towelling cream from her face.

'The wireless one. Something to do with the Aquarium.'

'Oh, Martin Seal? I expect he's busy.'

But the temptation mastered her. She had heard nothing from the lawyers, and was too much disgusted with the whole affair to approach them. The sun shone; London was hot; the papers promised an anticyclone. 'White Ladies,' a fresh breeze, the *Curlew* bowling down the Medway, and Martin—it would be bliss. After all, she deserved a little bliss. And they could still be good. She knew, she thought, how to manage Martin. She had only to whisper in his ear, 'Suppose the B.B.C. could see us——?' and he would put a county between them.

So here they were in the little green car, outside the stage door. Saturday night—and the usual cloud of gallery worshippers, girls, surrounded the car. 'Good night, Miss Moon!' 'Mary, you're wonderful!' 'Better than ever!' She had pressed gently through them, signing her name illegibly on programmes and scraps of paper, and in autograph books, held upside down. Martin, a sheepish and uncon-sidered male, the feeble tail of a comet, had struggled after her. He was divided, as usual, between fear that he would be recognized and resentment that he was not; the girls took no notice of the handsome youth, unless to complain about his elbows. But, grudgingly, they had permitted him to enter the car and sit beside their idol. And here they were. Florrie, the faithful dresser, was packing Bootle and the baggage in the back of the car. Foster, the theatre's fire-man, stood with a friendly grin by the door, holding off the more impetuous of Mary's admirers. How nice, she thought, everybody was! Always the same, especially on Saturdays, when she made her little speech after the final curtain. It was cheering to hear their good-nights, to have their good will, as she drove off alone. But to-night there was Martin by her side: and he was to drive her into the country, into the cool air, into the dark. Some one, for a change, to take the labour of the journey; hold out his hand at the London crossings, and peer at sign-posts in the country lanes. They would talk for a little, as they drove, and then, for she was tired, she would put her hand on his knee and her head on his shoulder, and be driven, drowsy, uncomfortable, but happy, through the night. What was to follow she knew not: but this, she knew, would be bliss. So she said, 'Curtain up, Martin!': the cloud of girls pressed forward, crying, 'Good night, Mary!' and away they went.

John Adam felt a queer sensation—that what was hap-pening to him at this moment had somewhere happened to him before. And so, of course, it had. There they were, embarrassingly ushered by a very small boy into the same, clean, cheerless hotel bedroom. Exactly the same inoffensive but dreary wall-paper (the good old rose pattern would have been better than this drab discretion), the same large bed, and little bathroom, the same cold fireplace, the same information about the Russian Baths, Massage, and Vibrant Hair Treatment, the same instructions for the summoning of servants, by bell or telephone, and almost the same view of the English Channel, which lacks variety. There was his lady again, trying the lights, patting the pillows, and peering a little critically into the bathroom. Only, this time, it was Folkestone, not Brighton, and Tott, not Myrtle.

Miss Tott began to take off her things.

'I think I'll go for a stroll,' he said, 'before dinner.'

'All right,' she said. 'I'll have a lie-down. I've got a bit of a head.'

He hoped that his paramour was not going to be ill. In the train she had been much less talkative than usual, and had complained of a cold.

'Chilly, isn't it?' she said, and shivered.

'I don't feel it. But I'll light the fire for you.'

'Do, dear. And you might send up a cocktail, will you?'

'Routine as usual,' he thought, and went out.

'*No*, Martin, *no*,' said Mary, almost fiercely. 'The car is *not* going to break down, and we are *not* going to stop at Rochester or anywhere. We sleep at 'White Ladies' and nowhere else——'

'But, Mary, darling——'

'If you don't drive on at once, Martin, I shall scream like a virgin in the Second Act. . . . Darling'—she changed her tone—'you do understand. We *must* be patient. John's doing something, I know. Drive on, darling, and to-morrow we'll go sailing. Kiss me.'

'Damn you,' said the Voice. But he kissed her and drove on sulkily through the dark.

His long walk on the Leas did Mr. Adam good.

He returned to the hotel refreshed in body and spirit. All, he thought, would soon be well. True, there was the

distasteful ritual of to-morrow morning to be faced, but
even that had lost some of its terrors. With the shrewd
and sensible Laura all things would be easier. He wished
she would not talk so much, but they were now firm friends,
and he had no fear that the Myrtle troubles would be repeated. This time he would not make the mistake of
over-tipping the chambermaid.

There was no reason why Mary should not have her hotel
bill by Tuesday.

And to-night he would have a little of his favourite claret
—none of that dangerous gassy stuff. Laura would not
want that. Almost eagerly he asked at the bureau for the
key of 27.

The reception-clerk said, 'The doctor's with Mrs. Adam
now, sir.'

What next?

As he hurried along the corridor the doctor came out of
the room.

'Mr. Adam? Ah, yes. I'm afraid, Mr. Adam, your wife
has developed measles.'

Mr. Seal woke up and wondered where he was. He
perceived that he was in a strange but delightful room, low-
ceilinged, panelled, full of old furniture and prints, and
looking out through narrow windows on to an orchard
splashed with sun. A man in a black coat was stealthily
and, in some indefinable way contemptuously, unpacking
the few clothes Mr. Seal had brought with him and hiding
them away in various drawers. Mr. Seal watched him
through half-closed eyes, deliciously drowsy and content.
What a bed, and what a good sleep! He was at 'White
Ladies', that was it—the famous 'White Ladies', in the
Orchard Room. His first week-end away with Mary.
Somewhere in this very house Mary had been sleeping too.
All day he would be with her, and part of Monday too.
And this morning he was going to church with Mary and
the family: for Mary had said that he must make a good
impression and be asked again. Not that he minded going
to church: he was a God-fearing Christian and liked nothing
so much as an old-fashioned village church, with bells and

hearty singing. There had been talk of a sail down the
Medway: but, over sandwiches and whisky last night, it
had been decided that that was impossible, because the
tide was wrong. So they were going to church, and he
must get up: it was ten o'clock already. The man in black
said aloofly that he would prepare the bath, and went out
with the grey suit under his arm. Beside the bed was a
little tray with a delicate blue tea-set, a toy tea-set, a fairy
tea-set. Mr. Seal sat up and drank some tea, three cupfuls,
from cups as light as eggshells and of about the same
capacity. How delicious to live always in a house like this,
with Mary in command! There was a sort of spiritual
flavour in a fine country house, where all was order and
dignity and taste. It exalted one, said Mr. Seal to himself;
he felt very happy, and, in some misty new way, good.
He was sorry now that he had made that silly suggestion
about stopping at Gravesend or Rochester. He had not
intended it very seriously; and Mary, he knew well, would
not have listened to him if he had. Still, it was a pity, and
this calm old room made him feel ashamed of himself. But
all was well; and he would know better another time. The
man in black returned with the grey suit and said that the
bath was ready. Mr. Seal shaved and sang the 'Preislied'
in his bath, till he thought of Verena Simmons, and was
suddenly silent. There had been, he knew, some cloud at
the back of his contentment, and that was it—Verena
Simmons was staying in the house. Verena Simmons had
gone to bed when Mary and he arrived last night—this
morning: but she was in the house somewhere, and he had
gathered that she was here quite often. He could not
imagine why.

He had known Verena Simmons for many years: they had
worked together in the old days on the 'Children's Hour'.
He had been an Uncle and she an Aunt. Even then she
had made him feel uncomfortable, he never knew why.
He had nothing against her: she was bright and bird-like,
was earnest and seemed kind, he thought, and was even
good-looking in a cold, refined style. Then he had become
an Announcer and she had been transferred to Talks. They
met from time to time in the endless corridors; and still
she was bright and he uncomfortable. Some fool had told

him one day that Verena had a passion for him, and that
this was common talk. He had not thought much of that,
though he remembered trying to be more genial than his
habit was the next few times they met. Then she had left
the Corporation altogether, and taken to writing. Plays,
chiefly. She had sent him two plays she had written for
the Wireless and asked him to intercede for them with the
entertainment side. He had done his best, but nobody
wanted them. And somebody, he remembered, had said
that she was not a kind woman at all, but spiteful. He
remembered vividly the phrase that was used, because it
was a terrible phrase: 'The sort of woman who writes
anonymous letters.' He did not believe that of 'poor
Verena' (as most of them called her). But, still, it was a
pity, perhaps, that she was at 'White Ladies' this week-end,
his first week-end away with Mary. Ten to one, she would
write a play for Mary, and it would be no good. Poor
Verena. However . . .

Humming the 'Preislied', he returned to his room. The
grey suit, brushed and neatly folded, lay on the sofa. His
shoes, brightly polished, were under the dressing-table.
His razor-strop, in a seamanlike coil, lay behind the
looking-glass; and two pipes, a crumpled pipe-cleaner, and
an envelope with tobacco in it, which might well have been
left in the bag, were disposed in an orderly group on the
other side of the table. It was wonderful, he thought, for a
poor man to receive so much attention: to tread this lush,
expensive, purple carpet, and dress like a lord in this ancient
lovely room! He began to dress. That is, he began to look
for his vest, pants, and shirt. Where were they? He
opened the dressing-table drawers. In the left-hand top
drawer were two handkerchiefs and a gold safety-pin: in
the right-hand top drawer were two stiff collars and a
black tie: the other drawers were empty.

But on the opposite side of the room was a beautiful old
chest of drawers, polished, mellow, curved like a crescent
moon. Everything, no doubt, would be in that. 'Louis
Quinze,' thought Mr. Seal, who knew little about furniture.
In one of the top drawers of the 'Louis Quinze' he found his
flannel collars and in the other his Old Salopian tie: in the
second drawer the jersey which he had brought for sailing

10

and his grey flannel trousers: and in the bottom drawer some female garments smelling of camphor.

But there were many other pieces of furniture in the room, all old and lovely: and Mr. Seal, still humming, began a systematic search of the room. In the great tall-boys he found, on one side, his tennis shoes, and in the other his vest and pants, and parts of his evening dress: but still not the shirt which he proposed to wear at church. He found, however, as well, two old curtains and some muslin frocks.

In the second chest of drawers, humming no longer, he found the rest of his evening dress and some part of the uniform of a Guards officer.

Still no shirt or socks. And it was half-past ten. Mr. Seal's modest equipment for the week-end could have been disposed, without much untidiness, in a single drawer of moderate dimensions: and Mr. Seal began to wish that this had been done. No doubt the man in black had wished him to feel that all the fine furniture was his to enjoy: perhaps he had thought that walking exercise was good for him; but Mr. Seal would be late for church, and where was his shirt?

He now perceived an old lacquer cabinet in the south-west corner of the room. He walked over and opened the doors of this piece, expecting to see old china or nothing within: but behind the doors were drawers, and in three of these drawers he found his shirts and his socks.

With the sensation that he had won some refined game of hide-and-seek Mr. Seal began to hum again, and prepared to dress. He had everything now. . . .

'But where the hell are my braces?' said Mr. Seal aloud.

A little irritated, he searched the numerous old pieces again. The childish pleasures of the man in black had ceased to be amusing: and before he had finished his search he fiercely pressed the bell-push. He looked in the tallboys, both chests of drawers, the lacquer cabinet, the dressing-table drawers, the little drawers of the writing-table, and an old oak chest full of curtains and rugs. There were no braces anywhere.

'Probably,' thought Mr. Seal, 'the damned fool thinks that I have two pairs of braces. But I'm not that sort of man.' He rang the bell again.

But he could hear no bell. Perhaps it was broken. It

was twenty-five to. He could not go to church without his braces. He had brought no belt. He had brought only one tie, besides his black dress tie, and that would not go round his waist. . . . The situation was ridiculous. He rang the bell again, but the thing must be broken. He went out into the passage. More thick purple carpet: dusty sunlight streaming through windows: a bath 'running' somewhere: but nobody about. On the long march to his room last night he had seen somewhere the notice, on a brass plate, 'BACHELORS' WING'. If he was in the Bachelors' Wing he could slip into some bachelor's room and ring his bell. There was a door open a little way along the corridor. He listened outside, but heard no sound, and knocked gently on the door.

'Come in.'

Mary's voice!

He stepped inside: and there was Mary in night-gown and a kimono, all royal blue and dragons, clasping a large sponge with one hand and brushing her golden hair with the other.

'Good morning, Martin. Why aren't you up?'

That was so like her, he thought—no coy 'Go away!' or 'What are you doing here?'

'Can I ring your bell?' he said. 'They've gone off with my braces, and I can't make any one hear.'

'Of course, darling: ring away. How did you sleep?'

'Fine, thanks. And you?'

'So-so.'

She continued her busy brushing. He pushed the door back a little and went to the head of the bed and rang.

He looked down at the tumbled bed. In this bed she had slept—though only so-so. Exciting, sacred bed. How lovely she looked like this, with her hair as ragged as an April cloud, and the sun shining through the tops of the tangle. He had not seen it so before.

'You'd better go, dear,' she said, coolly, 'before they answer the bell.'

'All right.' He walked towards her. 'Give me a kiss. You look lovely.'

'I'm a sight,' she said, and kissed him quickly.

There was a burst of laughter, and 'Oo!' said a shrill voice, 'Do that again, Aunt Mary.'

The door opened wide: and in the doorway stood Simon
and Peter, aged six and three. And behind Simon and
Peter stood Nanny, almost the last of the British Nannies,
grey-haired, white-clad, and absolutely square, face and
body and mind.

'I'm sorry, Mrs. Adam. They're terrors for peeping. . . .
Come along, you—you and your Red Indians.'

'No, no, no!' cried Simon. 'We stalked Aunt Mary—we
stalked her, didn't we?'

'You stalked me,' said Mary gravely. 'Now go and stalk
Mr. Seal's braces, because he's lost them, and I must have
my bath.'

'No, no, no, we want to stalk Aunt Mary.'

'Come along with you,' said Nanny.

Mr. Seal, less at ease than Mary, moved towards the door.

'Nurse,' he said over the children's heads, 'if you should
see the valet, or any one, would you say—— Ah, there
he is. I say, could I have my braces, please?'

'Your braces, sir?' said the man in black, with pained
surprise. 'I think you'll find them in the Queen Anne, sir.'

Mr. Seal followed him back to his room. The man in
black went straight to the 'Louis Quinze' and opened the
second drawer.

'I looked there——' Mr. Seal began.

The man in black unfolded the grey flannel trousers and
there, neatly folded also, like a snake in its lair, lay the braces.

There were many things which Mr. Seal might have said.
He might have sworn: he might have pointed out that he
never wore braces with those particular trousers: and that
if his braces must be hidden away it would have been better
to hide them in the grey trousers on the sofa. Afterwards
he was sorry that he had not said these things. But now
he was flabbergasted; he was in a strange house and reluctant
to seem offensive; and he supposed that he was in the
presence of some sort of eccentric. So he said weakly,
'Oh, thanks. Very sorry. I did look there.'

Mary laughed heartily as they walked to church.

'All very well,' said Mr. Seal. 'But I hope those children
don't talk about it to Verena Simmons.'

Measles! Of all things! Of all the inappropriate back-grounds to an illicit week-end! There was no rash yet, but the temperature, the sneezing, the running eyes, and certain little spots in the mouth left little doubt in the doctor's mind. Why in the world couldn't the thoughtless creature have had measles in her youth? And why nurse a sick child if she hadn't had it?

The unfortunate husband drank his claret alone, while a nurse looked after the feverish woman in Room 27. He was badgered with compassion by the head waiter and his staff. Even the manager was kind, though he deprecated, it was clear, the importation of infectious diseases into his hotel. He had dropped hints about the lady being more comfortable in hospital, but John protested strongly. For if Laura went off to hospital the whole expedition was in vain. But the doctor had said it was not essential, and the manager yielded.

So here he was, married to Miss Tott for at least a fortnight. She would be in bed for ten or twelve days, and infectious for fourteen. And, at her age, the doctor said, there might easily be complications. Having brought the woman there as his wife, he could not go home and leave her with a nurse, as if she were a stranger. Apart from his own sense of decency, it would be dangerous, he felt, if the King's Proctor heard of it. He would have to travel down to Folkestone every night during the week. But Joan's half-term holiday was next week and he had hoped to spend an evening or two with her. What a business! To say nothing of the expense—a doctor, a nurse, and now another room for himself. At this rate Miss Tott, whose own terms had been so reasonable, would cost him nearly as much as Miss Myrtle.

And at the back of his mind there was the disturbing question: Would even a fortnight with a woman who had the measles count as adultery in law? Would it be necessary for the measles to come out? He would see Boom on Monday and inquire. 'Damn,' said Mr. Adam, and reck-lessly ordered a glass of port.

'We shan't make it,' said Mary, and put the tiller hard down. 'The wind's died on us, and the tide as well.'

The *Curlew* turned her head slowly into the dying breeze; and they faced the setting sun. The little yacht carried hardly enough way to take her round, and she hovered in stays for a moment or two, bowing uncertainly to the crimson sky. But the jib, backed to starboard, took her over at last, and she lay on the other tack, her mainsail flapping lazily, and drifted gently sideways towards the sea.

They were at the bottom of Long Reach in the River Medway, four or five miles from home. A desolate corner. Flat saltings and marshes, threaded with creeks, bounded the river north and south. The nearest dwelling-house was miles away. No craft was to be seen except a single sailing-barge, gliding down from Rochester on the first of the ebb; a lovely silent shape cut out of the gaudy sky. Mary and Martin had sailed away from 'White Ladies' soon after breakfast, and had a magical day. Low Water, by the tables, was about two o'clock at Sheerness. They would sail out into the Thames and cruise about in the neighbourhood of the Nore till the flood began. That would give them five hours—plenty—for the beat back up the Medway, and bring them home in time for dinner.

But a following breeze on a sunny morning may blow time-tables and good resolutions away. The *Curlew* went roaring down the Medway, as the bargemen say, straining at the sheets. Driven on by wind and tide, she swallowed up the little Medway, and raced out into the wide estuary of the Thames before it was noon. Here there was rough water but a strong wind on the quarter, and the green boat plunged ahead as quickly still, leaping through the waves like a greyhound in the long grass, tossing her head and shaking herself and challenging the world. She was a stout little boat, but a wet one, and the two in the cockpit were bombarded with spray, whipped with salt water, wet and blinded, and cold, but happy, drunk with sun and the spirit of the water. They were alone, really alone, for the first time: the world could not touch them, until they deigned to touch land again: even Verena Simmons was many miles away. Yet they spoke of Verena even now, as they plunged eastwards towards the Nore. Verena the jest: Verena the bore: but Verena the menace. Mary feared that she had mortally offended Verena: for last Sunday Verena had given

her a play to read, and this morning Mary had told Alice
what she thought of it: and Martin, who had been sitting
with Verena on the veranda, thought that Verena had
heard. That was terrible: and Mary, her face dripping with
cool spray, said she felt hot to think of it. And Verena had
wanted to come on this trip with them. That was too
much; and kindly Alice had shooed her away. Poor Verena:
it was a shame! And they were ashamed. Yet they laughed
to think of her, with the blissful scorn of lovers.

Now they could wave to the men in the Nore Lightship.
There was talk of heaving-to, to keep the poor men company, and eat the sandwiches. But the breeze was too
lively, and the day too beautiful, to lie and roll in one place
for the sake of sandwiches, or punctuality. They must go
on. 'This wind will hold,' said Mary, accustomed to obedience. 'We've plenty of time.' They must go on. Who
could sit still this morning, when all things moved, and
sparkled and flashed: the white woolly clouds scurried
across the river: the low, grey shores of Essex glittered and
heaved; the mad horizon tried to climb the sky: the sailing-
barges by twos and threes came striding down from London?
The wind, the water, the world were racing out to sea this
morning, and how could the *Curlew* sit still? They must go
on. They went on, steering for the Mouse, beside the
tawny Maplin Sands, where the sea-gulls stood by regiments
in the sun. They turned a little before the tide, and began
the beat back, keeping close to the flats on the Essex shore,
because the ebb ran slackly there. Martin marvelled at
the things his Mary knew, and he marvelled at the strength
of her, clinging to the tiller with her small, cold hands,
though he had to help her when the squalls caught them
and the *Curlew* pulled like a runaway horse. She wore
yellow oilskins and a yellow oilskin hat, the fringes of her
hair were drenched and her face a bright pink: and nobody
in the gallery queue would have recognized their Mary
Moon: but Martin, because he loved her, thought that she
was lovely still.

But the summer breeze fell light, and a summer haze
crept up the river, about the time they left the Essex
shores and headed across for Sheerness. The sun was
warming now, and Mary took off her yellow hat to dry her

celebrated but soaking hair. 'I'm a lunatic,' she said. 'What will my public say?' A heavy curtain of purple haze hung over Sheerness and the Isle of Sheppey: Sea Reach, westward, was grey and misty and eastward the sea was grey. But here in the middle river the sun drew a circle of gold and glitter. And through the heart of the circle, across the bows of the little *Curlew*, proceeded slowly, silent, imperial, a full-rigged sailing-ship, one of the wheat-fleet, bound from Australia for the Millwall Dock. Her yards were bare, and far ahead, at a reverent distance, one little tug with a bright red funnel drew the noble old vessel quietly along. Her yards and rigging, picked out in gold, were like a pattern painted on the Kentish haze. Somehow, occupied with their tacking and their talk, the two lovers, unseamanlike, had not seen her before, and now saw her suddenly. 'Oh, look!' whispered Mary, and could say no more: and Martin, at last taking his eyes off Mary, looked ahead to windward and, just off the starboard rigging, saw the lovely ship. 'My God!' said Martin, and they gazed at her in silence.

She passed like a golden phantom out of the circle of sunlight, and disappeared too soon into the mists of Sea Reach.

'Wheat?' said Martin.

'Yes,' said Mary. 'Makes you feel small, doesn't she?'

Martin put his arm round the yellow oilskin. For many minutes they sailed in silence, Martin tending the jib-sheets whenever they went about. The wind fell lighter still near the shore, and at last Mary said, 'If we're not careful, my lad, we'll never make Sheerness.'

Indeed, it was a near thing that they were not swept up Sea Reach by the swelling flood. But they made a long leg south-eastward on the starboard tack, and at last they glided past the Point into the Medway. They tacked back and forth on the dying breeze, and drifted rather than sailed, as long as the tide endured.

But now the tide was done. The *Curlew's* head moved slowly towards the saltings: but sideways, all the time, the tide carried her back towards the Thames.

'We don't want to go back to Sheerness, do we?' said Martin.

He spoke in a low voice, because the world was suddenly so quiet. The *Curlew* moved so gently now that she made no sound in the water. The sailing-barge had gone by, and they could hear the noise of her tackle as she jibed: but nothing more.

Mary said slowly, 'It might be better. There are trains from there.'

'Trains! Awful thought.'

'Sunday trains, too. But it might be better.'

'Why?'

'When have you got to be back, Martin?'

'Monday afternoon. Why?'

'I was thinking.'

'What about?'

'The tides.'

'What about them?'

'They're all wrong.'

'He's not helping at all,' thought Mary. 'What shall I do?'

'She's very serious,' thought Martin, and he stooped down and looked up into her face. That was very serious too: she stared ahead and would not look down. They were so close, standing together at the tiller on the silent river; and yet they seemed so very far away. He drew her to his side and said, 'Cheer up, darling. What do we do—anchor?'

'Yes. Unless we go back to Sheerness. We can't land here.'

'Would that be all right? Sheerness, I mean.'

'I don't know. I've never been there. It might be difficult. And I shouldn't like to leave the boat. Of course, I could land you, and stay in the boat myself.'

'That's a rotten idea,' said Mr. Seal. 'Let's anchor. Say when, and I'll do the work.'

'Not yet.' She held his arm. 'There's a creek a little way below here. With any luck we might just make it—if we don't foul that buoy.'

'What happens there?'

'Nothing but sea-gulls and herons and things—and miles of marsh.'

'Nice.'

'It's a lovely place. I spent a night there once with the Merridews.'

'Sounds fine.'

'Martin?'

'Yes, darling?'

Now she looked at him: and he thought that suddenly she seemed pathetic, wistful, defenceless—what was the word? Whatever the word was, it was the most surprising thing, for he had always thought of her as the dominant one.

'Martin, the tide won't turn before two and we shan't get back before breakfast—if then.'

'All right, Mary. That's plenty of time.'

There was a pause while they cleared the great buoy. Then she said, 'Martin, will you be good?'

But she thought—what an insane and dreadful thing to say!

He thought, 'Well, I'll be serious too,' and said, 'Probably not, Mary.'

'You must, Martin.'

'I'll try.'

'You must, Martin. Please.'

'All right, Mary. Whatever you say.'

He was the strong one now, he thought, and must live up to the part.

'There's the creek,' she said. 'We'll make it.'

Nobody could be cross with Laura Tott. She was the real 'patient', cheerful, uncomplaining and penitent. On Sunday the temperature was down a little. Mr. Adam sat with her all the afternoon while the nurse went out, and listened to her brave attempts to gossip. He liked the queer creature more and more. She said he was not to bother about her but to come back the following week-end, when she would be well, and they could arrange about the evidence. But Mr. Adam was only the more determined not to desert her. Joan, he was sure, would understand.

On Monday morning the rash was out and the temperature was up again. Miss Tott smiled bravely through her rash at him, as he left for London. He promised to return as early as he could. Would she like a few grapes?

'No,' said the sick woman. 'Bring me some nice scandal!'

.   .   .   .   .

They dropped anchor beyond the first corner in the silent creek. They stowed the sails and hung out the riding-light; the sun was not yet down, but he was smothered with low clouds and a pallid mist was rising on the saltings. Mary said, 'Martin, there's nothing to eat, I'm afraid,' and went into the little cabin. Martin followed, and together they searched the lockers and the cupboards. They found a pot of Bovril, a tin of biscuits, and a half-bottle of whisky. Martin lit the Primus stove and Mary the hanging paraffin lamp. They sat down on opposite sides of the swinging table and looked at each other: and were afraid. They were so close to each other: so sheltered from the world; and yet they were as far away as two strangers passing in Piccadilly.

Mary stood up suddenly, and, stooping, looked in the tiny glass. 'Perhaps it's a pity,' she said, 'we didn't bring Verena Simmons.'

'I believe we did,' said Martin, suddenly fierce. 'I feel she's here.'

'My God!' said Mary, laughing, pushing her damp hair back. 'What *would* my public say?'

'What would Verena say?'

'You seem to have that woman on your mind.'

'You put her there, my dear.'

Heavens, they were nearly quarrelling, at the end of their magical day.

'The kettle's boiling,' Mary said.

They munched dry biscuits and drank hot Bovril with whisky in it. Mary said, 'I shall never forget that sailing-ship.'

'I never saw one before—not moving.'

They talked about the sailing-ship, and about their voyage, but still like strangers at afternoon tea. The little cabin was warm and confiding, but it was charged with suspense and uneasiness, as if a thunder-storm lay bottled up in one of the lockers.

They washed-up together, and Martin went on deck. Mary fiddled with her hair before the glass, and sighed: and said 'Oh, God!' and followed him, and stood beside him.

The night was breathless. The sun was just down, the moon just up. The mist had crept from the saltings to the water. The *Curlew* seemed to be riding on a moonlit cloud.

No sound of man was to be heard—only the lap of the tide against the stem, the croak of herons flying over, and the cries and chuckles of waterfowl among the reeds. The sky above, the water beneath, the desolate saltings for miles about them—these two were at the end of the world.

Far off in the Edinburgh Channel a great ship hooted twice, and was answered twice by another.

'Then some one else is alive,' whispered Mary.

Martin put his long arm round her, and fiercely gripped her little arm. Out here in the soft evening no thunderstorm was present.

'Oh, dear,' said Mary.

He kissed her quietly, and they sighed together, like two brave people who know that they are doomed.

'I wonder,' said Mary, 'why beauty and silence make me feel so ill.'

'Beauty is Truth, Truth Beauty,' said Mr. Seal, desiring now to keep seriousness away.

'Idiot!' said Mary; but she thought 'Beauty is Truth. . . . If I let him love me it will be Truth, God knows. But will it be Beauty? And will it in the end be even Truth?' She said suddenly, 'Damn that woman!'

'What woman?'

'Verena What-is-it. I keep on thinking of her—I don't know why.'

'Damn Verena! Forget her.'

'Oh, dear,' said Mary. 'Martin, I'm afraid.'

'Oh, my love,' said Martin: and kissed and comforted her.

Every evening John Adam took the train to Folkestone; and every evening, like a faithful bird, he brought in his beak some little morsel of gossip, some choice smoking-room story, with which to comfort his imprisoned mate. It was not easy for him: for it was not his habit to tell 'stories', or even to listen to them with much attention. He generally laughed in the wrong place, and could seldom remember the merry tale ten minutes later. The only scandal to be heard at the office was rather literary and professional, the manœuvres of other publishers and the sales of their authors, poor stuff for the hungry Laura. But at the club, to the surprise of the 'pink gin' group, he began to take a glass of sherry in the smoking-room before lunch; and there he heard one or two things about débutantes, Members of Parliament, foreign noblemen and colonels' wives, which delighted Laura. And, if the hunt discovered nothing there, a little politeness in the Pullman car—and perhaps a glass of sherry—was sure to extract a good story or two. The stockbrokers and business men knew at once that John was not the sort of man who would have heard any of their stories, and enjoyed the rare pleasure of un-loading their oldest ones without fear of being stopped.

The chase cost him a good deal in sherry: but John thought that it was worth it. Miss Tott thought that he was sweet, relating diffidently and badly his precious anecdotes: and she never flinched, however often she had heard the tale before. They talked much about education too, and played piquet.

As the days went by, Mr. Adam was more and more disquieted by the sight of the chambermaid who attended Rooms 27 and 28. Violet Mitchell was very different from Rose Parkins: she was young, pink-cheeked, and cheerful, with rich bronze hair—too young, he thought, and innocent to be entrapped into his horrid enterprise. She was devoted to Miss Tott, who made her laugh, and friendly to himself. She did her work with energy and zest: she sang as she cleaned the bathroom and she called him with a smile: a simple unspoiled country girl. And, regardless of her doom, she was giving her unstinted toil and trust to one who was deceiving her. The case was worse, far worse, than Rose Parkins: for Rose had been a tough old soul, he thought, and they had known each other for two days only. But this was a mere child, and already they were old friends. Her parents, he had found out, lived in a tiny village under the Downs and kept the post office. Probably they would be outraged to see their Violet (an only child) hauled into the Divorce Court, if only as a witness.

He spoke of this to Miss Tott. But she said, 'You're soft. Don't worry.'

For Miss Tott, the first day the fever left her, had told

Violet all about Mr. Adam and his business there: and had instructed Violet in her duties.

And Violet was delighted: for she had never gone to London. That was one of the reasons why she sang in the bathroom and called Mr. Adam with a smile.

Laura was thorough: she was determined that this time there should be no bungling and no uncertainty about Mary Moon's divorce. There must be not one 'tea-in-the-morning-performance', or two, but several. So five times Mr. Adam rose early and went to Room 27 and asked the laughing Violet to bring up tea for two. And on the fifth and last morning Miss Tott said, 'Well, if the King's Proctor isn't satisfied now we'll take the bed into Court.'

'As a matter of form, Mrs. Adam—purely a matter of form, I know—I must ask you the question I put to you once before. Will you yourself have to ask the Court to exercise its discretion in your favour?'

'No,' said Mary.

'Quite,' said Mr. Freebody. 'And now about your proof——'

The same old business. The same old interviews and affidavits and documents and photographs. There were a few slight differences. Laura Tott for May Myrtle. And Clause 5 of the petition referred to the abortive proceedings in the Myrtle suit. And adultery was alleged not only at Folkestone but at the respondent's flat. ('Proof of Ernest Wilkin.') And Mary had had an anonymous letter warning her against a dark woman who had been seen with her husband in Soho. And as a result of that she had given instructions for her husband to be watched.

There was, this time, too, a muddle about the identifications. It was arranged that Laura and John should be in the Adelphi Terrace flat at a given hour and show themselves together at the window on receiving a telephone message from Mr. Boom's clerk: at the same time Mary and Mr. Wilkin were to be in the street below and were to look up, behold, and identify the guilty couple—Mary to identify the man as her husband, and Mr. Wilkin Laura as (1) the woman he had seen leaving the flat at two o'clock in the morning, and (2) the woman in the photograph identified by Violet Mitchell.

Mary raged furiously against the undignified affair: but it was better, Mr. Freebody persuaded her, than a confrontation of all four together in a room. Indeed, he said, the contrivance was chiefly designed for her own benefit. John, growing harder through experience, had come to regard such antics almost as natural and necessary; Laura thought it was fun; and Mr. Wilkin was paid for it.

It was found difficult to fix an hour convenient to all parties. It was the old trouble, that John worked by day and Mary by night; and John was working late and Mary had to be at the theatre by seven-thirty. And Mary was not going to give up a Sunday in the country in order to stand in a street with Mr. Thomas and a private detective and identify John Adam as her husband. At last the strange rendezvous was appointed for seven p.m. on Wednesday (a matinée day). Mary rested in her dressing-room after the matinée, was collected by Mr. Thomas, and proceeded, simmering, to Adelphi Terrace. She was introduced to Mr. Wilkin, and disliked him. She looked up at the window said (by Mr. Thomas) to be John's, and waited. Men passed in and out of the Savage Club, a few yards away. Most of these, by some wicked chance, were men she knew—actors, dramatic critics, playwrights, journalists. Some noticed her, some did not. Some who saw and recognized her pretended that they did not: but all who recognised her wondered what Mary Moon was doing, standing about in Adelphi Terrace with two such seedy little men.

Two of the Savages came across the road and asked her what she was doing there. To the first, Mr. Edward Apple, the humorist, she said, with no extravagant geniality, that she was waiting for somebody. The humorist passed on rapidly into the club. Mary looked up at the empty window and swore softly: for she liked Mr. Apple and had no wish to hurt him. At that moment the telephone bell rang in Mr. Adam's flat. Laura Tott took off the receiver and said 'Hullo!' (which is, and always has been, an extra-ordinary way of opening a conversation with an invisible interlocutor).

'Miss Tott?' said a quiet and cultured voice.

'Speaking.'

'Will you and Mr. Adam,' said the voice, 'kindly show yourselves at the window? The other parties are ready below.'

'Mr. Adam's not here.'

'Oh, hell!' said the quiet and cultured voice.

'There was a message,' said Laura, 'that he'd gone to the House of Commons to see the President, and might be a little late——'

'The President? What President?' said the voice with apprehension. To the owner of the voice there was only one President.

'I don't know. The President of the Board, I suppose.'

'What's all this? *What* Board?'

'The Board of Education. Mr. Adam's on a deputation. There's a Bill, or something, in Parliament, I think.'

'Oh, hell!' said the voice again. 'Hold the line, will you?'

Miss Tott obediently 'held the line'. She heard mutter-ing. Then silence.

Outside Mr. Ronald May, the film critic, crossed the road and said brightly: 'Hullo, Mary! What are *you* doing here?'

'GOD KNOWS!' said Mary, with the face of an angel and the voice of a fury.

Mr. Ronald May passed also into the club.

Miss Tott became tired of holding the line. She had looked forward to a dramatic encounter this evening, and the drama seemed to be departing before it had arrived, so to speak. Uppermost among her anticipations had been the thought that she was to confront the famous Mary Moon, and in so intimate a manner—from a window, true, but an upper window, and as the Woman in the Case who had (technically, at least) supplanted Mary Moon in her husband's affection. Well, Mary Moon was out there waiting and she, Laura, was wasting her opportunities here holding the line, without, so far as she could see, much satisfaction to any one. And, from what she knew of famous actresses, Mary Moon would not wait long. The temptation was too potent. Laura deserted the telephone. She looked in the glass, she powdered her nose, she patted her hair at the sides, she walked to the window, 'feeling her part', and she looked down at the Terrace. She stood very still in what she felt was a dramatic attitude, one hand high up on a curtain, the other on a hip. Yes, there was Mary Moon. She gave her a long, steady look, and moved into the room.

'That's her!' said Mr. Wilkin suddenly.

Mary looked up and met the eyes of her Supplanter. And, when Laura was out of sight, Mary was overcome with laughter. She did not know what she had expected, but she had not expected Laura's thin face and pointed nose, and that mirth-compelling vampish poise. She could not stop laughing: she put a handkerchief in her mouth and turned away, for she did not wish to hurt the woman, and Laura might look out again. She stammered, 'It's too much,' and opened the door of the little green car; she waved her hand to the astonished Mr. Thomas, and, still shaking with laughter, drove away.

So the thing had to be done at Mr. Freebody's office: and this time, for various reasons, Mr. Freebody employed another set of tactics. It was arranged that John and Laura Tott should arrive at his office at three-thirty and be taken to Mr. Freebody's room. On their way they would pass a room in which were Mr. Thomas, Mary, Mr. Wilkin and the maid Violet Mitchell (these three were to be there by three-twenty). The door of this room would be ajar: and, when the guilty couple passed, Mary would say, 'That is my husband'; Mr. Wilkin would say, 'That is the woman who was with Mr. Adam at his flat, the Red Elephant Restaurant, the Zoo, and the Tower of London'; and Violet Mitchell would say, 'That is the couple who spent a fortnight in Room 27.' But John and Laura were a little late. Mary disliked Mr. Wilkin: she tried to talk to Violet Mitchell, but Violet was too shy to say much to the famous Miss Moon. Mary had promised not to bring Bootle this time, hated the idea of seeing John with Miss Tott, and after a quarter

of an hour's wait was inclined to bolt again. But at last a
buzzer sounded, Mr. Thomas whispered, 'Here they come,'
and the three of them were marshalled by the doorpost.
'There was a time,' thought Mary sadly, 'when all this
would have seemed quite funny.' John and Laura, under
instructions, walked very slowly past, followed at a distance
by Mr. Boom. Violet began to whisper to Mr. Thomas,
and all was going according to plan. But Laura Tott, who
suspected that she was going to be done out of her meeting
with Mary Moon, after all, turned her head and saw Mary.
Without a moment's hesitation she left the procession and
entered the room. At last she had her wish and was face
to face with Mary Moon, not far-off on the other side of
the footlights, not in a surge of women at the stage door,
but intimately, in a private room. She gazed, adoring, for
a few seconds: then she took a little book from her bag
and said simply, 'May I have your autograph, dear?'

Mary said, 'Of *course!* Have you a pen, Mr. Thomas?'

Meanwhile, John had followed Laura and was being
merrily greeted by Violet Mitchell, who was delighted to
see him again: and Mr. Freebody and Mr. Boom, con-
verging at the door, surveyed together a disgraceful scene
—the wronged wife giving her autograph to the adulteress,
and the unfaithful husband in cheerful conversation with
the principal witness against him.

The party was firmly dispersed: and Mr. Boom said
afterwards that it was the most irregular incident in the
whole course of his professional experience.

Adam, M. R. v. *Adam, M. J.*, was in the list for hearing on December 9th, 1930, before Mr. Justice Cole,
a King's Bench Judge on loan to the P.D.A. Division.
A much earlier date had been expected by the solicitors,
but a number of unforeseen collisions and shipwreck cases
had kept the Divorce Judges busy with Admiralty work.
All concerned congratulated themselves that the case was
not taken by the President. Mary in particular did not
want to face those armour-piercing eyes again.

Yet she found, like John, that experience had stiffened
her. Waiting to be called, she was not oppressed, as she

had been in the Myrtle case, with the thought that she was about to go into the box and tell lies. She felt rather as if she were going to play a poor part (under-rehearsed) at a Charity Matinée. She hoped only that it would soon be over and that she would not disgrace herself.

That was one thing, she reflected, about the dreary affair. She had learned to tell lies almost without minding.

Mr. Justice Cole was a dear old soul, she thought—bored but benignant. She felt, as she watched him consign spouse after spouse to (provisional) freedom, that this Judge took the same view of the 'Undefended List' as she did—that it was a messy, distasteful, but unavoidable business, and must be disposed of as quickly as possible. She loved the little sigh with which he said 'Yes' at the end of every case, and the way he peeped over the top of his spectacles, as if he were hiding behind them.

Even the Court itself had a more human note—not quite so large, she thought—red curtains, not green, and no canopy over the witness-box. And no great brass anchor hanging like an ecclesiastical sign above the Judge's head. More like a room, this Court, and less like a bit of a cathedral. 'Heavens!' she thought, 'if any one had told me I should come to this—preferring one Divorce Court to another . . . !'

'On that evidence, my lord, I ask for a decree nisi, with costs.'

'Yes,' said Mr. Justice Cole wearily, and put the papers aside. The tone was the tone of a housewife giving an extra night out to a housemaid whose mother is ill again.

Free!

Mary could hardly believe it. She wanted to kiss the little maid, Violet Something, who had done so well. She wanted to sing 'Love me, laddie!', her present theme-song. She wanted to send a telegram to John and another one to Martin. But she walked out of Court with a set, sad face, as if she were walking out of church. Outside, in the wide corridor, she saw Violet. She hurried to Violet and took her hand and said, 'Violet, you were splendid!' Which pleased Violet very much: for though she had enjoyed her trip to London it had grieved her parents, as John had feared. The lady's evident joy made her feel that she had done a good deed. But Mr. Freebody seized Mary's elbow and marched her away. Mr. Freebody lectured her all the way down the Central Hall and, still lecturing, put her into a taxi.

But she did send a telegram to John.

Darling marvellous so grateful for all you've done what a time you must have had with Tott love Mary.

Free!

She rang up Martin, who was at the B.B.C. 'Darling, it's all right! Isn't it marvellous?'

Mr. Seal rang off at once.

Pig! Never mind, she would see him to-night.

Free!

But the severe Freebody and the austere Seal had chilled her mood.

She was not free at all, she remembered, not for six months. After six months her lawyers must apply for the decree to be made absolute: and then she might be divorced or become a fully married woman again.

Perhaps she would not see Martin to-night. She had to be careful now, Mr. Freebody said: and what she thought was being careful would be frantic recklessness to Martin, she knew.

Six months. Well, it was not so long. But what a childish arrangement! To say, 'Yes, you ought to be free, but in six months' time I may say "Yah, I didn't mean it!" ' Why couldn't the Court make up its mind once and for all, as other Courts did? There were women, somebody had told her, who used the decree nisi as a sort of instrument of blackmail—refused to apply for the decree absolute until they had got more money out of their husbands. What a world!

Six months. It was a long time, really. It might not seem a long time to Mr. Justice Cole. But he had not been waiting for three years in a state of suspended neutrality to life, neither virgin, wife, nor widow. Six months was not a long time to a free man, but it was an age to a man in jail, or even to a suspect with a charge hanging over him.

And she was that. Neither maid, wife, nor widow, nor any kind of woman: but a special class of being, restricted by special laws and curfews. Mr. Freebody said that it would be wise to go home as early as she could, never to be so much as 'dropped' at her home by a man late at night, and to be seen with men as little as possible. Anything she did might be seen and reported. She was like a convict on ticket of leave.

Six months. It was a very long time.

And she—strange thought—was the 'innocent party'. John, who was the 'guilty party', could do what he liked, and nobody would care or question.

A very hard world, thought Mary.

Well, she would be good—and careful. She would not meet Martin at the Savoy that night.

She went straight home after the show: and had a lonely little supper. But she rang up Martin, and comforted the sad young man with the promise of bliss in six months' time. She told him merrily that she had looked under the bed for the King's Proctor: and they both laughed heartily.

His Majesty's postman dropped twenty-seven anonymous letters into the letter-box at the King's Proctor's Office, 12 Old Queen Street, Westminster. The Assistant Chief Clerk to the King's Proctor read and considered them all.

The one relating to Mrs. Adam's private affairs was more circumstantial than most of them. It mentioned a gentleman's name—a yachting trip—and goings-on at a country house near Rochester.

The King's Proctor's Office and staff were modest: and its activities were limited by the watchful Treasury. If each of the twenty-seven anonymous letters had pointed indubitably to a naughty case the King's Proctor could not have pursued them all. He could only put his hand into the rag-bag of dirty linen and select this or that affair, more or less haphazard, for his cleansing activities. Like a Customs officer, he must divide his time between frowning and winking, for he could not search everybody: and so, sometimes, the very guilty might escape, while those less guilty were caught by a capricious pounce. Since justice ought to be the same for all, this was not, he knew, a defensible state of affairs: but it was not his fault.

The King's Proctor, Sir Percival Frost, himself considered the anonymous letter about Mr. Adam, wearily and sadly. All his duties as King's Proctor wearied him: the very name was a burden to him. For the world, the ignorant world outside Whitehall, supposed that he was the King's Proctor and nothing else: and even his friends could think of him as nothing else. He was like the hangman, haunted by his office. Facetious acquaintances would sometimes introduce him as 'Sir Percival Frost—the King's Proctor, you know,' and tell the young ladies that they would have to be careful. And the ladies would giggle. Even if he was spared that, sooner or later, at house-parties or clubs, or dinners, he would hear some one whisper excitedly, '*He's the King's Proctor*': and he would catch strange ladies eyeing him as if he were some fearful but fascinating monster.

Yet his Proctorial duties were but a small part of his official life. He was, primarily, His Majesty's Procurator-General and Solicitor to the Treasury. Nobody, however, introduced him as 'His Majesty's Procurator-General'. Nobody whispered at tennis-parties, '*He's the Treasury Solicitor!*' He was a King's Counsel and Fellow of All Souls: he had had a brilliant academic career and done much valuable public work outside his own department. To all this the great world was blind: branded on his forehead the great world saw only the slightly discreditable words 'King's Proctor'. 'Discreditable,' yes, for they thought of him not as an officer charged to see that the law was not evaded and mocked, but as a Nosey Parker who pried into other people's love-affairs and had an unwholesome interest in adultery.

Sir Percival Frost sighed. 'Adam, M. J.' The name, and the initials, stirred something in his mind—something, he thought, to do with a fishy case—a rejected petition—a—— Ah, yes—he remembered. He had noticed the case, because the wife was that pretty actress—what was her name?—Mary Moon. So now they were trying again.

Sir Percival Frost sighed. He had a mind to drop the accusing letter in the waste-paper basket. He hated anonymous letters, and despised their authors. He would have liked to leave Mary Moon alone—for her performances had given him pleasure. But the King's Proctor was a just man, with that passion for strict equity which sometimes tends to produce inequity. Whenever personal inclination urged him to leave a particular case alone it was his rule to pursue it, if the circumstances seemed to call for it. People could not be let off because they were well-known actresses: for that way lay not only injustice but scandal.

The King's Proctor sighed. And the Registrar was asked to forward the file of papers in the suit of *Adam* v. *Adam*.

An ex-policeman named Rigby rode up on a motor-bicycle to the servants' door of 'White Ladies'. He wanted to sell tickets for a concert in aid of police charities. The cook, who was keen-eyed and Caledonian, observed that the place of the concert was Tottenham, London, and that it had taken place two years ago. Mr. Rigby then explained that the concert was a minor feature of his mission. He wanted, if he could, to see the housemaid about a legal matter—nothing against the young lady, of course.

Doris, the junior housemaid, could not help him much, though, of course, every one knew that Mrs. Adam and the wireless gentleman were very thick. 'Quite a case.' But here was Harriet. She might know.

Harriet, the senior maid, was dressed in her best. 'Going into Rochester?' 'Yes.' 'Like a ride on the back of the bike?' Well, she wouldn't say 'No'—not if he was a careful man. Had been going by the bus: but a ride on the pillion would make a change, certainly. Have time to go to the pictures? Well, you never could tell, could you? She was meeting a friend, but he might be late. Mr. Rigby and Harriet rattled off to Rochester: and Doris asked Nanny what exactly was it she had seen that Sunday morning.

At the pictures, Mr. Rigby, in his deep, gruff voice talked busily to Harriet: and, next day, many citizens in Rochester were discussing the goings-on at 'White Ladies'.

'Christmas in Manchester!' thought Mary. 'Oh, dear!'
The curtain fell for the ninth time. The National Anthem

came through the curtain, muffled, like the bath-water of the
man next-door, and Mary, sighing and depressed, tripped
away to her dressing-room through the busy crowd of stage-
hands. Everything was marvellous: the play was a winner
and herself the winning jockey. The audience loved her—
for a 'second night', even on a Christmas Eve, they had
been 'grand'—and dear Figgie was pleased with her, and
loved her, and thought she was marvellous; and he said the
play would be even more of a winner in London. To-
morrow was Christmas Day, a whole free day at last, without rehearsals, performances, or fusses, no 'shop' at all
except perhaps for a word or two with Figgie over a glass of
champagne. And yet, ungratefully, she sighed and was
depressed. The truth was, she wanted to fling off her Third
Act dress, hurry into an old coat and skirt, have one drink
at the hotel for luck, dash away to the station and catch
the midnight train to London. Always before, after a
Christmas opening at Manchester, she had done that: and it
was fun to drive through London in the foggy dawn of
Christmas morning, tired, grubby, but happy.

This time she did not dare. The first thing she would do,
she knew, would be to ring up Martin: and the next thing,
they would be arranging to meet in the evening and have
their Christmas dinner together at the Savoy: and then
perhaps there would be a party somewhere, she would stay
out after curfew time, something indiscreet would happen,
and the King's Proctor would hear of it. So she would stay
in Manchester for Christmas and be good.

In the morning she would ring up Martin. Or Martin,
probably, would ring up her. And, after all, he was always
with her on the wireless. No King's Proctor could come
between her and her Martin's celebrated 'Good night'. Not
that she could hear it often: for in London, when Martin was
delivering his eleven o'clock 'Good night', she was in the
middle of the Third Act Finale. But here, in the Provinces,
where they opened at seven-thirty——

'Florrie, what's the time?'

'Twenty-five to, dear.'

She could just do it.

'Quick, Florrie!'

'What's the hurry, dear?' said Florrie, unfastening the

Third Act frock with maddening deliberation. 'We're not going to London, are we?'

'No, Florrie. Never mind. Tell John I want a taxi *now*.'

Florrie went out, mystified and slow, for, as a rule 'we' dawdled at the end of the show, hung about and talked to people and kept Florrie from her bed. And Florrie expected to know everything, sentimental secrets and all. But Florrie was not going to know this particular sentimental and ridiculous secret: though if Florrie did not know Florrie would not consent to hurry.

Once out of the frock 'we' could do without Florrie. But it was going to be difficult to escape in time. Christmas Eve, and there must be tippings and presents—the callboy, the stage-door keeper, the fireman, Florrie. . . . And dear old Figgie would be round in a minute with one of his dear little fusses. 'Played the Telemachus scene too slow again, my dear.' Quite right, but what was one to do in a house the size of a cathedral? By the time the gallery had seen the point of one line the stalls were laughing at the line that followed. And outside there would be the usual cloud of fan-girls, hungry for smiles and handshakes and autographs.

She would take off her make-up at the hotel. That would save time, though it might shock the hotel.

'Good night, Florrie, bless you. Lovely Christmas, here's a little something for the tribe, and there's something special for you in the drawer, wrapped up.'

Mary kissed Florrie, and, buttoning her coat as she went, ran out of the dressing-room just as Figgie, making his slow imperial rounds, approached it.

'Darling, can't stop now,' she bubbled; 'you're perfectly right about that scene—see you at the hotel, shall I?—in the Restaurant?' and dashed up the stairs.

'Miss Moon going to London?' the astonished manager inquired.

'No, Mr. Figg,' said Florrie with faint disapprobation. 'We're not going to London. We're just excited, and we won't say why.'

All through Christmas this unprecedented secretiveness was a worry to Florrie.

Mary pressed notes and bundles of silver into eager hands,

kissed the old fireman for Christmas, and dashed out through the rain so swiftly that only two of the fan-girls caught her. Six minutes to. She had done it.

The hall and lounge of the hotel were thronged with gay citizens gathering for the Gala Supper. Mary hurried through them, her stage make-up attracting little notice among so many pillar-box lips and manufactured cheeks. She came, panting, to her room on the second floor, and switched on the wireless. A red eye glowed richly in the little box beside the bed, and from it emerged softly a Christmas carol. She was in time.

Room 218 looked on to the inner courtyard and was quiet. Heavy curtains and carpets, heavy eiderdown, and heavy heated air. In the bathroom the central-heating apparatus grunted and groaned like a caged boar faintly resenting the sound of Anglican carols. Mary sat alone and waited, laughing at herself a little. What a situation for a hard-boiled actress of twenty-nine! In a minute or two the carols would cease, and she would hear Martin's voice—he was 'on' to-night, she knew. He would say a few special words for Christmas, and then the 'Good night, everybody. Good night.' But he would say it in the special way, with the subtle upward inflexion at the end of 'everybody', which meant 'Good night, everybody, but especially Mary'. Thousands of Martin's innumerable admirers had speculated upon that little variation: hundreds had written to inquire the reason for it. Only Mary knew. It was her own invention: she had rehearsed him in it that night on the Medway: and how they had laughed under the moon as Martin, time after time, murmured 'Good night, everybody' to the misty saltings. It was to be used, they had agreed, only on special occasions, or when she was far away, not in London when they might meet ten minutes later. He would use it to-night: and she, like a sentimental girl, was waiting, out of breath, to hear it.

The carols ceased. There was absolute silence, except for a single subdued 'honk' from the radiator.

Mary put her hand to her breast. What a soft little fool she was!

A voice began to speak, a gentle, purring man's voice. A few words about Christmas. And then 'Good night——'

'Damn!' said Mary and switched the gentleman off. It was not Martin's voice.

'Honk!' said the radiator loudly.

'Going down, miss?'

Mary stepped into the lift, depressed but dazzling. She was not going to mope like a schoolgirl because her senti-mental indulgence had been denied her. And she was not going to creep into the Gala Supper in an old coat and skirt, though she was a lonely decree-nisi mongrel of a woman. Figgie was dressed, and she would put on something nice to please him.

She did. The one-armed liftman admired her sidelong in the little glass as they descended.

She stepped out of the lift bravely, looking like a queen without a care. All who saw her nudged their neighbours and said, 'Look!' And the first person she saw was Mr. Martin Seal, waiting to sign the register at the bureau.

'Just arrived. Got away unexpectedly, as Wycherley wanted to have the New Year off. Couldn't bear it,' he whispered. 'Had to come.' Naughty Martin. But Mary pressed his arm to her side and did not care who saw her—she was so glad to have him there. The King's Proctor, Mr. Freebody, all were forgotten. She was going to have a happy Christmas Eve with Martin after all.

A broad, burly man just behind Mr. Seal waited patiently for his turn to sign the book.

'Three-eighteen,' said the sleek young lady.

'Is that quiet?' said Mr. Seal. 'The last room I had here seemed to be on Platform 4.'

'Very quiet, sir. It's on the inside court.'

'Funny,' said Mary, as they moved away. 'Mine's two-eighteen.'

'This is too easy,' thought the broad, burly man: and he asked for a quiet room on the third floor.

Figgie had an extra place laid for Mr. Seal and made him welcome. But he could not be expected to believe that

Mary had not known about Martin's coming. Why, otherwise, had she hurried from the theatre and put on a smart frock? Not for Figgie's bright eyes, said Figgie. Mary laughed at his little jokes and did not care whether she was believed or not. She disliked, as a rule, this gaudy Golden Restaurant, where the whole Cotton world stared at her as she ate: the hot air tired her and destroyed her appetite: she could never think of anything to eat but oysters, and the waiters were noisy with the plates in the corner But to-night, she thought, it was charming and gay, though the noise of revellers was deafening: she would have a dozen oysters and a *vol au vent* to follow. She would have champagne and pull a cracker with Figgie. She sat between the two men on the sofa side, facing the room; and she did not care who stared at her to-night, for she was proud of her handsome lover, and she was happy. Jacques, the obsequious head-waiter, presented her with a Souvenir Fan: she pulled a cracker with Martin and put the cap on Figgie's head.

Figgie gently removed the cap. He was glad to see his leading lady happy, for he was fond of her in a fatherly fashion. She had worked hard and loyally for him and deserved to be happy. Besides, it was good business to have a happy leading lady. He could remember three different leading ladies sitting in tears at that very table. But he knew that it was dangerous for this leading lady to be happy at the present time: and he was a little worried. Mary was a good girl, he thought, but impetuous. A little excitement was natural this evening: the strain of rehearsals over, the play safely launched, Christmas Eve, and a handsome lover descending without warning from the skies— but her mood, Figgie thought, was a little too mad and merry to be safe.

He and Mary had made the usual bad jokes about the King's Proctor till they were tired of them. But now, he thought, a bad little joke would be the best way to serve his benevolent purpose.

He whispered in her ear, 'Which is the King's Proctor's table?'

Mary turned her shining eyes to him, and laughed. 'Oh, darling! They couldn't, could they? Not to-night. It wouldn't be Christian!'

Figgie looked round the room. It was difficult, certainly, in that crowd of paper caps and squeakers, crackers, false noses, popping corks and good will to all men, to believe that any one could be spying upon two young lovers. Nevertheless——

But Mary saw that her kind Figgie had serious thoughts, and she too became serious. She took his hand and whispered, 'Don't worry, Figgie, bless you. I'm going to be a good girl—really I am.'

Figgie was comforted and patted her hand: but he said, 'I'm sure you'll be good, my dear, but will you be careful?'

Outside in the Byzantine Lounge Mr. Rigby yawned and ordered a whisky-and-soda. He wanted beer: but in the Byzantine Lounge, for some reason unknown, they would not serve beer. In the Golden Restaurant a man might drink beer, but not smoke a pipe. So those who, like Mr. Rigby, wanted to smoke a pipe and drink beer, were in a difficulty.

But the Golden Restaurant was no place for Mr. Rigby, in any case: it was too rich, and he would be too near the parties he was interested in. So he sat and yawned in the Byzantine Lounge, and gazed with some contempt, as a good Londoner, on the gay inhabitants of Manchester. From his table he could keep an eye on the party of three through the open door of the restaurant: Mary's flushed and radiant face, Mr. Seal's, pale and intellectual, and the old man's, the colour of a turkey's wattle. That, he knew from the papers, was Mr. Roger Figg, the theatrical manager.

Yes, thought Mr. Rigby, it was a clear case, and no mistake. All very well to be chaperoned by an old boy at supper-time, but what about afterwards? The expedition, he thought, would be justified; it would need to be, for it was hard on a retired constable to be at work on Christmas Eve. Just about now, by rights, or a little earlier, he should have been creeping into the kiddies' room in his Father Christmas outfit, and thrusting oranges into three long stockings. For Mr. Rigby was a good-hearted, domestic father and husband, and he enjoyed the Christmas

ritual, first to last. When he got the message from his
friend the porter at the flats to say that the party was going
to Manchester that night, he had had half a mind to say,
'Well, let him go.   Good will to all men.   Leave 'em alone.'
Nobody would blame him for not going off on a wild-goose
chase to Manchester on Christmas Eve.   Indeed, he might
catch it from the boss for going.   But Mr. Rigby had always
been a one for duty: he was a fair man and kindly, but the
first law of his life was to obtain a conviction whenever
possible.   He was not very happy about the evidence so far
—that yachting affair was fishy, certainly, but not, he
thought, final, though it would be useful stuff if there was
any more like it.   Christmas, now, was just the sort of time
to catch people off their guard, young people, late parties,
and that.   On the other hand, he had no authority to go.
There was very little money in King's Proctor's work, he
knew.   The K.P., as a rule, employed local people for local
work, and if a bill was presented for railway fares to Manchester and a room at a rich hotel there might be trouble.
He couldn't consult anybody—the office was closed for the
holidays.   But by the time the office was going again the
party would be back in London, perhaps.   Instinct and
training told Mr. Rigby that this was a case for action, for
taking a chance.   Just for the one night.   He bade his
clinging family a sad farewell.

And here he was, ready for action.   He had explored the
ground already.   He knew exactly by what route Mr. Seal
would proceed from Room 318 to Room 218 on the floor
below—by the 'service' staircase which was twenty yards
from both of them.   Chance had made the thing easy for
all parties: and Mr. Rigby had only to wait until the unsus-
pecting prey walked into the trap.   He filled another pipe
and hoped that the lovers would soon have had enough
to eat.
    Hullo!   There they were, coming out together, crossing
the lounge!   They had left the old man alone.   Quick work!
Mr. Rigby prepared himself for motion: but he did not
move.   They might be making for the Oval Room, where
the dancing was.   Beyond that was the lift.   He thought it

unlikely that they would slip off upstairs so early and so openly. But if they passed the Oval Room entrance he would have to follow.

Mr. Seal, with Mary hanging on his arm, pressed sideways through the crowd and disappeared among the jigging dancers. Mr. Rigby lit his pipe.

No ethical scruples disturbed Mr. Rigby's reflections. Nor did he form any moral judgment upon the guilty couple he was pursuing. He had no desire to interfere with anybody's fun, and did not intend to: the couple would have their fun all right. But if they came up against the law they were 'for it', and that was their look-out. As for the law, it was the law: he had never even asked himself whether it was a good law or not. It was not his business. He knew that there were people who fussed about Divorce Law Reform: but that, he thought vaguely, would only mean all this American hanky-panky. What he meant by that he could not have explained: but he knew that it was bad because it was American. If any one had told him that he was engaged upon the work of a dirty spy, prying into the private lives of two good citizens who had committed no crime and done no harm to any living person, he would have been surprised and resentful. One had to spy on people who broke the law: and one law was the same as another. Most of the last year of his time with the Force he had passed in disguise, spying upon his fellow-citizens, not upon the murderer, blackmailer, or incendiary, but upon those who drank beer at midnight, or sold each other sweepstake tickets, or placed shilling bets for the poor, or pretended to tell fortunes, or sold French books; and he had been taught to believe that anything was fair if it secured a conviction So no ethical scruples disturbed Mr. Rigby's reflections.

Almost motionless in the herd of dancers, Mr. Seal tightened his grip and fiercely pressed his Mary to him. His hand upon her bare back was hot, but she liked it. He was sweating a little on the forehead, but she loved him. His embrace was hardly modest, but it pleased her. And so thick was the crowd that immodesty was unavoidable, and imperceptible. Their elbows were pinned to their sides:

his left hand crushed her breast. She smiled up at him and said. 'Darling, it was grand of you to come.'

He bent down and whispered in her ear, 'Shall I come down and say "Good night" to you?'

'No, Martin.'

She was firm and serious, and shook her golden head.

'Yes.'

'No.'

'Why not, darling?' he pleaded.

'We must be good. It's not safe.'

'Yes, it is. Here.'

'Besides, I want to be good.'

'Come off it,' said the Announcer inelegantly.

'Yes, I do. It's Christmas or something.'

'But, darling, I shan't see you for ages. I've got to go back to-morrow. When do you come to London?'

'February. We do Glasgow and Edinburgh first.'

'My God!'

'I know, darling. But it can't be helped.'

'I wish I hadn't come.'

'Oh, Martin, I was so happy. Don't spoil it, darling.'

'Sorry, Mary, I didn't mean that. But I don't see——'

The band stopped playing.

'Let's go back to Figgie.'

Figgie was tired before most of the revellers, but he conceived himself to be a watch-dog on duty, and he was determined not to leave the young couple together. He would be cruel to be kind and escort Mary to the lift himself. He could do no more.

He, therefore, once or twice, expressed the opinion that Mary was exhausted by her labours and should be sure to get a good sleep. Mr. Seal said that he thought she looked wonderfully fit and fresh, considering all things. But Mary at last agreed that she was tired: Figgie signed the bill, and the three moved slowly into the Byzantine Lounge. Mr. Rigby followed: and since, at that hour, only one lift was working, he followed them into the lift.

Mr. Rigby stood in the corner; Mary glanced at him but did not give him a thought. Only the observant Figgie, talking busily to the others, noticed his build, noticed his feet, and said to himself 'Policeman?' But Figgie had no reason to suppose that the police were after Mary, and he thought no more about the man.

Figgie said to Mr. Seal, 'Which floor are you?'

'The third,' said Mr. Seal, gloomily: for he had hoped to keep this information dark and leave the lift with Mary at the second floor.

Now he had to shake hands formally and say 'Good night' at the second. 'See you to-morrow,' said Mary, and disappeared. Mr. Seal, volcanic with anger, was carried up to the third floor with Figgie and Mr. Rigby.

'Good night,' said Figgie to the liftman: and to Mr. Seal, 'Come along to my room and have a night-cap.' Mr. Seal reluctantly consented: for this, after all, was the great Mr. Figg, and in the ordinary course of things he would have been excited by the invitation. Also, he must give Mr. Figg no reason to suspect his dangerous intentions. So he followed Figgie down the endless corridor, consoling himself with the thought that he was being cunningly deceptive. Mr. Rigby watched him go: Mr. Figg marched ahead of him, humming softly: and the young man's mind was an open book to both of them.

Figgie longed for his comfortable bed, and he drank nothing himself at this time of night; but he detained Mr. Seal for three-quarters of an hour, plying him nobly with whisky and reminiscences. Mr. Seal wanted to go, but could not. He admired the old man, and knew that he was being honoured. Thousands of men and women would have thought themselves fortunate to sit there and listen to Figgie's talk, the story of his youth, his failures, his successes, even his love-affairs: any newspaperman would have paid large sums for it. But he, Mr. Seal, sat there cursing in his heart: and Figgie talked and talked, cursing and yawning secretly: and Mr. Rigby, at the door of 322, cursed secretly and yawned. And, on the floor below, Mary, the cause of all this cursing, lay like a long, pale waterlily in a very hot bath, and told herself that she was a very good girl.

Mary yawned, stretched, switched off the light over the

12

bed, and wriggled like a dog into a comfortable curl. She was tired, but still happy: she had had a glorious bath and smelt pleasantly of verbena. She had thought that Martin might ring her up from his room and say 'Good night': but perhaps it was better not. She felt not only happy, but, in a sort of spiritual way, exalted. She had resisted temptation and felt the better for it. She was sorry for Martin, and for herself: but she had faced him firmly and kept him off: and that, in itself, was a satisfaction. But, above all, the glow of being good possessed her: it might be Christmas, it might be humbug and the fear of being found out: but there it was. On the whole, she thought, it was Christmas. She thought of her old father and was pleased by the thought, for he would be proud of her to-night, if he knew. The firelight flickering on the ceiling was good company: she watched it for a little and closed her eyes.

'Honk!' said the radiator: but Mary was asleep.

The telephone bell rang.

She woke painfully, her heart thumping. Who on earth ——?

Martin, of course. . . .

'Hullo?'

'Mary?'

'You woke me up.'

'So sorry. I've been with Figg.'

The voice was infinitely remote and soft, as if the speaker were surrounded by enemies, none of whom must hear a syllable: it was the purr of Savoy Hill reduced by a master to the lowest pitch of audibility.

'I'll come and say "Good night", shall I?'

'No, Martin.'

'Yes—I've hardly seen you.'

'No, Martin. Please!'

'Only for a minute.'

'But I'm asleep.'

'I'll tuck you up.'

'Better not, dear.'

'I'm coming.'

A pause, while Mary thought.

'Well, if it's really only for a minute——'

'All right.'

'Promise?'

'Yes.'

'You'll be good?'

'Yes.'

'And careful?'

But Mr. Seal had gone.

'Honk,' said the radiator. 'Curse!' said Mary and jumped out of bed.

Mr. Seal, in green silk pyjamas, a purple dressing-gown and bedroom slippers, stealthily closed the door of 318 and looked up and down the long, dim corridor. Not a sound, not a soul in sight. Manchester, even on a gala night, went early to bed. He turned to the right and walked quickly to the staircase. 'And about time too,' said Mr. Rigby to himself.

The 'service' staircase was uncarpeted, and the heels of the bedroom slippers flapped on the stone, making, it seemed to Mr. Seal, a monstrous noise; so he slackened his pace and put his feet down delicately. Mr. Rigby, who was dressed in grey woollen pyjamas and a dark blue dressing-gown, halted at the top of the stairs, round the corner.

At the turn of the stair Mr. Seal stopped suddenly and looked back. Soft footsteps behind him, surely. But now not a sound. He went down three steps and heard the soft pad-pad again. The long girdle of his dressing-gown was trailing behind him, and at the end of it was a heavy tassel which dropped from step to step like a diminutive dog. Mr. Seal picked up the girdle, and, feeling both frightened and foolish, hurried down the remaining steps to the lush carpet of the corridor below. This too was empty and dim: a light burned far away, but it was too dark here to see the numbers on the doors. Mr. Seal had wisely brought with him a small electric torch. It would never do to knock at the wrong door. What was this? 210. 12—14—16—18—four more. That would be the one—where a dim light came through the fanlight of a bathroom. He put the torch out.

Mr. Rigby, who had nothing on his spacious feet, sped down the stairs like some huge fairy, magically nimble and noise-less. He thrust his nose round the corner, and was in time to see a quick flash of the cautious torch and Mr. Seal, his head bent, knocking, or rather caressingly scratching, on a door.

Mr. Seal disappeared; and Mr. Rigby noted that the gentleman was admitted without a word being spoken—a bad sign. Mr. Rigby listened at the door but could hear low voices only, no words. He too had an electric torch; he had a little note-book also: and in the note-book he wrote down carefully Room 218, and the time, one-seventeen a.m. From the other pocket of the blue dressing-gown he took a thread of black cotton and a little wax. He fastened the cotton taut across the doorway, from doorpost to doorpost: he took a pair of Mary's shoes, and two pairs of men's shoes from neighbouring doors, and he arranged them in a kind of pyramid on the mat before the door, so that they looked like the work of some tipsy practical joker. The first pyramid fell down with a faint clatter. But the young people, no doubt, would be too busy to notice that.

He put his eye to the keyhole, as a matter of form, but could see nothing: and now he could hear nothing—another bad sign. On the same side of the corridor as Room 218, but farther away from the 'service' staircase, was a Gentlemen's Lavatory. Mr. Rigby went into one of the compartments, propped the door open with a toilet roll, sat down, lit his pipe, and patiently resigned himself to a lengthy vigil.

'Somebody's at the door!'

Mary whispered the words, her eyes large with alarm. She stood before the dying fire; Martin's arms were round her: she put a finger on her lover's lips: and thus they remained for a minute, mute and trembling, staring at the silent door. He could feel her heart racing, as his was racing.

The silence was crushing.

'Honk!' said the radiator.

She took her finger from his lips. He whispered, 'I thought I heard somebody behind me on the stairs.'

She said with mild reproach, 'Then why did you come, you silly boy?'

'I thought it was my dressing-gown.'

She made no comment on this strange remark, but said, 'I'm sure I heard somebody. Go, my dear.'

He said, 'But if there's somebody there I'd better wait till they've gone.'

There was reason in this: and she did not know what to say. She was not alarmed now, only indignant that such things could happen to her, that to be in love should bring such trouble. 'Oh, dear,' she said sadly, and laid her head upon his breast.

Mr. Rigby told himself that he was a smart fellow, and if everybody had their rights he would be one of the Big Five now instead of a retired man doing fancy-work for the K.P. Nevertheless, a job was a job, and he liked to do it properly, whatever it was. The stone floor of the lavatory struck cold on his bare feet, but the glow of the chase was warm in his breast. His birds were trapped: he would get a conviction. All he had to do was wait. Many a man would have gone off to bed now, content with what he had got. After all, he had seen the gentleman go into the lady's room at one-seven-teen a.m. and that should be enough. But he liked to do things thoroughly, finish a job off. To pass the time he wrote in his little black book: 'Seal came out of 218 . . .' and left a blank space for the hour. He hoped the gentleman would not make too long a job of it. Might be all night, of course. And he, Mr. Rigby, might fall off to sleep: he was sleepy enough, and comfortable enough. But then, with any luck, the gentleman would upset the shoes and make a clatter. He had thought of drawing-pins, but that might be dangerous. 'Inflicting bodily harm.' Mr. Rigby yawned. It was Christmas morning already, he thought: and it wouldn't be long now before those kiddies of his were waking up and taking a peep at their stockings. They never slept much on Christmas Eve night, the little bastards, bless 'em. Nor would their poor old dad, at this rate. Never mind. Good will to all men.

'But, if you're right, Mary, we may as well be hanged for a sheep as for a lamb.'

'Then I'm not right. Anyhow, darling, you must *go*!'

.   .   .   .   .

The detective's feet were cold. The lavatory seat was hard. A little walk, he thought, won't do no harm. And while he was about it he would get some more clothes. Socks and shoes, for instance. It was not so important now that he should not be heard. Nevertheless, he proceeded on tiptoe, like a retired, burly ballet-dancer, to the door of 218. The pyramid of shoes still stood, the thread of cotton was intact. He listened but heard nothing. He went up to his own room, put on socks and slippers, and a woolly waistcoat. Leaving the room, he turned this time to the left. It might be useful to know of another way up, and there must be a public staircase somewhere. There was: about six rooms to the westward. Mr. Rigby walked down it, chewing some nut-chocolate, and returned to his post in the Gentlemen's Lavatory.

Go, darling, go.'

Martin whispered, 'Why all this whispering? We're not criminals, are we?'

'There's somebody there again.'

'I heard nothing.'

'I'm not sure that I did. But I *know* there's somebody. I feel it.'

'Then I shall stay here.'

Martin was now the bold one, or seemed to be.

'Martin, this mustn't happen again. I can't stand this hunted feeling. We're *not* criminals—but they can make us feel we are. And it's not worth it—that's the point.'

'It *is* worth it.' And he hugged her.

'You say that now. But what about your job?'

'There's nobody there, darling. It's all imagination.'

'Wait. I'll put out a pair of shoes and see. Kiss me.'

They kissed.

'You go into the bathroom.'

'Put something on.'

She put on over her night-dress a little coat of white fur; and Mr. Seal, not so bold now, went into the bathroom.

Shoes in hand, quietly but bravely, Mary opened the door and stepped into the dark. Martin heard a scuffling sound, and a muffled, shuddering exclamation. He came out of the bathroom. Mary stood motionless in the doorway, staring down at an untidy heap of shoes, as she might have stared at a dead body in her doorway. Martin took her arm and drew her back: but before he shut the door he peered quickly, right and left, along the corridor. Nothing was to be seen or heard. He shut the door softly.

'What's the matter, darling?'

'The *shoes*!'

She was pale and shaking, as if she had seen a ghost.

'What about them?'

'They were all *arranged*. In a sort of *heap*. They weren't there when you came?'

'Couldn't have been. But what's the trouble? It's the boot-boy, probably. That's what you heard.'

'Who's whispering now?' she whispered, and walked across to her dressing-table. 'The boot-boy?' she said aloud, clutching at hope. 'May have been. *Oh, God, what's this?*'

'What?'

Mary was staring at her reflection in the looking-glass. He went quickly to her and looked over her shoulder. A long thread of black cotton lay in a loop below her breasts, caught on either side by the fur of the little coat. She detached it carefully, slid her fingers to the end of it, and held it up, like a dead serpent.

'What d'you make of that?' she said.

'Nothing. Black cotton.'

'There's no black cotton in my room. You saw me put on this coat. Did you see any black cotton then?'

'No.'

'I must have picked it up outside.'

'Why not?' said Martin, but his eyes were anxious, watching her anxious eyes in the glass.

'Oh, darling, don't you *see*? It's a *trick*. It was fixed across the door somehow—to catch *you*! Oh, darling, somebody saw you come—somebody's out there watching us. Oh, darling, why *should* they—what shall we *do*?'

And Mary, worn-out, wept upon his breast.

He hugged and comforted her. It was a joke. It must be a joke. After all, it was Christmas Eve. Figgie, perhaps. One of the company?

Mary quickly recovered her composure, and considered

the joke hypothesis, but without conviction. Figgie could never do such a thing; and no member of the company, she thought, would dare. Except Lizzie—and she had gone to London.

Some total stranger, perhaps?

Perhaps. But why?

'Drunk'.

'Maybe,' said Mary. 'Anyhow, don't worry, darling.' She was the strong one, she felt, and must remain so. 'I'll ask Figgie to-morrow. But go now, Martin, my sweet. I want to sleep.'

'I want to stay.'

'No, you don't. You're frightened. So am I.'

'With all those people watching, I'm safer here.'

She smacked his face gently, and suddenly everything was a joke again.

'When we are married——' she sang.

'We'll have sausages for tea.'

'We're not married yet, darling.'

Mary was the master, and Martin went. And she was right—he was frightened. It was no joke slinking through the silent corridors, and up the cold stone staircase, looking over his shoulder, and clutching the girdle of his dressing-gown.

Mr. Rigby, much more quickly, went up by the public staircase. Peeping round a corner and between two fire-buckets, he saw Mr. Seal slink into his room. He made a note of the time in his little black book, and went, yawning happily, to bed. He would be back in Fulham in time to light the candles on the Christmas-tree.

Mary saw Martin off by the midday train to London. The station was dark, dank, gloomy, and deserted. The few passengers and porters went about silently, resenting the necessity for travel on Christmas Day. Outside it was raining; inside the station every inanimate thing seemed to be sweating—and sweating black. The trollies sweated, the platforms oozed a dismal black, the handle of the carriage was clammy and left a black smear on Mary's glove. The two lovers, sitting in the empty carriage, talked sadly

in whispers, as if there might be listeners under the seat.
Both confessed that they had slept little and unquietly;
and in the daylight their fantastic fears were as strong as
before. Mary, as jocular as possible, had accused Figgie of
playing practical jokes outside her bedroom door, and he,
with some surprise, had protested his innocence. They
could think of no explanation but the sinister one: but
both were feebly pretending to think nothing of that.

'We won't worry, anyhow, will we ?' said Mary.

'No, darling. I'm sure it's all nonsense.'

'And we won't give them a chance to upset us again, will
we?'

'No, Mary. Kiss me. Good-bye, my love.'

'Darling!' she whispered: and, suddenly, '*Look out.*'

Mary quickly withdrew her face. A large man in a bowler-
hat and a blue overcoat was passing the window. He gave
the couple a long, straight look and went down the platform.

'Who was that?' said Mary, still in that guilty whisper.

'I seem to know his face.'

'I do. I remember. He was in the lift last night—with
you and me and Figgie.'

'Nothing in that. But—I know. He came up on the same
train as I did. I remember wondering how he could afford
a first.'

'My God!' Mary whispered. 'That's the man! I *know*
it is.'

'Seen anything of our wireless friend?' Figgie sat on the
green sofa in Mary's dressing-room, disturbed. It was the
Wednesday of the last week in Manchester; he had not
intended to come up before the Friday, for he had much to
do in London. Henry Hake, his stage-director, was a
Napoleon of his kind, and all, last week, had seemed well
with 'Penelope'.

But Henry, over the telephone, had confessed, with
caution, to worries and doubts: not about the play, or the
music, not about the company or even the public, but about
the leading lady. She was not, to cut it short, giving such a
good performance.

'She's not ill?' said Figgie.

'No. But nervy. Made a fuss last night about a stage-hand standing in the wings. Not a bit like her.'

'H'm,' said Figgie and thought, 'Love-trouble. Has that young man been up again?'

'Not that I know of.'

'H'm,' said Figgie. 'I'll come up to-morrow and sit through the show. Don't say I'm coming.'

He asked no more questions. Henry was not the man to utter such baleful opinions without good cause.

Now he had sat through the show with Henry, conscientiously making notes on the 'Accounts' pages of his diary; and he agreed that Henry was distressingly right. Technically, there was nothing to complain of—nothing, that is, that the public would consciously detect: and the audience, though 'sticky', seemed to enjoy themselves as usual. But, to those who knew, something was absent, which in the long run made all the difference, the imponderable extra which captured an audience without their perceiving it. There was less life, no electricity. It would not be fair to say that Mary was walking through her part, for that would mean laziness or stupidity: and Figgie could never accuse her of either. But the mind seemed to be elsewhere: she missed a music cue and said two of her best lines like a woman talking in her sleep; and twice the vigilant Figgie caught her looking off into the wings, when eyes and attention should have been fixed upon another actor. Most unlike Mary, as Henry had said: and something must be wrong. If this had been the hundred-and-thirty-seventh performance he would have said she was stale and thinking of her next play: but this was only the twentieth, and she loved the part. In three weeks (after the fortnight in Scotland) they would be facing London, the fastidious audience of a Figg First Night, and the critics, terrible as an army with newspapers. Secretly, he could not be sure that the play would capture London, though every word he spoke about it expressed a quiet confidence. It was not everybody's meat: his productions never were; and that was why everybody had at least a nibble at them. To make the multitude take a hearty meal was always the problem: and to make them gobble up 'Penelope' he was counting on

one attraction more than any other—the vibrant personality and charm of Mary Moon. If that failed him the
whole production, he feared, might fail.

The first thing was to diagnose the trouble. Perhaps, he
thought, Mr. Seal had basely turned to another. And so he
said:

'Seen anything of our wireless friend?'

She had her back to him, sitting at her table: but in the
mirror he could see her face, on which she was smearing an
unbecoming coat of white grease. She looked up sharply,
stopped her greasing, and sought his face in the glass. There
was fear in the movement, suspicion in the eyes: and Figgie
was shocked. Why in the world should she be afraid of
him?

'No,' she said. 'Not since Christmas.' Figgie never
wasted time, and the next thing he said was, 'What's the
matter, Mary? Something's the matter.'

He knew that everything in the world could be discussed
before Florrie.

But Mary said, 'Pop along to the stage door, will you,
Florrie, dear, and see if there's a letter for me.'

Florrie said, wounded, 'We know very well there's no
letter for us at the stage door, because if there was it would
be here on our table. If we want to talk secrets to Mr. Figg
why don't we say so?'

'Sorry, Florrie. You're quite right.'

'It's of no consequence, dear,' and Florrie went out,
wagging her head.

'Worse and worse,' thought Figgie. 'Secrets from Florrie!'
but he said, laughing, 'You've done it now.'

But Mary did not laugh: and things were bad indeed if
Mary could not laugh at Florrie's tantrums.

She said, 'Have you ever been followed, Figgie?'

'Followed? Only by a Countess who wanted to play
Alice in Wonderland.'

Still Mary would not laugh at his little joke.

She said: '*Followed*. Spied upon?'

'No. Why?'

She towelled off the last of the grease, and turned round.
Figgie was accustomed to seeing his lovely ladies in the
unbecoming stages of make-up: but Mary's face frightened

him. He discounted the pale and sticky cheeks: but there
was trouble in the eyes, and trouble on the trembling
mouth, and a cloud of trouble on the brow.

'It's filthy,' she said. 'Figgie, they're after me. I'm
sure they are.'

'Who?'

'Detectives. That grimy King's Proctor, I suppose.
Figgie, I can't bear it!' Figgie feared she would cry, and,
leaning forward, took her hand.

'Steady, dear. Now tell me slowly.'

Figgie could nearly always stop a leading lady from crying
if he put his mind to it. But sometimes he let them cry:
because that was best.

Mary, with her hand in dear old comforting Figgie's, was
calm already.

'You remember Christmas Eve, when Martin came up?
Well, he came to my room that night—after he left you——'

'Oh, dear, I thought I'd prevented that.'

'Darling old Figgie!' She patted his hand. 'But he
wasn't there long, dear, I promise you. Anyhow, I thought
I heard somebody snooping about outside: and when I
looked out, there was a thread of black cotton across the
door and a heap of shoes——'

'Shoes?'

'All *arranged*. Like a shop window. *You* know. Must
have been done on purpose——'

'But why?'

'God knows. For Martin to trip over, I suppose, when
he left.'

'But what would be the point of that?'

'I don't know.'

'Sounds more like a practical joke to me.' Figgie was
relieved. If this was all the trouble——

'That's what Martin said. You remember I asked you if
you'd been funny that night—the next day, Figgie?
Though I never thought you had, of course.'

'Thank you, dear.'

'But that day, Christmas Day, when I was seeing Martin
off at the station, we saw a sort of police-looking man—he
was going back to London on the same train. I was all
of a jump and noticed him, because I remembered he went

up in the lift with us that night. Do *you* remember him,
Figgie—you were in the same lift, weren't you—a sort of
wall of a man, with a face like a sponge and the most
elephantine feet——? An absolute stage detective?'

'Hell!' thought Figgie: but he said seriously: 'Yes. As a
matter of fact, I do.'

'You do? Well, Martin didn't notice him in the lift:
but he did think he'd seen the man before, coming up from
London on the same train on Christmas Eve. So, what with
one thing and another, it looks pretty ominous, don't you
think, darling? He follows Martin up to Manchester, watches
him all night, and goes back to London on the same train
as Martin.'

Figgie wished that he had confessed to being a practical
joker. But it was too late for that now. He said, 'Steady,
my dear. How do you know he was watching all night?
You didn't see any one prowling about, did you?'

'No, darling. But the whole point of detectives is that
you don't see them prowling about. That's what they're for.'

'It might be a coincidence,' said Figgie feebly.

'It might. But I feel it isn't. And when I *feel* anything
it's generally right. I didn't really *hear* anybody outside
that night—I just *felt* there was somebody there—long
before the shoes or anything. And there was.'

Figgie had had so much to do with so many women that
he was not inclined to brush aside what Mary called her
'feelings' as nonsense. The more she said the more disturbed
he was: and the more calm and unconvinced he seemed to be.

He summoned all his powers of persuasion and comfort:
he held her hand tight, and looked into her eyes, and said,
'Mary, dear, do you know what I think? You're tired,
you're overworked—and you're just imagining things; I've
done it myself. And now we'll go to the gilded pub and
share an oyster and a bottle of the best.'

She took her hand away, turned towards the glass, and
set to work upon her face again.

'I agree to the oyster, Figgie darling, and even the bottle,
but not the rest,' she said.

'You've nothing to go upon, really.'

'I know. That's the awful thing. If it was certain I
wouldn't mind so much. I mean, if the man had knocked

at the door and taken our names and addresses—like a motor-accident—it would be bearable. One would know one was in for it. You see that, Figgie?' She went behind the screen to put on her frock.

'Yes,' said Figgie. He remembered the weeks of secret apprehension he had suffered, thinking that he would have to have an operation; and how, when at last the doctor had told him that there would have to be an operation, it had been almost a relief. After that it had been a straight-forward, natural event to look forward to—almost a joke. He *knew*.

'But you haven't seen the man again?' he said.

'No, darling. But I expect to—everywhere. Wherever I go I feel there's *somebody*. It's *terrifying*, Figgie. The other night I thought I saw him standing in the wings—in the Telemachus scene. I nearly screamed—did Henry tell you? But it was only a stage-hand I hadn't noticed before.'

Figgie thought, 'This is awful,' but said nothing. Behind the screen the sad tale continued.

'And how do I know it will always be the same man? Anybody in that crowd at the stage door may be one of them. I hardly dare to go back to the hotel with Henry. I've told Martin not to ring me up. Oh, Figgie, darling, it isn't fair—is it, Figgie?'

'No,' he said. 'Can't you speak to your lawyers?'

'I daren't. They're not supposed to know about Martin, you see. Figgie, you'll have to help me somehow.'

She came out and stood before him. Figgie looked at her piteous face, and thought, 'Now she had better cry.' So he took her hands and said. 'I will, dear. Don't worry. It'll be all right. Anyhow, you gave a beautiful performance.'

'I didn't. You know I didn't. I gave a *foul* performance. And you were a pig not to say you were coming.'

And Mary cried.

While she cried Figgie patted her hand and thought busily, wondering how in the world it was to be all right. In his rich experience of life and the stage he had never en-countered a similar difficulty—a sensible leading lady being driven into a nervous breakdown by private detectives, perhaps imaginary. Probably imaginary—he said to himself:

for he knew little of the law, and could not believe that it was quite so barbarous as Mary thought. But the practical need was to persuade Mary that her detectives were imaginary. So long as she believed in them she would be miserable—and no wonder, poor girl. To feel that she was being watched by unknown men—afraid to consult her own lawyers—afraid to telephone to her lover—he could think of nothing so likely to upset a leading lady. But what was to be done? Wild expedients occurred to him. Could one go to the King's Proctor and ask him point-blank if he had put detectives on a certain woman? Probably not—for that might suggest to the fellow that the lady had something to hide. Who was the King's Proctor, anyway? Where did he live? 'Damn and blast the King's Proctor!' said Figgie to his secret heart. 'Isn't the theatrical business difficult enough without *him*?'

Mary stopped crying and felt better. Figgie was confident and comforting. He said it was all moonshine. He said he was sure they didn't do things like that, not in cases like Mary's; but he said he would speak to a good lawyer he knew, and make sure: and Mary felt better still.

'And now for that oyster,' he said.

'All right. You pig, Figgie, I shall have to do my face again.'

Figgie did all things thoroughly, promptly, and expensively. Having ordered the oysters in the Golden Restaurant he sent for a page, and commanded a personal call to London—Mr. Timothy Barter, K.C. While he prepared his oysters, with a fine air of absorption in that important business, he watched Mary cunningly, and noticed how, with equal cunning, she looked from table to table, seeking a proctorial gentleman. 'It's an obsession,' he thought. 'Something drastic must be done.' He remembered how they had looked for the King's Proctor on Christmas Eve and laughed about it. It was no joke now.

'Your call to London, Mr. Figg.'

Mr. Barter, the well-known divorce advocate, was not in Court the next day and had not much to do. He was an old friend of Figgie's and had advised him often: he readily

consented to come up to Manchester for lunch unofficially
—almost the strangest mission, he said afterwards, of his
career.

'Figgie, you are sweet.' He came back to the restaurant
with a confident and happy smile on his face. And Mary
felt the sort of relief that comes when the doctor has been
sent for. She had no idea who Mr. Barter was, or what he
would do. But Figgie had sent for the man, and he would
do something. She enjoyed her supper and slept well.

Mr. Barter enjoyed his day-off at Manchester. He liked
Figgie and admired Mary, whom he had not met before.
Mr. Figg was not quite sure of his ground: there might be
some sensitive little spot of etiquette which would prevent
Mr. Barter from advising in such a case—one never knew
with lawyers. So Figgie thought it wise to let the lawyer
talk himself into a good humour, and be attracted to Mary
(perhaps) before he was asked to assist her. Mr. Barter
drank Hock and told cheerful stories of the Divorce Court.
Amusing stories. But to Mary it was like lying in a nursing
home the night before an operation for appendicitis while
the night nurse sat on the bed and told cheery anecdotes
about abdominal cases which had not gone well: and she
listened in silence, her confidence diminishing with every
story. Doctors and lawyers were very nice, but very
much alike, she thought; to hear them talk, you would think
that the human race was no more than the raw material for
their professions, fit only to become 'abdominals', 'petitioners', or 'co-respondents'. But all professions were the same,
perhaps: nobody in her own could come into a room without
'making an entrance', and every unusual remark was 'a
good line' or a 'gag'. The film people could not look at St.
Paul's Cathedral, or a sunset, without discussing whether the
spectacle would not make a good 'shot'. Mr. Barter, she
thought, was nice, but tiresomely 'shoppy': and he seemed
to have no pity at all for his 'respondents' and 'interveners':
they were just jokes. Nor had he a word of criticism for his
prehistoric law; he took that as a matter of course.

'Talking of detectives,' he said. Mary stiffened and
shivered in her soul. 'One of the most extraordinary cases

I remember. I was for the respondent—we'll call her Lady A—in a defended suit: and we'll call the co-respondent B.'

'B being the naughty gentleman?' put in Figgie: both he and Mary had found it hard to follow some of the stories, who was the 'petitioner', the sex of the 'respondent', and so on.

'Yes. There was plenty of money and no expense spared. The "sleuthing" alone must have run the husband into thousands. They followed her all across France to Monte Carlo. She went there with her sister—we'll call the sister C. Now it so happened that at the same time C was being very actively pursued by a colleague of mine—a very distinguished "silk", with a large divorce practice. I won't tell you his name——'

'We'll call him D?' suggested Figgie helpfully.

'Yes. D. As a matter of fact it was old Humphrey Galloway. However. . . . well, on a long job like that you can't, obviously, have the same sleuth at work the whole time. It's a twenty-four-hour job. One sleuth takes the parties as far as Boulogne, say, or Paris, and then he hands over to another. The result of that, sometimes, is that they get on the track of the wrong person, and that's what happened in this case. As it happened, B was never on the train at all——'

'Half a minute. I've forgotten who B is.'

'B's the co-respondent—our man—that is, my client's lover.'

'Oh, yes.'

'The man who *was* on the train, standing the ladies drinks and so on, and seen, by the way, coming out of one of their compartments—forgive me, Miss Moon—was my distinguished colleague D.'

'The K.C.?'

'Yes.'

'I see. I've got it now. Do you follow, Mary?'

'Yes,' said Mary flatly. This, she thought, was a hateful story, and confirmed all her fears. If 'sleuths' could prowl about at night in French express corridors, why not in Manchester hotels?

'Well, before the trial we got to the bottom of all this, and we were pretty sure that we could prove that there'd

13

been a mistake. The trouble was that we didn't want to have to bring it out that the man on the train was D. On the other hand, we couldn't go to counsel on the other side and say, 'Look here, if you don't shut up you'll land our dear colleague D in the soup; so we had to keep quiet and do the best we could. Well, A went into the box——'

'That's the wife?'

'Yes. She did very well. Cleverest woman I ever saw in the box. But towards the end of her cross-examination counsel on the other side—we'll call him E——'

'Haven't we had an E?' said Figgie.

'No, A's the wife, B the co-respondent, C the sister, D the K.C., and E is the petitioner's counsel——'

'The husband's?'

'Yes.'

'Call the husband F?'

'If you like,' said Mr. Barter shortly. 'The husband doesn't really come into the story. Well, E handed up to A a sheet of paper with a number of rather smoking-room stories written on it, found by the husband in the wife's bureau. And he said—that is, counsel said—"Do you know the handwriting those stories are written in, Lady A?"

' "Certainly," said A.

' "Isn't that the handwriting of the co-respondent?"

' "No."

' "Whose handwriting is it, then?"

' "I'd rather not say."

' "Why not?"

' "It's nothing to do with this case, and would only cause unnecessary scandal."

'You see,' said Mr. Barter, 'as A knew perfectly well, the handwriting was the handwriting of D, the K.C. He'd been at her place a good deal, while he was after her sister.

'Well, there was the usual business. The Judge said she must answer, and started rumbling about contempt of Court: and then Lady A threw a convenient faint. It was late in the afternoon and the Court adjourned till the following day.

'Well, we could do nothing to help her. . . . You know the rule, of course?'

'What rule?'

'While your witness is in the witness-box you leave her alone, mustn't prompt or advise her. It isn't done.'

'No, I didn't know that,' said Figgie. One of the unexpected decencies, he thought, which made the legal world so difficult to understand.

'And we couldn't tell the other counsel what we knew. So we had to sit tight till the morning and pray. And, I can tell you, we were in a considerable stew.

'The next day Lady A goes into the box, and D—I mean E—says to her, "You were just going to tell us, Lady A, the name of the gentleman in whose handwriting these unpleasant anecdotes are written?"

'She says, "I can't tell you." The Judge says, "You must." She says, "Well, milord, may I write it down?" The Judge agrees. He looks at the bit of paper—all the Court in a fever, as you can imagine—and he says, "I think you two gentlemen at the Bar had better look at the name the witness has written."

'Well, then I thought the fat was in the fire. E looked at the paper first: he's got grand control, and never blinked: but when I got a peep at the paper I nearly burst. What do you think she'd written—of all the impossible names—?

' "Mrs. Stanley Baldwin." '

Mr. Figg laughed heartily, and even Mary smiled.

Mr. Barter repeated the impossible name with relish, and said: 'It was a brilliant stroke. Quite brilliant. You see, they couldn't challenge her without calling Mrs. Baldwin, or bringing out the name anyhow: and I suppose she betted on their not wanting to do that.

'After that we won in a canter,' said Mr. Barter, and passed on happily to another story.

'Funny,' thought Mary. 'The only thing the lawyers worried about was the reputation of the K.C. They don't care a hoot how much *our* private affairs are discussed in public.'

But Figgie, at last, had come to business. He was putting a hypothetical case—he made it hypothetical for fear of running on to some hidden snag of etiquette. In such and such a case—— Would it be likely——? What exactly did the King's Proctor——? In a hotel like this, for example——.

Mr. Barter was clear and decisive. He was not deluded by Figgie's artifice, but blandly pretended that he was. He said that the King's Proctor was not nearly so active as people supposed. He had a very small staff and was kept very short of money by the Treasury. His whole Budget, Mr. Barter thought, did not exceed £7,000 a year. He had, he thought, a few regular sleuths of his own, though Mr. Barter was not sure of that: but, as a rule, for local work, he employed local solicitors or the ordinary agents—and paid them badly. He could never afford, for example, the kind of trans-continental chase described in Lady A's case. Nine times out of ten he acted on an anonymous letter, where the parties were poorish and the case was simple. Mr. Snooks got a decree and a kind anonymous person wrote to the King's Proctor and said that for the last twelve months Mr. Snooks had been living with Miss Green; local solicitors were instructed to make inquiries: they knocked at Mr. Snooks' door and Miss Green opened it. But for the elaborate pursuit of the rich the Proctor had not the means: and in a case such as that described by Figgie the parties would be very unlucky to find the Proctor after them, unless, of course, there was some special scandal he couldn't leave alone, or he had instructions from the Court. Sometimes, for example, the Judge would put a query on the papers when the decree nisi was given. But nearly always it was an anonymous letter. Many people made the mistake Mr. Figg had made: they read about the King's Proctor, they read about detectives in 'defended' cases, and they jumped to the conclusion that the King's Proctor used the same methods. But he didn't. He ought to—if he was any use at all. But he couldn't afford it.

This discourse, though they did not understand all of it, was a warm relief to Mr. Figg and Mary. It acted like the sympathetic address of a specialist assuring his patient that she is suffering not from cancer but a little indigestion, and needs a sea-voyage. Her fears melted away. Mr. Barter went back to London with a large cigar, a little mystified but mellow. Mary told Figgie that she would worry no more, and that night he told her, truthfully, that he had never seen her in better form.

.   .   .   .   .

The Attorney-General, Sir Antony Farrow, a big man with a capacious brow, picked up the papers in *Adam, M.R.*, v. *Adam, M. J.*, and wearily removed the red tape. He had had a difficult day; a Revenue case in the High Court that morning, a tiresome Friday debate in the House in the afternoon about some Private Member's proposal to establish a Ministry of Justice; and he had to make a speech this evening at a dinner of the Worcestershire Association. He liked the President and had promised to speak for him, but he had thought of nothing to say about Worcestershire, and was not quite certain where it was. And now, at his chambers, he found this little pile of King's Proctor's intervention cases.

One of the duties which entertained him least was the direction of the King's Proctor in matrimonial causes. Most laymen, he knew, thought of the King's Proctor as a kind of Matrimonial Star Chamber, an English Ogpu, a relentless official Department which went about secretly seeking whom it might devour. In fact, the poor Proctor rarely acted on his own volition: he was instructed by the Court, or goaded by a private person to make inquiries. And, having made inquiries at the instigation of others, he could not act upon them in Court without the Attorney-General's direction.

The King's Proctor did all the dirty work, spying on the parties and preparing the cases; but the responsibility for proceeding was his, Sir Antony's. Yet not one in a thousand citizens knew that he had anything to do with divorce matters.

It was not an easy duty to discharge. Sir Antony was a strong churchman, and anxious to preserve the ideals of Christian marriage. But he was broad-minded, and did not consider the law to be perfect, even from the churchman's point of view, though, as a politician, he maintained that no Government could face the question of a material alteration. Meanwhile, whatever the law was, it must be obeyed and enforced: and he heartily applauded Lord Hawkhurst's labours in that direction. What puzzled him was his lordship's increasing willingness to exercise his discretion and grant relief to an erring and deceitful petitioner. For this, in a sense, appeared to be losing on the swings what was gained on the roundabouts. What was the use of delivering on Monday an elaborate anathema against trickery and deceit, if on Tuesday, when deceit was confessed, the Court said that it would be forgiven? Accordingly, once or twice, Sir Antony had declined to allow the King's Proctor to intervene in what he thought was a clear case; for, said Sir Antony, if the guilty petitioner was to be allowed to ride off on the discretion the net result would only be a waste of public time and money, and the guilty petitioner might as well be left alone. Then he would receive reproachful letters from the Treasury Solicitor, suggesting that he, Sir Antony, was opening the way to abuses, injuring morality, and weakening the law. Yet he thought himself as good a churchman as his lordship.

Here, then, was another case, the usual squalid anecdote: evidence of nurses, reports of sleuths. A gentleman called Rigby, who wrote like a policeman. 'I then proceeded to the vicinity of Room 218 and kept observation on the door of same. . . .' 'Rigby'—yes, Sir Antony remembered the name now—one of the regulars. It looked a clear case, and a pretty bad one. Misconduct both before the petition and after the decree: flat defiance of law and decency. What sort of people were the parties? A publisher, an actress, and—hullo!—somebody on the B.B.C. All mixed up with the entertainment business. Sounded like one of these 'Bohemian' sets—all that night-club stuff. They were the sort of people who wanted jumping on; the heart of the nation was sound enough. Who was the actress? Stage name 'Mary Moon'. Ah, yes, he had heard of her; never saw her: hadn't been to the theatre since Barrie's last play. She was a favourite, he believed, but he couldn't help that: on the contrary, if well-known people were let off it got about, and that was when trouble began. On the other hand, if old Hawkhurst was going to let her off, what was the good? But, probably, with an actress, and a lot of 'Bohemian' talk about, he would not be so amenable. His duty seemed clear: it was a bad case, *prima facie*, and, on the whole a case for intervention. He wrote: 'I direct intervention. A. Farrow,' and put the papers together. And now what the deuce was he to say about Worcestershire?

.　　　.　　　.　　　.　　　.

'Miss Moon?' the stage-manager called respectfully.

There was no answer. There was no Miss Moon. The stage waited.

'Miss Moon?' called the assistant stage-manager, and scampered off towards the dressing-rooms.

Mr. Figg broke off a conference with the dress-designer, and came down the central gangway of the stalls.

'Hasn't Miss Moon arrived yet?' he asked quietly. Figgie was always quiet at rehearsals: no nerve-racking yells from the dark dress circle: just as much voice as was necessary to reach the stage.

'No, sir.'

'Send some one to her dressing-room, will you?'

'Yes, Mr. Figg. Jack's gone.'

The stage waited. Figgie did not fuss. There was plenty of time still. The first full dress rehearsal for the London production, band, costumes, scenery, lighting-effects, and all, was to be at eight o'clock that evening, and now it was three: but Figgie did not fuss. Or rather, he fussed, but fussed quietly, so that it did not look like fussing. They had only to get the 'Flight of Athene' right now, and all was well: and that was a purely mechanical business. No reason for his leading lady to hang about while they got the mechanics right. He had told her not to come before two-thirty. She was late, but there—she was the leading lady, the pinnacle of the whole production. The author led him away to the side of the stalls, and complained of the way in which the comedian was speaking certain lines. Figgie listened to the author, all courtesy and attention. The stage waited.

The stage was a strange sight. It was a scenery-without-dress rehearsal, which is the strangest sight the stage has to offer. The 'set' (by Mr. Roland Burtle) was an imaginative presentation of the courtyard of the House of Ulysses in the Isle of Ithaca. From the front of the dress circle, and from high up in the top boxes, the strong sun of the Mediterranean beat down upon stately columns, palms and cypresses, upon two Greek (but anachronistic) statues, and a lovely little fountain. And the stage was peopled with a crowd of men and women in modern English dress. The day was cold, and the men walked about among the palms

in overcoats, of which the collars were turned up pro-
tectively. The young ladies of the chorus, more hardy, but
not more Homeric, were in 'practice-dress', their plump
legs naked from their 'trunks' to their ankles. Mr. Tom
Rogers, who played Ulysses, sat in front of the fountain,
surrounded by pale, chubby legs, and from time to time he
affectionately slapped a leg or two to keep them warm.
The goddess Athene, who alone was dressed for her part,
stood by the footlights with very little on, discussing with
Mr. Burtle how much more she could safely take off. Mr.
Burtle thought, quite a lot; but the goddess Athene had
respectable parents who lived in Kensington.

'Mr. Carter,' said Figgie to the producer, 'we might run
that through again, while we're waiting for Miss Moon.'

Mr. Figg was seized by his publicity expert and carried
off to the back of the pit.

Mr. Rogers rose wearily, and said, 'Where's my indecent
goddess?'

The Flight of Athene had caused much trouble. At
Manchester and Glasgow Ulysses had returned to his home
in Ithaca, according to the legend, by ship, and there had
been some attempt to be faithful to the deliberate tale of
the poet Homer—the old-man disguise, the privy plot with
Telemachus, and the old nurse Euryclea: even the affecting
episode of the wanderer's dying dog had been included.
But the play was too long and had to be cut somewhere.
The author, goaded to the verge of desperation by com-
plaints about the length of his work, had at last suggested
a drastic cut, for which, theatrically, there was much to
be said. In Homer, and at Manchester, the goddess
Athene, the particular patron of Ulysses, disturbed by the
insistent pressure of the Suitors on his wife, had met him
on the sea-shore of Ithaca, disguised as a shepherd, and
given the complicated instructions on which the rest of the
story was founded. The author's idea was to cut the cackle
and come to the Suitors. Athene was to be not less disturbed, but more practical than the goddess of the legend.
She was to descend upon the slow Phæacians' ship, pick
up Ulysses, carry him swiftly across the seas, and (herself
invisible to mortals) deposit the hero in the heart of his
domestic circle at the critical moment when the loathly

suitors Antinous and Eurymachus were about to try their strength with the great bow of Ulysses. One of them (for all the audience could tell) would be successful, and poor Penelope was in a sad state, having promised to give herself to the successful archer. Down comes a poor old beggar from the skies, seizes the bow, does the trick, disperses the Suitors with a gag or two, and turns out to be Ulysses himself.

The proposal had many merits. It was dramatic and quick: it had a flavour of pantomime which seemed to fit both the Christmas season of England and the known habits of the Homeric gods. It gave Tom Rogers an effective entrance: and, as a 'cut', it was thorough, a heroic slash and not a half-hearted nibble. On the other hand, it cut out an enormous chunk of the great Tom Rogers' part. This did not worry the author greatly, for he thought that Tom Rogers was miscast and clumsy. But it worried Mr. Figg, who had to keep his stars not only bright but twinkling: and he said at first, 'Peter Pan stuff. Too complicated.' And Henry Hake, with the sad experience of a stage-manager, said, 'No wires, for God's sake. If you'd ever had anything to do with wires——'

But Figgie thought about it and held that it was good, though Henry Hake still shook his head and muttered, 'Wires!' And when Figgie thought that a thing was good he allowed neither personal nor practical troubles to stand in the way of it. Tom Rogers was a loyal old soul, and, properly handled, would not rebel. The goddess Athene was a very attractive show-girl who would look nice flying; and, as the play stood, not nearly enough was seen of her legs.

The 'flying' expert, Mr. Flack, was engaged: a new dress was hastily designed and made for the goddess Athene, and Figgie had a satisfactory lunch with the loyal Mr. Rogers.

When the operation was first attempted it seemed impossible. The scene was brilliant with Mediterranean sun, and in that light the wire which supported a flying goddess, to say nothing of a flying beggar, would be distressingly visible to the audience against the columns and the azure sky. The lighting scheme, then, had to be altered for the flying act. That was easy. At the approach of a goddess by air there would naturally be thunder and lightning and manifestations of alarm among the mortals present. All the lights would go out while the thunder raged and the chorus excitedly rushed about and muttered 'Rhubarb!' But the arrival of the goddess, though it must be invisible to the Suitors, would lose much of its effect if it were quite invisible to the audience. There must be general darkness, punctuated with lightning, but a brilliant light upon Athene and Ulysses as they descended from the clouds (or rather the high step-ladder placed in the wings (L)). This light must shine the instant they appeared, and not an instant before; it must follow the pair of them to the ground, and it must follow Athene as she flew away. Also there must be a light upon Ulysses, dramatically deposited. But there must be seen no shadows of wires moving across the back-cloth or scenery: and there must not be so much light that the audience would perceive the business of detaching the wire from the back of Ulysses for the goddess Athene to carry away with her into the clouds.

Moreover, the goddess Athene had been engaged for her figure and not for her wits, which were less evident. Mr. Tom Rogers, in spite of his age and bulk, took to the business of flying with surprising ease and even a touch of grace. ('There's a good old trouper for you!' said Figgie with approval.) But the goddess Athene made her first descents as if she were reluctantly attached to a parachute, her legs wide apart and feebly waving, like waterweeds agitated by a vigorous current. Her silver cloud of invisibility attached itself to bits of scenery, to the weapons of the Suitors, or the beard of Ulysses. The awkwardness of her actions seemed to emphasize the inadequacy of her attire. A dog doing clumsy tricks suddenly strikes the beholder as being naked. But the goddess, though not a natural genius, was a trier, and could learn. After six or seven flights she was making a better job of it. Then, however, the lighting gave trouble. If the big front lights were used they cast a strong wire-shadow on the back of the stage; so after much argument and shouting they were eliminated. But the 'perch' lights, at the side, were difficult to direct on to the moving target, and they caused more shouting. The light would shine brightly on a group of chorus-girls while Athene and Ulysses flew down in darkness. And when at last the two were properly illuminated the flying expert also was clearly visible detaching the wire of Ulysses. Mixed up with all these difficulties was the eternal question of what and how much the goddess Athene ought to wear. In one light she would look decent, though exciting; but in another, although in fact she had more clothes on, she appeared, from the stalls, to be quite naked. From time to time she was summoned to a conference at the side of the stage with Mr. Figg and the dress-designer, and there, in full view of all, nonchalantly removed a wisp here or replaced a wisp there. The goddess Athene, who had not previously made much impression on the company, became more and more important and popular: and the principal actors, kicking their heels during these proceedings, regarded her and the management with less and less favour. Even the patient and agreeable Penelope had begun to make remarks about the goddess's intelligence: and at that point Figgie had tactfully sent Mary home.

But now the various mechanical problems seemed to have been well and truly answered: and it only remained to try the scene with the dialogue—with the band—and, most important, with Penelope. Mr. Figg and the author, sitting in the stalls, waited anxiously to see how the final trial would go. While Ulysses was still climbing his ladder in the wings, Mary walked quickly on to the stage from the other side. She put her hand under her eyes, to shade them from the footlights, and looked about the stalls for Mr. Figg. 'I'm sorry, Mr. Figg. I was kept at Rexon's about the shoes.'

'All right, my dear,' said Figgie placidly. 'We're only just ready for you.' But to the author he muttered, 'What's the matter with her? She's upset about something.'

The author said, 'It's this Athene business, I think. She was jumpy yesterday.' The author thought that the 'temperaments' of actors were excessive and ought not to be encouraged.

'No,' said Figgie, who knew more about his actors. 'Mary's not that sort. There's something up. Look at her.'

Mary was not, as usual, chatting happily to the chorus-girls, who loved her because she had so little 'side', but was

standing alone by the proscenium arch reading a long
document. She was pale and seemed restless: from time
to time she put a hand to her head: she tapped on the stage
with one little heel; she looked over her shoulder as if
somebody might be trying to read her document. But no
one was looking at her except the two men in the stalls.

'Nerves,' said Figgie. 'Have you sprung some new lines
on her, Terence?'

'No,' said the author, shortly. His 'new lines' were a
sore point.

'Then what's she studying so hard?'

'God knows!'

'All ready, Mr. Rogers?' the producer called.

'Aye, aye, sir,' said Ulysses, off.

'Places, everybody!'

Mr. Figg intervened, gentle but compelling.

'Mr. Carter, we have Miss Moon here now. Would you
like to try the whole scene through?'

'Certainly, Mr. Figg.'

'Do you mind, Mary? You know your new lines?'

'I think so, Mr. Figg.' She smiled feebly across the footlights, and her voice was dim and far away.

'Oh, dear,' muttered Figgie. 'I don't like the look of
her.'

Mr. Carter deferentially led Mary to her place and
whispered a few instructions. The greatcoats, the bare legs,
the bowler-hats and bathing-dresses, huddled together,
an incongruous crowd, round the graceful fountain. Dead
silence.

'Eurymachus!'

'Now, fair Penelope,' said Eurymachus (who was quite
bald, and wore brown boots), 'your future lord will show
you what he can do.'

Eurymachus took the bow of Ulysses. There was a
loud click from the prompt corner and all the lights went
out. Thunder and lightning followed immediately: the
crowd moved about in an agitated manner, and said 'Zeus!'
'Rhubarb!' 'Some portent!' and other things provided by
the careful author. Suddenly a bright light shone, and
two figures, perfectly lit, descended together from the left
of the stage. Unfortunately the goddess Athene descended

stern-first, and, alighting close to Penelope, displayed a lightly-clad behind to the stalls. The chorus, according to orders, were silent, and Penelope said angrily, 'Oh my God!'

There was a quiet titter among the chorus: but Mr. Figg called, 'Never mind! Go on! Go on!'

'Lighting perfect,' he muttered to the author.

The wire-work had been swiftly done: the goddess Athene rose into the air, and, this time the right way round, disappeared into the wings.

'Go on!'

The divine phenomena being done with, the Mediterranean sun blazed out again. The beggar crouched on one knee, gazing up into the eyes of Penelope. And Penelope said, 'I think, Eurymachus, that this poor Proctor could draw a bow as lustily as you.'

'*Hey, what's that?*' called the author from the stalls.

'Shut up,' whispered Figgie.

Mary covered her face with her hands, one of which still clasped the document. The company stared at her. And at that moment the goddess Athene reappeared, high up on the left, and, still suspended by her wire, swung slowly across the stage towards the fountain. Her invisible cloud was clutched in her left hand, and, as she swung, she rotated, like a corpse on a gibbet.

She reached the fountain, perched there precariously, and said, 'I'm awfully sorry, Mr. Figg. I slipped off the ladder.'

The company laughed now without restraint. But Mary, after one look at the apparition, gave a shrill, high, frightening scream, covered her face again, and burst into tears. The long grey document fell to the floor.

'My hat! Hysteria!' said Mr. Figg, and rushed for the pass-door.

When Mr. Figg reached the stage Penelope was still sobbing, attended by Euryclea and one of the chorus-girls. The unfortunate Athene had been unhitched and led away, sure that in some way she had driven the leading lady mad. The rest of the company stood about and whispered, trying to pretend that nothing unusual had happened. Mr. Figg said, 'We'll break now, Mr. Carter. Call the whole company back at seven o'clock, Mr. Hake.'

'All back at seven, please, ladies and gentlemen.'

The stage emptied quickly.

Mr. Figg strode across to Mary, red-faced, anxious and affectionate. 'What is it, my dear? We've worked you too hard.'

'No, no,' said Mary, with trembling lips. '*Look* at the filthy thing!' and with one small foot she kicked the document towards him. 'I'm awfully sorry, Figgie darling —but they served it on me as I came in.' She began to sob again.

'Take her to her dressing-room,' said Figgie. 'I'll come in a minute.'

The women led her away: and Figgie, much distressed, picked up 'the filthy thing'.

The author stood at Mr. Figg's elbow, and they read the document together:

In the High Court of Justice

PROBATE, DIVORCE AND ADMIRALTY DIVISION

(DIVORCE)

BETWEEN

<table>
<tr><td>MARY ROWENA ADAM</td><td>*Petitioner*</td></tr>
<tr><td>*and*</td><td></td></tr>
<tr><td>MERVYN JOHN ADAM</td><td>*Respondent*</td></tr>
</table>

THE KING'S PROCTOR SHOWING CAUSE

His Majesty's Procurator-General showing cause why the decree nisi pronounced in the above suit on the 9th day of December 1930 should not be made absolute, saith:

1. THAT material facts hereinafter mentioned have not been brought to the knowledge of this honourable Court.

2. THAT on the night of the 6th–7th July 1930 the Petitioner committed adultery with Martin Percival Seal of 27 Porchester Gardens Bayswater in the

County of London in a boat or vessel named the *Curlew* in the County of Kent.

3. THAT on the night of December 24–25th 1930 the Petitioner committed adultery with the said Martin Percival Seal at the Heart of England Hotel Manchester in the County Palatine of Lancaster.

4. THAT the Petitioner has frequently committed adultery with the said Martin Percival Seal.

His Majesty's Procurator-General therefore prays that the Court will rescind the decree nisi made herein and will order that the Petition be dismissed and that the Petitioner be condemned in the costs of the King's Proctor and will make such further order as the Court may think fit.

DATED this 10th day of February 1931

'That,' said Mr. Figg, 'is a nice little Valentine to give to a leading lady just before a dress rehearsal.'

Mr. Freebody read the King's Proctor's plea of intervention with a slight cloud on his face and a heavy one in his mind. This was the first case of his to be called in question by the King's Proctor or any other authority, and his professional pride was touched. Moreover, if the King's Proctor was right, it meant that his judgment was at fault: he had been deceived in, and possibly by, his client: and he had believed in Mary more firmly than in most of them. If she had let him down, the Courts might call him a rogue, but he must certainly call himself a fool.

'That's a pity,' he said at last, and looked up.

'It is,' said Mary. 'What does A do now?' She was very pale, but cool and determined.

'That depends.'

Mr. Freebody leaned back in his chair, and considered. He never liked the task of asking ladies whether they had or had not committed adultery: and even at the present crisis he preferred to approach the question indirectly.

'On what?'

Mary, equally, was not disposed to answer the question until it was put.

'On whether the charges in the King's Proctor's plea are true or not.'

'Yes, and No. Bootle, lie down!' said Mary, jumping up. 'Bootle, you're a shameless hound!'

The dog Bootle had extracted from the waste-paper basket a draft Power of Attorney and was playing football. Mr. Freebody wrote on his pad a note for his clerk—'No Dogs'. They invariably caused a disturbance at the critical moments. Now, as like as not, he would have to begin again. The dog Bootle having been reduced to immobility, he said, 'Yes, and No? Forgive me, Mrs. Adam, but I don't quite understand.'

'Yes, about the boat. No, about the hotel.'

'One has to trust this woman,' Mr. Freebody thought. 'She's so beautifully direct.' But 'Yes, about the boat'— what was this?

'Yes, about the boat,' he repeated gravely. He picked up the King's Proctor's plea, and looked for a date. 'That is the first charge—July 6th?'

'Yes.'

'And you have no answer to that?'

'No. Except that it was an accident. We were caught by the tide. We never meant——'

Mr. Freebody raised a deprecating hand, as if to say that the dramatic origins of adultery did not at the moment interest him. He spoke very slowly and kindly:

'That's not my affair, Mrs. Adam. What is troubling me a little is that you don't seem to have been quite frank with me. You will remember, when you first came to me, I said to you that I assumed that you would not yourself have to ask the Court to exercise its discretion in your favour.'

'Yes. And I had no idea what you meant.'

'What did I say then, do you remember? There are various ways of putting——'

'You asked if I had been living with anybody. And I said "No." And that was true.'

'I'm sure it was. But that was the first petition. Now, before we began the present proceedings—in, when was it, July—I think I asked you the same question?'

'All that about the discretion? Yes.'

'And your answer, again, was "No"?'

Mary nodded.

'Did you know what I meant that time?'

'Yes.'

'Oh, dear!' thought Mary. 'I'm tired of all this.'

'Well, my dear Mrs. Adam, was that quite frank,' continued Mr. Freebody with a charming smile, 'in view of what you've just admitted?'

'I wasn't living with him—I hadn't lived with any one. It was just once——'

Mr. Freebody was silent for a moment or two, looking at Mary. Mary patted her dog, but looked straight at Mr. Freebody. His smile disappeared; but he spoke at last as kindly as before.

'Mrs. Adam, if I may say so, I have a particular respect for your character and intelligence. What you have just said might be a good get-out for many people—and we may, outside these four walls, have to stick to it. But, just between yourself and me, are you quite satisfied with that answer?'

'How nice he is,' thought Mary; 'and how right about everything!'

'No,' she said with a sigh. 'I'm sorry, Mr. Freebody. But that's the foul thing—for the first time in my life I've been made to tell lies.'

'Nobody's made you tell lies,' said the lawyer gently. 'If you had taken me into your confidence we could have gone to the Court and asked for discretion. Old Hawkhurst has tightened things up in many ways, but he's made things much easier in discretion cases, where the circumstances call for it. Of course, one can never be certain, but——'

'You mean, confess everything?'

'Certainly.'

'But you don't understand. I wanted to keep Martin—Mr. Seal out of it altogether. He'd lose his job. That's why I couldn't even mention him to you.'

'What is Mr. Seal's job?'

'He's on the B.B.C.'

'Ah, yes, of course. A very virtuous Corporation. Tell me, if it's not impertinent, do you and Mr. Seal propose to marry?'

14

'Yes. . . . Down, Bootle!'

'And—again you must forgive me—does Mr. Seal put his job before you?'

'He doesn't see why he shouldn't have both. Neither do I.' Mary sighed wearily and looked down at the dog. 'It all seems such terrible nonsense.'

'Oh, dear,' thought Mr. Freebody, 'she's going to cry.'

'Well, isn't it?'

She raised her head: her voice was challenging but her eyes were wet.

'So brave,' thought Mr. Freebody, 'and yet so feminine.' She moved him: she touched his heart: but he said lightly, 'It is. I think I told you that in Scotland you would have been spared much of this trouble.'

'Don't tell me that again, *please*, Mr. Freebody,' said Mary laughing. 'What are we going to do in this part of the world?'

'One moment. Before I answer that let me be quite clear. We admit the first charge—but we deny the second, the hotel episode?'

'Absolutely.'

'And there's nothing else that we have to confess?'

'Kisses.'

'Kisses, no doubt. But kissing is not yet a criminal offence. Kisses. Affection. Indiscreet conduct. We admit all that. But to be plain, we have not committed adultery, technically, except upon the one occasion.'

'No,' said Mary, and thought, 'How sweet!'—all this delicate talk about 'we', all this protective verbiage—and Mr. Freebody's delightful mixture of legalism and colloquial humanity.

'Mrs. Adam,' her adviser said, 'I believe you entirely——'

'Thank you, Mr. Freebody.'

'And I'm not going to cross-examine you, as I should, I may tell you, most clients in such a case. But, so that I may know where we stand, tell me about the hotel, will you—just the simple story, so far as you know it. I must know, you see, what the charge is based upon.'

Mary told him all she knew, and almost enjoyed the telling. It was such a relief to tell the truth without fear.

'Well?' she said at the end.

'H'm,' said Mr. Freebody. He stood up and walked about the room. He stood before the fire for a little and looked at Mary's back. He stooped and patted the dog Bootle's head, which Bootle, being now asleep, did not value highly. Then he returned to his seat.

'Mrs. Adam,' he said, 'we have now two courses of action —no, three.'

'Yes?' said Mary. She was surprised to hear that there were so many. And how comforting that 'we' was!

'I'll take the easiest and the least attractive first. You've asked for a divorce. You've got a decree nisi. The King's Proctor says you don't deserve a divorce because he's found you out. He hasn't found you out so badly as he thinks— but still he's found you out. Now, the first thing you can do is to give in to him, admit the charges (one of them), and your petition is dismissed. That won't cause much fuss in the papers—just a paragraph or two, because you're a well-known person—but you'll still be tied to your husband, and you won't be able to marry Mr. Seal. On the other hand, it's just possible that Mr. Seal's name might be kept out of the papers—one can never be sure about that, these days, but it's possible. In that case—you won't think I'm insulting you?—the relations between yourself and Mr. Seal would be nobody's business, except your husband's. And if both of you were prepared to remain married in name but not in fact, that might be a solution. It's highly unsatisfactory, but it happens very often. Far too often.'

'My husband wants to marry,' said Mary. 'A school-teacher.'

'Oh, dear. Well, that brings us to Number Two. You abandon your petition—and the thing is begun again from the other end. Your husband files a petition against you; but, owing to the present proceedings, he will now have to ask the Court to exercise its discretion in his favour. That is, he will have to confess to the Court the acts of misconduct which he has tacitly admitted in the present suit, and ask the Court to give him a divorce in spite of them.'

'It all sounds like a parlour game,' said Mary. 'Snakes and Ladders, or something.'

'It's very like Snakes and Ladders,' said Mr. Freebody. 'The farther you get the more obstacles there are.'

Mary put her hand to her head.

'Let's think. I'm in such a muddle. In that case Mr. Seal would be the co-what-is-it?'

'Co-respondent? Not exactly. And not necessarily. You might, of course, provide yourself with a new admirer. But, if so, you would probably have to find a new solicitor as well.'

'More lies?'

'Yes.'

'And both of us would be lying then—John about his woman, and I about my man?'

'Possibly.'

'What a world! I won't do that. Besides, I don't see why John should be troubled any more. He did it this way for our sakes—for my sake, anyhow—and we've muddled it——'

'*Please!*' said Mr. Freebody, 'you mustn't say things like that to me, Mrs. Adam. That sounds painfully collusive.'

'*Please!*' said Mary, indignant. 'If you're going to talk humbug, Mr. Freebody, I shall begin to despair.'

'I know, dear lady,' said Mr. Freebody gently. 'I entirely sympathize. But those of us who are trying to do this business decently—that is, to run with the law and hunt with humanity—have a very difficult job; and you mustn't make it more difficult. We can work for a long time on what is called a decent fiction, but the moment it's allowed to become an indecent one we're done.'

'I understand,' said Mary, penitent as suddenly as she had become indignant. 'I'm sorry, Mr. Freebody. Where are we now?'

'We are hovering between Alternatives One and Two. I'm speaking now as your friend and not as your lawyer; for in Number Two I could perhaps play no part at all, and Number One would, professionally, be a bit of a blow to me (but I don't want you to think about that). There is no golden road out of your difficulty. Somebody, I fear, must suffer. You don't like Number One because it would, or might, mean the exposure of Mr. Seal, and the suffering of your husband, who wants to marry. You don't like Number Two, because you think your husband has done enough: because, again, it would mean the exposure of Mr. Seal or the taking by yourself of a temporary lover——'

'Oh God!' said Mary. 'What's Number Three?'

'Number Three? You asked me just now whether you couldn't still "ask for the discretion"—which means, couldn't you confess your wrongdoing and throw yourself on the mercy of the Court? The answer to that, to borrow your own expression, is "Yes, and No." To ask for the discretion of the Court on an original petition for relief is a very different thing from asking for discretion upon an intervention by the King's Proctor. In the first case you confess to misconduct: in the second case you confess not only to misconduct but to the deliberate deception of the Court and its officers. And that, in the eyes of the Court, is almost worse than misconduct.'

'Well, I agree with that,' said Mary. 'I do think that lying is worse than—the other thing. If they think that too——'

'Ah, but they don't take a confession of lying so well as they take a confession of adultery. In the one case you have only outraged your husband and the marriage laws, in the other you have outraged the whole system of justice —you have wasted public time and money, you have made the Court look foolish by successfully deceiving it——'

'Gosh!' said Mary. 'Have I done all that?'

'I'm just giving you the point of view of the Court, that is, the Judges. If they forgive you for deceiving them they think they may encourage others to deceive them. All the same, they sometimes do it: only there must be a very good excuse for the deceit. Where the parties are poor, ignorant, badly advised, and really don't know what they're doing, for example. But in the case of well-to-do, educated people, properly advised, the excuse has got to be very good indeed——'

'Well, can't I say that I didn't want Mr. Seal to lose his——?'

'Mr. Seal's departure from the B.B.C. will not, I fear, count for much with the Court. I can't pretend it counts for much with me, though I understand your feelings. No, what you can say is that your act of—that what you did was a single, unpremeditated act, induced by accidental circumstances and never repeated—and, that being so, you did not realize that you ought to disclose it. You did not, in short, wilfully withhold a material fact, because you did not know it was material. It will have to be made clear that your solicitor put certain questions to you, but your answer is that you thought he meant a definitely guilty association—to use your own words, "living with" somebody. But you are anxious now to tell the whole truth, and you are doing so. It's pretty thin, but——' Mr. Freebody paused. The dog Bootle woke up and yawned with a plaintive sound.

"All this, however, is assuming that you can persuade the Court that you are speaking the truth now. If the Court concludes that you not only deceived them before the decree was granted but have been deliberately committing misconduct ever since, you haven't a dog's chance: and you have to face the possibility that, having admitted the first charge, you won't be able to repel the second. As to that, it's hard to say, and I should like to have counsel's opinion before I did say. It looks bad, in a way. They've all the right foundations—long association, proved affection, and the opportunity. But the superstructure's weak. The Court is never keen on "paid watcher's" evidence, and generally requires some corroboration: which, in this case, I don't suppose there is. You don't know of any one who would have been snooping about after you and Mr. Seal that night?'

'Not a soul. Neither of us saw anybody. Only that man at the station, and in the lift.'

'H'm. Yes. Well, I wouldn't say this to every woman, Mrs. Adam, but I believe that you might get away with it. You're a good witness, you've made me believe you, and there's no reason why you shouldn't have the same effect upon a Judge. Only, mind, this is not a thing that the best lawyer in the world can bet about. You're not going to ask the Judge to give you something you've a right to have: you're going to ask him to exercise his discretion in your favour: that means, in law, he can do as he pleases, and it means, in fact, that he may do as his liver pleases that morning. A thousand and one accidents may upset him— the state of the weather—something you say in the box; he may take a particular dislike to your counsel, or he may decide that morning that it's time he made another example in your kind of case. You've got to grovel to get the discretion, and even if you do grovel it's still a gamble. Apart from that, it won't be fun. Fierce cross-examinations. More publicity. Forgive this lecture, Mrs. Adam, but I want you to be quite clear.'

'Have I got it right?' said Mary slowly, as if she were fumbling with her words at an early rehearsal. 'Number One means surrender—a bit of a stink in the papers—and nobody any better off. Number Two means lying all round —and perhaps parting with you, Mr. Freebody. It might be better for Mr. Seal, but it would be worse for my husband?'

'In many ways, yes.'

'And Number Three means telling the truth, fighting the thing, and taking a sporting chance?'

'And no escape for Mr. Seal,' said Mr. Freebody quietly. 'Yes. I see.'

Mary was silent for no more than five seconds. She looked at the dog, she looked at Mr. Freebody, and decided swiftly.

'Well, I say Number Three,' she said. 'Face it and fight it. What do you say?'

Mr. Freebody stood up and held out his hand. 'I agree. And, if I may say so, I think you're a fine person.'

He had not for a long time been moved so deeply at a professional interview. He had not thought that a blonde could have so much stuff in her. The urge to battle was in him too. His first thought was for his client always: but, if he could advise a fight with a good conscience, he enjoyed a fight. Thus the good fox-hunter, anxious to kill the fox for the farmer's sake, prefers a long run to a short one. The King's Proctor gave a particular glow to the thought of this fight. That official's first intervention in a Freebody case was no trifling matter, and the more he thought of it the more he resented it. To have to surrender to him would have been galling to Mr. Freebody and perhaps damaging to his firm: and to fight him and win would be a fine feather in its cap. With a sound case, a popular actress, and a good witness, it might be done.

He found suddenly that he was still holding Mary's hand, still looking with admiration into those brave grey eyes.

'Good luck to you, Mrs. Adam,' he said.

The dog Bootle barked, as if to say, 'Come off it!'

Mary went home, feeling very strong, clear-headed, and determined. She did not care a damn for their laws and their Courts, their King's Proctor and all the King's men. It was a monstrous castle of bricks and nonsense, and she was going to defy it and knock it down. This mood carried her triumphantly through the final dress rehearsal, which was as smooth as old brandy and as sparkling as champagne. Mary was the principal bubble, the essential spirit of the evening. There was a considerable audience—friends, relatives, and a critic or two—and she delighted them. She delighted Figgie too, and dismissed all his fears. He could not remember such a dress rehearsal. Even Henry Hake could not cast him down, gloomily reminding him that a good dress rehearsal meant a bad first night.

'Too good,' said Henry Hake.

'Too good?' said Figgie. 'Too good be damned!' And he hurried away to kiss Mary.

Figgie took her to supper at the Savoy with Mrs. Figg, a motherly person, devoted to her husband and every one who helped him. Delighted that all seemed to be well with Mary, she incautiously mentioned 'the horrid lawyers'. Figgie frowned. This was the last subject he would have mentioned that evening. But Mary was glad to relieve her mind and tell them about her endless interview with Mr. Freebody and the coming battle with the King's Proctor.

Mrs. Figg applauded Mary's valour, and patted her hand, sure that the battle was won already. But Figgie sat silent and serious. He knew little of the law but much of life, and he did not like the sound of this affair. He could not imagine himself as a member of a jury, being persuaded that Mr. Seal had been content to tuck Mary up in room 218 on Christmas Eve—though he could not see that it mattered, one way or the other. Presently his wife was greeted by some one at the next table: and while they talked Figgie said quietly: 'Mary, if there's anything I can do— you'll let me do it, won't you?'

'Thank you darling—but I don't think there is.'

'But, Mary, what about the Christmas Eve affair? I was about, you know: I was with you two all the evening. Why shouldn't I have been in your room as well as Martin?'

'But, darling, I don't need *two* co-respondents!'

'No, don't you see—we were all together—a sort of late party in your room—talking about the play?'

Mary stared at her manager, amazed.

'Figgie, would you do that for me? You sweet old thing!'

'Of course I would. Or anything else.'

'Commit perjury?'

'I shouldn't call it perjury—about a damn silly thing like this.'

'The lawyers would, if they found out. No, Figgie, you don't understand. The whole point is that I don't want there to be any more lying at all. "The truth, the whole truth", and all that. And if they don't like it they can do the other thing. All the same, Figgie, I think you're very, very sweet, and I'm very, very grateful.'

Oblivious of the crowd, she bent her head and kissed the side of Mr. Figg's white head.

'All right, my dear,' he said. 'But don't forget. You may change your mind.'

Mrs. Figg's conversation was over: and she turned in time to see the chaste salute.

'Only a gesture, Olive, dear,' said Mary.

'What's it all about?' said comfortable Mrs. Figg.

'I had a plan to get myself a little publicity,' said Figgie. 'But Mary's jumped on it. However, to be kissed in public is worth almost as much.'

The same valiant mood accompanied Mary into bed and to sleep. She lay in bed, tired but happy—happy about the rehearsal and Figgie's kindness and her resolution to tell the truth: and before she turned out the light she defied the King's Proctor and all his lawyers again. She saw herself in 'the box' at the end of a two days' cross-examination, pale but undefeated, still shattering some great K.C. with answers of high nobility and unusual cleverness. Crowds

waited in the street to hear the news of her victory. She
was 'splashed' in the newspapers as a sort of modern St.
Joan—the Woman who Dared to Tell the Truth. But to-
morrow was the first night, and she must sleep. She patted
the dog and turned out the light. But still, half asleep, the
Divorce Court, not the play, filled her mind. She invented
outrageous questions for the K.C. and blew them to pieces
with her sharp retorts. The Court 'rocked with laughter'
—and Mary fell asleep.

She woke at four o'clock. The dog had crept up under
the eiderdown and laid his wet nose on her neck. But that
was his normal behaviour. Something else had wakened
her, oppressive and menacing. She had a first night to-
night, but it was not that. The first night would be
alarming, but exciting and successful. 'All right on the
night,' she murmured drowsily. Then she remembered
suddenly and was afraid. She had challenged the law, she
had undertaken to defy the King's Proctor. She stared
into the darkness and saw herself in the box again. But
now she was not the triumphant St. Joan. She was a feeble
creature, frightened and ashamed. The lawyers shot the
same questions at her, but she had no clever retorts for
them. She could not endure the darkness and turned on
the light. Four o'clock. The dog blinked and crept back
under the eiderdown. Four o'clock—the terrible hour: the
silent hour when the sleepless are alone with their doubts
and troubles, when conscience bullies and courage fails.
Mary stared at the wall-paper and tried to think of the
play. She muttered in her mind the words of her songs.
She began to make up a little speech of thanks to the
clamorous first-night audience. She stepped down shyly
towards the footlights and said, 'Ladies and Gentlemen,
your wonderful reception . . .' But all the time she was
in that dreadful 'box', perched up like a chained parrot,
high above the gaping crowd, alone and defenceless, stared
at and stuttering. Nobody believed her: and what was
believed was shameful. The Judge would speak of her as
he had spoken of poor Margaret: 'The woman Moon . . .'
She felt cold in the stomach and hot in the head. What a

fool she had been! Why go and tell that lawyer everything?
She could have brazened it out, denied everything, and
played the injured innocent. It was too late for that now.
And there was Martin. Poor Martin! He did not know yet
what had happened; what she had decided and what was
before him. That was another job for this full, terrible
day—to tell Martin. Wasn't it enough to have the agonies
of a first night without so much other trouble? And a
sleepless night on top of all. Five o'clock. If she could
only sleep! She opened the small cupboard by her bed and
swallowed an aspirin tablet. Her head ached. It might
be better to get up, but she must try to sleep because of
the play. And the thought of Martin, which should have
been consoling, worried her now. How would Martin take
the news? He would be upset, she knew, because of his
job. He was so devoted to his silly old Wireless. But
would he be unpleasantly upset? Would he be angry with
her? Did he, in short, love her well enough to be nice about
it? She was not sure—a sad confession, but she was not
sure. Six o'clock. Her head would burst. Yes, that would
be the last straw, if she and Martin were to quarrel about
this. To-night, probably, that fool of a girl would bungle
the flying business and the play would be a flop. But what
a fool she had been herself to go to the lawyer without
consulting Martin first! She had not intended to tell Freebody everything, but her fatal habit of truth-telling had
been too strong for her. What a fool! It was all very well
to be high and mighty about telling the truth—but one
ought to think what it would mean to others. Poor Martin.
If he was angry she would deserve it. And poor John.
How would he feel when he heard the news? More scandal
and newspaper stuff. And perhaps no divorce at the end
of it. It was one thing to tell the truth, it was another to
make people believe it. Perhaps, after a terrible trial, she
would not get the discretion, or whatever it was. A nice
hole they would be in then. Martin sacked, and nobody
able to marry anybody. There was another milkman.
Half past six. What was this? Mary put her hand to her
neck. Wet. Sweating—with funk. Mr. Freebody's brave
girl. Ha! Who wouldn't sweat with so much to worry her?
For it was all her fault. She should never have let poor

John behave like a gentleman—never have sent those silly telegrams. What a fool! She would deserve whatever came to her. But then, she had no idea it was all so serious and difficult. Everybody had said it was easy. What a fool! What laws! When would the case come on? Anyhow, she was glad she had said 'No' to Number Two. That would have been too much—to make poor John start all over again. And go off herself with a strange professional 'co'. But now she had sacrificed Martin instead. Well, that was right, perhaps. He was the wrongdoer, really, not John. If anybody was. But she could not see that any one had done any wrong. They were all like so many mice, trapped in the cruel laws. Seven o'clock. Half-past seven. And still the tired brain ran round and round the cage, and buffeted itself against the bars. It was light now. She would get up, first night or no. She looked in the glass. 'My God,' said Mary, 'I look fifty and feel a hundred.'

'Hullo.'

'Martin?'

'Hullo, dear.'

Mr. Seal was surprised. Since Mary's return they had spoken once only, and then only to arrange not to meet again.

'I must see you.'

'But I thought you said——'

'Something's happened.'

The voice was urgent, and Mr. Seal was disturbed.

'What?' he said.

'Something awful. I can't tell you now.'

More and more disturbing—Mary being cautious on the telephone.

'All right,' he said. 'Lunch-time?'

'If you like. Where?'

'Where is there?'

'I don't know.'

'Not the Savoy.'

'No.'

'Well, where then?'

'Wait. Let's think.'

There was silence, while they tried to think of some place in which two persons about to marry could safely take the midday meal.

Mary said, 'Isn't there some quiet place in Soho?'

'At those quiet places you meet everybody you know.'

'I know.'

'I don't know. Where do you think?'

'What an imbecile conversation!' thought Mary.

'I know,' she said at last. 'The theatre. In the stalls.'

'What?'

'There's no call this morning, and there'll be nobody about, much. Go straight through the foyer as if you owned the place. If anybody notices they'll think you're Press or the author or something. But they won't.'

'Is that all right?' asked Mr. Seal, dubiously.

'Sit down in the back of the stalls. I'll come through the stage way.'

'All right, dear. What time?'

'Quarter to one?'

'Right.'

'Good-bye.'

'Come Bootle. Leave the nice policeman alone.'

The policeman, Mary thought, looked sharply at her as she left her house. Bootle, too, seemed to think that he was suspect, and he barked. Probably the Chief Constable had her name on his decree-nisi list. But she smiled at the policeman, and the policeman smiled back, and, marching away, she thought, 'Who cares?' Everything was open and above board now, and she had nothing to conceal (except, of course, this meeting with Martin). She felt better now, in her mind, though her eyes and body were tired and her head foggy. She was ashamed of the terrors of the night. In the brave daylight, after breakfast and a long bath, she knew that her decision was right. Fear nothing and tell the truth. And now, at least, she was going to see her Martin again. Secretly, as if they were burglars—but still—— Poor Martin. He would be in a state. How she hoped that he would be nice. Though, if he was not, she could not blame him. Dear Martin. She longed to see him: and yet she was afraid. But that was against the rule. Fear nothing.

Martin Seal walked to the Underground with a heavy heart; and before he turned each corner he glanced behind him to see if there was any sleuthlike person on his track. Not that it mattered much now, he supposed, if there was. He had little doubt what Mary's news would be. The worst had happened. Since Christmas he had hoped faintly, but increasingly, for the best. Twice, late at night, he had seen the burly gentleman in the bowler-hat: the porter at the flats, he noticed, took a new interest in his movements, and, if Martin went away to the country, would innocently inquire about his destination. But this might be a favourable sign. If they were still spying it might mean that they had not yet enough evidence to act upon; and now they never would, for till Mary was free they were going to be not only good but careful. Poor Mary! She had always wanted to be good, and he, if any one, was to blame for everything. What a fool he had been to go up to Manchester! And yet, was that so very wrong? He truly loved Mary, had hardly looked at any other woman, and meant to marry her. And it was not as if he were stealing her away from a devoted husband. He had harmed nobody and thought no harm. This terrible offence, for which he was being pursued by the forces of the law, was, after all, a mere technicality, not driving dangerously, but driving without a licence. Yet for this he might lose his job—his career. It seemed hard, sighed Mr. Seal. Well, it was his own fault. He knew the laws and customs of the land: and when Mary had tried to keep him off he had pestered her still. Poor Mary. It was worse for her. Her first night to-night, and now this trouble. Poor Mary. She could say, 'I told you so,' now, with a vengeance. She might be furious with him. Not like her, but she might be. He hoped not. Dear Mary.

Mr. Seal took a seat near the back of the dusky stalls. The curtain was up, Penelope's Bed-chamber was set, and two electricians in shirt-sleeves stood by Penelope's bed, busy with flex and fuses. There was an air of hushed activity in the theatre, as in a camp on the eve of battle, when the troops are at rest after the fever of drilling and preparation, and only the despised staff and supply-services are still at work. Two charwomen swept and panted at the side of the stalls, speaking to each other in cautious whispers. Henry Hake sat in the front row, huddled up in a greatcoat and staring at the stage. He had got rid of managers and producers and actors at last, and was smoothly rehearsing his own department, the changes of scene and lighting. From time to time he gave a quiet order to an invisible person called Joe about Batten Number One, about a border or a perch, a flat or the floats; and from some unseen height a subdued voice answered respectfully in terms unintelligible to Mr. Seal.

Mr. Seal had not before seen the intimate mysteries of the theatre in operation: and, though on principle he thought that all forms of entertainment and instruction, when set beside the B.B.C., were as the toys of children or the bladders of fools, he was impressed. There was present, he felt, the same unobtrusive, compelling efficiency which worked the wheels of his own Corporation. All who saw the work of the unsmiling, unbending, unerring Mr. Hake were impressed in a like manner: but, like Mr. Seal, they did not always give the credit to Mr. Hake. Mr. Seal thought proudly that it was the power and spirit of his Mary which inspired the place. To-night, upon that stage, she would be the Queen: and here in the stalls, where now he sat alone with the charwomen, the wealth and intellect of London would sit enthralled and render homage. He, Martin, would not be among them: he would be at Savoy Hill reading the News and the Fat Stock Prices; announcing the programme of the Pitts-Arundell Quartet, perhaps for the last time. Yet the Queen of this theatre, the Queen of to-night, was his promised lady and no other man's: and that was a proud thought. In a theatre all men think in the way of the theatre: and Mr. Seal, sitting there alone, was a bolder person than he had been on the Underground, clinging to a strap in a smoking-compartment. His love for Mary swelled up and filled him: and he said to himself that for such a woman no sacrifice was too severe.

At that moment Mary walked quickly across the stage, bound for the pass-door. She might have slipped round behind the scenery, but she knew that Mr. Hake would see her, sooner or later, and thought it best to show herself openly.

She halted and looked at Penelope's Bed: the chief electrician looked up and said, 'Good morning, miss. Good luck to-night, miss.'

The invisible Joe, an old ally, called down, 'Going to knock 'em to-night, Miss Moon?'

'You bet, Joe.'

'That's right. Mind your head, miss. There's a batten coming down.'

Mr. Hake did not wish her good luck, for he never wasted words on the obvious: but he said, 'Morning, Mary. How d'you feel?'

'Fine, Henry, thank you.'

'Then clear the stage,' said Mr. Hake. 'We're busy.'

She blew him a kiss and disappeared. Henry Hake thought, 'My God, she looks like death.'

These exchanges thrilled Mr. Seal, for they supported his Queen theory: but he too thought, 'How tired she looks.'

Then she came to him, tripping up the centre gangway, without a sound, like a dancing ghost. He took her hand and they gazed at each other. It was so long since they had seen each other and held hands and kissed: and they were so glad that both almost forgot the reason they had met; forgot that they were suspect persons meeting against the law. And Mary took a look at the back of Henry Hake, and another at the busy charwomen: and, reckless creature, she kissed Martin quickly, and then they sat down.

At first they could talk nothing but foolishness.

'How are you, darling?'

'How are *you*?'

'You look fine.'

'You look tired, darling—but very sweet.'

'Do I? I had a terrible night. And you?'

'I'm all right. But you? You mustn't have terrible nights.'

'Never mind. How's your old Wireless?'

(Always she teased him by calling his British Broadcasting Corporation 'the old Wireless'.)

'All right, funny one. How's the play?'

'All right, I think. We've put some flying in. It's fun.'

'I wish I was coming.'

'I wish you were, darling. Will you think of me?'

'I will, Mary.'

'Will you send me a telegram?'

'Two. And one little flower.'

'Pig! Only one?'

They were suddenly silent.

'It seems years since I saw you, Mary.'

'It is years, Martin.'

She sighed, and took his hand.

'This won't do, Martin. We must talk. Listen. . . . Oh, dear!'

She was silent again, and gazed at the stage, where Batten Number One was now slowly ascending behind a border of vine-leaves.

'Go on, darling.'

'Listen, Martin. It's happened. I've had an awful *thing* from the King's Proctor. Haven't *you* had one?'

'No. But I guessed it was that.'

In the dim light she looked at him, wondering. He seemed so calm. But he had not yet heard her dreadful confession.

'It came the day before yesterday. Perhaps I ought to have told you—but I didn't know what to do. Anyhow, I've been to Freebody's, and—Martin, I expect you'll be cross with me—do you know what I've done?'

'No, darling. Go on.'

Still he gripped her hand strongly, and seemed to be quite without anxiety.

'Well, darling, I've said we'll fight it.'

'Fight what?'

'The *thing*. The King's Proctor.'

'All right. What does that mean?'

'Well, it means there's a frightful *case*—and I have to ask for the *discretion* or something—and then perhaps I may get my divorce after all. Only I have to grovel and confess everything—I mean about keeping things dark, and

15

sleeping with you on the boat—it's all terribly complex, but the lawyer thinks that that's the best way.'

'I see,' said Martin, studying her earnest face. What had they done to his laughing lady?

'Yes, darling, but do you?' she went on anxiously. 'I'm afraid it means that you'll be in the soup too, Martin. It will all come out—you may have to give evidence, the lawyer says—and then what will your old Wireless say?'

'*Imshi!*' he said, smiling. 'Which, being interpreted, means "Bunk!"'

She stared at him, amazed and delighted by his coolness. 'But, darling, are you sure you don't *mind*?'

Martin said quietly, taking both her hands now, 'Whatever you think is right, Mary, I'm with you.'

Now, at last, she was persuaded—and overjoyed; and she burst out, 'Oh, Martin, you are a nice person. I'm so glad you're so nice!'

What feeble words to express so much! She wanted to kiss him, to jump up and sing, to dance down the gangway and shout in Henry's ear that her lover was the finest fellow in the world!

'I'm not, Mary. I've caused all the trouble.'

'No, you haven't. It's the silly laws. Why *should* they chase us about like this?'

Still, it was warming to hear Martin taking the blame. Perhaps they would admit now, Figgie and Henry Hake, and Alice Merridew, and all of them, that her Martin was a fine fellow. She knew very well what most of them thought about him—that he was not good enough for her; one of those good-looking but feeble boys of the B.B.C., too much of the feminine in him, no guts. Now they would see that he had as much guts as any of them—unsuspected depths of character—as soon as the test came. It was easy enough to make that mistake when a man had nice manners and a gentle voice, and did not go about with a red face proclaiming to the world that he was a great big hearty he and did not care a damn for any one. She had nearly made the same mistake herself, and she was penitent.

'Never mind, Mary. I'll get another job. Writing plays for you, perhaps.'

'Darling, I wish you could.'

'But we'll go away somewhere first, when all this is over. I've saved some money.'

'Where shall we go, darling?'

'Anywhere. Ceylon.'

They sat and whispered, sweet electric nonsense, very straight in their seats now, for Henry Hake, saturnine and weary, was on the stage, giving orders to the lighting staff and facing the stalls.

'I wish we were in the *Curlew*, Mary.'

'I wish we were, Martin. . . . Oh, dear.'

It was hard to think of the *Curlew* and not to be able to take her in his arms.

'I'd better go, Martin. I must try to sleep this afternoon. I think I shall now—now I've seen you.'

'Do, darling. Shall we go?'

'Better not together, p'r'aps. And Bootle's at the stage door. I'll go that way.'

It was hard to think of the *Curlew* and have to slink away by different doors. And yet, she thought, remote and respectable in this public place, they were nearer than they had been in the *Curlew*, nearer than they had ever been.

'Oh, dear,' she sighed.

'Don't be sad, Mary. All's well.'

'That was a happy one. Martin?'

'Yes?'

'I'm happy, Martin. I love you.'

'And I love you.'

She looked about her. The charwomen had departed. Henry Hake had turned his back and was talking about battens to the invisible Joe.

'Kiss me, darling,' said Mary. 'It's mad, but kiss me.'

They kissed.

'One more. We mustn't meet again till it's over.'

'Good-bye, my love. Good luck.'

Mr. Rigby, peering through the glass panel at the back of the stalls, put his note-book in his pocket. It was time, he saw, to go.

But Mary did not sleep that afternoon. She went home uplifted, fixed in resolution, glowing with pride,

understanding at last, she thought, the meaning of love.
And she found in the Wedgwood bowl a letter from her
father. Goodness, a long, long letter! Poor old thing: she
had not seen him for months—

THE RECTORY
CHATHAM PARVA

MY DEAR MARY,

'I hope you are well and wish that I saw more of
you. I see that you are returned from the North, and
had hoped that you might, perhaps, run down here for
a night or two while you are resting.'

'Resting!' Mary thought. Poor darling—if he only
knew! But heavens—he *did* know! What was all this?
'I have been worried about you. . . . Mrs. Partridge . . .
staying in Sussex . . . gossip about you . . .' It was one
of those letters so evidently dreadful that the mind cannot
endure to take the words in carefully at the first reading.
Mary's eye leaped swiftly down the pages, collecting only
the general sense. 'I think the name was Simpson.' Verena!
Verena Simmons was going round the country telling tales,
and now the tales had reached the Rectory. Cruel! 'I do
not, of course, believe any part of what I was told, but it
has upset me, and I think you ought to know what is being
said. . . .' Poor darling. And now he was back at the
old texts again—'Whom God hath joined . . .' But God
didn't join us, Daddy! . . . 'Cleave unto one woman . . .'
Oh, dear, oh, dear! Miles and miles of it. But the writing
was shaky towards the end. He was old and tired. . . .
'I find that my work in the garden takes it out of me more
than it did—the stooping . . .' Poor old thing—he would
never roll the croquet-lawn again. She must go down and
see him on Sunday. No, that might be fatal, for she would
have to tell him the truth. Better perhaps to write first,
and try to *make* him understand. Then, if he never wanted
to see her again, he need not. Poor old thing! But why
should any one be allowed to lay down the law for other
people's lives . . . because of a few old texts two thousand
years behind the times? Christ, she was sure, would never
have done that: the Bible wasn't a law-book; but her father
talked as if it was an Act of Parliament. Oh, dear!

Now she must rest. All the life had gone out of her again. Verena Simmons! The Christian!

She lay down. But at once in her mind she began to write that long letter to her father, true but tactful, keeping nothing back but *making* him understand.

She must do it now. She left her bed and began.

At six o'clock she tore up many pages and began again.

At seven o'clock, in the dressing-room, Florrie said, 'What's the matter now? We look like a ghost.'

Mr. Figg, making a little tour of the principals' dressing-rooms before the curtain rose, came to the star's room, and knocked and called his name with caution. This was always a moment at which to approach leading ladies with caution. Sometimes they were weak with nerves, and threatening to be sick, sometimes (but rarely) confident and cool, sometimes overflowing with sentiment and kisses, sometimes in a violent rage—somebody had not sent them flowers, the new shoes did not fit, or the last-minute hat was quite impossible. None of these moods was Mary's now. She was lifeless—the worst and rarest mood of all. 'Come in,' she said in a flat voice, and showed him a blank face: no excitement, interest, nervousness, temper—nothing.

'Are you rested, dear?' said Figgie.

'No, Figgie.'

'We're played out,' said Florrie.

'Figgie, do you think that's a good letter?'

Figgie, wondering, took the numerous sheets and raced through them as Mary had raced through her father's letter. What in heaven's name was all this? . . . 'St. Matthew . . . St. Mark . . . Dean Inge. . . . Since all this began, darling, I've read the Royal Commission. . . .' Had the poor girl gone mad? . . . 'quite clear that Christ never meant to lay down *laws*, only *ideals* and principles, or as Dean Inge said, "A counsel of perfection" . . . John and I did try hard to stick . . . but it couldn't be done . . . everything else the law has driven us to . . . and really, darling . . . if the law's bad . . . dear old people like you . . . *rather* responsible, darling. But don't think . . .'

'Overture and beginners, please!' sang the callboy.

Figgie put the strange screed down among the greasepots and hare's-foot and eye-black and small discoloured face-towels.

'I must go. Put it out of your mind, dear,' he said earnestly. 'I'm sorry. . . . Lunch with me to-morrow and we'll have a talk. But forget it now, if you can. So much —so many people, depend upon you, dear. Good luck—and thank you.'

He kissed the top of her head and went out, almost for the first time completely beaten by a situation. He could have calmed nerves, placated temper, prescribed for sickness: but a leading lady exhausted with legal worries and agitated by the meaning of St. Mark x.—this was beyond his powers.

He went to his box and said to Mrs. Figg, 'We're done. Mary's down and out. They're driving the poor girl mad.'

Not a 'flop', but a disappointment. 'Three months,' the knowing critics said. They were puzzled to account for their disappointment. 'Signs of under-rehearsal,' said one or two of the less intelligent, though that was never a charge to be laid against a Figg production. Most of them took the easy course and blamed the author. 'Lifeless dialogue.' . . . 'Mary Moon worked hard and loyally at an unconvincing part.' . . . 'Not all Miss Moon's arts and graces could overcome . . .'

'Bad luck, Terence,' said Figgie. 'But never mind. We'll be all right when we get our Mary back'—though he was not too sure of that. 'She played like a dead woman.' 'She was, poor thing.'

She acted like a cold machine—like an engine with only one cylinder firing. Half of her mind was muttering all the evening, 'He'll die. . . . Whom God hath joined . . . It isn't *fair*.'

The frozen mood of the star affected the whole company. The Flight of Athene went wrong. The scanty trappings of the goddess caught in a buckle on the shoulder of Eurymachus and could not be released. There was a struggle, a loud tear, and Athene ascended into Heaven, nearly naked.

As this scene approached Mary had become obsessed with the fear that she would say something awful, as she had at the dress rehearsal—a fascinating fear familiar to the actor. Over and over she repeated her correct line, till it must, surely, be fixed in her mind. But at the loud disrobing of the goddess the line fled from her again. She stared at the beggar, wondering what in the world she had to say to him. Nothing, nothing was in her mind except the words, 'If a woman shall put away her husband and be married to another she committeth adultery.' The prompter spoke, but she did not hear: and he had to speak three times. That episode, perhaps, was 'Penelope's' last straw. Figgie, by that time, was resigned to gloom. 'That old clergyman,' he muttered mildly, 'is going to cost us twenty thousand pounds.'

'MY DEAR MARY,
'Thank you for your long letter. Your news has grieved me deeply, as you feared, though it is better to have had it from you than from the newspapers, and I can be glad of your honesty, at least. But it grieves me most, my dear daughter, to know that there is still, in thought, so great a gulf between us, a gulf which not even the Word of God can bridge. While this is so, I think it better that we should not meet. I should dearly love to see you, and I am grateful to you for saying that you will come down: but the gulf, I fear—— But there, I am too old and tired for disputation and will say no more. I do not condemn you, my dear, for anything that you have done; but I pray that God may bring you to a better understanding.
'Your loving Father'

'Oh, dear,' said Mary—the whimper of a hurt dog. She was so miserable that she could not even cry.

'Up to the intervention of the King's Proctor,' said Mr. Freebody, 'the whole costs will fall on your husband. They're not substantial, and we may expect to get them.

We may possibly be allowed some of the costs of the
King's Proctor's intervention, assuming we succeed. But
that is uncertain, and the proceedings may be expensive.
We ought, I think, to take in a leader——'

'What's that?'

'A silk. A K.C.'

'Oh, yes.'

'And probably the other side will do the same. If we
win we're all right. Meanwhile, if you don't mind——'

'All right, Mr. Freebody. I'll send you a cheque.'

'I want you to be clear, Mr. Seal,' said Mr. Freebody.
'You are not bound to give evidence in these proceedings
at all. If you appear it will be as a witness called by Mrs.
Adam. We could, of course, subpœna you: but I understand that Mrs. Adam would not wish to do that. And, if
you do appear, you are not bound to answer any questions
tending to show that you have been guilty of adultery.
Mrs. Adam will already have confessed that she has committed adultery with you: but that does not decide that you
have committed adultery with her. Indeed, there have
been cases in which the Court has found that a respondent
wife has committed adultery with the co-respondent, but
not that the co-respondent has committed adultery with
the respondent. The law is a little strange, but——'

'You surprise me,' said Mr. Seal. 'But don't worry, Mr.
Freebody. Go ahead. I shall be there.'

Mr. Seal sat in a little cabinet in the corner of the big
studio listening to a comic opera about eighteenth-century
life. The orchestra was in full blast. Five singers stood
on the small platform, singing a loud quintet with dainty
words about Love and the Spring, smiling archly at the
microphone and glancing anxiously at the conductor.
Beyond them stood the chorus, in two compact bodies,
divided carefully by sexes. Mr. Seal watched them through
the glass side of his cabinet and thought suddenly, as
perhaps the fish thinks, peering out from his tank, 'What
fools they all look!' Still, it was sad to think that this was

his last night. He had resigned, mysteriously, giving no reason but a vague inclination towards literary work. He was not going to wait for the sack. Still, it was sad. His chiefs had been surprised, disappointed, kind: but his successor was already named. Nobody was indispensable to the vast machine. And to-night, for the last time, he would say 'Good night' to the world. Sad. But still, it was a silly job—he saw that now. Nothing vital or creative in it—a mere transmitter—little better than a telephone instrument—much less important than the microphone. Sad, all the same—to have to go for such a reason. The quintet was coming to an end, and the chorus, with expressions like over-worked post office assistants at Christmas time, were chanting merrily, in six parts:

> All the world loves a lover!
> In the merry spring
> When Love's on the wing
> All the pretty birds sing,
> For we all love a lover.

'All the world loves a lover.' Does it? thought Mr. Seal. Does it love, for example, a man charged in the plea of His Majesty's Proctor showing cause why the decree nisi——

But the quintet was over, and he must explain to the puzzled world the present situation in the complicated comedy.

'Miranda, the Duchess's maid,' he told the world, with that persuasive purr which seemed to say, 'Believe me, if you will only listen you really will enjoy this.' 'Miranda, the Duchess's maid, afraid that her little plot is on the verge of detection, decides to make a clean breast of it to the Duke. Hearing from Ferdinand of the Duke's assignation with the lovely Isobel, she goes to the arbour at the appointed hour, and believing the masked Lorenzo to be the Duke . . .'

The Finale began. 'All the world loves a lover.' 'What bilge!' thought Mr. Seal. He would like to tell the world what he thought of it to-night—just before he said his last 'Good night'. 'That concludes our operetta "Love and Laughter",' he would say, 'and I hope you enjoyed it, you sponge-faced humbugs—especially the theme-song "All the world loves a lover". Well, I'm a lover, and I'm losing my job because of it. *That's* how much the world loves a lover. If I hadn't resigned I should have got the chuck. Some of you would think that it was right for me to go: a few of you would write shocked letters if I didn't go: not one of you would dare to write and say that I ought to stay—though most of you would think so. Because those of you who are not sponge-faced humbugs are afraid to say "Boo!" to the sponge-faced humbugs. I've done no harm to any one: but I'm a lover, and I've been unlucky. And this makes me unfit to read out the Fat Stock Prices. I can't tell you why, but there it is. All the world loves a lover and Joy's on the wing. By the way, I'd like to tell you something about the young gentleman who's getting my job. You'll like him: and I'm quite sure that he'll never appear in the Divorce Court: but of the two of us I shouldn't mind betting that I'm the better man. However, all the world loves the King's Proctor. Good-bye, everybody. *Good*-bye.'

The Finale was over.

'That was the end of the operetta "Love and Laughter",' said Mr. Seal, silkily. 'And that concludes our entertainment for to-night. Good night, everybody! *Good* night.'

Almost the only thing, Mary thought, that she had not experienced was a Consultation with Counsel. It was a 'Consultation', Mr. Freebody said, if it was with a K.C. and a 'Conference' if Counsel was only a junior—a delicious distinction. Now in the taxi, whirling down to the Temple, Mr. Freebody hurriedly explained to her what it was all about. It appeared that the barristers were engaged in the preliminary skirmishes called 'pleadings', and the King's Proctor had asked for 'particulars'.

'By your Answer,' said Mr. Freebody, 'which was drafted by Counsel, you admitted an isolated act of adultery and prayed for the discretion of the Court. The King's Proctor has now asked for what are called 'particulars' of the facts relied on in support of your prayer for the favourable exercise of the discretion. And Barter wants to see you before he settles. The question is, you see, how much to say. Here we are!'

    .   .   .   .   .

Mr. Freebody had decided that it would be best to 'take in' a leader, and they 'took in' Mr. Timothy Barter, K.C., M.P. Mr. Barter was forty-two, one of the five most able advocates of his generation, and one of the two most successful. He had an expansive general practice, but had done much work in the Divorce Court. He was Irish and fearless, and, though a reputed Tory, directed most of his speeches in Parliament to criticizing the Tory leaders. In Court he had had his biggest triumphs with his worst cases. He seemed to thrive on a hopeless cause: no one could advance with such an air of candour and inevitability a bold, and, at first sight, impossible argument. He was a brilliant, and an economical, cross-examiner. Mary had murmured that she had met him once and rather liked him. The choice seemed a good one.

Mr. Barter, as a rule, did not meet his lay clients at this early stage in the proceedings: but the case seemed difficult, and his client, from the solicitor's account, unusual: and he wanted to judge for himself whether she had the stuff in her to carry a bold case through. At Manchester she had said little, and he had formed only a cloudy impression of an attractive but reticent blonde.

In these new relations, Mary had confidence in him at once. She liked his fresh face and friendly smile: and he gave a warm welcome to Bootle, which no other lawyer had done: for Mr. Barter, at week-ends, was a hunting-man, and had dogs and horses of his own.

The consultation was in every way a more impressive affair than a visit to Mr. Freebody. The solicitor's office had always, she thought, an air of dust and untidiness—little rooms full of black boxes and documents. But this was a wide, well-furnished, well-lit room, with a thick carpet, and shiny rows of leathery Law Reports instead of black boxes. Mr. Barter was neat and elegant in his black coat and striped trousers. He sat at his great table, and the rest of them sat in a reverent semicircle on the other side of it—Mr. Ransom, his junior, with a large note-book, Mr. Freebody and herself. Mr. Freebody addressed the great man with deference, and Mary felt that for the first time she understood the mysterious difference between barristers and solicitors.

Mr. Barter was quick, alert, and direct.

'The point is this, Mrs. Adam. I never like to tell the other side more than is necessary by way of particulars at this stage: because whatever you tell them gives them a chance for ferreting about and digging up what may be dangerous. But we've got to tell them something more—and the question is, 'How much?' Now, Mrs. Adam, if you wouldn't mind—without any embarrassing details—I'd like to hear from you, first, the whole story of the yachting expedition. I'm no sailor myself and want to get it clear. Would you mind?'

Mary found that she didn't mind. She felt, as she had felt at Manchester, that Mr. Barter would do her good.

'Thank you,' said Mr. Barter briskly at the end. 'I think I see my way clear now.' Like Mr. Freebody, he believed every word that Mary said. He asked her a question or two about Manchester, and the lawyers plunged into an animated discussion, very little of which was intelligible to Mary. She stroked the dog's head and fell into a sort of doze, as weary soldiers sleep upon the battle-field while the shots fly over them.

'Are you at all afraid of *Ostick and Ostick*?' she heard Mr. Freebody say at last. 'Rayden—page 342.'

'Do we know the case, Ransom?' said Mr. Barter, smiling, to his junior.

The junior took down a large book and read: 'Where there is a substantial admission of adultery by the petitioner, and the petitioner puts forward an excuse for it, it is for the petitioner to begin. King's Proctor showing cause—1917. Probate, page 20.'

'Ah, yes. I remember. But I fancy that 'substantial' is the important word there: and our admission is not substantial. Besides, there's the other matter in dispute. Oh, no, I don't think we begin, Mr. Freebody. But we must look up *Ostick*.

'I don't think we need keep you any more, Mrs. Adam,' he said charmingly. 'Good-bye; I wish you could bring your dog into Court, but we'll do what we can without him.'

Bootle barked, as was his custom now at the end of a legal
discussion, whether a consultation with a K.C. or a mere
interview with a solicitor: and Mary gratefully retired.
Mr. Ransom was already reading from another book:
'. . . Where the adultery set up by the King's Proctor
is admitted by the petitioner to the whole or a very considerable extent . . .' She did not want to sit and listen
to three men discussing whether her adultery would or
would not count as 'substantial' or 'very considerable'.
Though now, strangely enough, such a conversation no
longer seemed strange. 'Am I mad,' she whispered to
Bootle in the taxi, 'or are they?' But Bootle was asleep.

'We shan't come on before twelve-thirty. Probably not
before lunch.'
'Hullo?'
'Yes?'
'Did you say Court One, Mr. Freebody?'
'Yes.'
'Thank goodness!'
Slightly puzzled, at the other end, Mr. Freebody said:
'Oh, yes, Cole's a good Judge. But so's the old man. There's
not much in it.'
'I didn't mean the Judge, Mr. Freebody—I meant the
Court.'
'What about it?'
'Oh, nothing. Just a woman's whim. You wouldn't
understand, Mr. Freebody.'
'Oh, come!' Mr. Freebody thought that he had an un-
usual understanding of that difficult branch of knowledge.
'Have you ever noticed the red curtains? Never mind.
I'll be there.'

Curtain up at two o'clock.
This time Mary sat in the front and lowest bench of all,
just in front of Mr. Barter, and between Mr. Freebody and
Mr. Seal. To see the Judge she had to look up, as the first
violin looks up from the orchestra-pit to see the stars.
On the level of her eyes was an almost empty book-case,

holding only one row of Probate Reports, a Law List, *Rayden and Mortimer on Divorce*, a jug of water, two tumblers, a bowler-hat and an overcoat. Beyond and above the shelves sat the Registrar of the Court and the official shorthand writer, who was a chubby, pink-faced man and used a handsome fountain-pen. His light-grey suit looked out of place, she thought, just under the sacred Bench and next to the black-gowned Registrar of the Court. Above them were the red curtains and dull brass rails, then the Bench, the Judge's reading-lamp, square oak panels, dark brown or sooty, and then the bare, pale stone climbing up to the high glass roof. Except for the stone, Mary thought, it looked just like the 'Library' set in any drawing-room comedy. That panelling was not real at all, but a thin partition of ply-wood and canvas: and there was the curtained door (U.L.C.) through which the actor-manager would presently 'make his entrance' on to the raised gallery. Very effective. But Mr. Freebody was whispering: 'That's Sir Humphrey.' A tall, clean-shaven barrister, with aristocratic features and fine grey hair almost matching his wig, was rustling along the bench on which Mr. Barter sat.

'Afternoon, Tim,' he said, sitting down.

Since the petitioner had 'taken in' a leader, the King's Proctor had briefed Sir Humphrey Galloway, K.C., well-known in that Court for his smooth and able advocacy and in public life for his high principles and strenuous defence of the English Sunday.

Mr. Barter leaned forward and whispered, 'Did I tell you at Manchester a story about a K.C. and a railway-carriage—the "Mrs. Baldwin" story?'

'You did.' Mr. Barter jerked his head a little leftwards and chuckled. 'That's the man.'

'Is it really?' This was cheering. He must be human, then, though appearances were against it.

Mary glanced back at the refined, ascetic face, and tried to imagine Sir Humphrey stealthily entering a 'sleeper' in dressing-gown and bedroom slippers. She couldn't.

Then the Judge made his entrance: the congregation stood up: and the play began.

.   .   .   .   .

It began with a brief legal argument about *Ostick* v. *Ostick*. The Judge ruled that since the petitioner's admission of adultery related to an isolated act, and not the only act charged, it was for the King's Proctor to fire the first shot. Mr. Barter was pleased: for he wanted to know what sort of shot Sir Humphrey had.

Sir Humphrey Galloway opened his case briefly: for he had only a Judge to deal with; and a Judge sitting alone was a very different matter from a Judge and jury. The Judge wanted to hear not eloquence, but evidence: he was an expert in the one and needed little assistance in appreciating the other. Moreover, Sir Humphrey had a shrewd notion that the best part of his case would be provided by the witnesses for the other side.

'My lord, in these proceedings I appear for the King's Proctor, who intervenes by the direction of the Attorney-General to show cause why a decree nisi granted to Mrs. Adam by this Court on December 9th last for the dissolution of her marriage to Mervyn John Adam should not be made absolute. The grounds of this intervention, my lord, are that the petitioner, at the hearing of her petition, withheld from the Court the material fact that a few weeks before her petition was filed she herself had been guilty of adultery with the person named, Mr. Martin Seal, and that since the decree nisi was granted she has again been guilty of adultery with the same person. Evidence will be called, my lord, and, in the ordinary course, I should not think it necessary to say much more at the present stage. But the petitioner, by her answer, has taken a course which makes it necessary to go a little further. By her answer, my lord, the petitioner admits the truth of the first charge in the King's Proctor's plea, that is, the act of adultery prior to the hearing of the petition: but she denies that she has committed adultery on any other occasion, that is, she traverses directly the second charge set out in Paragraph Three of the King's Proctor's plea. And the petitioner is asking the Court to exercise its discretion in her favour, and to grant relief in spite of her admission that she has deceived the Court and once, at least, been guilty of adultery. It is, of course, open to the

Court to exercise its discretion in such a case if the Court is satisfied that there was some excuse for the original deceit, that no deceit is being practised still, and that either the circumstances of the case or the public interest make it desirable that her conduct should be overlooked. My lord, it is for my friend to satisfy the Court that all these conditions are present, and I will not attempt to anticipate the defence. But I think it right, my lord, to say at once that in the view of those by whom I am instructed this is not a case in which the discretion of the Court ought to be exercised in the petitioner's favour . . .'

'If he says discretion again,' thought Mary, 'I shall scream.'

But he was still at it.

'. . . to grant discretion to one who even now, in the submission of the King's Proctor, does not come into Court with clean hands. I am not going to weary the Court by outlining evidence which will speak clearly for itself: but, my lord, certain evidence will be called the relevance of which may not immediately appear, evidence relating not merely to the two specific charges, but to the whole course of the petitioner's conduct, and going to show, my lord, that that course has been one of consistent and deliberate deception not confined to the single act which is now tardily admitted. My lord——'

Mary passed into a sort of mental sleep, gazing at the stiff white shirt-cuffs and gold cuff-links of the Judge. She woke up suddenly and heard Sir Humphrey say:

'Miss Constance Cannon.'

'Miss Constance Cannon.'

'Who's she?' whispered Mary to the air: and though she had made a vow not to show her face to the jackals behind her she had to turn her head to see who Constance Cannon was.

'Nanny!' she whispered. 'Oh, what a shame!'

Far back in the eighth row of the stalls old Nanny was startled by the sound of her name, and trembled. No one had called her Miss Cannon since her last visit to an agency (and that was five years back): she never saw her name

written except upon her Health Insurance card or the rare
letters her sister sent her. To her little world, which was,
for her, the whole world, she was 'Nanny', neither more nor
less. But it was clear that the man in the wig meant her,
and, trembling, she made her way to the box. Trembling,
but determined not to show that she trembled. She repeated the oath in a voice that was determined: she seized
the edge of the box and stared straight at the wall before
her, high up, just below the window, and waited, her lips
drawn tightly together: but her face was grey, and, do what
she would, the little finger of her left hand twitched.

Mary said to herself, 'This is the worst thing they've done.'

It was the worst thing that Nanny had ever done. She
had not meant any harm, had not even thought any harm.
It was nothing to her what the gentry did, provided they
maintained a continual supply of delicious babies and small
children for her to nurse and bath and bring up and worship.
She had always liked Mrs. Adam, who was nice-spoken and
friendly and played with the children whenever they appeared in public. She, Nanny, had thought no harm of the
gentleman being in the lady's room, even if, as the children
said, the gentleman had kissed the lady. For all she knew,
the lady was a widow, and they were going to be married.
And, if that sharp fellow Lawrence had gone off with the
gentleman's braces and didn't answer the bell, what was
the poor gentleman to do? Having dressed a good many
boys in her time, Nanny knew the importance of braces.
Which was more than Harriet and Cook could say. But
those two, who knew nothing, would talk about everything.
Harriet, who had ears like sponges, had heard the children's
tales of stalking Mrs. Adam and catching her kissing: and
then there had been that foolish talk in the kitchen, Harriet
and Cook nodding their heads and showing-off about the
things they knew. And Nanny, God forgive her, tired of
Cook and Harriet pretending they knew so much, had
spoken up and told them what *she* knew—and that was that
there was nothing to know. But that had been enough for
nosey Harriet to talk about when the man on the bicycle
called and took her to the pictures. And so, here she was,
poor Nanny, stuck up before a crowd of people, having
sworn to tell the truth, the whole truth, and nothing but

16

the truth. Well, she could do that, but what did it matter, what she could tell?

It seemed to matter very much. She had to say how the lady and the gentleman were dressed, and where exactly they stood, and what they said. But before they arrived at that point there was an argument about what little Simon had said, peeping round the door, poor lamb.

'And then, Miss Cannon,' said the good-looking lawyer, 'did you hear one of the children make an exclamation?'

'Yes, sir. He give his war-whoop, same as he always does, when he's stalking any one, as he calls it. Red Indians, like.'

'His war-whoop? Was that all?'

'No, sir. He said, "Stalked, Aunt Mary! Do it again." '

'One moment.' This was the Judge: and Nanny stared at him in alarm. But the Judge looked at the lawyer and said, 'Sir Humphrey, I don't know what answer you expected: but is what the Red Indian soldier said evidence?'

There was gentle laughter from all those who had read or heard of the *Pickwick Papers*, and Mr. Timothy Barter rose lazily to his feet.

'My lord——' said Sir Humphrey.

'My lord,' said Mr. Barter, 'my client has nothing to conceal, and, if your lordship had not intervened, I should have been prepared to let the question pass. But formally, my lord, I must object to the question——'

Sir Humphrey, rather ruffled, said, 'The question I asked was "Was that all?" '

'Meaning, unmistakably, "Was that all the child said?" '

'My lord, my learned friend has no right to make that suggestion. At the same time, my lord, in my submission, my lord——'

There was then an extraordinary argument, which passed over Nanny's head, as mysterious as a fugitive storm. Throughout the argument Mr. Barter maintained his attitude of righteous indifference: he did not, it was clear, care what the end of the argument might be, but he was profoundly shocked by the low standards, ethical and professional, of Sir Humphrey Galloway. At last the Judge decided that what the children had said before the door was opened wide was not evidence: and Nanny was taken on to the clothes, conduct, and conversation of the grown-ups.

Mr. Barter rose to cross-examine, and showed at once what he was made of.

'Miss Cannon,' he said, 'I only want to ask you one question. Mrs. Adam has nothing to conceal, so don't be afraid to answer it. Did you understand from what the child Simon said, either at that time or later, that he had seen Mr. Seal kissing Mrs. Adam?'

'Well, yes, sir, I did.'

'Thank you, Miss Cannon.' And Mr. Barter sat down with an air of great satisfaction, as if he had won the case already.

'I wonder,' thought Mary, 'they don't put little Simon in the box. Now Alice, I suppose.'

Alice Merridew swore by Almighty God that she would tell the truth, the whole truth, and nothing but the truth. But nobody seemed to pay the smallest attention to this bold and important announcement. The Judge was talking to a man who was standing on the Registrar's chair and presenting an enormous tweed-clad posterior to the Court. Sir Humphrey was reading Mrs. Merridew's 'proof'. Mr. Barter was talking to Mr. Ransom. The audience chattered. Even the usher, who had invited the lady to repeat the oath, did not appear to be listening to what she said, but gazed with a nebulous expression at the clock, as if he were thinking (as in fact he was), 'It's a long time till they open.'

Mr. Freebody bent his head and said to Mary, 'They do this better in Scotland. The oath *is* an oath there. The Judge administers the oath himself (I think, as a rule, he stands up), and the witness has to swear that he will tell the truth "as he will answer to God at the Great Day of Judgment", or something of the sort. That's the way to stop perjury in a God-fearing country. This woman might as well be reciting a passage from the telephone book. I'm not sure that any one would notice if she did.'

'How nice Alice looks!' thought Mary. 'And how she must hate this!' That had been one of the worst shocks, to hear that Alice had been dragged in. Alice Merridew did hate being there. She looked down and saw Mary in the front row, and for a moment their eyes exchanged sympathy. It would have been bad enough to be brought there on Mary's side, to help Mary. But to be subpœnaed by the enemy to give evidence against her friend and guest: and then to have the name of her lovely house splashed about in the newspapers, probably described as a sort of brothel, where loose behaviour was the regular thing—Alice Merridew was miserable. It was very hard, she thought, that this trouble should be brought upon her by her kindness of heart. She did not care twopence for Mr. Seal, but she cared a lot for Mary and had only wanted to see Mary happy.

Sir Humphrey looked at her curiously. 'Doesn't look like the leader of a fast set,' he thought. 'Pale, fragile, sensitive type, all elegance and breeding. Looks as if she might crumple up if you said "Boo!"; but very often that sort is the toughest in the end.' A slight snub nose, a good jaw: and he had a note from the solicitor, 'Will say as little as she can.' Always a difficult job examining-in-chief a witness on subpœna who didn't want to talk. Mustn't ask them leading questions or nasty questions. It was like fighting with one arm tied behind one—like cross-examining without the weapons of cross-examination. If they turned really nasty one could ask leave to treat them as hostile witnesses; but if they did no more than refuse to give the answers expected it was difficult to get the leave.

Yes, she had known Mrs. Adam for many years and Mrs. Adam had often visited her for week-ends. She had not known Mr. Seal so long, but met him in Mrs. Adam's dressing-room, and in July invited him too. What were the relations between them? Friendly. Nothing more than that? Not to her knowledge. Sir Humphrey wanted to say, 'Quite sure? No signs of affection?' but it wouldn't do: he must be patient.

'What made you ask Mr. Seal to your house if you had not met him before?'

'I liked Mr. Seal and wished to meet him again.'

'Very well. On the first occasion that Mr. Seal came to your house was there any talk of a yachting expedition?'

'Yes.'

'Whose suggestion was that?'

'Mrs. Adam's.'

'And who were to form the party?'

'Mrs. Adam and Mr. Seal.'

'Nobody else. Did that expedition come off?'

'No. The tide was wrong.'

('How do they know all this?' whispered Mary. And Martin whispered back, 'Verena.')

'Would you mind explaining that, Mrs. Merridew?'

'It was High Water about three: so it would be impossible to go for a long expedition down the river and get back in the evening."

'I understand. Did Mr. Seal ever visit your house again?'

'Yes. The following week-end.'

'Why did you ask Mr. Seal to come again so soon?'

'Mrs. Adam was coming too, and——' Alice Merridew stopped suddenly: she had said the wrong thing, she was sure: but what else could she say? 'I liked Mr. Seal so much I wanted to see him again'? The next thing, there would be a scandal about herself.

'Yes, Mrs. Merridew?' said Sir Humphrey smoothly.

It was too late to go back, anyhow. She said: 'And the tide was right for sailing. Mr. Seal was very anxious to have a sail.'

'And did Mr. Seal in fact go sailing that week-end?'

'Yes. On the Sunday.'

'With whom?'

'With Mrs. Adam.'

'Nobody else?'

'No.'

The Judge leaned forward and looked over the top of his glasses, as if he had suddenly seen Sir Humphrey and was astonished by the sight.

'Sir Humphrey, how does all this help us? The petitioner, by her answer, admits that she was guilty of adultery on this yachting expedition. Unless Mr. Barter insists, I don't see that all this is necessary.'

Mr. Barter rose and said, 'So far as my client is concerned, my lord, it is quite unnecessary. My client admits affection. She admits previous association. And she admits adultery on this isolated occasion.'

Sir Humphrey said, 'My lord, the submission of the King's Proctor is that this was not an "isolated" act at all, brought about by some sort of navigational accident, but that it was part of a long and calculated course of misconduct and deceit: and therefore, my lord, the circumstances which led up to it are important, not as proof of the act, which is admitted, but as showing the character and state of mind of the petitioner, and throwing some light upon the second charge, which is denied.'

Mr. Barter rose again, now very lofty in tone, and slightly indignant. 'My lord, if my friend is going to take that line, let the whole story be told, by all means—if your lordship pleases. My client is most anxious that it shall not be said that we kept anything back.'

The Judge thought for a moment, and then said, 'Very well. Go on, Sir Humphrey.'

Alice Merridew, during this colloquy, forgotten by all, had been far away. She was on the sunny little wharf at 'White Ladies', with the breeze flattening her skirts against her, and the grey Medway gliding by. Verena, rather cross, stood at her side; Sam Hardy sat in his dinghy, watching the *Curlew* glide away; and Mary, looking so happy, waved her hand across the water, her arm rising straight from her shoulder like a little mast, with a tiny pink handkerchief for pennant. She went back to the house with Verena, so glad to have made her friend happy that she cheerfully endured the cross Verena all day. To think that that happy little scene had landed them all in this world of wigs and interminable argument! What a sense of proportion! What did it matter, after all, to any one whether Mary had slept with Martin or not?

But they had finished that little jaw. Mr. Barter sat down and said to himself, 'Capital.' Now he would be able to make something of that absurd stuff of Mrs. Adam's about her adultery being a sort of accident. The less said about that the better, he had thought, but now he could say a lot.

Sir Humphrey said, 'Was there any suggestion that any one else should accompany these two on the expedition—yourself, for example?'

'My husband and I were going to church.'

'But you had other guests? Did none of them want
to go?'

'I think Miss Simmons said something about it.'

('Oh, dear,' whispered Mary. 'You're right.')

'What did she say?'

('Oh, *dear*!' thought Alice Merridew. 'Where are we
getting to?')

'I believe she said she would like to go.'

'You "believe"?' said the Judge. 'Don't you know?
Did she use those words or not?'

'Yes, my lord.'

'Very well. Be open, please.'

'Was that in the presence of Mrs. Adam?'

'Yes.'

'Is there room in the boat for more than two?'

'Oh, yes. Plenty.'

'Then can you say why Miss Simmons did not go?'

'I—I wanted Miss Simmons to stay with me.'

'Was there any other reason?'

Alice Merridew was silent, cold and prickly with apprehension. She remembered vividly the fearful scowl that
Mary had made. The thoughts raced through her head,
'What shall I do? That Judge suspects me. If I don't tell
the truth they'll get it somehow. And if I do—perhaps it
doesn't matter.'

'Come, Mrs. Merridew, you heard the question?'

'I didn't think she would—mix very well with Mrs. Adam
and Mr. Seal.'

The Judge interposed briskly, 'Come, come, Mrs. Merridew—what you really mean is "Two's Company, Three's
None," isn't it?'

There was laughter, and every one felt better.

'Yes, my lord.'

'Then why not say so? But I still don't see where all this
gets us, Sir Humphrey?'

'My lord, I was just going to ask the witness whether Mrs.
Adam expressed any opinion upon the proposed addition to
the party.'

The Judge, having scored a laugh, had blossomed into a
genial humour. 'I don't see how she can have done that, in
the other lady's presence. Unless, of course, she made a

face or kicked the witness under the table. Perhaps she
did. Did she, Mrs. Merridew?'

Alice was at ease now, cheered by the laughter and the
sensible, nice Judge, and she said without hesitation: 'Yes,
my lord. She made a face.'

And now there was loud laughter.

'Well, Sir Humphrey, you have your answer. The petitioner made a face when it was suggested that another lady
should go to sea with her. I see nothing surprising in that.
I have no doubt Helen of Troy would have done the same.'

Now there was much laughter, and the reporters sighed
for the good old days before the Act of 1926, when they
could have given all this evidence in full, and there would
have been head-lines about 'Helen of Troy'. But those
delights were limited now to queer cases about 'enticement',
which were not covered by the Act.

The Judge, with a pleased half-smile, wagged his head
from side to side. Sir Humphrey stood, an immobile rock
in the sea of laughing people, smiling deferentially, but
thinking, 'Laugh, my hearties, but you wait till my final
speech. This won't do the lady any good.' And Mr. Barter
thought, 'Thank God there's no jury.'

Sir Humphrey at last said. 'Did you see the two go off in
the boat together?'

'Yes.'

'And when did they return?'

'About eight o'clock the next morning.'

'Did you see them return?'

'Yes. I saw the boat coming up the river, from my bedroom, and went down to meet them.'

'Thank you.'

Sir Humphrey sat down.

Mary had been whispering to Mr. Freebody, and Mr.
Freebody whispered to Mr. Barter; and now Mr. Barter rose.
His cross-examination was short and swift.

'Mrs. Merridew, does Miss Verena Simmons write plays—
or try to write plays?'

'Yes.'

'And had she, to your knowledge, submitted a play to
Mrs. Adam for her opinion?'

'I believe she had.'

'And had Mrs. Adam, that Sunday morning, expressed an opinion adverse to Miss Simmons' play?'

'Yes.'

'Knowing something of artists and authors, Mrs. Merridew, were you surprised when Mrs. Adam, as you have told us, "made a face"?'

'Not very.'

'Thank you.'

'Samuel Hardy.'

Sam Hardy, the 'White Ladies' boatman and gardener, stumped heavily across the Court, sailed into the box like a barge before the wind, put the helm hard over, and brought up all standing. Or so he afterwards described his movements. Sam had been skipper of a sailing-barge till the freights became too few. He roared out the oath as if he were telling his mate to drop the 'torps'l' in a squall. He would never look right on land: and in that assembly of pale and painted faces he looked as wrong as a ballet-dancer at a barge's wheel. His face was as highly polished as a billiard-ball and almost as red: he wore a thick blue jersey under his neat blue coat: and his knuckles, on the ledge before him, had the surface of a walnut. He blew like a breeze of personality into the quiet Court. He admired Mary and had taught her all she knew about the water: he understood that she was supposed to have done wrong and was in danger of 'going to loo'ard'. But since he had been called into the business, he supposed that it must be to give the Court his assistance as a waterman. There was no doubt that Mary had disregarded his advice as a waterman: and it was fixed in his mind that that was the important question to be decided.

The solicitors had warned Sir Humphrey that Mr. Hardy —subpœnaed, like Alice Merridew—might be difficult also, but for the contrary reason that he would say too much. He had been a trouble to the gentleman who took his 'proof', always wandering off into voluble descriptions of the weather, the state of the tide, and many memorable voyages of his career. A nuisance to the solicitor, no doubt, but possibly a help to counsel: for a witness with a full mind, anxious to talk, would not be so clever at keeping things back. Solicitors, thought Sir Humphrey, were nearly always wrong about evidence.

Sam testified that he had got the *Curlew* ready for the lady that Sunday morning and saw her sail away with the gentleman. He was an Essex man and spoke in the racy tongue which is shared by the bargemen of both sides of the Thames. He used the word 'that' always where common mortals say 'it'.

'Yas, sir, I had the mains'l set, and all ready to rights, time they mustered away. About eleven, sir. That blowed a nice little breeze from the Sou'-west.'

'Who, did you understand, was in charge of the vessel, the lady or the gentleman?'

'The leddy, sir. She were skipper, certainly.'

'Had you seen the gentleman before?'

'No, sir.'

'Did you know anything of his capacities as a navigator?'

'Pardon, sir?'

'Was he able, to your knowledge, to take charge of the vessel?'

'I knowed nothing about him, sir. I could see he'd been in a boat before, sir, by the way he come aboard; but I wouldn't say I'd ship mate with him before I knowed some more about him.'

'What would you say of Mrs. Adam's capacity to handle a boat?'

'Miss Mary, sir?' Sam Hardy looked down at Mary with a great grin. 'She knows as much as a bag of monkeys, sir.'

There was loud laughter: but again Sir Humphrey thought, 'The laugh, I think, will prove to be with us.' He said; 'Do you mean by that that she knows a little or a lot?'

Sam Hardy, refreshed, like the Judge, by the healthy air of laughter, answered excitedly, 'There's nowt she don't know about that little old boat, sir. I've been ship-mates with her time and again. I larned her all she knows —didn't I, Missie Mary?'

Again, the happy Court laughed at Sam's proud face and pointing finger.

The Judge said, kindly, 'Mr. Hardy, you must address yourself to me.'

'Aye, aye, sir,' said Sam. 'Beg pardon, sir, but what's in my mind, sir, that comes out.'

'Mr. Hardy,' said Sir Humphrey, 'you say you often "go shipmate" with Mrs. Adam. Was anything said about your going on this occasion?'

'Why, sir, I said I'd go along with the leddy and the gentleman if they wanted a hand, but Missie Mary said, "No, thank'ee, Sam, you go to church." I had to laugh.'

And so did the audience.

'Why did you have to laugh, Mr. Hardy?'

'Because Missie Mary knows very well I ain't been to church since I was married!'

'I see. And had you any anxiety for their safety, seeing them go off alone?'

'Nary a one, sir. That blowed a nice breeze, and the glass setting steady. Proper summer weather, sir, and that had all the appearance of holding.'

'And had you complete confidence in Mrs. Adam's capacity and judgment or not?'

'I had, sir. That's right.'

'Was anything said about their destination?'

'Yas, sir. There an' back, as the smuggler said.'

'What do you mean by that?'

'They weren't going to make a passage nowhere, sir—only cruise about and come home on the flood.'

'Was any particular time mentioned for their return?'

'Back before dark, they said, sir.'

'Do you ever, Mr. Hardy, give advice to Mrs. Adam, or to other guests of the house, before they go sailing?'

'Yas, sir. I tell 'em the tale, the way the weather looks, an' that.'

'Did you give Mrs. Adam any advice on this occasion?'

'Yas, sir, I believe I did.'

'Can you remember what you said?'

'I said, "Don't you go roaring out to sea, missie, if you want to be home before dark. That's a nice fair wind you have now," I said, "but coming home, that'll be turning all the way——"'

' "Turning all the way"?' said the Judge. 'What do you mean by that?' His lordship was better acquainted with steamships than with sailing-barges.

'Turning,' said Mr. Hardy, gazing at the Judge in some surprise that one so great should know so little, 'turning to windward, sir. What the yacht-folk calls tacking, I believe.'

'Ah, yes. Of course.'

'The witness means, I think, my lord,' said Sir Humphrey, unnecessarily, 'that while on the outward voyage, the wind being fair, the vessel would proceed on a more or less direct course, on the return journey, with the wind adverse, it would be necessary to tack to and fro, so that it would take much longer to cover the same geographical distance. Is that right, Mr. Hardy?'

'Aye, aye, sir.'

The Judge said, 'Anyhow, you advised Mrs. Adam not to go too far?'

'"I wouldn't go no farther than the Nore," I said, "That blows nicely now," I said, "but that won't hold," I said, "I'll lay. Proper summer weather, that is," I said— "sun down, wind down. Five o'clock," I said, "and that'll be flat calm. Then you'll lose your tide." '

'I see, Mr. Hardy. Did you see the boat return?'

'Yas, sir. Next morning. 'Bout eight o'clock.'

'Did Mrs. Adam say anything?'

'Yas, sir. She said they'd run out nigh as far as the Mouse, an' had to bring up in Long Reach, tide-bound.'

'And what did you say?'

'I said, "What did I tell you, missie? You ought to known better. You ought never to have went so far." '

Sam looked down at Mary with a kindly smile, the fatherly reproof of a teacher disobeyed. But now there was no laughter in Court. Mary did not look at him, and Sam felt that in some strange way he had 'gone to loo'ard'.

Feeling uncomfortable, he turned back to the lawyer and found that he had sat down: and another lawyer had popped up to windward of him.

'Mr. Hardy,' said Mr. Barter, 'you have made many voyages in sailing-barges in the tidal waters of the Thames Estuary. Were you ever able to say for certain that you would reach a particular place at a particular time?'

'No, sir. Nothing's certain in sailing-barges—not even the brass.'

'The brass?'

'The money, sir.'

'Ah, yes. Would it be fair to put it this way: You might say "I hope to reach such-and-such a place before dark" —but you wouldn't bet on it?'

'Bet on it? Never, sir,' said Sam emphatically. 'No bargeman ever knows where he'll be bringing up, with the wind baffling about and them humbugging tides.'

'If you were caught in Long Reach at nightfall, Mr. Hardy, with a foul tide and no wind, what would you do?'

'Let go my anchor, sir, and put the sooky on.'

'What is the sooky?' said the Judge.

'The sooky? The kettle, sir.'

'Ah, yes. Thank you.'

'At that part of the River Medway, Mr. Hardy, is there any convenient place at which to land?'

'Not that I knows of, sir. There's nowt but saltings— marshes and that. It's a humbugging kind of a place, sir, for yacht-folk.'

'Thank you, Mr. Hardy.'

But now the first one had popped up again: and Sam stared at him, wondering how long this Jack-in-the-box business was to continue.

Sir Humphrey said, slowly: 'Suppose that you had been in charge of the *Curlew* that day, Mr. Hardy: and suppose that Mrs. Hardy had told you that she must be back by dark: do you think that you might have got her back before dark?'

And Sam, without a moment's thought, meeting by instinct a challenge to his professional skill, said heartily: 'I'll lay my life I would, sir!'

Now there was a gust of laughter. Sir Humphrey sat down, well-pleased, and Sam, bewildered, returned to his seat.

'One up,' thought Sir Humphrey. Mr. Hardy had been most fruitful: and the solicitors wrong, as usual.

The Judge looked at the electric clock, and said, 'At half past ten to-morrow.'

Mary, a few minutes late, had to press through a crowd of barristers and sightseers to reach her seat, and, as she pressed, she looked up and saw the red, round face and bosky moustache of the Manchester man, hanging above the witness-box like the forbidding totem of a cannibal tribe.

'What happened next, Mr. Rigby?'

'Rigby,' so that was the foul creature's name!

'Looks like a bobby,' she whispered to Mr. Seal.

'It is. Listen.'

'Acting upon information received I proceeded to Manchester by the six-fifty p.m. train from Euston. Mr. Martin Seal travelled on the same train. I engaged a room on the same floor as Mr. Seal. I ascertained the number of the room occupied by Mrs. Adam—Number 218.'

'How did you do that?' said the Judge suddenly and sharply.

'I overheard a conversation between the parties.'

Filthy fellow! Mary noted with pleasure the Judge's sharpness. Mr. Freebody had told her that the paid sleuth was not attractive to the Court: and evidently Mr. Freebody was right. Filthy fellow! Looking back, she could not think of any conversation in which she had told Martin the number of her room. Yet she had named it somewhere, and this nasty red man had been listening at her elbow. The tale of Mr. Rigby's peregrinations about the Heart of England Hotel was slowly extracted and recorded. His language was unfailingly correct and constabular. From a convenient situation he had observed the parties at supper, at which they were accompanied by a third party, believed to be Mr. Figg. . . . He had observed Mr. Seal's movements from the time he left the lift with Mr. Figg. . . . His room was in the vicinity of Mr. Seal's. . . . Mr. Seal returned to his room at one-eight and left it again at one-fifteen. . . . He was then in dressing-gown and pyjamas. . . . Witness followed. . . . Mr. Seal proceeded down the staff staircase and knocked at the door of Room 218. . . . Witness saw him enter. . . . Did he hear any exclamation from the person who opened the door? . . . None. . . . Was there any discussion before Mr. Seal was admitted? . . . None. . . . The time was then one-seventeen. . . . He recorded the time at the time. . . . He kept observation on the door. . . . While waiting, on three occasions he listened at the door. . . . He could hear no conversation. . . . At two-five

the door opened and a woman looked out into the passage.
. . . She was wearing a night-dress and some sort of wrap.
. . . He recognised her as the woman who had had supper
with Mr. Seal. . . . Could he point to her in Court to-day?
. . . Yes. A few minutes later the door opened again and
Mr. Seal came out. . . . He returned to his room. . . .
That was at two-twelve. . . . Mr. Seal returned to London
that day. . . . Did he ever see the petitioner and Mr. Seal
together again? . . . Yes. . . . When was that? At the
Joyful Theatre, on the morning of February 13th. . . .
They conducted a conversation, sitting in the stalls. . . .
At the end of the conversation he saw them kiss. . . .
Twice.

'Oh!' Mary gasped and bit her lip, and went white with
indignation. Not that it mattered. But the meanness of it!

Mr. Barter leaned forward, and whispered, 'Is that true?'

'Perfectly. It was after that thing came from the Proctor.
We met about that——'

Mr. Barter nodded, listening with his other ear to Mr.
Rigby.

How did the witness come to see them at the theatre?
. . . He saw Mr. Seal by chance in the street and followed
him. . . . Was he keeping continuous observation on the
parties at that time? . . . No.

Mr. Barter rose, and the eager audience looked forward
to a fierce cross-examination, in which Mr. Barter would
put it to the witness that the story he had told was a 'tissue
of lies.'

But Mr. Barter disappointed them. He was very quiet;
very gentle, almost friendly; and the first questions puzzled
the audience.

'When you followed Mr. Seal downstairs, Mr. Rigby, were
you close behind him?'

'No, sir.'

'Can you say how far behind him you were?'

'I waited till he turned the corner, sir, at the foot of the
stairs. Then I slipped down.'

A titter or two.

'By "slipped down" you mean, I suppose, that you ran
down?'

'I wouldn't say "ran", sir.'

'But you were in time to see Mr. Seal knock at the bed-room door?'

'Yes, sir.'

'So that you must have come down much faster than Mr. Seal?'

'I suppose so, sir.'

'As fast as you could?'

'Yes, sir.'

'How much do you weigh, Mr. Rigby?'

'I couldn't say, sir, to a pound or two.'

'But you can say to a stone or two?' (Laughter.) 'I don't want to be rude, Mr. Rigby, but you're not a feather-weight, are you?'

'About fourteen-ten, sir.'

'Nearly fifteen stone.'

The word 'stone' gave Mr. Barter a notion.

'Was the staircase carpeted?'

'No, sir. Only stone.'

'What sort of shoes were you wearing?'

'None, sir. Nothing.'

'Bare feet? Yours is an arduous career, Mr. Rigby. But you wore some clothes, perhaps?'

Laughter. The stalls enjoyed this.

'Dressing-gown, sir. And pyjamas.'

'And as you came down the stairs—as fast as you could—fifteen stone—it's possible, isn't it, that the dressing-gown rustled a little?'

'Maybe, sir.' Mr. Rigby could not make out what the fellow was driving at.

He changed his position and put his right hand on his hip.

'And that you made even more noise than that?'

'I don't think so, sir.'

'You were a little out of breath, perhaps?'

'No, sir.' A touch of indignation, as if to say, ' My lungs are as good as another's.'

'Would it surprise you to hear that you were heard by Mr. Seal?'

'Yes, sir.'

'You tell the Court, do you, that you conducted these lightning movements so quietly that the man you were following could not have heard them?'

'Well, sir, he never looked round.'

'You have told the Court how you observed the door of Bedroom 218 that night. Were you continuously in view of the door from the time Mr. Seal entered the room till the time he left it?'

'No, sir. I was round the corner part of the time.'

'Then can you be sure that no one else entered the room during that time?'

'Yes, sir,' said Mr. Rigby, confident.

'How?'

'I took precautions.'

'Precautions?' Mr. Barter repeated innocently. 'What sort of precautions?'

'Well, sir.' Mr. Rigby hesitated, and put both hands on the ledge of the box again. 'I fixed a length of black cotton across the door, and from time to time I confirmed that it was unbroken.'

'Very ingenious,' said Mr. Barter, with frank admiration. 'Why didn't you tell the Court about that before?'

'I wasn't asked, sir.' (The reason of that was that Sir Humphrey had thought, 'Better not. Sounds too much like a detective story.')

'Didn't you tell the King's Proctor's representatives about it?'

'Yes, sir.'

'You did? I see. Very well. So you fixed some black cotton across the petitioner's door? And did you take any other precautions?'

'Yes, sir. I put a pile of shoes on the mat.'

'With what object?'

'So that I should be sure of hearing the gentleman when he came out.'

'*I* see,' said Mr. Barter in a very encouraging and approving tone. 'How much do you weigh, again?'

'Fourteen-ten,' said Mr. Rigby, tired of this emphasis upon his weight.

'And you think that nobody in the room could have heard your operations?'

'No sign of it, sir.

'Very well. Thank you, Mr. Rigby.'

Mr. Barter left it at that. He had indicated to the Judge

17

a possible line of defence, of which he might or might not make more later on. He was not sure. It had its dangers. And that closed the case for the King's Proctor.

Mr. Barter opened the case for the petitioner. The prospect of seeing the petitioner in the box had filled the Court to an almost insanitary degree: and all day long the officials at the doors were turning people away. The barristers' benches were crowded with young advocates, anxious to study obscure points of law or the instructive methods of leading counsel. In the next Court the learned President of the Division had before him a Probate case of high legal importance: but the barristers' benches were not uncomfortably full.

Mary had slept little, but longer than she expected, with the help of one of the doctor's 'dopes'. And she had come into Court unexpectedly cheerful. But that was easy to understand. It was not the first night that mattered but the waiting for the first night. This time to-morrow the worst might be over; anyhow, it was going to happen at last.

And Mr. Barter's speech was cheering. His voice was refreshingly natural and youthful after 'Heavy Humphrey's' pompous tones. And his point of view was refreshingly contemporary. For the first time since the case began Mary felt that she was situated in the real world and not in some fantastic region invented by lawyers. Mr. Barter was talking the same language as herself. And he talked it with ease and confidence, as if he knew no other language, and meant every word that he said.

He was saying, not with adjectives or passion, for the opening speech is not the place for them, but by implication, all the fine brave things which she had whispered to herself so many lonely nights in bed. Sir Humphrey and Sir Humphrey's witnesses, and all the intimidating paraphernalia of the Court, had begun to make her wonder whether she was quite so right as she had thought. Perhaps, after all, she was mad. But now, listening to Mr. Barter, she was sure again that she was right. Odd! She would never have guessed that she could ever be glad to listen to a public speech about her private life: but now she was.

Mr. Barter knew as well as Sir Humphrey that, before a Judge sitting alone, the general rule was 'The less said the

better—let him have your evidence'. But Mr. Barter's
problem was very different from Sir Humphrey's. Sir
Humphrey had opened on the crest of the wave, and Mr.
Barter was opening in the trough—a damaging admission,
and much more of a case against him than he had expected.
The facts were the sort of facts that could be twisted into
any shape; what mattered here was the general impression.
Mr. Barter hoped that his witnesses would produce a general
impression of a favourable character: but he thought that
it was a case in which he might assist them by preparing the
ground. The question was, How much could be said without wearying the Judge?—a very delicate question.

'My lord,' said Mr. Barter, 'the line of argument which
has been developed by the other side compels me to
say rather more than, at this stage, I had intended. As I
have already indicated to the Court, I do not complain in
the least of the calling of certain evidence which seemed, at
first sight, to your lordship to be irrelevant, and still seems,
to me, to be unnecessary. For, as I have said, and say
again, there are in this case no facts which my client wishes
or is attempting to conceal. But she is entitled to resent,
and she will in that box presently reject, the construction
which my learned friend has endeavoured to place upon the
admitted facts.

'What are the facts? My client, as the Court can perceive
without my assistance, is a young, vigorous, and attractive
woman. She marries at an early age, in the exceptional
emotional circumstances which affected so many young
persons during the period of the Great War and after. The
marriage proves to be an unhappy, indeed an impossible
one. Not without patient and protracted effort on both
sides, the marriage at last breaks up. The husband leaves
the wife, and, after an interval of two years, he forms an
attachment for another woman. He provides his wife with
evidence which gives her lawful ground for a divorce. At
once she files a petition. On a technical point of evidence,
some error for which she is in no way responsible, the petition is rejected. Consider her position. It is nearly three
years since her husband left her. She too has formed what

seems to be an enduring affection for another, the person
named in these proceedings, Mr. Seal. They wish to marry.
They are young, eager, healthy, and in love. It is three
years, perhaps, since the petitioner has enjoyed that
satisfaction which is the right, and may become the physical
necessity, of a married woman. By an accident of legal
procedure—to describe it no more hardly than that—she
finds herself still, against all expectations, bound by the law
of marriage to a man who no longer means anything to her
in terms of marriage; a man who has, by default at least,
admitted publicly that he no longer has any claim upon her
in terms of marriage. Yet that bond subsists and will sub-
sist, for all she knows, indefinitely. In that situation, my
lord, humanly speaking, though not legally speaking, it
would have surprised no one if this woman, despairing of
the law, had committed herself irrevocably to a lawless
union with the man she loved. As you will hear, she did not
lack persuasion to take that course—and you will hear that
not from her own lips but from the lips of Mr. Seal, who is
prepared to go into that box and testify to that effect, cost
what it may. That is the situation, my lord, that is the
temptation, in the summer of last year: and that temptation,
as you will hear, is strenuously resisted. There is affection
between the parties—much more than affection: there is
association: there is indiscretion—all this is openly admitted:
but there is nothing more. Then Fate, Accident, Unwisdom
—call it what you will—creates, without premeditation or
calculation, on either side, an opportunity, a temptation, so
powerful, so irresistible, that in my submission it would be
too much to expect any two mortals, placed as these two
mortals were placed, to fight against it. All the apparatus
of romance, all the incitements to passion are present—the
moon, the water, a solitary ship, the man she loves: the
world remote, no fear of discovery, and, my lord, may I add
no hope of escape—is it a cause for wonder that this woman
yielded to so overwhelming an armament of temptation?
But still, my lord, I am going to submit that the act was, in
a sense, a very true sense, an accident—not premeditated,
and, what is more important, never repeated. I am not going to say that my client was ashamed of it, or ought to be,
because I do not want to use the language of humbug——'

'Golly!' thought Mr. Freebody. 'Tim's going it.' Mary, without turning her head, took a look at the Judge, and was not surprised to see him lift his eyebrows.

'But, my lord,' the confident voice went on, 'my client had some slight acquaintance with the law, and more than an ordinary sense of probity. She knew that, as the law stands, she could not come to this Court and ask for her marriage to be dissolved if she was herself committed to an irregular union with a man not her husband. And therefore, as you will hear, my lord, she did refuse to convert the accident into a habit and to do deliberately that which she had been persuaded to do by exceptional circumstances. What happens? Her husband again provides her with the necessary evidence on which to found a petition. Her solicitor, Mr. Freebody, very properly, puts to her the usual questions to assure himself that his client will come into the Court with "clean hands". My client genuinely believes that, in the real sense, she has clean hands: on a previous occasion she has been asked whether she is "living with any one", and she believes, quite honestly, that that is what her solicitor means. She answers truthfully that she is not: she honestly believes that the single slip of which she has been guilty—if guilty is not too strong a word—is not a material fact which she need bring to the notice even of her legal adviser. Humanly speaking, if I may for a moment speak so, my lord, it is a tender memory, not to be shared with any one unless the compulsion is obvious. With a perfectly good conscience, then, she obtains her decree nisi. She resolves to see nothing of the man she loves until the statutory six months are past. A hard, indeed, my lord, as many would think, in all the circumstances, an inhuman restriction—but she accepts it, voluntarily. But, my lord, her lover is not so amenable to the discipline of the divorce laws. It is Christmas Eve, and, unexpectedly, he is off duty. He hurries to Manchester: he takes supper with her: and, as he will frankly tell you, he does all he can to spend the night with her. As he will tell you, as they will tell you, she sends him away. There was no adultery that night, though there was, we freely admit, indiscretion—compromising circumstances. Unhappily, whether by Fate or——'

'Mr. Barter,' said the Judge drily, 'I am never drawn

towards litigants who are consistently the victims of Fate.' ❀

Mr. Barter laughed as merrily as any one in Court: but he thought, 'Better cut the cackle' and he said, 'I am much obliged to your lordship, and I heartily agree. My lord, I was going to say "Whether by Fate or Malice". If your lordship pleases, I will withdraw Fate and leave Malice standing—for that I believe to represent the true facts of the case. By malice, then, or some other influence, my lord, the attention of the King's Proctor is drawn to the affairs of my client, out of all the many hundreds of women in her unhappy position: and the King's Proctor's very proper inquiries, my lord, disclose these undoubted, these compromising acts of indiscretion. As a result, my lord, he makes two charges against my client. The first charge she admits, though it would have been easy to deny it; the second charge she denies, though, of the two, it may be the more difficult to repel. That, in brief, my lord, is my client's story—the story, I shall submit, of an honest woman who deserves the favourable exercise of your lordship's discretion. Mrs. Adam.'

Mary said to herself, 'Fear nothing,' braced her spirit, and rose. But the Judge said, 'At two o'clock.' Lunch.

'No luck,' said Figgie, hurrying her down to the horrid little restaurant. 'Like lunching on the guillotine. What about a whisky-and-soda, dear? Put some stuffing into you. I always like something before I make a speech.'

'Figgie, I believe I will.'

After lunch there was an *ex parte* application in Admiralty about a foreign ship which some one wanted to arrest. The matter annoyed the Judge, for the practice was strange to him, and the delay was agony to Mary. But at last the Admiralty man got what he wanted and went away.

'Hold the Book in the right hand, please, and read the oath aloud.'

Here she was, then, for the third time, looking down at the kindly usher, swearing that she would tell in public the whole truth about her private life.

Here she was, for the third time, telling the world who she was and when she was married, and where she lived. This time, too, there was a row of formal questions about her petition and her decree nisi. Now she felt strangely cool.

Then Mr. Barter plunged suddenly *in medias res*. 'Mrs. Adam, I want his lordship to be perfectly clear about your position. Have you heard all the evidence which has been called by my learned friend in these proceedings?'

'Yes.'

'Do you wish to deny any statements of fact which these witnesses have made?'

'No.'

'Did you commit adultery with Mr. Seal on the night of the 6th of July last?'

'Yes,' said Mary, firmly enough: but she felt suddenly faint, and she felt herself blushing—what a fool! She gripped the ledge and stared at the shorthand-writer's beautiful pen, which hung poised like a hawk above his pad, ready to swoop upon the next question.

The Judge was writing laboriously in longhand, and Mr. Barter, with his rump resting comfortably on the top of the desk behind him, waited.

'On the night of December 24th did Mr. Seal come to your room, as was described by the witness Rigby?'

'Yes.'

'Did you commit adultery that night?'

'No.'

'Or on any other occasion?'

'No.'

'Did Mr. Seal kiss you, as the witness Rigby described?'

'Yes.'

'Has he kissed you on any other occasion?'

'Often.'

'Apart from the night of——'

All this was slow and tiresome, but easy. There was never any doubt what answer ought to be made: and Mary, trained to the apprehension of an audience, felt that this

one, so far, was with her. Certainly, it was held. No cough-
ing or rustling: hardly a whisper. But the slowness of the
dialogue was painful, the waits between questions while the
Judge wrote in his book. She did not know where to look
during the waits. If she looked at Mr. Barter, she would
see behind him some face in the crowd, the eyes staring at
her, and she would wonder what the mind was thinking about
her. She tried looking down at the floor of the Court, but
that made her feel guilty: she tried looking straight ahead,
high up, at one of the oak panels, a particular panel, darker
than the others: but that, she felt, was awkward and
theatrical. On the whole, the safest place to look at was the
fountain-pen of the official shorthand writer, or the top
of his bald head. Except when she spoke too low, he never
looked at her.

Mr. Barter took her safely through the story of the *Curlew*:
though this was not so easy. The roundaboutness of the
questions was extraordinary. He couldn't, it seemed, say,
'Did you mean to get back that night?' He had to say,
'Did you intend to return at any particular time?' and she
said, 'Yes.' And then he said, 'At what time?' And she,
'By dinner-time.' Four speeches instead of two—like a bad
playwright. She had been warned about this—some stuff
about 'leading questions'—but when there were so many
questions, and every question meant another uncomfortable stare at the fountain-pen, it was hard to bear. Still,
that part of it was all right, and surely nobody now would
believe that she had deliberately worked for a night-out
with Martin. Poor Martin. What was he feeling like? She
dared not look at him. And once, when she looked at Mr.
Barter, for a change, her eyes went past him and found John.
His face very white, his spectacles very large, his hair, she
thought, thinner still. Fancy John being there! Poor
John. Not looking at her, of course, the thoughtful fellow.
John was always staring at the Judge, very serious, but,
she thought, very angry. No wonder. Poor John.

The part about the 'concealing a material fact' was not
so easy. For here she had a double duty, to show that Mr.
Freebody did not know about her adultery in the *Curlew*,

and to show that she had honestly misunderstood his questions. The Judge intervened, and it was difficult: difficult because the Judge was kind, and Mary felt that he believed her, and was on her side. And he said, so slowly and gently, looking over the top of his spectacles, like some nice grandfather at a Christmas party:

'Mrs. Adam, you've given your evidence, so far, very frankly. Don't be afraid—it's your own counsel, you know, who is putting these questions, and I am quite sure that there is nothing which Mr. Freebody wishes to conceal. I want you to tell me, as clearly as you can remember, what was in your mind at this time with regard to your duty before the law?'

This was the worst moment yet. Mary gripped the ledge: and the hated word 'DISCRETION' swelled up in her head and threatened to burst; but she could form no sentence about it.

'Well?' said the Judge, sweetly.

'My lord, Mr. Freebody said he supposed I shouldn't need the discretion—and I didn't quite know what he meant.'

'Yes? Was that all?'

Oh, dear—now she was getting Mr. Freebody into trouble! She would have to explain that there were two times. But it was too difficult to explain everything: better, she thought, perhaps, to telescope the two times into one.

'No, my lord. He said something about—had I been living with anybody? And I thought that meant—living with somebody—something permanent. And as there was only this one time, my lord—I thought it didn't mean—it didn't matter so much.'

The Judge looked straight at her for a moment or two; and Mary felt that she was under a microscope, being very carefully weighed by an infallible machine. But she met the dangerous gaze steadily, and four men in Court said to themselves, 'She's fine!'

The Judge said at last, 'I see,' and returned deliberately to his normal pose, like a tortoise drawing in its head.

Saved!

And then Mr. Barter himself must underline things and put her into a state of confusion again.

Mr. Barter said, 'Whatever was said, or was not said,

Mrs. Adam, did it ever occur to you that you ought to disclose to any one what happened on the night of July 6th?'

'No.'

But that wasn't really true! She had known, really, that she ought to tell Mr. Freebody, and ask him if it mattered: but she had been so anxious to keep Martin out of the case. She longed to say now to the nice Judge, 'As a matter of fact I didn't say anything because of Mr. Seal's job,' but Mr. Freebody, though he had never put it into definite words, had made her understand that she must not say that, for it was not a good excuse. But why didn't he warn Mr. Barter not to ask silly questions? Here she was, to all intents and purposes, lying again—and all her brave talk about telling the whole truth was nonsense. For the first time, during the wait, she looked at Mr. Freebody with a little frown, her eyes following her mind. And Sir Humphrey, watching her closely, followed both.

The audience was not so quiet now. There were coughs and movements. The Court was still crowded: standing people blocked the gangways: and every seat abandoned was quickly seized. But there seemed to be more coming and going. After one of Mary's answers the Judge said sharply, 'Keep quiet, please.' The usher pushed through the standing audience to the second row from the back, and whispered fiercely to an old man reading a newspaper, 'Put that paper away! No papers in Court!' Mary, with her theatre sense, not looking at the crowd, felt a difference in the atmosphere, but could not tell what it was. She thought, 'They don't like me. They know I've lied.' And she thought, 'Heavens, if this is my own counsel what will it be like when the other man begins?'

But the rest of the examination-in-chief was less perilous. Mr. Barter conducted her delicately through the whole story of Manchester: and here, being able to tell the simple truth simply, she was not afraid. Martin's surprise appearance— her resolution—their telephone call—her weak but innocent acquiescence—the noises heard at the door—the discovery of the shoes—the black cotton: all was told. Yes, before that she had had an idea that somebody was outside, watching: and Mr. Seal had thought he heard somebody. The light dwindled: a faint flush of rose came through the great windows behind her and for a few minutes played on the panels across the Court. Then suddenly it was dark: and, high up, the two rings of lamps were lit, a soft light, like twenty-four large luminous pearls.

Under the roof, above the twenty-four globes, hung a wintry mist, but the well of the Court was cosy: the green-shaded lamp on the Judge's table lit up one side of his face and gave it the genial glow of an old man sitting before the fire. Some of those who had their doubts about Mary began to take a gentler view. Once more she was asked whether she had ever committed adultery except in the *Curlew*, and, once more, firmly, she said 'No.' She looked at her little watch. Twenty to four. Mr. Barter must have nearly done now, surely, but there was no hope, she supposed, of their finishing her cross-examination to-day. The Court 'rose' at four-fifteen. Another bad night ahead. And she must play this evening, whatever happened. It would be awful: but she would face it. That put Florrie into her mind. Florrie had vowed that she would get a seat in Court somewhere. Where was Florrie? Between two questions, Mary, for the first time, glanced up at the public gallery. Full of people, all staring down at her. An alarming sight, and she lowered her eyes quickly: but she had seen Florrie for a second. Florrie was sitting in the front row, next to the Judge's private gallery (full too): and her devoted old eyes, fixed upon Mary, were trying to say, 'We're quite all right. We'll show 'em, won't we, dear?' It was sweet of Florrie to be sitting up there, looking like that, and Mary, in that second, got the message and was comforted.

Now, then—'Heavy Humphrey' had the stage.

'You present yourself to the Court, Mrs. Adam, as a woman who is telling the whole truth?'

'I do.'

'You are keeping nothing back which, to your knowledge, the Court ought to know?'

'Nothing.'

'How long have you known Mr. Seal?'

'Four or five years.'

'And how long have you been on terms of affection?'

'About two.'

'Can you remember when it was he first kissed you?'

'Well, about the same time.'

'Two years. But you say that until the night of Sunday, the 6th of July, that is, nearly eighteen months later, you never committed adultery?'

'No.'

'Your counsel suggested that that was not for lack of persuasion. Is that correct?'

'Yes.'

'But you were a virtuous woman, still tied to your lawful husband, and until Sunday, the 6th of July, you resisted temptation?'

'Yes,' said Mary doubtfully. What a foul way of putting it!

'But on the previous Sunday morning, the 29th June, Mr. Seal was in your bedroom and kissed you?'

'Yes.'

'You were in your night-gown?'

'And kimono.'

'And kimono. Very well.' If you really think that helps you, Sir Humphrey's tone seemed to say. . . . 'Wasn't that a little incautious, Mrs. Adam?'

'I saw no harm.'

'Had Mr. Seal ever been in your bedroom before—either at "White Ladies" or elsewhere?'

'No.'

'Not the previous night?'

'No,' said Mary a little fiercely.

'Are you in the habit of receiving gentlemen in a night-dress—and kimono?'

'No. But Mr. Seal was different——'

'How?'

'We—we were old friends.'

'Old friends. But if it is true that you were virtuously resisting the dishonourable proposals of this—old friend, isn't he the last person you would invite into your bedroom?'

'I didn't invite him. He knocked and looked in——'

'Can you say how he knew that that was your room?'

'My lord——' said Mr. Barter, jumping up quickly: but already Mary had answered: 'I don't think he did. He couldn't find his braces, and——'

There was a squall of laughter, with a tang of ribaldry in it. One usher looked up at the gallery and said, 'Quiet, please'; the other ferociously said 'Silence!' and with his hands made gestures signifying 'Bad dog, down!'

Mr. Barter was on his feet: and he said, 'My lord, Mr. Seal is to be called and will account for his movements, if necessary. This witness cannot be expected——'

'My lord, my learned friend——'

'My lord——'

The Judge said, 'I saw nothing objectionable in the question, Mr. Barter. The witness might have told this gentleman which was her room. They might have said "Good night" at the door the night before. But I don't see that it will help us much, Sir Humphrey.'

'If your lordship pleases,' said Sir Humphrey, well pleased himself with the little passage. And the Judge, as if determined that all should have fair play, turned to Mary. 'Is your answer this, Mrs. Adam? You've already told us that Mr. Seal knocked at your door, and asked permission to use the bell because he could get no attention in his own room. And now you say that, so far as you know, he did not know when he knocked that the room was yours?'

'Yes, my lord.'

The Judge gave both K.C.s a kindly look, which seemed to say, 'See how easy it is if you leave it to me.'

'How many rooms,' said Sir Humphrey, 'are there in that corridor, Mrs. Adam—roughly?'

'I should say about twelve.'

'About twelve. And it was quite by chance, so far as you know, that Mr. Seal, having lost his braces, happened to knock at your door and not at one of the other eleven?'

'As far as I know. He may have knocked on all of them. But mine was half open——'

Mary stopped: she must not, she knew, say too much: and she wanted to say more and more. She gripped the ledge tightly: she must not let this smooth, insinuating fellow

rattle her. But she was beginning to be rattled, she felt
wobbly and weak—and over this ridiculous little incident,
to which she had never given a thought. What *was* the use
of telling the truth?

'Yes, Mrs. Adam! Your door was half open, you were in
your night-dress—*and* kimono—and somebody knocks, you
say "Come in"—is that right?'

'Yes.'

'And in walks a gentleman whose dishonourable proposals you have been resisting?'

Oh, dear—everything sounded so dreadful in this twisted
language! But:

'Yes,' said Mary.

'Were you surprised?'

'A little.'

'Were you alarmed?'

'Why should I be?'

'Answer the question directly, please,' said the Judge
gravely.

'My lord, I'm not a child. I can take care of myself!'

Oh, dear—she ought not to have said that. She was
talking too much. But the questions were so maddening—
so ludicrous. Did they think one committed adultery just
after breakfast in some one else's house—with children
running in and out of the room?

'What steps,' said the smooth voice, 'did you take to
protect yourself on this occasion?'

'I don't understand.'

'Did you ask Mr. Seal to leave the room?'

'Not at once.'

'What happened, then?'

'I told him he could ring the bell, and he rang it.'

'Where was the bell?'

'At the head of the bed.'

'So Mr. Seal came into the room and, at your suggestion,
rang the bell at the head of your bed?'

'Yes.'

'And you then permitted him to kiss you?'

'Yes.'

'Wouldn't it have been wiser, in all the circumstances,
to have sent Mr. Seal away? You might have said, "I'll

ring the bell and when the maid comes tell her you want something." Wouldn't that have been wiser?'

'Perhaps.'

'But that course never occurred to you?'

'No. I never thought there'd be all this fuss about it.'

'You mean by that, don't you, that you didn't expect to be found out?'

'No.' Mary's voice flew up in a little eddy of anger. 'I mean there was nothing to be found out!'

'That what happened was nothing out of the ordinary?'

'Nothing to be ashamed of.'

'This gentleman comes into your bedroom, you are in your night-gown, and he kisses you. Do you really say, Mrs. Adam——'

But the Judge was talking, bless him!

'Sir Humphrey, you know, there are kisses and kisses, and it is easy to make too much of the word. Young people in these days——'

'My lord——'

But the Judge was off. He seldom missed an opportunity to show that he was not one of those dry-as-dust lawyers the novelists wrote about, but a man-of-the-world, acquainted with the facts of life, and keeping pace with the movement of the times. He continued amiably, 'There is the mistletoe kiss, the passionate kiss, the kiss of young love, the morning kiss of husband and wife.' ('Oh, Lord!' thought Mr. Barter.) 'You're not suggesting, are you, Sir Humphrey, that adultery took place that morning?'

'Not that morning, my lord. My lord, perhaps, arising out of your lordship's observations, I might ask the witness to describe the kiss, so far as she can——?'

'Very well, Sir Humphrey, if you think it will help. You are an actress, Mrs. Adam, and no doubt have to act various kinds of embraces—how would you classify this one?'

'It was just a little one, my lord.' And Mary for the first time, smiled: and her smile was so charming, and her answer had such a note of wistful deprecation, as if she had almost begun to despair of finding sanity in the raving world, that all the neutral hearts in Court were swept suddenly over to her side.

'Would it be fair,' began Sir Humphrey, and already she

knew that whenever he looked up at that point above the Judge's head and asked if it would be fair, the question was going to be a nasty one—'would it be fair, Mrs. Adam, adopting one of his lordship's phrases, to say that it was in the nature of a "husband-and-wife morning kiss"?'

Yes, this was dangerous, she felt, though she could not at once perceive why. And it was difficult to answer too. . . .

'If you mean it wasn't very exciting——' she began. There was laughter, and the impartial public credited her with another point.

But Sir Humphrey was not even smiling, and he faced her now: and his tone said that he had done with sparring and was proceeding mercilessly to the knock-out.

'I'm suggesting, you see, Mrs. Adam, that your relations at that date *were* those of husband and wife, that you received this gentleman in the casual manner you've described because it was not his first visit—because he was quite at home in your bedroom.'

'*It's not true!*'

Mary was angry now; her lips trembled, she went pale, and she rapped the back of one small hand on the ledge of the box.

'What a pathetic, feeble little gesture for a leading lady!' Figgie thought.

'You still tell the Court, then, do you, that at that date you had never committed adultery?'

'I do.'

'Very well. Now about the yachting expedition?'

But the Judge looked at the large clock, and said, 'Would this be a convenient moment, Sir Humphrey——?'

'Certainly, my lord——'

There was a little discussion about the next day's programme.

'Probably not before twelve, then,' said the Judge at last, and with surprising swiftness disappeared, like a wise old rabbit bolting into his hole.

The audience, standing up respectfully to see his lordship go to ground, thought 'A pity.' A good entertainment had come to an end too soon. Mary had the mixed feelings of one who is told by the dentist that that will be all to-day—

it was blessed to have a respite, but hateful not to get the whole thing over.

Mr. Barter, in the wide corridor, nodded kindly to her, and hurried away to a consultation.

Mr. Freebody said, 'You go home now and have a good sleep.'

She said, 'I'm going to play to-night.'

'Must you?'

'No, but I'm going to.'

'Well, well'—he stopped himself from saying, 'My God, what guts!'—'I think I may come. Could I get in?'

Figgie, standing by, said, 'I'll tell them to keep seats for you.' (That, alas! was easy. Mr. Freebody could have four boxes if he liked.)

'Lovely,' said Mary. 'Come round and see me afterwards, Mr. Freebody.'

'No,' he said. 'Better not. You're in the box still. Good night.'

Figgie explained, leading her down the great Central Hall and talking busily, as he thought was best. 'The idea is, you see, that your lawyers mustn't get at you and tell you how to correct anything you said to-day, or what you ought to do to-morrow. It's a queer business—the law. So fair in many ways and so foul in others. You know, the more I see of the law the more I respect the lawyers—and the less I respect the law. It isn't their fault, after all, what the law is—they've got to run the thing as they find it; and I think they put up a jolly good show. Look at this, now.'

They stopped and looked back up the dark Hall. The February fog had crept in and hung like a flimsy curtain over the windows and the upper arches. The place was parsimoniously lit by two great globes, high up and hazy, like two moons on a misty night. The feet of lawyers and litigants, hurrying away across the polished pavement, were shockingly loud in the Gothic gloom, sending echoes far up beyond the two moons, and seeming impious, like noise in a cathedral.

'Fine show,' said Mr. Figg, the showman.

Mary shivered. 'It's an awful thing to be up against.' She was so little and the law so large. How had she ever

18

thought she could pit herself against this great gloomy pitiless place?

'Don't worry, dear,' said Figgie, and took her arm again. 'You'll win all right. I felt that all day. But that's the cleverness of it, you know—it's all such a good *show*—all the robes and the wigs and the Gothic and the long words —it all makes you feel you're in church: and that makes you feel that what they say is all right, when all the time you know it's raving lunacy. Look at to-day—all that stuff about Martin being in your room that morning. Well, I can see exactly how that might have happened, without meaning a thing—like somebody running into your dressing-room at the theatre: but the way that soft-soaper put it—I really began to think it mattered myself. Anyhow, the Judge didn't, and that's the great thing.'

'Think not, Figgie?'

'Sure, dear. Taxi!'

What a comfort Figgie was!

'Why not till twelve to-morrow?'

'Something to do with that ship.'

The next morning the charming versatility of the Probate, Divorce, and Admiralty Division was beautifully displayed. The President was occupied with the fantastic will of a wealthy religious woman which had embroiled a great number of relatives with a great number of charities. Mr. Justice Fish, and his brother Gregory J., had both fallen ill with influenza. And the hearing of *Adam* v. *Adam* (*King's Proctor showing cause*), *pt. hd.*, had to be suspended for the consideration of the urgent affairs of the foreign steamship *Regen*, which had damaged a British ship in the Lower Hope and now proposed to leave the Port of London. Mary heard some of the proceedings, fascinated but bewildered by the talk: ships being arrested, writs nailed to masts—the ship, she gathered, wanted to bail herself out—underwriters, charter-parties, demurrage, overtaking vessels, and a foreign sea-captain giving evidence with difficulty and indignation. She admired her Judge still more; for, though he had not known the meaning of 'turning', he seemed to be as confident in Admiralty as in adultery. Indeed, as he remarked to a King's Bench colleague at lunch-time, he was doing his best to make a show with 'one foot in the sea and the other in the sewer'.

But he seemed, she thought, less genial this morning: he jumped on a persistent junior who would not take 'No' for an answer, and he complained to the usher about draughts. It was a bitter, easterly day, and Mary remembered gloomily a saying of Mr. Freebody's that in the end the 'discretion of the Court' meant 'the liver of the Judge on that particular morning'.

It was nearly one before Sir Humphrey had the stage again, and the Judge turned his attention from the *Regen* to the *Curlew*.

Sir Humphrey, this morning, seemed to take an even more unfavourable view of her character and veracity. There was a lot of 'Now, now'-ing. 'Now, now, Mrs. Adam, that wasn't the question I asked you. Will you listen, please? What was the *real* reason why you made a face at Mrs. Merridew, when it was suggested that Miss Simmons should accompany you?'

'I didn't want Miss Simmons to come.'

'Oh, no. Wasn't the real reason that you didn't want *any one* to come—that you wanted to be alone with Mr. Seal?'

'Well, yes.'

The Judge looked at her. 'Now, Mrs. Adam, you know, you could very well have said that before.'

'I'm very sorry, my lord, but everything I say he twists about so.'

But this made matters worse.

'If you are not treated fairly,' said the Judge, more in sorrow than in anger, 'you may be sure that your counsel will object, and I shall protect you.'

Mary whispered, 'I'm sorry, my lord,' and felt as if she had been threatened with a whipping, though she had still no notion what it was that she had done wrong. 'Oh, dear,' she thought, 'if they're going on like this I shall cry or scream or something.' She bit her lip: and Martin Seal swore in his soul: and Figgie muttered to Mrs. Figgie, 'Bad beginning.'

'And you didn't want any one to accompany you, Mrs.

Adam, because you had no real intention of returning that night?'

'Yes, I had.'

'I suggest to you that all this story of your being caught by the wind and the tide, and the rest of it, is an ingenious fabrication of your own?'

'Well, you're wrong.'

Oh, dear, she must control herself: but how she hated this smooth, soapy fellow!

On he went, ignoring her rudeness, steady as a snail.

'If you really intended to return before nightfall, why didn't you take Mr. Hardy's advice?'

'I didn't think. I was happy.'

This answer was not sullen, but very quiet, and infinitely sad. A heavy hush and stillness held the Court, such as the name of Christ might bring upon a Board-meeting. For the first time there was a little break in the easy rhythm of Sir Humphrey's questions; and the Judge stared at Mary without writing her answer down, as if the mention of happiness in that place had shocked them both.

'He told you, didn't he,' Sir Humphrey said at last, 'not to go farther than the Nore?'

'Yes.'

'And, in fact, upon the outward journey, you say you went nearly as far as the Mouse?'

'Let me see—how far exactly is the Mouse?' said the Judge.

'My lord——'

Charts were handed about, and his lordship found the Mouse Lightship on the chart and measured the distance from the Nore: and while he was about it, had a look at the Medway: and observed that there was a town called Queenborough not very far from Long Reach. And Mary looked down and met Martin's eyes. Each smiled sadly and looked away: for in this strange world a look might be illegal. But Mary, waiting for the next question, thought of the *Curlew*, the *Curlew* solitary in the creek, the only place in the world: and the mist creeping slowly, like a sea, across the saltings: and the warm russet moon, a short-sighted, friendly moon, peering through the mist as an old lady through her glasses: and the tide sucking at the

Curlew's sides: and the waterbirds rustling and calling in the reeds: and Martin and Mary, magically alone and free, and in love. Now all that magic and happiness had become a shame and a disgrace: a thing for lawyers to paw and pry into, a matter of 'adultery' and 'inference of guilt'—'a material fact which ought to be disclosed'. 'A material fact!' Such words for such a night!

Mary wanted to cry—or to throw things: and Martin, again looking furtively her way, feared that she would. But she thought now, 'What was it Figgie said last night? "It isn't the lawyers who are to blame—but the law".' Poor lawyers. She must keep her temper.

So she was very mild and acquiescent during the next ten minutes—mild and acquiescent, but despairing. For Sir Humphrey, she felt, was convincing the whole world that her night in the *Curlew* had been a thing carefully planned and calculated by a wanton woman, and not a lovely gift from the lawless gods. The main thought in her mind now was that she was beaten, whatever she said. There was a moment when Sir Humphrey seemed to be suggesting that they had never gone out into the Thames at all, but had made straight for the secluded creek. And when at last Sir Humphrey said, 'I put it to you'—he was always 'putting it' now—'that you never had any intention of returning to "White Ladies" that night?'—she answered, 'All right, have it your own way.'

The Judge gave her a sharp look: but he said kindly, 'Come, come, Mrs. Adam. Keep control of yourself. Ask the question again, please, Sir Humphrey.'

But already she was ashamed of herself. She caught a glimpse of Mr. Freebody's profile, very still—Mr. Freebody, who believed in her. 'I've no guts at all,' she thought. And this time she answered firmly, 'Of course I did!'

The Judge said, in that slow, confiding manner, which always made her feel that, after all, there was some sanity and safety in the world, 'Tell me this, Mrs. Adam—and don't be afraid to answer frankly.' He paused, thinking out the best and fairest form of words. 'You say that you did intend, when you started out, to return before dark? If you had really given your mind to it, and ordered the voyage accordingly—I'm not saying that you did not—but, if you had, do you think that you could have carried out that intention successfully?'

'Yes, my lord. Easily. But when one's sailing—— My lord, it's so difficult to explain——'

'Nevertheless, I think I understand,' said the gentle voice, letting the words fall like drops of syrup into the Court. 'When one is sailing—and one is with the individual one loves—and one is happy, as I think you said—one does not think—one forgets discretion—and anything may happen. Is that what you want to say?'

'Yes, my lord,' said Mary, fervently. What a lovely old man he was! If only all of them——!

'At five minutes past two,' said the lovely old man.

'Thirty-five minutes for lunch,' said Figgie admiringly. 'My hat, these lawyers are whales for work!'

Mary looked across the room. Martin, with his back to her, sat alone at a little table. Poor boy! They had arranged, upon advice, not to see each other during the case—but she couldn't think why. Considering that they were confessing to adultery they might surely have had fried plaice together. And the moment she escaped from the box he would be in it. Oh, dear! And it would be worse for him—much worse, after all the things she had had to say about him. She was the virtuous female, resisting dishonourable advances; but he was the unsuccessful villain. She longed to go to him. And he was having some trouble about his food. He kept appealing to waitresses for something, but they hurried by, disowning his table. He looked cross and upset. Oh, dear! 'What about a whisky-and-soda?' said Figgie. 'Put some stuffing into you.'

'Figgie, I believe I will.'

After lunch Sir Humphrey passed to the hotel at Manchester: and Mary met him with a better spirit. But this part of the ordeal was worse than anything before: for now she was admitting almost everything, but denying everything else. Why, if her intentions were really virtuous, did she permit Mr. Seal to come to her room at all? This wasn't a case, was it, of just after breakfast, in a friend's house, with people about? It wasn't a case, was it, of a lonely boat, and a woman caught in circumstances in which, according to my learned friend, resistance to temptation was humanly impossible? It was a case, wasn't it, of a large hotel, at dead of night, when detection was highly improbable? It wasn't a case, was it, of a violent man hammering at her door, making a scene? It was a case of a gentleman, by telephone, requesting permission to visit a lady, and receiving that permission? And the gentleman had already, hadn't he, received the highest favours the lady could grant? But on this occasion there was no intention to grant those favours again? What, then, was the intention in permitting the gentleman to come? To say 'Good night'? Was that all? Quite sure? Was that quite fair to the gentleman—in all the circumstances? Perhaps not. According to evidence the gentleman was in the room for nearly an hour. Was that right? Probably. Rather a long time to spend saying 'Good night', wasn't it? No? What happened? Talked? Remember what you talked about?

'Yes,' said Mary, suddenly fierce again. 'We talked about your beastly detectives.'

'I beg your pardon?'

For the first time since the case began Mary felt that she had scored a winner. Sir Humphrey's flow of inevitable insinuation was checked: he diverted his eyes from their favourite target over the Judge's head, and stared at Mary, with his mouth a little open, as if mortally wounded by the suggestion that he was the kind of person who employed detectives—a sort of *solicitor*!

Mary continued, breathless but triumphant. 'That's what we talked about—how he was to get away! If it hadn't been for that he wouldn't have been there five minutes.'

But Sir Humphrey's agile mind had already perceived how this assault might be used to his own advantage.

'I see, Mrs. Adam,' he said, as cool and smooth as if he had been working up to this point throughout his cross-examination. 'So that, believing yourselves to be observed, you had no mind for love-making?'

And Mary could not resist the temptation: 'Would *you* commit adultery,' she said, 'with a detective at the key-hole?'

Oh, dear, she shouldn't have said that! Even as the words came out she knew that they were wrong. But out they would come, like a comedian's gag. Still, the whole world was laughing, even Sir Humphrey—and what a thing it was to get a good laugh again! But the old Judge wouldn't like her any more. She glanced at him, alarmed. He was going to say something, clearly: but his amiable eyes twinkled and she thought his lips twitched.

He said, 'Mrs. Adam, you are not here to put questions to learned counsel.'

A little ripple of merriment, more subtle, ran about the Court.

Sir Humphrey said, and his eyes were sliding up the wall again: 'Is it your case, then, that you were prevented from committing adultery by the supposed presence of a detective?'

'No.'

'How soon, do you say, after Mr. Seal's arrival did you suspect the presence of a detective outside?'

'As soon as he came.'

'As soon as he came? In that case, wouldn't the wisest thing have been for Mr. Seal to leave your room at once?'

'I suppose it would'—doubtfully. What a devil the man was!

'Your "Good night" story would then have been more easy to believe?'

No answer.

'But, in fact, he stayed for nearly an hour?'

'We weren't sure that it was a detective.'

'Are you sure, Mrs. Adam, that you didn't commit adultery?'

'Yes.'

The devil! In two or three sentences, Mary thought, Sir Humphrey had deflated her again. But Mr. Figg knew the value of a good laugh: and he said to himself that she had scored heavily on points. He whispered to Mrs. Figg, 'An inspiration!' which was not quite fair to Mary's legal advisers. 'And how *true*!' he chuckled. ' "Would *anybody*

—with a detective at the keyhole—marvellous!' Mr. Figg always said that every laugh in a play was worth thousands of pounds to him.

Yes, he thought, the thing was going better now. A few more of Sir Humphrey's serpentine questions, a few rather sullen replies, and then one of the Judge's slow, sobering interventions.

'Nobody is trying to trap you, Mrs. Adam. But, you know, you're asking the Court to believe a good deal that is difficult—I don't say that you won't be successful—but Sir Humphrey is only doing his duty in testing the truth of what you say.'

Mary at once was all penitence and sweetness: and she said in the gentle voice the old Judge could always draw from her, 'I'm sorry, my lord. I know it all sounds difficult. But I'm telling the truth. And if I'm not believed I can't help it.'

They looked straight at each other; and those in Court had the impression of two honest souls touching and understanding, a welcome thing after the wit-play of cross-examination. Figgie said to himself, 'He does believe her.' And the wise Sir Humphrey asked no more questions about the Manchester hotel.

But, as in some classic steeplechase, every fence seemed stiffer than the one before. Now it was the Concealment of a Material Fact and her excuse for it. She was an educated woman, wasn't she, with some knowledge of the world? Her present petition for dissolution was not the first she had brought, was it? Before that petition was filed she had had, no doubt, many interviews with her solicitors? And probably discussed the divorce laws with her friends? She knew, didn't she, that a woman could not ask for a divorce if she herself had been continuously guilty of adultery, unless that guilt was disclosed to the Court? Did she know that, or not, when the petition was filed?

'Yes—if it was continuous—I knew. But I thought if it was only once——'

'You thought, did you, that if there was only a single act it did not matter?'

'Yes.'

This seemed a nice, helpful question: but it must be a trap: for Sir Humphrey's eyes were higher up the wall than usual.

'Did you know that, in law, a single act of adultery is sufficient ground for a divorce?'

'Yes.'

'You knew that in such a case a single act *does* matter?'

'Yes.'

'What reason, then, had you to suppose that in your case, where adultery must be disclosed, a single act "did *not* matter"?'

'Oh, my God!' thought Mary. She opened her mouth, but no sound came forth. A terrible moment—like 'drying up' on a first night.

But the beloved Judge came to her rescue. Turning back the big pages of his note-book, he said, 'I think, Sir Humphrey, we've had that clearly enough. The witness told us that she drew a wrong conclusion from her solicitor's phrase about "living with anybody". "I thought",' the old man read, ' "that meant living with somebody—something permanent. And as there was only this one time I thought it didn't matter so much.' "

'Yes, my lord, but, if your lordship permits——'

Sir Humphrey, secretly, was discontented with his lordship. A cross-examination was a scientific process, a careful balancing of brick on brick: and just when the topmost brick was being delicately put into place this old egoist would intervene and send the whole thing toppling over.

But the old egoist thought that he knew as many ways as Sir Humphrey of arriving at the truth.

'Look at me, Mrs. Adam,' he said.

Mary looked at the dear old man: and she said to herself, trembling, 'This is the crisis.'

The old man, before he spoke again, slowly wagged his head, once to the right, once to the left, and once to the right again.

He said then, so slow, so inescapable, 'Do you tell me, Mrs. Adam, that what you have said is the truth—and the whole truth?'

'Yes, my lord.' But was it? The whole truth? Looking

straight at this old man who believed in her, could she stop
there? She couldn't. Though it was all nonsense, raving
nonsense, she must be square with the old man. 'But also,
my lord——'

She mustn't: she would ruin everything.

'But also——? Yes?'

'My lord—also—I wanted to keep Mr. Seal's name out
of it—even from the solicitor—because of the B.B.C. My
lord—I was afraid he'd lose his job.'

There!

Mr. Barter, to his secret soul, said 'The fool!' and, bending
forward, whispered in Mr. Freebody's ear. She saw Mr.
Freebody shake his head vigorously. She looked back at
the Judge. The old man was fumbling among his papers
and wagging his head again. He's upset, she said, looking
at his mouth.

He said—but in how different a voice, 'You were afraid
that if you disclosed your adultery, even to your solicitor,
Mr. Seal would lose his employment, because of the scandal?
Is that it?'

'Yes, my lord. He has.'

The old man's body swayed a little—as if he were dodging
some irritating insect. 'He's upset,' she said, 'but holding
himself in.'

'But, you see, Mrs. Adam'—the voice was patient still,
but she could hear the disappointment in it—'you see, Mrs.
Adam, in the statement of facts which I have before me—
the facts relied on in your prayer for my discretion—there
is nothing about your anxiety for Mr. Seal. You say there,
as you have said in Court, that you did not realize that what
took place between you and Mr. Seal was important enough
to demand disclosure. That is one thing. It is quite another
thing to say that you kept quiet in order to shield your lover.
The first may or may not be an acceptable excuse. The
second could never be. Which do you——'

But the despairing little voice broke in, 'Oh, my lord,
why not?' It was the voice of a disciplined witness no
more, the voice of a tragic actress facing disaster in the
Third Act. All was over now, she felt, by the way the old
man looked and spoke, and instinct said that it was no
more use to pretend and be obedient. The words poured

out, unplanned, unordered—and all the old man's attempts at interruption could not stop them.

'Oh, my lord, why not,' cried the pitiful voice. 'What better excuse could there be? My lord, if I've done wrong, I'm sorry: but I don't understand—it all seems nonsense— I've done no harm to any one, my lord—my husband doesn't want me—and I've done nothing, my lord, but love somebody. Is that a crime? My lord, you've been very kind —but why *should* he lose his job because he loves me?— why *should* our private lives be spied upon—and messed about in a Court like this? My lord, I've tried so hard to do right, and tell the truth, but everything I do seems wrong, and I am so tired, so very tired of it all.'

The voice sank as she finished and sadly died to nothing at the end: the witness put her hand to her face and wept bitterly.

The same shocked stillness held the Court as when she had said that she was happy. Such alien, terrible words— 'happiness' and 'love'—they should not burst like bandits into a Matrimonial Cause. And those worse words—about 'private lives being messed about'!—as well tear off the Judge's wig, or put a match to the Courts of Justice.

Figgie wanted to cry with Mary.

The usher went to her with smelling-salts. Mr. Barter, glad of the interlude, debated swiftly in his mind certain professional points, and whispered with Mr. Freebody. 'This may do us a bit of good,' the solicitor whispered. 'And we'll need it,' said Mr. Barter grimly. The Judge, with a dab of his hand, restored Sir Humphrey to his seat. This was a pity, he thought. A nice little woman, and he had believed in her—perhaps did still. 'I'm doing too much,' he thought. 'Ought to have left all this to counsel.' But he would try her once again.

'Would you like to stand down for a little?' he asked kindly.

'No, thank you, my lord. I'm quite all right. I'm very sorry, my lord.'

Again that fugitive, enchanting smile! And Figgie muttered, 'Little devil! Wonder if she cried on purpose.' For the stalls, at least, he thought, were her slaves again. But Mary was thinking, 'What a fool!' And what a sight she must be! Mary Moon messy with tears in public!

The Judge said, 'Mrs. Adam, I am prepared to overlook certain expressions you have used under the stress of emotion. But, you see, I am asking myself——' He checked himself suddenly. 'Go on, please, Sir Humphrey.'

'And about time too,' Sir Humphrey thought. Sir Humphrey had not many more questions, but they were scorpions. Until this moment she had concealed from every one, hadn't she, the second of her two reasons for concealment—her desire to shield Mr. Seal? Yes. She must say 'Yes'—to save Mr. Freebody; but, oh, Lord, another lie! Could the Court be sure that there was nothing else she was concealing? Did she still say that she did not know that she ought to disclose the *Curlew* episode? Suppose that she had understood perfectly well, wouldn't she still have kept it back for the sake of Mr. Seal? Mr. Barter objected to that—a hypothetical question—but the Judge said it was permissible, and Mary answered 'No.' Then Sir Humphrey put it to her that her real and only reason for concealment was her anxiety for Mr. Seal. He put it to her that she had knowingly and deliberately deceived the Court. He suggested to her that the night of July 6th was not the only occasion on which she had committed adultery. And he asked—his last question—'You are an actress, are you not, Mrs. Adam?'

Then Sir Humphrey sat down, conscious of a job well done. And if the old man had left him alone, he thought, they would have been where they were much earlier.

What worried Mary was that the old man never looked at her now. She had lost him, she was sure.

Mr. Barter was in a hole, but not so deep as Sir Humphrey fancied. He thought the solicitors had bungled things—there was always a discreet way of preventing an intelligent witness from blurting out that sort of thing. But the point was not a substantial one, after all, though much had been made of it. The important question was how far his client's credit had been shaken in the Judge's mind. Mr. Barter believed in her still, and his voice was as breezy and confident as before.

He asked four questions only:

'Having decided in your own mind, Mrs. Adam, that you were not bound to mention to any one what happened on

the yacht, was there any reason why you should mention
to any one the name of Mr. Seal?'

'No.'

That was a fine question. Already the fog seemed thinner.
Figgie, too, who had been increasingly perplexed by the legal
manœuvres, now saw everything clearly and muttered,
'Of course. Quite right. What *was* all the fuss about?'

'Before you decided to oppose the King's Proctor's plea
in this Court, were you advised of certain other possible
courses which might be expected to involve much less
publicity for yourself and Mr. Seal?'

'Yes.'

'And, having had that advice, did you, in consultation
with Mr. Seal, decide to face the charges in open Court, as
you are doing?'

'Yes, I did.'

'Is the evidence you have given in this Court the truth
or not?'

'The truth.'

'Thank you, Mrs. Adam,' said Mr. Barter coolly. 'Mr.
Martin Seal?'

'One moment, Mr. Barter.'

The Judge had something to say. The usher shooed Mr.
Seal back to his seat.

'Mr. Barter, you know, I am wondering whether I want
to hear this evidence.'

The rustling Court froze into stillness.

'My lord, Mr. Seal will confirm in every particular——'

'Yes, yes, we will assume that, as to the facts, he tells
exactly the same story as the petitioner. It will surprise
me very much if he does not.' ('Old devil,' muttered Mr.
Freebody.) 'But what is troubling me now, Mr. Barter, is
not so much what the petitioner did as what she did not
disclose, and the reasons she gives for not disclosing it.
What have you to say about that, Mr. Barter?'

Mr. Barter, very innocent, 'Is your lordship referring
to——' A little too innocent.

The Judge said, 'You know very well to what I refer,
Mr. Barter.'

'If your lordship has in mind my client's frank admission that, apart from any other consideration, her anxiety to shield her lover would have made her reluctant to make what she believed to be an unnecessary disclosure, I submit, my lord, that too much weight can be given—and has been given—to that. It's quite clear, my lord, from her answers that that was not the primary consideration in her mind. It's clear that she made an honest decision: no doubt it was a welcome one, for the reasons mentioned. But it's clear, my lord, in my submission——'

'Is it clear, Mr. Barter? If it was clear to me I should not at this stage be discussing the point.'

'My lord——'

'You see, Mr. Barter——'

The old head wagged again, and Mr. Barter waited reverently.

'You see, Mr. Barter, you're asking me to exercise the discretion in your favour, in your client's interest. But in making my decision I must be guided not only by the interest of the parties but by considerations of the public interest. It is not in the public interest that persons found to be guilty of adultery should be allowed to escape free of all penalty. One of the penalties—and, still, I think, in spite of changed conditions and altered standards, one of the most powerful sanctions of the marriage laws—is the publicity—now limited, it is true, by Statute—which attaches to the proceedings of this Court. That operates in two ways, to mark the guilty with a social stigma, and, in some professions and callings, as we have heard, to expose them to the material risk of losing their employment or position. It may be thought hard, by the unthinking, that in some classes and spheres of occupation the revelation of adultery has very little consequence, and in others may bring social and material ruin. On the other hand, it would be intolerable if it could be said that those in high places, in important offices under the State, for example, were free to infringe the moral law without fear of consequence. It is often right that there should be, or appear to be, one law for the rich and another for the poor.'

'Glory!' thought Mr. Barter, 'is the old boy writing a book, or what?'

'For these reasons I must do nothing which might encourage the belief that persons in the position of the petitioner are entitled to conceal their own wrongdoing from motives of perverted chivalry, in order to protect their partners in guilt from social and material damage. If the petitioner had come to the Court and said directly, "I did commit adultery, but I concealed it to save my lover," these proceedings would have concluded at an early stage—if they had ever been permitted to begin. And the question upon which you have still to convince me, Mr. Barter, is whether that is not, substantially, the position to-day.'

Mr. Barter listened to this address with increasing inward dismay: but the expression on his face suggested that few previous utterances of the human voice had roused in him so much admiration and approval.

'My lord,' he said, with polite unconcern, giving the tail of his gown a twitch round his legs. 'I confess that I rely in the main on the transparent honesty of my client, as shown not only by her demeanour in the box but by the whole course of her previous conduct. Entirely of her own volition, my lord, she has chosen the course which was bound to result in the maximum of publicity, both for herself and her lover——'

'You know the old saying, Mr. Barter: "As well be hanged for a sheep as a lamb——" '

There was a little laughter, a little mystified. Mr. Barter thought, 'What the deuce is the point of that?' But he said respectfully, 'Yes, my lord; but it is a little hard, if having taken that course, the course of absolute openness, my client is now to be regarded as a person lacking in openness, for reasons which—with great respect, my lord— are not, in my submission, substantial.'

'I agree that the way in which she gave her evidence impressed me, Mr. Barter. But I have to remember that she is an actress, accustomed to playing a part——'

'My lord!' Mr. Barter was really shocked.

'I don't press that, Mr. Barter: but there it is. Nor can I entirely ignore certain expressions which fell from her, under the pressure of sudden emotion, it is true, but the more likely, for that reason, to represent the real mind than

the studied answers of a clever woman. Again, I would
not press the argument unduly: but those expressions did
suggest to me that your client, in her heart of hearts,
denies the moral authority of this Court to adjudicate upon
her matrimonial affairs at all——'

'Really, my lord, with great respect——'

But there was no stopping the old horse now.

'And, if I am satisfied that she has come into Court in
that frame of mind, denying the force and authority of the
law, I am bound to regard with some suspicion the assurance
that she has conscientiously done everything which, to her
knowledge, the law requires her to do. To put it plainly,
Mr. Barter, in one breath she tells us that the law is an old
fool, and in the next that she has throughout scrupulously
respected and obeyed the old fool.'

'Really, my lord, with great submission, is not your
lordship giving a little too much weight to the emotional
outburst of a highly-strung woman who has been under-
going a prolonged nervous strain?'

Mr. Barter's tone was masterly—the respectful, affectionate reproach of a child to a beloved grandfather. It
said, 'You are the best and wisest of mortals—but please,
please, be nice to-day.'

'I don't want to do that, Mr. Barter.' The old man paused,
and said, 'I will ask the shorthand writer to read out the
words to which I refer.'

'Oh, *dear*!' Mary whispered.

The chubby shorthand writer swiftly turned back his
pages: and in flat, mathematical tones, without pause or
expression, he read the fatal passage:

'Oh — my — lord — why — not — what — better —
excuse — could — there — be — my — lord — if — I
— have — done — wrong——'

Mary went cold within. It sounded dreadful. Like the
stage-manager reading the soubrette's part at an under-
study rehearsal.

To the audience, too, it sounded dreadful—without the
appeal of Mary's voice and the sad charm of her face.

'——be — messed — about — in — a — Court — like —
this——'

Bald, foolish, rebellious, unbalanced, rude.

19

'——I — am — so — tired — so — very — tired — of — it — all.'

The Judge wagged his head twice, and looked at Mr. Barter, as if to say, 'Sound's pretty putrid, doesn't it?'

And Mr. Barter, to himself, said, 'True. But does it matter? What's biting the old boy?'

He said boldly, 'My lord, a belief that the law is in need of amendment is by no means incompatible with perfect obedience to the law. Even His Majesty's Judges, my lord——'

But his lordship had his eye on the clock. 'Well, Mr. Barter,' he said, 'it's four o'clock now, and, in any case, little is to be gained by calling Mr. Seal to-day. Let him be here at half past ten to-morrow. Before that we shall both of us have an opportunity for reflection. At any rate, you now know the trend of my mind. At half past ten to-morrow, then.'

He rose, and, with a whisk of his black robes, was gone. The public went out chattering and bewildered.

Mr. Seal pressed Mary's hand and whispered, 'You were marvellous, darling.'

Figgie took her arm and said, 'Fine show. How d'you feel? They've made my head ache. Did you understand it all?'

'Not a thing,' said Mary. 'And I'm beginning not to care.'

'S'sh!' said Figgie. 'Well, anyhow, you've done your piece.'

'Thank God. I wouldn't do it again for three hundred a week.' What a relief it was to have escaped from that box —win or lose!

'You're not going to play to-night?'

'Yes, I am.'

'Sticky wicket,' said Mr. Barter to Mr. Freebody. 'What's the matter with our Albert to-day?'

'Trouble is, I think, he likes her—but doesn't want it to be said that he was vamped.'

'I like her too—but, my God, she talks too much. Good night.' And Mr. Barter hurried away to a consultation in the Guano case.

No one was left in Court but the ushers, tidying a little.

The junior usher said: 'Old boy's on the war-path.'

'These discretion cases are always a toss-up. Might as well back horses.'

'Albert said he's got a boil on his bottom.'

'Shouldn't be surprised. Well, coming across?'

It was scientifically correct to say that Mr. Justice Cole had a painful boil, not yet ripe, on his behind: but it would have been quite untrue to suggest that this had affected his conduct of the Adam case. He went home, thinking about the case, worried by the case, and had a worrying evening. His wife was large, dyspeptic, extravagant, and querulous; no doctor could persuade her that the symptoms of her indigestion did not point to heart disease: and she was ever seeking for new doctors who would at once make her perfectly well but keep on assuring her that she was seriously ill. Her only other interest in life was a strange card-game called Bridge, at which she invariably lost money. She could not lose as much as she had been in the habit of losing, because of the financial position: but she still lost enough to infuriate and distress Sir Albert. His salary had been cut down by the taxes to the earnings of a rising junior or freelance journalist. He had three married daughters, each of whom, in spite of an expensive education, had married impecunious and unsuccessful men—a painter, a writer, and an architect. Each of these, his wife said, was in trouble again: and the two favourite daughters had come to lunch that day and had timidly suggested, poor dears, that their allowance was inadequate and ought to be increased. This—and her heartburn—had so upset their mother that she had had to go off to the club and lose twenty pounds at Bridge. 'Twenty pounds! Good heavens,' said the Judge. 'Do you realize that that is more than twice our daily income?' Twenty pounds was two years' subscription to the golf club from which he had nobly resigned. He complained about his boil, but Lady Cole said shortly that in that case no port this evening would be a good idea. After dinner he tackled a Will case in which he had deferred judgment, not knowing what to do. He still did not know what to do; he had had no port, his boil hurt, and the testator's real intentions seemed this evening to be both uninteresting and unimportant. He went to bed early, and lay for a long time in a very hot bath, since that might benefit the boil. Lying in the bath he thought with a sense of irritation about the attractive little petitioner in the Adam case. A nice woman: he liked that colour hair—real gold: these 'platinum blondes', or whatever they were called, he thought, were silly. If he were young again—— And he had believed in her—perhaps did still. He had quite looked forward to finding in her favour, praising her honesty, giving her the 'discretion' like a sort of wedding-present for a nice niece, wishing her luck in the new life, and so on. But now, he was afraid, she had done for herself, though he wasn't quite sure. A pity. Not that she would worry very much, he thought, soaping his neck. In that sort of circle, he believed, it mattered very little if one was married or not, nowadays. Artists and actors. All over the place. No rules: no conventions. The young man had lost his job: but what was a job at the B.B.C.? He turned the hot tap again, and delicately felt the boil, to see if it was any softer. No. Hard as a billiard-ball, and painful. Poor little woman. But what were her troubles—any of their troubles—compared with his own? She was rich, probably, compared with him: earned three or four times as much as as he did, in a week. She was not tied up to a complaining, spendthrift, Bridge-fiend; she had not three penniless married daughters to worry about; she had not to sit in Court all day listening to other people's troubles with a boil on her behind. If she wanted to commit adultery she could do so and not be a penny the worse. No tradition, no rules, no responsibilities, no appearances to keep up. Though why any one should want to commit adultery when they saw what came from that kind of thing he didn't know. Three penniless daughters, all expecting to be kept alive by him, although they were married. Mr. Justice Cole stood up and gloomily scraped at his back with a loofah. All this talk about adultery. As if that was the only thing that mattered, the one marital pleasure, the sole marital sin. If that was so, how could we go on saying that human marriage had a special quality that made it superior to the mating of animals? If human love was distinguished by its spiritual splendour, the union of minds and souls and so forth, then the test for divorce ought to be whether that higher union had broken down, not whether somebody had slept in the same bed as somebody else. Discourage that, by all means, as we discourage pilfering and committing nuisances, but don't say that it's the one thing that matters. . . . And then blame the newspapers because there's so much talk of adultery. Who made the old divorce reports disgusting—before the Act of 1926? Not the naughty newspapers—they were mirrors reflecting the true facts—but the law which made it impossible to get a divorce without proof of adultery. The boil seemed a little easier; he would lie down and have another soak in the soothing water. A lot to be said for the Americans, really, though we turned up our noses at their laws. They saw, at least, that the real marital offences were not always physical. We had the cheek to call their laws 'indecent', but, goodness! . . . which was the more indecent, a divorce because of 'mental cruelty' or 'incompatibility', or a trumped-up hotel divorce case about a bogus act of adultery? That sulky, good-fornothing, gambling female at the other end of the flat— absurd to think that he could only be rid of her, if he wished, by the commission of 'adultery' by one side or the other! He had no other hold upon her at all; she could spend all his money, against his orders, and he must pay her debts— or face a public scandal, which she knew very well that a Judge of the High Court could not do. If she went to her horrible Bridge Club and, while she squandered his money on some brainless effort at a Dam Slam, or something of the sort, she slandered her neighbours, as she was quite likely to do, *he*, her husband, would be liable for damages, according to the lunatic laws of England. If she never gave him a moment's help or comfort, if she made it impossible for him to save a halfpenny, that was nothing to the law. She might drive him to the verge of madness with her complaining and her indigestion, her fits of temper, her extravagance and inefficient housekeeping; but if he left her (which he would never dare to do) he must pay her a third or more of his income as long as life lasted, because long ago she had chased him and compelled him to sleep with her. The one event that could save him now was the inconceivable event that somebody would want to sleep with her, and she with him. That, and that only, was the glorious test by which the fitness of a wife or husband was judged by the most intelligent country in the world. No wonder the women of England were said to be solid in defence of the divorce laws! Those laws were the most powerful instrument ever invented for the extraction by the female of ease and comfort and money from the male. They were never defended upon that ground, but that was the truth of it. They were upheld as the sure shield of morality and chastity and. . . . 'Bah!' said his lordship, aloud, 'what bilge!' And, swept by a storm of anger, he plucked the loofah from the water and hurled it passionately against the wall of the bathroom.

His lordship gazed in some surprise at the wet imprint of the loofah on the wall. A sobering sight. 'This won't do,' said his lordship, and slowly left the bath.

That night he dreamed, a wild, alarming, interminable dream—an exhausting dream: for, apart from the terror, it continually imposed upon him a mental effort. His tired brain was always working, arguing, composing a speech, preparing a judgment, fumbling for words, wrestling hopelessly with slippery ideas. He was on the Bench when the dream began, explaining Section 178 of the Judicature (Consolidation) Act, 1925, to a golden-haired lady of extraordinary charm; but when he explained to her that she ought not to play Bridge because the King's Proctor would show cause if she did, she soared out of the box and stood beside his bath, gripping the edge of it, her face pale and her lips tight: and he wanted to say that he loved her and would she be his wife instead of the Woman Named, whose name he simply could not remember: but he could only say, 'I am in the King's Bath: this raises an irresistible presumption of adultery.' But she replied, 'Adultery! Adultery! Adultery! Adultery! Adultery! Adultery! Adultery! Adultery! That's all you seem to THINK about!' And after that, whatever else happened, the word 'Adultery!' was always in the background, ringing like a bell, or going trickety-prank, like a railway train, or roaring like the London traffic, or ticking slowly like a great clock—Adultery! Adultery! Adultery! Adultery! All the time irregular, appalling things were happening—things against which there must be some convincing argument, some shattering precedent, some glorious Statute, but he never had time to think it out, because the woman kept shouting, 'Adultery! Adultery!' And suddenly Sir Humphrey was in the bath too, looking exactly like an enormous loofah: and Sir Albert picked Sir Humphrey up and quickly threw him against the wall, a little doubtful about his ruling, nevertheless, and not at all surprised when the usher said 'Silence!': but because of the 'Adultery! Adultery!' noises he could *not* think of a precedent for throwing Sir Humphrey at the wall. And then this delicious, golden-haired lady with the enchanting smile, said, 'With *great* respect, my lord, you have a boil on your bottom!' And he said, 'If it pleases your ladyship—— Stand down if you'd rather.' But she said, 'Adultery! Adultery! Adultery! Adultery! I put it to you that you *have* got a boil on your bottom! I suggest to you that you have a BOIL on your bottom.' Then all the people in the bathroom, or the Court, or whatever it was, began to sing, in unison, 'I put it to you—I put it to you—that you HAVE got a boil on your bottom!' There was loud laughter after this, and Mr. Barter said that that was the case for the petitioner. And while the Judge was trying to find the papers in the case, which were always disappearing behind a sponge, his wife came in and saw the golden-haired lady, who had taken all her clothes off and was sailing a boat in the bath. His wife said crossly, 'Oh, well, if you've got a boil I shall go and play Bridge.' And then the golden-haired lady, who was wearing her night-dress now, said, 'What's more, you're concealing your false teeth from the Court.' And he said, 'With great respect, I have a good excuse.' But she said, 'All very well, but how would *you* like it if you had to stand up in the bath and hold the loofah in the right hand, and speak the whole truth about the material facts of your false teeth?' Then everybody in the bath stood up and held loofahs in the right hand and read the oath aloud—and this was the most terrible part of the dream.

'Adultery! Adultery! Adultery! Adultery! His lordship's—material—teeth are false! I put it to you! I put it to you! I put it to you! I put it to you! His lordship's —material—teeth—are—FALSE!'

Then his brain became at last extraordinarily clear, and he knew exactly what he ought to say. But now he could *not* get anybody to say it to: everybody slipped away like bits of soap in the water, or flew about like loofahs, or put on wigs and hid behind the witness-box, where, of course, he could not reach them; and they all made a terrible noise with their 'Adultery! Adultery!' so that, although he shouted at them, he could not make them hear. But at last he saw the golden-haired lady, alone in the witness-box, which was sailing about the Court like a little boat, with somebody's night-shirt for a sail; he had to run and run to catch her, and climb over the rocks and sponges, and his knees were weak, and Sir Humphrey kept pulling him back or standing in front of him and suggesting that he had a boil; but in the end, with a frantic effort, he caught and seized the golden-haired lady, who was now in a green coat and skirt drinking port in his dining-room. He said, 'You're perfectly right. The whole thing's NONSENSE!' She smiled at him very sweetly and the Judge woke up, sweating.

He lay for a little, remembering the dream. Then he got up and lit the gas-ring and boiled a little hot milk; and as he sipped at it, he said: 'This won't do. This won't do at all.'

The Judge sat down delicately, for the boil was worse this morning; but, almost before the manœuvre was complete, he said:

'Mr. Barter, I think I ought to say that I see no reason to modify anything that I said last night. But I am anxious, in this difficult case, that everything in the petitioner's favour should be before me, so you had better call your evidence. Have you any witnesses other than Mr. Seal?'

'No, my lord. My lord, I do not think his evidence need take up very much of the time of the Court.'

'Don't you be too sure,' muttered Sir Humphrey.

So Martin went into the box, bewildered, but believing, on the whole, that all was already lost. He wore the light-grey suit: he looked athletic and handsome and honest, but, in the bright light of the morning, very anxious and pale: the women in Court liked him; the men were not so sure, for half of them envied him his luck with Mary Moon. While he took the oath a little wave of sibilants ran across the crowded Court, as a hundred mouths whispered, 'The B.B.C. Announcer.'

Mary looked up at him and clenched her hands. The high cliff of the box was so close to her that she had to put her head on one side to see him. It was more hateful to see him up there, exposed like a criminal to the peering mob, than to be there herself. And the mob, she knew, would not be so kind to him. He had to say worse things than she had: and he was a man. Why, she raged, should the mob be there at all? If all this filthy 'publicity' was necessary to keep the nation pure, let the case be published in the papers, but keep the sightseers out of Court! How tired he looked, poor boy: but how nice, how brave!

Accustomed to the microphone, he spoke too low. Mary longed to whisper, 'Speak up,' for she was sure that somebody else would do it, and hated the idea of that.

Mr. Barter's questions were not numerous. In two or three words Mr. Seal confirmed the whole of Mary's evidence; and then Mr. Barter summed up the past and future in four sentences:

'Before the failure of the petitioner's first petition for the dissolution of her marriage did you ever commit adultery with her?'

'No.'

'Did you commit adultery with the petitioner on the night of July 6th?'

'Yes.'

'Have you ever committed adultery on any other occasion?'

'No.'

'Is it your intention, if the petitioner's marriage is dissolved, to marry her?'

'If she will have me.'

'What was that?'

'Speak up, please, Mr. Seal. The answer was, my lord——'

'If she will have me.'

'If she will have me?'

Sir Humphrey, too, was quicker this morning. The first

question was a nasty one. 'Can you tell his lordship where your braces were ultimately found that morning?'

'In my own room—hidden away in a drawer.'

'In your own room? So that your expedition to Mrs. Adam's room was, in fact, superfluous?'

'I couldn't find them.'

'Very well.'

Sir Humphrey passed on to the *Curlew*. Mr. Seal was quite sure that they had both genuinely intended to return before nightfall: and kept saying so, in spite of puttings and suggestings. As to Manchester, he was equally firm. No, he had not been really content with the information that he was to stay for one minute only; certainly, he had hoped for better things, but equally certainly they had not happened. The petitioner was agitated by the detective talk; and, both in the ball-room and on the 'phone, she had strongly resisted his proposals.

All this was terrible to Mary, because, she thought, it put Martin in a bad light, the unsuccessful villain. But she was wrong: the 'public' liked him: a passionate lover defending his lady and telling the plain truth, it was clear, without thought for himself. Figgie whispered to Mrs. Figgie, 'A jolly good boy.'

The Judge liked Mr. Seal. He had got the pitch of the Court now, and gave his answers well, his restful voice just touching every corner; he was confident but not aggressive; he looked clean and orthodox. His experience with the B.B.C. gave him a better understanding of the official mind than Mary had, and made him think a little more before he answered. He was both more respectful and more cautious. Figgie whispered, 'We shall win yet.'

Then Sir Humphrey turned to the old bugbear. Did the witness ever express to the petitioner the opinion that if he appeared in the Divorce Court he would be dismissed from his employment? Probably—yes. He could not quite remember when. The witness knew, didn't he, after the yachting episode, that Mrs. Adam was filing a petition for divorce? Did the petitioner ever discuss these proceedings with him? Of course. When? Many times. Just before the petition was filed? No—well, she had said vaguely that she was getting a divorce—nothing more. Did they never discuss between them whether the adultery in the *Curlew* should be disclosed or not? No. Quite sure? Yes.

'But you were anxious, were you not, because of your employment, not to figure in divorce proceedings?'

'As a co-respondent—yes.'

'And you had made that plain to the petitioner?'

'Yes.'

'I suggest that you again made your desires and your position plain when she was about to file her petition?'

'No.'

'I suggest that you made your anxiety so plain that she decided that your name must not be mentioned?'

'It never occurred to me that I need come into it at all.'

'Do you swear that, Mr. Seal?'

'I'm swearing everything.'

There was a feeble but approving titter, and Sir Humphrey said quickly, 'I beg your pardon, Mr. Seal. There are some witnesses who require to be reminded of their oath. I don't suggest for a moment that you are one of them.'

'Thank you, sir.'

'How nice the lawyers are,' thought Mary, 'even when they're being nasty.'

But now the Judge lent a hand, and Martin turned towards the Bench. Seventeen ladies admired his profile, and several gentlemen envied it.

'Have I got it right, Mr. Seal?' said the old man. 'Although very much in love with the petitioner, you never proposed to run away with her, because you did not wish to appear in Court as a co-respondent?'

'No, my lord.'

'But you honestly thought that there were ways and means by which *she* could get a divorce without your name being publicly mentioned, although you had committed adultery together? Is that right?'

After a little pause, 'Yes, my lord.'

Mary stared at the water-jug on the bookshelf, paralysed. Figgie muttered to himself, 'Oh, Lord!' What wizards these lawyers were! Within a few minutes, two or three sentences —they could make black look white—and white look black again. They were conjurers—and what showmen! They had the theatre beat. Figgie, who always swore that he

knew what the bulk of an audience was thinking by looking
down at the stalls from a box, was sadly sure now that
those about him were against Martin now, and thought
him a bit of a worm—even if he were telling the truth,
which was now not certain.

The old Judge was wagging his head again—a bad sign.

And Sir Humphrey said: 'Mr. Seal, were you in Court
yesterday when a certain passage in Mrs. Adam's evidence
was read aloud by the shorthand writer?'

'Yes.'

'Do you agree with the general purport of those expressions?'

'I don't quite follow.'

'Do you hold the same attitude to the law of divorce—
let us put it in this way: Do you hold, as Mrs. Adam seems
to do, that your "private lives" ought not to be—"messed
about" was, I think, her expression—I would rather say
"inquired into"—by this Court?'

Horrible silence. Mr. Seal did not know what to say.
Whatever he said, he thought, would be dangerous, might
be disastrous. One could never tell, because one never
knew up what perilous garden-path these lawyers were
leading. He glanced at Mary, but Mary was still staring
at the water-jug. There was only one rule—Mary's rule.
Tell the truth.

Mr. Barter rose. 'My lord, with great respect, is that
quite a fair question? There never was a witness who
thought that his private affairs ought to come into Court.'

Salubrious laughter.

'I was thinking the same,' said the Judge. 'What exactly
are you after, Sir Humphrey?'

'My lord, you yourself suggested that the petitioner,
holding these views, may have deliberately deceived the
Court. If she did, it is very probable that she discussed
the matter with the witness: and if he holds the same views
it is very probable that the matter was the subject of
conversation between them.'

'That sounds very like a conspiracy to defeat the ends
of justice. You're not suggesting that, are you, Sir Humphrey? If you are, the witness must be warned.'

'No, my lord, I was directing myself to the state of mind

of the petitioner, as to which her lover may be able to assist the Court. But, my lord, I don't wish to press the question——'

'I think, perhaps, Sir Humphrey, it is taking us a little far,' said the Judge, who was now a little fogged about the whole affair.

And then, when all was well, there came an unexpected voice from the most unexpected and unconsidered quarter, the witness-box:

'My lord, I don't mind answering,' said Mr. Seal, rather breathless. 'I do think the same! We've done no harm to any one, my lord—and I don't see why—just because we——'

But 'No, no, no, *no!*' his merciful lordship interrupted. 'No voluntary statements, Mr. Seal! Take my advice and wait for the questions. Go on, Sir Humphrey.'

'Oh, Lord,' said Mr. Barter bleakly to himself. 'These people who will tell the truth!'

Sir Humphrey, having got more or less what he wanted, like manna from Heaven, sat down.

Mr. Barter, in re-examination, had only one question— very careful and slow:

'Did the petitioner ever discuss with you whether she should or should not disclose to the Court the fact that she had committed adultery with you?'

'No, sir.'

'That is the case for the petitioner, my lord.'

'Extraordinary people,' thought Figgie. 'They don't seem to be bothering about the girl's being naughty. The only thing that worries them now is why she didn't make a song about it.'

And then Mr. Barter made his great speech. Secretly, he feared that a good case was going down the drain, as good cases mysteriously do; but he had captured forlorn hopes before, and thought that, with boldness and tact nicely adjusted, he might do it again.

'My lord, in this case, after the evidence you have heard

from the petitioner and Mr. Martin Seal, I ask the Court
with all the earnestness at my command to exercise its
discretion in the petitioner's favour. My lord, I appreciate
as well as any one the difficulties of the Court in such a case
—anxious to do what is best for the individual but bound
to do what is best for public morality and the rule of law.
But, my lord, is this not one of the cases in which the pursuit
of those two interests most clearly leads to the same conclusion? This is not the case, my lord, of a wanton woman,
promiscuously misconducting herself with Tom, Dick, or
Harry. It is now three years—three and a half—since her
husband left her: but still the name of only one other man
is coupled with hers, the name of the man who has gone
into that box and confirmed alike her confessions and her
denials. If your lordship says "Yes" these two persons,
young, healthy, responsible citizens, will marry, and in the
ordinary course of nature breed children——'

'The petitioner has not bred any children yet,' said the
Judge dryly.

'No, my lord; but the original foundation of these
proceedings is that she and her husband were unsuitably
matched, from which, my lord, may proceed more con-
sequences than it would be proper to consider now. But,
my lord, if your lordship says "No", these two persons—
divided by law but united in love—think what you will of
them—will live together still, but in a lawless, unconsecrated
union, or, as the simple phrase goes, in sin. There may, or
may not, as your lordship has hinted, be children: but if
there are they will be born out of wedlock and carry through
life the ignoble name of bastards. On the other hand, my
lord, there is the husband, found guilty of adultery by this
Court and perhaps himself desirous of marrying again a
mate with whom he can more surely hope for a happy and
a fruitful union. If your lordship says "No" he too will be
condemned either to an unnatural celibacy or to lawless
love. It is in your lordship's power to say that both these
persons shall have at least the opportunity to repair past
errors, and lead respectable and normal married lives,
according to law, to public policy, and the tenets of religion.
Can it be doubted, my lord, in which direction the public
interest reposes?

'My lord, I am well aware that there might still be circumstances which would compel the Court to say "No"—as, for example, if the petitioner had been shown to be a liar and a cheat: for such must not ask or receive favours from the Court, lest others be encouraged to lie and cheat. My friend suggests, and will no doubt suggest more strongly still, that my client, even now, is not telling the truth. But, my lord, if that were so, it would have been very easy for my client to deny *both* the charges in the King's Proctor's plea. And if she were a calculating woman, who thought, "It will be wise to admit a little and deny the rest," the obvious course would have been to deny the first charge and to admit the second. For the first charge is the more damning of the two, since it exposes her, if it is true, to the accusation that she is guilty not only of adultery but of deliberate deception: and it is, of the two, by far the less easy for her accusers to substantiate. As to the first charge, the yachting episode, there was no direct evidence of any kind, except what the parties themselves provided: no mortal soul knew where the *Curlew* was or what she was doing during that night; it would have been easy to invent some cock-and-bull, heroic story to show that all through the night the *Curlew* was struggling against wind and tide in Sea Reach or elsewhere: and no man would have been able to adduce any evidence to confute that story. If it were denied, the first charge would rest upon nothing but the purest presumption. But it is not denied. Why? Because my client believes in telling the truth. Take, then, the second charge. That, if only one of the two was to be admitted, is the obvious one to admit. Of the two it is the less serious, for it does not involve the deception of the Court: and all kinds of human excuses could be made for such a lapse, if it were admitted openly in Court. Moreover, of the two it is the more difficult charge to refute, for, at first sight, appearances are all against her. And yet, my lord, this charge is strenuously resisted. Why? Because my client believes in telling the truth. In short, my lord, she has taken the course exactly opposite to that which would be expected if she were a calculating and dishonest woman. She admits the greater and denies the lesser charge; she admits that which would be easy to repel and denies that which is difficult. That is not the course of a liar, my lord. Nor has her demeanour in the box been that of a liar. Indeed, my lord, I do not propose to dwell upon the details of the evidence in these proceedings, for I am sure that no argument of mine could add any force to the plain and candid assertions my client has made, supported in every particular by Mr. Seal, whose utterances also bear the stamp of honesty. My lord, it may well be that, if the happiness of these two stands in jeopardy to-day, it is because the habit of truth is too strong in them. As we have seen, my lord, in the racy language of the witness Hardy, "What's in their minds, my lord, that comes out." I do hope, my lord, that in this of all Courts, that not too common candour will not be allowed to operate to the prejudice of my client.

'If I were to presume so far as to attempt to interpret your lordship's mind, I should say that the only question which troubles your lordship in this case is directed to my client's relations, not with Mr. Seal or any other man, but with the law—the question whether she has honestly discharged her duties to this Court according to law. And it may be that upon that question some spark of doubt in your lordship's mind has been kept alive by certain expressions of my client tending to show that she is lacking in respect for the law which it is your duty to administer and hers to obey. My lord, I beg you to dismiss that consideration, those expressions, from your mind. My lord, unhappily, there are very many in the land, many of our own profession, many even, if your lordship will forgive me, among those who practise in this Court, who are not wholly satisfied with the condition of the laws, and do not in their hearts respect them. But that is not to say that they do not dutifully observe them: and my client is equally entitled to belief when she tells the Court that she has done the same.

'My lord, you and I, loyal servants of the law, know very well that we must keep our own counsel in these matters, whatever we think of the law. But is it a cause for wonder that this woman, who is not a servant of the law, and has suffered much through the law, should reveal, at a moment when her mind is opened wide to the world, some little disrespect for the law? Let us try to put ourselves in the woman's place. What, my lord, has the law done for her that at such a moment she should sing its praises? The law made it easy for her to enter into an unhappy marriage, but makes it—rightly, as you and I believe, my lord—difficult to escape from it. For the third time, my lord, within the space of a few months, she finds herself in a public Court, still bound upon the same hard quest: and in the course of this, the third ordeal, believing strongly in the justice of her case, she is persuaded, rightly or wrongly, that the law is still inhumanly determined to violate her happiness, her sense of decency, her natural right to live her own life according to her conscience. My lord, is it to be counted against her that at such a moment, after so much trouble, that protesting, that rebellious cry should be wrung from this brave but almost despairing spirit?'

'Bravo!' muttered Figgie: and all the lay world thought the same. The debonair and breezy Mr. Barter had disappeared: gone were the high and confident tones. This was a passionate, pugnacious Barter, whose voice was charged with anxiety, with moral indignation, and profound conviction. The voice rose and fell now, rose suddenly and sharply to a vital word, a humane challenge, and fell to unsuspected depths of feeling, to thrilling murmurs almost unheard. The people watched the tabs of his wig bob up and down like puppet dancers on his gown; they were drugged by his eloquence, enjoyed the drug, and were sure that he was right. The Judge sat with one hand supporting his chin, steadily staring at Mr. Barter over his glasses, his face as solemn, as unchanging as a statue's. And Sir Humphrey, drawing faces on a note-pad, said to himself, 'Good effort, Tim, old boy, but you're sunk.'

'My Lord, I will go further,' said Mr. Barter, shifting the pitch of his voice again, as an organist suddenly pulls out a new stop. 'I will imagine the worst that in this case I can imagine—which is, my lord, that after all has been said that can be said you should still conclude that this woman, when she concealed her solitary lapse from virtue, was mainly moved by her desire to shield her lover and not entirely by her lack of understanding of her obligations. My lord, even if that were proved, I should still appeal to you to overlook it and exercise your discretion in——'

20

'Oh, come, Mr. Barter, do you really mean that?'

'My lord, after all, would the offence be so grave? The concealment, not of half a dozen promiscuous infidelities, but of a single surrender to the man she loves: the motive not to save herself from shame but to preserve the livelihood of the man she hopes to marry. My lord, by all means let us see that the law is properly regarded, but let us preserve a keen sense of the realities. The law, my lord, was made for man, not man for the law: the law, if it demands respect, must, like the litigant, deserve it. The law insists, my lord, that this woman shall come into Court with "clean hands": but'—here came a sensational whisper, 'has the law, my lord, "clean hands" where it has touched this woman's history? Let us look back, my lord, beyond the concealment to the act concealed, and remember the occasion of it. That act, my lord, that single surrender, that solitary lapse from virtue, did not follow quickly after my client's separation from her husband: it was not a hasty or a careless act of defiance: it did not come, my lord, *until after she had appealed to the law, in this Court, to give her her freedom, and the law, through no fault of her own, had failed her.*'

Mr. Barter rammed the last sentence home with hammer-heavy tones and an agitated fist. And then he paused a moment, as if to gather his strength for the final shattering assault, or perhaps to give the Court time in which to absorb a new idea.

'And so, my lord,' he continued, 'I submit, with all conviction, that this is not a case in which the law is entitled to say that because it has not been regarded it cannot be gracious. It is not a case in which to examine with a microscope the minutiae, the technicalities, but to look with a generous eye over the whole field of my client's history and to see in which direction the broad and unmistakable road of natural justice leads us. Nor is it a case, my lord, in which the Court need shrink from generosity for fear of creating a perilous precedent: for there is in this case no trace of downright wickedness, and in all the circumstances there is a peculiar character which is not likely to be repeated. Besides, my lord, is it not the great beauty of the discretionary procedure that it need neither follow precedent nor fear to create it, since, like the royal favour, it knows no master but itself, and draws its bountiful decisions not from the books but from the justice of every case considered on its merits?

'Lastly, my lord, this is not a case where the dignity of the law and this Court is endangered. There are times, my lord, when he who stands upon his dignity comes nearer to losing it than he who does not seem to regard it. The dignity of the law, my lord, will not suffer if it forgives this woman her fault: but the dignity of human lives and human loves, my lord, will suffer loss if it does not. I submit, my lord, that, so far from being a deceitful wanton, my client, by her conduct both in this Court and out of it, has shown herself a woman of high character and purpose, one who has an exceptional regard for the truth, and deserves to be looked upon with favour by this Court, where truthfulness is so highly valued and properly insisted upon. I ask you, my lord, to grant this woman's prayer for your discretion, that she may be free to marry the man she loves.'

Mr. Barter sat down, saying to himself, 'Damn! that last bit went wrong.' But a murmurous approval fluttered the crowd. Mary turned round and gratefully smiled at him. Figgie said, 'Well, surely that's done it.' And Mr. Freebody turned and said, 'Fine. I think you've got him.'

Sir Humphrey rose. But the Judge looked at the clock. One o'clock. And at half past one the doctor was coming to his private room to consider the boil, perhaps to lance it. He said, 'At two o'clock' and went out.

Figgie and Mary had an almost jubilant lunch: all was nearly over, and Figgie was confident that the day was won. She was not to play that night, Figgie insisted, or at the matinée on Saturday, but to come back to her delighted public on Saturday night. 'You'll get an ovation,' he said.

'Perhaps I'll be booed.'

'Not if you win,' said Figgie. 'Not anyhow,' he added quickly.

The Judge's clerk placed a cushion on the judicial chair. His lordship, supporting his weight on the arms, lowered himself carefully into position, winced, and said at once, without calling on Sir Humphrey:

'Mr. Barter, I listened with close attention and interest to your eloquent and able address. But I have come to the conclusion that this difficult case is not one in which I ought to exercise my discretion.'

Mr. Barter stared at the Judge, and murmured calmly, 'If your lordship pleases——' as if he did not care two hoots what conclusion was arrived at. But Mary's head sank low. She knew now the meaning of those words, once so mysterious: she knew that, after all, she had lost, and she wanted to cry, but swore that she would not. Even Figgie, by now, knew what the words meant, and muttered, 'Damn.' Mr. Seal knew too, but he stared up at the Judge, as straight and stiff as Mr. Barter: and the usher, watching him, thought: 'He's a tough one, though he don't look it.'

The old Judge was plodding on, placid, kindly, inexorable, cold: 'I have reached this conclusion with some reluctance, for at first I formed a very favourable impression of the petitioner, and I agree, Mr. Barter, that, if you look at the whole history of her married life, much that has happened to her is to be accounted her misfortune rather than her fault. But in this Court, Mr. Barter, we cannot look so far afield. If we could, we should have to direct our gaze even farther than you have suggested: it would not be right to stop at the married life of persons who come before us; we should inquire into their education, their upbringing, their parentage; and there would be no end to it. I, at least, must confine myself within the limits, narrow or not, laid down for me by the law of the land and the practice of this Court.

'Whatever view may be held of the long chain of circumstances which have led the petitioner into her present position, it is my duty to consider her conduct as it comes before me: and upon that, though in many ways I sympathize with her, I am bound to say that I am not satisfied that even now she has told the whole truth in this Court. I thought last night—and the opinion has been fortified to-day—that she knew much more about her lawful duty than she has represented. She is neither ignorant nor poor: she is intelligent, well-educated, well-advised, and a woman-of-the world—I use that term in no derogatory sense.' (The old boy glanced at Mary, and, sad and stricken though she was, she had to give him a little bow and a pathetic little smile; for, after all, he was still a dear old thing, and perhaps, at his age, in his position, he could not be blamed for being insanely wrong). 'I think she knew very well that she ought to disclose to her solicitors and to the Court the fact of her adultery on the night of July 6th, 1930, and I think that the main reason why she did not do so was her desire to shield her lover from harm. Mr. Barter has made a very clever attempt to brush this accusation aside as if it were unimportant, and even, if true, might be creditable to the petitioner. I can understand that in a novel or play much agreeable material might be drawn from this heroic piece of inverted chivalry: but this is a Court of law and not of romance. The matter is of high importance, not only for the direct reasons which I mentioned last night and need not, I think, recapitulate to-day, but for the shadow which it casts upon the general credit of the petitioner: for where one falsehood is found it is natural and right to look for others.'

His lordship paused and slightly shifted his seat, for the boil was hurting him. And John Adam, sitting behind his counsel, clenched his fists and muttered, 'Now's the time.' For a sort of madness had entered the quiet soul of John Adam. He had not meant to come to Court to-day, but some compelling force had brought him. He knew very well to what conclusion the Judge was labouring, and rebellion bubbled in him at last. What was the use of all these people sitting here and listening to all this nonsense? He, John Adam, could clear the whole thing up. The Judge was going to find that because both he and Mary had committed adultery neither of them could be divorced. But he, John Adam, knew very well that John Adam had never committed adultery, never thought of it. He had only to stand up and say so, and all would surely be well. He would stand up suddenly and say, 'My lord, I want to say something. You say my wife can't divorce me because she's committed adultery: but I never committed adultery so I can divorce her, can't I? Well, do it, you old fool, and do it now. I tell you the whole thing was a put-up job. Laura Tott had measles the whole time, and if the Court thinks I look the sort of man who would commit adultery with a perfectly strange woman who has the measles then the mind of the Court is more of a swamp than I thought. My lord——' Mr. Adam's lips moved; violent words poured through his mind, which seemed suddenly to have become strong, clear, and drained of all uncertainty and fears. The man next to him looked at him with apprehension, wondering what was the matter with the quiet-looking gentleman. But no words came from Mr. Adam's mouth; and his lordship was off again.

'The petitioner has sworn that she never committed adultery except upon the one occasion. (I would observe, in passing, that it is not an uncommon thing in this Court for a woman to confess readily enough to a single lapse but shrink from owning to two or three.) But what happened in Mrs. Adam's bedroom at "White Ladies" on the morning of Sunday, the 29th of June, although it does not point directly to adultery, shows a degree of intimacy which is at least compatible with a previous adulterous association. And the evidence with regard to the hotel at Manchester, looked at in the light of the known history of the parties, raises a presumption of adultery so strong that, at the best, it could not easily be rebutted. I am not going to say that, in both cases, the inference of guilt might not be negatived. I do not say that, if the petitioner's credit had remained unshaken in my mind, I might not have found as a fact that there was no adultery at the hotel in Manchester; and I do not say now that I am prepared to find as a fact that there was. It is not, I think, necessary for me to do so. The act of adultery admitted is sufficient in itself to disentitle the petitioner to a decree of dissolution, unless she can persuade me to employ the discretion: to do that she must satisfy me that she is speaking the truth, and I am not so satisfied. Having found as a fact that she has in one material particular practised a deliberate deception, I must require the strongest assurance that she is not still practising others: and this assurance, with the best will in the world, I am unable to discover. Therefore, in the public interest, I am bound to say that she has not made good her

claim that she deserves the exercise of my discretion. The
benefit of any serious doubt, in such proceedings as these,
must go to the King's Proctor, that is, to the side on which
the public interest lies, and not to the individual claiming
relief. Mr. Barter has painted a graphic and moving picture
of the petitioner's position, divided irrevocably from her
lawful husband yet debarred from marrying the man she
loves. I am very far from being insensible to the force of
that appeal. But what is the other side? If I were to say
that, although I am not satisfied as to her *bona fides*, she
may go free, because I am sorry for her, I should be offering
a direct encouragement to every discontented spouse to
commit adultery, to conceal it, and to come to this Court
for relief with pitiful but unsubstantial tales, which must
either be accepted, to the confusion of the law, or investi-
gated at great expense to the State and to private persons.
And on the balance the evil would be immeasurably greater.

'As I have already said, I arrive at this conclusion after
much thought and with considerable reluctance: and I do
not wish my reasons for it to be misunderstood. I do not
find that the petitioner is a wanton or a wicked woman; but
she has not, in my judgment, come up to that standard of
absolute truthfulness which this Court must always require,
particularly in the exercise of its discretionary jurisdiction:
and that is the principal ground of this decision. The
King's Proctor's plea is allowed: the decree nisi must be
rescinded. Costs—what have you to say about costs, Sir
Humphrey?'

'My lord——'

'If your lordship pleases——'

They were at it again—three of them now, for Mr. Adam's
counsel had popped up and joined the fray. 'Come away,
darling.' Martin's voice: and Martin's hand was on Mary's.
Why not? At least they were together again: no more pre-
tences. And why should they listen to the lawyers any
longer? They went out quietly, Martin making a way for
Mary through the crowd, and leading her by the hand.
Some who saw them go thus thought that it was a shocking
sight: but more thought that it was beautiful and moving,

for they were a fine fearless couple and had had poor fortune. Mary held her head high; her face was innocent and proud, and she smiled that brave little warming smile at the men who made way for her. And one of these muttered, 'Good luck, miss—it's a shame.'

The faithful Figgie saw them go, and left the Court, and followed. But at the foot of the steps he halted. He wanted to be with them, but his work was done, and it would be kinder to leave them alone. They went slowly down the dusky Hall, arm in arm, their heads very close together, looking very small and forlorn in that wide and misty place. Figgie saw them disappear through the swinging doors, outcasts from the temple of the law. He said to himself, 'God bless them,' and hoped they would be happy. Which was more than the law had done.

John Adam did not see them go. He was still staring at the Judge, rehearsing in his mind what he would say when he did stand up: 'My lord, I wish to make a statement. I am the respondent and I never committed adultery——' The question of costs was satisfactorily settled, another case was called, and counsel in the case of *Adam* v. *Adam* tied up their papers and left the the Court. But John Adam, almost alone now in the public benches, sat and stared at the old Judge, muttering, but saying nothing. The Judge, wearily readjusting his cushion, caught sight of the strange-looking, wild-eyed man, and thought, 'Who is that? He looks a little mad.'

'Queer thing,' said Mr. Boom after his seventh oyster. 'Just an ordinary English collusive divorce case—thousands like them every year. And all goes well until people start telling the truth. *Your* part of it—the part that was all lies from beginning to end—oh, yes, *I* know—isn't questioned at all. More wine, please, Henri. What are you going to do, John?'

'Nothing. What can I do?'

'Well, there is one thing you can do (but don't take this too seriously). You can go to the Court and ask for a divorce yourself——'

'But I'm supposed to have committed——'

'I know: but you can tell the Court you never did. I suppose you could prove it—call Miss Myrtle, call Miss Tott, call Miss Mortimer too. The only thing is that you'd all be charged with a conspiracy to deceive the Court and pervert the processes of justice—and perhaps Freebody and myself as well. Your position is this, you see: either you have committed adultery, in which case you can't ask for a divorce: or you have not, in which case you can be sent to prison for pretending that you have. The Laws of England are a continual joy.'

'Do you know,' said John, slowly, 'in Court yesterday— at the end—I very nearly did do what you say. For a minute or two, while the old Judge was talking—I went quite mad. I wanted to stand up and shout out the whole story. I sat there——'

'In a way, I wish you had.' said Mr. Boom. 'Six months in jail might do us all good. And that's what's wanted, really—some blazing scandal. Nothing else will ever get the laws altered. The trouble is that since the Act of '26 you can't work up a blazing scandal, because the newspapers can't publish the parts of a case that matter——'

'How d'you mean?'

'They can only print the bare bones of a divorce case now—names and addresses, concise statement of charges and defences, the summing-up, judgment, and so forth. And the bare bones are so dull that, as a rule, most of the papers don't bother to print them; and when they do the public only gets the official point of view. Look at the reports of your wife's case this morning. The merest summary—and it doesn't do justice to your wife at all. All the public gets from that is that she's committed adultery and told lies. Fortunately the old man said she wasn't a wanton and something about her shielding her lover, and the papers have seized on that because it makes a head-line —"Wife Shields Lover"—so I think she ought to be all right. But if they'd been able to print her evidence in full, and the story of Mr. Rigby prowling about that hotel in the King's name and a dressing-gown, there'd be no doubt about it at all. Sometimes the Act saves people from damaging publicity who don't deserve it: but just as often it does harm to decent people, because only part of the

story comes out. And the great thing it does always is to
save the *law* from damaging publicity; and that's a bad
thing. Because what the public don't hear about the public
don't bother about.'

Mr. Boom paused and sipped his wine.

'What about your—young lady?' he inquired.

'Just been appointed Head Mistress.'

'Oh, dear, that's going to make things difficult.'

'It has,' said John slowly. 'We're not going to meet
again.'

'I'm sorry about this, John—very sorry.'

'It's all right. You warned me.'

'Yes,' said Mr. Boom, sighing. 'Well, anyhow, let us
hope that the law and the prophets are happy. Two or
three truthful people have been compelled to tell lies
(including, perhaps, a solicitor, for I suspect that Freebody
had to tell one or two). Three decent people have been
compelled to behave indecently (if we include the Misses
Myrtle and Tott). One chaste woman has been compelled
to commit adultery. Four people have been prevented
from marrying the person of their choice, and one man has
lost his job. But remunerative employment has been
provided for two Judges, one Attorney-General, one King's
Proctor, the Registrar and his staff, two solicitors and their
staffs, two King's Counsel and three juniors, two or three
detectives, one or two policemen, Miss Myrtle, Miss Tott,
and sundry servants of the law, not to mention the Court
servants and the domestic staff of the various hotels.
Console yourself, John, by the thought that all this bene-
ficial activity and flow of money has been caused by your
unselfish attempt to behave like a gentleman and free yourself from the fetters of an unsuccessful marriage. It is true
that you are as much married as you were before. But
Chastity, Decency, and Truth have been upheld, and the
institution of Christian marriage has been saved again.'

'Did you say "Christian"?' said Mr. Adam.

'I did.'

'I put it to you,' said Mr. Adam, very slowly, and with
that strange fierce stare the Judge had noticed, 'that
there's a parable or something about a woman taken in
adultery?'

'There is. But that passage is not so often quoted as certain others.'

'I put it to you that there's not *one* thing the law has done to us, or made us do, that Christ would not have condemned.'

'I think you may be right.'

'*Christ!*' said Mr. Adam with such force that Henri, the waiter, dropped a couple of plates. 'I wonder they dare to mention his name!'

'Steady, John,' said Mr. Boom.

The callboy knocked twice—'Miss Moon, please!'—and went away.

'Oh, Martin, I'm terrified.'

'Fear nothing, darling.'

'Pray for me, Martin. Keep the door open, Florrie, and you'll hear the boos from here.'

'We'll hear no boos,' said Florrie confidently. 'Come on, dear, hurry, or we'll miss our entrance.'

'I'm ready. Pray, Martin. But don't worry. I shan't mind if they do boo.'

'I shall.'

'So shall I. Farewell.'

Mary fled from the dressing-room, and Florrie, paying no attention to Martin, stood listening at the open door. She was confident no longer: her tongue and lips worked nervously, her hands, in front of her strong, round stomach, clenched and unclenched like two small machines. Mr. Seal watched her, smoking a cigarette and, by all appearances, quite undisturbed.

Florrie knew exactly when to expect the round of applause which always greeted Penelope's first entrance—Euryclea's song; then a few lines of dialogue with Telemachus, spoken through music; then four lines without music; then the orchestra began the soft Penelope Music; then Mary's cue from Telemachus, 'Where is my virtuous but unfortunate mother?' (the author had tactfully offered to alter this line, but both Figgie and Mary said 'No'); and Mary danced on, carrying her Web, and pursued by a crowd of pertinacious Suitors. The applause varied, according to the day of the week: but Florrie, standing in the dressing-room, could almost tell by the volume of the reception how much money there was in the house.

'We shan't get a big reception,' she said, without looking at Martin, 'not Saturday night. Saturday night's never so good, not for applause. They're sleepy, you see, with the fresh air—and the pictures.'

'Yes,' said Mr. Seal gently.

Mary ran on to the stage and took her Web from the Property Man. The Property Man, an old servant of the theatre, stood beside her in the wings, as he always did after delivering the Web. He was a rough-looking fellow, with a huge moustache, a wife and three children. Every day he looked forward to this moment, his little talk with Miss Moon in the wings; and most nights, later on, he would repeat what she had said to him to an envious audience in the bar of the 'Blue Moon'.

As a rule, the conversation was brisk and intimate: for Mary knew the names and ages (and from time to time the diseases) of all his family: and could even show an intelligent interest in the 'snips' for to-morrow or the doings of the 'Arsenal'. It was a great source of pride, this little talk, beyond the pleasure of it; for it was not as if Miss Moon was all by herself—there were four of the Suitors (one of them a principal) standing just behind her, ready to run on between the same two flats. But he, Props, was always allowed to stand in the forefront with her, and have his little talk. And not one of the Suitors (not even the principal) would have dreamed of interrupting this hallowed *tête-à-tête*.

To-night Props felt sadly that the responsibility was too much for him. He did not know what to say. Yet he had so much that was important to say. He had backed a winner in the three-thirty, 'Arsenal' had won again, and Alice had not got whooping-cough after all. There stood Mary at his side, as usual, wonderful in her white silk dress, with that green thing in her hair and the gold thing round her neck. But she was trembling; she put one hand on her breast and stared out at Euryclea, shivering. Would the silly song never end? This was worse than anything, she had discovered: worse than a first night, worse than the witness-box. What would they do? Would there be boos—hisses

—or a murderous silence? She did not know which would
be worst. But she must not stand here, stupidly silent.
What would dear old Props think of her? The song was
nearly over. She said, 'What's the house like, Props?'
Her voice broke a little. Suppose it broke on the stage?

'They're lovely, miss,' said Props, delighted to receive a
lead.

But he could say no more. She was staring out at the
stage again, quivering again. He knew very well what was
in her mind, and longed to say something that would help.
But to-night, he felt, she would not be interested in Alice,
in the Arsenal, or even the winner of the three-thirty.

The cue was very near now. She put out her left hand
and rested it on his sleeve, to get a touch of human comfort.
'Oh, Props,' she said; and said no more. She was not going
to confess that she was frightened.

Props knew then that a great task had been given to him,
and to him alone. It was for him to deliver to this admired
and anxious lady the message which all the company, all
the stage-hands, all the dressers, the wardrobe mistress, the
stage-carpenter, the fireman, the callboy, and even those
comical blokes in the band would like to give to her.

He put out his rough right hand and patted her strongly
on the back. 'You're all right, miss', he said huskily.
'What's it got to do with any one, anyway?'

'Oh, Props, you darling!'

The Penelope Music began:

'Where is my virtuous but unfortunate mother ?'

Mary danced on to the stage, with doubt in her heart,
a radiant smile on her face, and a small dusty mark on the
back of her white dress.

Figgie, standing at the back of the dress circle, had
waited as anxiously as Mary. He said afterwards that the
moment after her entrance was the worst he had ever endured in the theatre, where the bad moments are so many
and bad. He was not going to clap himself: he had forbidden Henry Hake to give the audience the delicate lead
which had so often shown an audience where they were
expected to applaud; whatever came must come genuinely

from the people. They were not a lively audience, and had some of the Saturday quality of which Florrie had spoken. For a moment, a long, dreadful moment, nothing seemed to happen: and Figgie thought 'They're going to cut her. Worse almost than a boo.' For an instant his resolution wavered. He thought, 'I'll clap, and be damned.' He took his hands off the back of the barrier. But in the stalls they were clapping already; some one high up had shouted throatily 'Bravo!'—and before Mary could open her mouth to say her first line there was what is called 'thunderous applause'. The thunder raged, and swelled, and fell a little, and then came back and continued, strong and indubitable. For a full minute, which is a very long time, it held: and Mary stood bowing and smiling sadly, and plucking at the front of her frock like a nervous *ingénue*. She bowed and smiled, and said to herself, 'Thank God! How sweet they are!' But after that the thought that strangely filled her mind was, 'Poor John. I wonder what he's doing now.'

In the dressing-room they heard the noise: and there was a queer change. The calm Mr. Seal stood up and said excitedly, 'That's all right. Listen to that, Florrie! Listen to that!' But the agitated Florrie turned away from the door, with a serene demeanour, and took down the Second Act dress from its peg, as if nothing particular had happened.

'It's no more than what I expected,' she said. 'I thought we should get a good reception to-night.'

'Florrie, you're a damned liar!' said Mr. Seal.

'Maybe,' said Florrie. 'It's more than we deserve, anyway.'

But Mary ran off the stage into the arms of Props, and Props received his first kiss from a leading lady.

'Oh, Props! I believe it was you who did it. You made me laugh at just the right moment.'

'Not me, miss,' said Props. 'Listen, miss,' and he whispered hairily in Mary's ear, 'Don't you mind about them dirty laws, miss; and don't you mind what the big stiffs say. You've got the people with you, see?'

John Adam, that Saturday evening, dined alone and early at his club, cursing not God, not the lawyers, but Parliament.

After dinner he posted two letters. The first was to a

firm of estate-agents, to say that he was no longer in the market for the little house in Smith Square, Westminster.

The second letter was to Miss Joan Latimer, at St. Bride's College for Girls. It was a sad and rather mad little letter; and, on Monday morning, it made Joan Latimer cry, between the Geography and the English Composition lessons.

Having posted his letters in the hall, Mr. Adam left the club and walked across St. James's Street, as usual. At the corner of Jermyn Street he noticed a young girl standing by the wall. She looked so young and fresh and pretty that he took her for a shop-girl waiting for a friend or lover—a waiter, perhaps at one of the clubs: and four or five other men had passed her, thinking the same. She worked all the week in a factory for twenty-five shillings, and sometimes took to the streets on Saturday nights for a pound or two. But Mr. Adam was surprised to see her smile. He halted. She said, 'Good evening. Coming any place with me?' She had chestnut hair, hazel eyes, and a wide friendly smile, and a faint brogue.

He said, 'You're American.'

'Sure.'

'And a bit of Irish?'

'You're smart. I know a nice place Paddington way.'

'How old are you?'

'Nineteen.'

'My God!' said Mr. Adam. 'But I don't care. Taxi!'

'Is that your club there? I see you come out.'

'It is,' said the wild-eyed man. 'But I don't care. I don't care a damn for anything or any one.'

'Be Jabers!' said the girl, 'is that the way you feel? Well, it's a free country—if you're not found out.'

'I'm going to behave like a gentleman—at last!'

'Come on, then!' she said. 'I'm married meself.'

PRINTED BY
JARROLD AND SONS LTD.
NORWICH

METHUEN'S
GENERAL LITERATURE

A SELECTION OF
MESSRS. METHUEN'S
PUBLICATIONS

This Catalogue contains only a selection of the more important books published by Messrs. Methuen. A complete catalogue of their publications may be obtained on application.

ABRAHAM (G. D.)
MODERN MOUNTAINEERING
Illustrated. 7s. 6d. net.

ARMSTRONG (Anthony) ('A. A.' of Punch)
WARRIORS AT EASE
WARRIORS STILL AT EASE
SELECTED WARRIORS
PERCIVAL AND I
PERCIVAL AT PLAY
APPLE AND PERCIVAL
ME AND FRANCES
HOW TO DO IT
BRITISHER ON BROADWAY
WHILE YOU WAIT
Each 3s. 6d. net.
LIVESTOCK IN BARRACKS
Illustrated by E. H. SHEPARD.
6s. net.
EASY WARRIORS
Illustrated by G. L. STAMPA.
5s. net.
YESTERDAILIES. Illustrated.
3s. 6d. net.

BALFOUR (Sir Graham)
THE LIFE OF ROBERT LOUIS
STEVENSON 10s. 6d. net.
Also, 3s. 6d. net.

BARKER (Ernest)
NATIONAL CHARACTER
10s. 6d. net.
GREEK POLITICAL THEORY
14s. net.
CHURCH, STATE AND STUDY
10s. 6d. net.

BELLOC (Hilaire)
PARIS 8s. 6d. net.
THE PYRENEES 8s. 6d. net.

BELLOC (Hilaire)—continued
MARIE ANTOINETTE 18s. net.
A HISTORY OF ENGLAND
In 7 Vols. Vols. I, II, III and IV
Each 15s. net.

BINNS (L. Elliott), D.D.
THE DECLINE AND FALL OF THE
MEDIEVAL PAPACY. 16s. net.

BIRMINGHAM (George A.)
A WAYFARER IN HUNGARY
Illustrated. 8s. 6d. net.
SPILLIKINS : ESSAYS 3s. 6d. net.
SHIPS AND SEALING-WAX : ESSAYS
3s. 6d. net.
CAN I BE A CHRISTIAN ? 1s. net.

CASTLEROSSE (Viscount)
VALENTINE'S DAYS
Illustrated. 12s. 6d. net.

CHALMERS (Patrick R.)
KENNETH GRAHAME : LIFE, LET-
TERS AND UNPUBLISHED WORK
Illustrated. 10s. 6d. net.

CHARLTON (Moyra)
PATCH : THE STORY OF A MONGREL
Illustrated by G. D. ARMOUR.
2s. 6d. net.
THE MIDNIGHT STEEPLECHASE
Illustrated by GILBERT HOLIDAY.
5s. net.

CHESTERTON (G. K.)
COLLECTED POEMS 7s. 6d. net.
ALL I SURVEY 6s. net.
THE BALLAD OF THE WHITE HORSE
3s. 6d. net.
Also illustrated by ROBERT
AUSTIN. 12s. 6d. net.

CHESTERTON (G. K.)—*continued*
ALL IS GRIST
CHARLES DICKENS
COME TO THINK OF IT . . .
GENERALLY SPEAKING
ALL THINGS CONSIDERED
TREMENDOUS TRIFLES
FANCIES VERSUS FADS
ALARMS AND DISCURSIONS
A MISCELLANY OF MEN
THE USES OF DIVERSITY
THE OUTLINE OF SANITY
THE FLYING INN
    Each 3s. 6d. *net.*
WINE, WATER AND SONG 1s. 6d. *net.*

CLARKE (Carlo F. Culpeper)
GREYHOUNDS AND GREYHOUND
RACING. Illustrated. 5s. *net.*

CURLE (J. H.)
THE SHADOW-SHOW 6s. *net.*
    Also, 3s. 6d. *net.*
THIS WORLD OF OURS 6s. *net.*
TO-DAY AND TO-MORROW 6s. *net.*
THIS WORLD FIRST 6s. *net.*

DUGDALE (E. T. S.)
GERMAN DIPLOMATIC DOCUMENTS,
1871–1914
In 4 vols. Vol. I, 1871–90.
Vol. II, 1891–8. Vol. III, 1898–
1910. Vol. IV, 1911–14.
    Each £1 1s. *net.*

EDWARDES (Tickner)
THE LORE OF THE HONEY-BEE
Illustrated. 7s. 6d. and 3s. 6d. *net.*
BEE-KEEPING FOR ALL
   Illustrated. 3s. 6d. *net.*
THE BEE-MASTER OF WARRILOW
   Illustrated. 7s. 6d. *net.*
BEE-KEEPING DO'S AND DON'TS
     2s. 6d. *net.*
LIFT-LUCK ON SOUTHERN ROADS
     5s. *net.*

EINSTEIN (Albert)
RELATIVITY : THE SPECIAL AND
GENERAL THEORY 5s. *net.*
SIDELIGHTS ON RELATIVITY
    3s. 6d. *net.*
THE MEANING OF RELATIVITY
    5s. *net.*
THE BROWNIAN MOVEMENT
    5s. *net.*

EISLER (Robert)
THE MESSIAH JESUS AND JOHN THE
BAPTIST
  Illustrated. £2 2s. *net.*

EWING (A. C.)
IDEALISM   21s. *net.*

FIELD (G. C.)
MORAL THEORY 6s. *net.*
PLATO AND HIS CONTEMPORARIES
    12s. 6d. *net.*
PREJUDICE AND IMPARTIALITY
    2s. 6d. *net*

FINER (H.)
THE THEORY AND PRACTICE OF
MODERN GOVERNMENT 2 vols.
    £2 2s. *net.*
ENGLISH LOCAL GOVERNMENT
    £1 1s. *net.*

FITZGERALD (Edward)
A FITZGERALD MEDLEY. Edited
by CHARLES GANZ. 15s. *net.*

FYLEMAN (Rose)
HAPPY FAMILIES
FAIRIES AND CHIMNEYS
THE FAIRY GREEN
THE FAIRY FLUTE *Each* 2s. *net.*
THE RAINBOW CAT
EIGHT LITTLE PLAYS FOR CHILDREN
FORTY GOOD-NIGHT TALES
FORTY GOOD-MORNING TALES
SEVEN LITTLE PLAYS FOR CHILDREN
TWENTY TEA-TIME TALES
   Each 3s. 6d. *net.*
THE BLUE RHYME BOOK
  Illustrated. 3s. 6d. *net.*
THE EASTER HARE
  Illustrated. 3s. 6d. *net.*
FIFTY-ONE NEW NURSERY RHYMES
Illustrated by DOROTHY BUR-
ROUGHES. 6s. *net.*
THE STRANGE ADVENTURES OF
CAPTAIN MARWHOPPLE
  Illustrated. 3s. 6d. *net.*

GIBBON (Edward)
THE DECLINE AND FALL OF THE
ROMAN EMPIRE
With Notes, Appendixes and Maps,
by J. B. BURY. Illustrated. 7 vols.
15s. *net* each volume. Also, un-
illustrated, 7s. 6d. *net* each volume.

GLOVER (T. R.)
VIRGIL
THE CONFLICT OF RELIGIONS IN
THE EARLY ROMAN EMPIRE
POETS AND PURITANS
   Each 10s. 6d. *net.*
FROM PERICLES TO PHILIP
   12s. 6d. *net.*

GRAHAME (Kenneth)
> THE WIND IN THE WILLOWS
>> 7s. 6d. net and 5s. net.
> Also illustrated by ERNEST H.
> SHEPARD.   Cloth, 7s. 6d. net.
>> Green Leather, 12s. 6d. net.
> Pocket Edition, unillustrated.
>> Cloth, 3s. 6d. net.
>> Green Morocco, 7s. 6d. net.
> THE KENNETH GRAHAME BOOK
> (' The Wind in the Willows ',
> ' Dream Days ' and ' The Golden
> Age ' in one volume).
>> 7s. 6d. net.
> See also Milne (A. A.)

HALL (H. R.)
> THE ANCIENT HISTORY OF THE
> NEAR EAST   £1 1s. net.
> THE CIVILIZATION OF GREECE IN
> THE BRONZE AGE   £1 10s. net.

HEATON (Rose Henniker)
> THE PERFECT HOSTESS
> Decorated by A. E. TAYLOR.
> 7s. 6d. net. Gift Edition, £1 1s. net.
> THE PERFECT SCHOOLGIRL
>> 3s. 6d. net.

HEIDEN (Konrad)
> A HISTORY OF NATIONAL SOCIALISM
>> 10s. 6d. net.

HERBERT (A. P.)
> HELEN   2s. 6d. net.
> TANTIVY TOWERS and DERBY DAY
> in one volume. Illustrated by
> Lady VIOLET BARING.   5s. net.
> Each, separately, unillustrated
>> 2s. 6d. net.
> HONEYBUBBLE & CO.   3s. 6d. net.
> MISLEADING CASES IN THE COMMON
> LAW   5s. net.
> MORE MISLEADING CASES   5s. net.
> STILL MORE MISLEADING CASES
>> 5s. net.
> THE WHEREFORE AND THE WHY
> ' TINKER, TAILOR . . . '
> Each, illustrated by GEORGE
> MORROW.   2s. 6d. net.
> THE SECRET BATTLE   3s. 6d. net.
> THE HOUSE BY THE RIVER
>> 3s. 6d. net.
> ' NO BOATS ON THE RIVER '
>> Illustrated.   5s. net.

HOLDSWORTH (Sir W. S.)
> A HISTORY OF ENGLISH LAW
> Nine Volumes.   £1 5s. net each.
> Index Volume by EDWARD POTTON.
>> £1 1s. net.

HUDSON (W. H.)
> A SHEPHERD'S LIFE
>> Illustrated.   10s. 6d. net.
> Also unillustrated.   3s. 6d. net.

HUTTON (Edward)
> CITIES OF SICILY
>> Illustrated.   10s. 6d. net.
> MILAN AND LOMBARDY
> THE CITIES OF ROMAGNA AND THE
> MARCHES
> SIENA AND SOUTHERN TUSCANY
> NAPLES AND SOUTHERN ITALY
>> Illustrated.   Each 8s. 6d. net.
> A WAYFARER IN UNKNOWN TUSCANY
> THE CITIES OF SPAIN
> THE CITIES OF UMBRIA
> COUNTRY WALKS ABOUT FLORENCE
> ROME
> FLORENCE AND NORTHERN TUSCANY
> VENICE AND VENETIA
>> Illustrated.   Each 7s. 6d. net.

INGE (W. R.), D.D., Dean of St. Paul's
> CHRISTIAN MYSTICISM. With a New
> Preface.   7s. 6d. net.

JOHNS (Rowland)
> DOGS YOU'D LIKE TO MEET
> LET DOGS DELIGHT
> ALL SORTS OF DOGS
> LET'S TALK OF DOGS
> PUPPIES
> LUCKY DOGS
>> Each, Illustrated, 3s. 6d. net.
> SO YOU LIKE DOGS !
>> Illustrated.   2s. 6d. net.
> THE ROWLAND JOHNS DOG BOOK.
>> Illustrated.   5s. net.

' OUR FRIEND THE DOG ' SERIES
Edited by ROWLAND JOHNS.
> THE CAIRN
> THE COCKER SPANIEL
> THE FOX-TERRIER
> THE PEKINGESE
> THE AIREDALE
> THE ALSATIAN
> THE SCOTTISH TERRIER
> THE CHOW-CHOW
> THE IRISH SETTER
> THE DALMATIAN
> THE LABRADOR
> THE SEALYHAM
> THE DACHSHUND
> THE BULLDOG
> THE BULL-TERRIER
> THE GREAT DANE
>> Each 2s. 6d. net.

KIPLING (Rudyard)

    BARRACK-ROOM BALLADS
    THE SEVEN SEAS
    THE FIVE NATIONS
    DEPARTMENTAL DITTIES
    THE YEARS BETWEEN
    Four Editions of these famous
    volumes of poems are now pub-
    lished, viz. :—
                Buckram, 7s. 6d. *net*.
    Cloth, 6s. *net*. *Leather*, 7s. 6d. *net*.
    Service Edition. Two volumes
    each book.   3s. *net* each vol.
    A KIPLING ANTHOLOGY—VERSE
                Leather, 7s. 6d. *net*.
    Cloth, 6s. *net* and 3s. 6d. *net*.
    TWENTY POEMS FROM RUDYARD
    KIPLING   1s. *net*.
    A CHOICE OF SONGS   2s. *net*.
    SELECTED POEMS   1s. *net*.

LAMB (Charles and Mary)

    THE COMPLETE WORKS
    Edited by E. V. LUCAS. Six
    volumes.   6s. *net each*.
    SELECTED LETTERS
    Edited by G. T. CLAPTON.
                    3s. 6d. *net*.
    THE CHARLES LAMB DAY-BOOK
    Compiled by E. V. LUCAS. 6s. *net*.
    THE LETTERS OF CHARLES LAMB
    Edited by E. V. LUCAS. Two
    volumes.   6s. *net each*.
    THE BEST OF LAMB
    Edited by E. V. LUCAS. 2s. 6d. *net*.

LANKESTER (Sir Ray)

    SCIENCE FROM AN EASY CHAIR
    First Series
    SCIENCE FROM AN EASY CHAIR
    Second Series
    GREAT AND SMALL THINGS
    Each, Illustrated, 7s. 6d. *net*.
    SECRETS OF EARTH AND SEA
        Illustrated. 8s. 6d. *net*.

LENNHOFF (Eugen)

    THE FREEMASONS   21s. *net*.

LINDRUM (Walter)

    BILLIARDS. Illustrated. 2s. 6d. *net*.

LODGE (Sir Oliver)

    MAN AND THE UNIVERSE
            7s. 6d. *net* and 3s. 6d. *net*.
    THE SURVIVAL OF MAN 7s. 6d. *net*.
    RAYMOND   10s. 6d. *net*.
    RAYMOND REVISED   6s. *net*.
    MODERN PROBLEMS   3s. 6d. *net*.
    REASON AND BELIEF   3s. 6d. *net*.
    THE SUBSTANCE OF FAITH 2s. *net*.
    RELATIVITY   1s. *net*.
    CONVICTION OF SURVIVAL 2s. *net*.

LUCAS (E. V.), C.H.

    READING, WRITING AND REMEM-
    BERING   18s. *net*.
    THE COLVINS AND THEIR FRIENDS
                    £1 1s. *net*.
    THE LIFE OF CHARLES LAMB
    2 Vols.   £1 1s. *net*.
    AT THE SHRINE OF ST. CHARLES
                    5s. *net*.
    POST-BAG DIVERSIONS 7s. 6d. *net*.
    VERMEER THE MAGICAL   5s. *net*.
    A WANDERER IN ROME
    A WANDERER IN HOLLAND
    A WANDERER IN LONDON
    LONDON REVISITED (Revised)
    A WANDERER IN PARIS
    A WANDERER IN FLORENCE
    A WANDERER IN VENICE
            Each 10s. 6d. *net*.
    A WANDERER AMONG PICTURES
                    8s. 6d. *net*.
    E. V. LUCAS'S LONDON £1 *net*.
    THE OPEN ROAD   6s. *net*.
    Also, illustrated by CLAUDE A.
    SHEPPERSON, A.R.W.S.
                    10s. 6d. *net*.
    Also, India Paper.
            Leather, 7s. 6d. *net*.
    THE JOY OF LIFE   6s. *net*.
        Leather Edition, 7s. 6d. *net*.
    Also, India Paper.
            Leather, 7s. 6d. *net*.
    THE GENTLEST ART
    THE SECOND POST
    FIRESIDE AND SUNSHINE
    CHARACTER AND COMEDY
    GOOD COMPANY
    ONE DAY AND ANOTHER
    OLD LAMPS FOR NEW
    LOITERER'S HARVEST
    LUCK OF THE YEAR
    EVENTS AND EMBROIDERIES
    A FRONDED ISLE
    A ROVER I WOULD BE
    GIVING AND RECEIVING
    HER INFINITE VARIETY
    ENCOUNTERS AND DIVERSIONS
    TURNING THINGS OVER
    TRAVELLER'S LUCK
    AT THE SIGN OF THE DOVE
    VISIBILITY GOOD *Each* 3s. 6d. *net*.
    LEMON VERBENA
    SAUNTERER'S REWARDS
                Each 6s. *net*.
    FRENCH LEAVES
    ENGLISH LEAVES
    THE BARBER'S CLOCK *Each* 5s. *net*.
    'THE MORE I SEE OF MEN . . .'

LUCAS (E. V.)—*continued*
OUT OF A CLEAR SKY
IF DOGS COULD WRITE
'. . . AND SUCH SMALL DEER'
Each 3s. 6d. net.
See also **Lamb** (Charles).

LYND (Robert)
THE COCKLESHELL   5s. net.
RAIN, RAIN, GO TO SPAIN
IT'S A FINE WORLD
THE GREEN MAN
THE PLEASURES OF IGNORANCE
THE GOLDFISH
THE LITTLE ANGEL
THE BLUE LION
THE PEAL OF BELLS
THE ORANGE TREE
THE MONEY-BOX   *Each* 3s. 6d. net.
'YY.' An Anthology of essays by
ROBERT LYND. Edited by EILEEN
SQUIRE.   7s. 6d. net.

McDOUGALL (William)
AN INTRODUCTION TO SOCIAL
PSYCHOLOGY   10s. 6d. net.
NATIONAL WELFARE AND NATIONAL
DECAY   6s. net.
AN OUTLINE OF PSYCHOLOGY
10s. 6d. net.
AN OUTLINE OF ABNORMAL PSYCHO-
LOGY   15s. net.
BODY AND MIND   12s. 6d. net.
CHARACTER AND THE CONDUCT OF
LIFE   10s. 6d. net.
MODERN MATERIALISM AND EMER-
GENT EVOLUTION   7s. 6d. net.
ETHICS AND SOME MODERN WORLD
PROBLEMS   7s. 6d. net.
THE ENERGIES OF MEN 8s. 6d. net.
RELIGION AND THE SCIENCES OF
LIFE   8s. 6d. net.

MAETERLINCK (Maurice)
THE BLUE BIRD   6s. net.
Also, illustrated by F. CAYLEY
ROBINSON.   10s. 6d. net.
OUR ETERNITY   6s. net.
THE UNKNOWN GUEST   6s. net.
POEMS   5s. net.
THE WRACK OF THE STORM 6s. net.
THE BETROTHAL   6s. net.
MARY MAGDALENE   2s. net.

MARLOWE (Christopher)
THE WORKS. In 6 volumes.
General Editor, R. H. CASE.
THE LIFE OF MARLOWE and DIDO,
QUEEN OF CARTHAGE 8s. 6d. net.
TAMBURLAINE, I AND II 10s. 6d. net.

MARLOWE (Christopher)—*cont.*
THE WORKS—*continued*
THE JEW OF MALTA and THE
MASSACRE AT PARIS 10s. 6d. net.
POEMS   10s. 6d. net.
DOCTOR FAUSTUS   8s. 6d. net.
EDWARD II   8s. 6d. net.

MASEFIELD (John)
ON THE SPANISH MAIN 8s. 6d. net.
A SAILOR'S GARLAND 3s. 6d. net.
SEA LIFE IN NELSON'S TIME
7s. 6d. net.

METHUEN (Sir A.)
AN ANTHOLOGY OF MODERN VERSE
SHAKESPEARE TO HARDY : An
Anthology of English Lyrics.
Each, Cloth, 6s. net.
Leather, 7s. 6d. net.

MILNE (A. A.)
TOAD OF TOAD HALL
A Play founded on Kenneth
Grahame's 'The Wind in the
Willows'.   5s. net.
THOSE WERE THE DAYS : Collected
Stories   7s. 6d. net.
BY WAY OF INTRODUCTION
NOT THAT IT MATTERS
IF I MAY
THE SUNNY SIDE
THE RED HOUSE MYSTERY
ONCE A WEEK
THE HOLIDAY ROUND
THE DAY'S PLAY
MR. PIM PASSES BY
Each 3s. 6d. net.
WHEN WE WERE VERY YOUNG
WINNIE-THE-POOH
NOW WE ARE SIX
THE HOUSE AT POOH CORNER
Each illustrated by E. H. SHEPARD.
7s. 6d. net. *Leather*, 10s. 6d. net.
THE CHRISTOPHER ROBIN VERSES
('When We were Very Young'
and 'Now We are Six' com-
plete in one volume). Illustrated
in colour and line by E. H.
SHEPARD.   8s. 6d. net.
THE CHRISTOPHER ROBIN STORY
BOOK
Illustrated by E. H. SHEPARD.
5s. net.
THE CHRISTOPHER ROBIN BIRTH-
DAY BOOK
Illustrated by E. H. SHEPARD.
3s. 6d. net.

MILNE (A. A.) and FRASER-SIM-SON (H.)

    FOURTEEN SONGS FROM ' WHEN WE WERE VERY YOUNG ' 7s. 6d. net.

    TEDDY BEAR AND OTHER SONGS FROM ' WHEN WE WERE VERY YOUNG '   7s. 6d. net.

    THE KING'S BREAKFAST 3s. 6d. net.

    SONGS FROM ' NOW WE ARE SIX ' 7s. 6d. net.

    MORE ' VERY YOUNG ' SONGS 7s. 6d. net.

    THE HUMS OF POOH 7s. 6d. net. In each case the words are by A. A. MILNE, the music by H. FRASER-SIMSON, and the decorations by E. H. SHEPARD.

MITCHELL (Abe)

    DOWN TO SCRATCH   5s. net.

MORTON (H. V.)

    A LONDON YEAR Illustrated, 6s. net.

    THE HEART OF LONDON 3s. 6d. net. Also, with Scissor Cuts by L. HUMMEL.   6s. net.

    THE SPELL OF LONDON

    THE NIGHTS OF LONDON

    BLUE DAYS AT SEA Each 3s. 6d. net.

    IN SEARCH OF ENGLAND

    THE CALL OF ENGLAND

    IN SEARCH OF SCOTLAND

    IN SCOTLAND AGAIN

    IN SEARCH OF IRELAND

    IN SEARCH OF WALES Each, illustrated, 7s. 6d. net.

NOMA (Seiji)

    THE NINE MAGAZINES OF KODANSHA : The Autobiography of a Japanese Publisher. Illustrated. 10s. 6d. net.

OMAN (Sir Charles)

    THINGS I HAVE SEEN 8s. 6d. net.

    A HISTORY OF THE ART OF WAR IN THE MIDDLE AGES, A.D. 378–1485. 2 vols. Illustrated. £1 16s. net.

    STUDIES IN THE NAPOLEONIC WARS 8s. 6d. net.

PETRIE (Sir Flinders)

    A HISTORY OF EGYPT In 6 Volumes.

    Vol. I. FROM THE 1ST TO THE XVITH DYNASTY   12s. net.

    Vol. II. THE XVIITH AND XVIIITH DYNASTIES   9s. net.

    Vol. III. XIXTH TO XXXTH DYNASTIES   12s. net.

    Vol. IV. EGYPT UNDER THE PTOLEMAIC DYNASTY By EDWYN BEVAN.   15s. net.

PETRIE (Sir Flinders)—*continued*

    Vol. V. EGYPT UNDER ROMAN RULE By J. G. MILNE.   12s. net.

    Vol. VI. EGYPT IN THE MIDDLE AGES By S. LANE POOLE.   10s. net.

PHILLIPS (Sir Percival)

    FAR VISTAS   12s. 6d. net.

QUIGLEY (H.) and GOLDIE (I.)

    HOUSING AND SLUM CLEARANCE IN LONDON   10s. 6d. net.

RAGLAN (Lord)

    JOCASTA'S CRIME   6s. net.

    THE SCIENCE OF PEACE 3s. 6d. net.

SELLAR (W. C.) and YEATMAN (R. J.)

    1066 AND ALL THAT Illustrated by JOHN REYNOLDS. 5s. net.

    AND NOW ALL THIS Illustrated by JOHN REYNOLDS. 5s. net.

    HORSE NONSENSE Illustrated by JOHN REYNOLDS. 5s. net.

STEVENSON (R. L.)

    THE LETTERS Edited by Sir SIDNEY COLVIN. 4 Vols. Each 6s. net.

STOCK (Vaughan)

    THE LIFE OF CHRIST   6s. net.

SURTEES (R. S.)

    HANDLEY CROSS

    MR. SPONGE'S SPORTING TOUR

    ASK MAMMA

    MR. FACEY ROMFORD'S HOUNDS

    PLAIN OR RINGLETS ?

    HILLINGDON HALL Each, illustrated, 7s. 6d. net.

    JORROCKS'S JAUNTS AND JOLLITIES

    HAWBUCK GRANGE Each, illustrated, 6s. net.

TAYLOR (A. E.)

    PLATO : THE MAN AND HIS WORK £1 1s. net.

    PLATO : TIMÆUS AND CRITIAS 6s. net.

    ELEMENTS OF METAPHYSICS 12s. 6d. net.

TILDEN (William T.)

    THE ART OF LAWN TENNIS Revised Edition.

    SINGLES AND DOUBLES Each, illustrated, 6s. net.

    THE COMMON SENSE OF LAWN TENNIS

    MATCH PLAY AND THE SPIN OF THE BALL. Each, illustrated, 5s. net.

TILESTON (Mary W.)
DAILY STRENGTH FOR DAILY NEEDS
                 3s. 6d. net.
    India Paper.   Leather, 6s. net.

UNDERHILL (Evelyn)
MYSTICISM   Revised Edition.
                 15s. net.
THE LIFE OF THE SPIRIT AND THE
LIFE OF TO-DAY   7s. 6d. net.
MAN AND THE SUPERNATURAL
               3s. 6d. net.
THE GOLDEN SEQUENCE
    Paper boards, 3s. 6d. net ;
    Cloth, 5s. net.
MIXED PASTURE :   Essays and
    Addresses   5s. net.
CONCERNING THE INNER LIFE
                 2s. net.
THE HOUSE OF THE SOUL   2s. net.

VIEUCHANGE (Michel)
SMARA : THE FORBIDDEN CITY
    Illustrated.   8s. 6d. net.

WARD (A. C.)
TWENTIETH CENTURY LITERATURE
                 5s. net.
THE NINETEEN-TWENTIES   5s. net.
LANDMARKS IN WESTERN LITERA-
TURE   5s. net.
AMERICAN LITERATURE 7s. 6d. net.
WHAT IS THIS LIFE ?   5s. net.
THE FROLIC AND THE GENTLE : A
CENTENARY STUDY OF CHARLES
LAMB   6s. net.

WILDE (Oscar)
LORD ARTHUR SAVILE'S CRIME AND
THE PORTRAIT OF MR. W. H.
               6s. 6d. net.
THE DUCHESS OF PADUA
               3s. 6d. net.
POEMS   6s. 6d. net.
LADY WINDERMERE'S FAN
               6s. 6d. net.
A WOMAN OF NO IMPORTANCE
               6s. 6d. net.
AN IDEAL HUSBAND   6s. 6d. net.
THE IMPORTANCE OF BEING EARNEST
               6s. 6d. net.
A HOUSE OF POMEGRANATES
               6s. 6d. net.
INTENTIONS   6s. 6d. net.
DE PROFUNDIS and PRISON LETTERS
               6s. 6d. net.
ESSAYS AND LECTURES   6s. 6d. net.
SALOMÉ, A FLORENTINE TRAGEDY,
and LA SAINTE COURTISANE
               2s. 6d. net.
SELECTED PROSE OF OSCAR WILDE
               6s. 6d. net.
ART AND DECORATION
               6s. 6d. net.
FOR LOVE OF THE KING
               5s. net.
VERA, OR THE NIHILISTS
               6s. 6d. net.

WILLIAMSON (G. C.)
THE BOOK OF FAMILLE ROSE
    Richly illustrated.   £8 8s. net.

METHUEN'S COMPANIONS TO MODERN STUDIES

SPAIN. E. ALLISON PEERS.   12s. 6d. net.
GERMANY. J. BITHELL.   15s. net.
ITALY. E. G. GARDNER.   12s. 6d. net.
FRANCE. R. L. G. RITCHIE.   12s. 6d. net.

METHUEN'S HISTORY OF MEDIEVAL AND MODERN EUROPE

In 8 Vols.   Each 16s. net.

    I.   **476 to 911.**   By J. H. BAXTER.
    II.   **911 to 1198.**   By Z. N. BROOKE.
  III.   **1198 to 1378.**   By C. W. PREVITÉ-ORTON.
  IV.   **1378 to 1494.**   By W. T. WAUGH.
   V.   **1494 to 1610.**   By A. J. GRANT.
  VI.   **1610 to 1715.**   By E. R. ADAIR.
 VII.   **1715 to 1815.**   By W. F. REDDAWAY.
VIII.   **1815 to 1923.**   By Sir J. A. R. MARRIOTT.

Methuen & Co. Ltd., 36 Essex Street, London, W.C.2